MUSE

Susan Irvine

Quercus

With thanks to Kate Constable, Gina Marcou, Susanna Scott, Simon and Alexa, Ben Ingham, Jeff Lounds and Jason.

First published in Great Britain in 2008 by

Quercus
21 Bloomsbury Square
London
WC1A 2NS

A CIP catalogue record for this book is available from the British Library

ISBN (HB) 978 1 84724 480 2
ISBN (TPB) 978 1 84724 481 9

10 9 8 7 6 5 4 3 2 1

Typeset by Lindsay Nash

Printed and bound in Great Britain by
Clays Ltd, St Ives Plc.

PART 1

1

You can't even write it down the way they say it.

Paghree.

Pachrhee

Pa-hurrh-eee

J'ai deux amours. Mon pie-ee et Pahurrhee where I'd come to shoot three stories. My big break as a stylist instead of an assistant. Babs over the top of the winged specs: this is your moment, Naomi, don't go off on one. This is costing us serious money you understand? I'd given her the nod of someone who understands, said I was thinking of Ryan Jackson. She said, if you can get him, brilliant. I'd rung Ryan Jackson's agent and spoken to her in crap French saying bon joor ji mapell Naomi Price eh ji sweezzun grond admeeratreese di son travaye. Not sure about admiratreese but she didn't bat an eyelid just said in hoity French to fax the details to him direct. Ryan Jackson was making a name for himself in the cool style mags. Our mag was supposed to be cool, on the borders of, but the truth was more real women read it which meant I was going to have to do a Suits for the Working Woman story. I just left that as a line at the end of the fax. I kind of implied we didn't really need to do it if he didn't want to. The rest of it I filled with sketches of my ideas for the other two shoots saying I was happy to discuss them. Put the number of the magazine with my extension but he didn't ring just faxed back my own first page with the date he was available and the amount of his fee scrawled on it.

*

When I got there the air-conditioning at the Hotel Milord was broken and there was a heatwave. I was in a cheap room at the top under the eaves. All the heat absorbed by the building during the day had to pass up through me on its way back out again at night. When I think about it. How I'd lie naked on the bed with my legs and arms spread out wide to maximise my surface area. I'd line up the quarter-bottles of wine from the minibar and the special size of Evian that held two handfuls of water. I'd drink my way through them while I watched the Russians standing about and the tanks outside a big white building. There was a military coup in Russia and it was there every time you turned on the TV.

My first morning waking up in Pahurrhee. They rang from reception to tell me it was time and I said mersee and closed my eyes again. I felt the early coolness and heard whee whee whee getting louder and then fainter again. After a while I figured it out. Swifts going past the open window. Swifts are the great travellers of the bird world. I got up and stuck my head out and saw roof tiles all round about me. Not saddo Coronation Street slates waiting for the sky to piss on them. These were curly golden crusts, fantasy pasties waiting to be broken off and bitten into.

It was August and the streets were deserted. The dust smelt like cake crumbs. As the taxi waited at traffic lights I watched an old concierge flicking her fingers in and out of a bowl of water to lay the dust. The taxi drove for a long time to the outskirts of the city and pulled up outside a building by a canal. When I rang the bell there was a humming sound then the front door clicked open. I went in and climbed up quite a few flights of stairs past padlocked doors. On the top landing the door was ajar. I pushed it open and felt my head dropping back. It was the size of the place and the volume of light. It plunged in from skylights all the way along the two slants of the roof and the windows on the two longer walls underneath. It seemed thicker than normal light, more like the whole place was pumped full of a volatile oil. Thin white cloth was nailed over all the windowpanes to diffuse the light and you couldn't see outside. I stood there for a few seconds before I noticed that there was a table away in the middle of the room with three people round it.

Tiny under the pointy roof. They were bending over the table. I saw the woman putting one side of her fist against her eye and then bending right over like that till the other end of her fist touched the table. She slid the fist around on the surface of the table, her face still attached to the top of it. I realised that she was looking at some contacts through a loupe.

I readjusted the bags in my hands and walked towards the table. The man was wearing a checked shirt and he had his hands on his hips looking at the woman. She was talking to him in French. I knew French but I couldn't understand a word. When I was about six or seven paces away the woman handed the loupe to the boy.

'You Naomi?' said the man. He didn't smile, he didn't even really look me in the eye. He had grey hair. I wasn't expecting him to be so old.

'Yeah, hi. You're Ryan, right?' I wondered if I should shake hands in a professional way or if that would be scarily uncool. Before I could make up my mind he was walking away.

'OK. Lets get started.' His voice over his shoulder.

I stood there holding my bags.

'Noy-me?' It was the woman. She had dark hair, shoulder-length with a shaggy fringe that completely obscured one eye. The other eye was something. She'd got a kohl pencil and just gone at the eye with it. It took me a moment to realise that this was how she pronounced my name. 'I'm Sylvie. Styliste at Paloma. This is Sergei my assistant.'

The tall boy was holding out his hand. 'Nice to meet you,' he said. 'Can I get you some coffee?'

I said I'd love some coffee. Styliste. I looked round for Ryan. He was off at the far end of the room talking to a boy I hadn't noticed before maybe his assistant. I probably should go over there and have a word with him. No wait a minute. Maybe she was just here to look through the contact sheets from another shoot. Maybe she was nothing to do with my shoot. Tones were soaking through the air and what could have been fast bells or digital wasps.

'Do you like it?' She cocked her head to show she meant the music.

'Lovely.'

'My son. His first – how you say? – disque.'

I could see Sergei twiddling the knobs on the stereo next to the kitchen area.

'You have a grown-up son?'

'He is seventeen. But he makes music since six years old. Shall we sit down?' She pointed to a chair and hoisted her skirt slightly so she could sit with one buttock on the edge of the table. As she did it I saw that she had a black ribbon tied round her bare thigh. Her skirt fell back over it. I sat down in the chair.

'Is that too loud?' said Sergei. He was coming back across the studio holding a big cup in both hands.

'No, it's fine,' said Sylvie, speaking to him French. 'But look at her sitting there. She's so English. What a dream.'

I realised she must be talking about me. Sergei handed me a cup. 'Who did your skirt?'

I told him. It was white rubberised lace. I was wearing it over a black leotard. I looked through the lace at my thighs. I had thought my legs should be browner for the look to work but maybe their tea-biscuit colour was edgier.

'OK,' said Sylvie, 'so please you talk us through your stories.'

Sergei propped himself beside her on the table. They both looked down at me.

'Shouldn't we wait for Ryan?'

'He won't come until we are ready to shoot.' She added, 'American.'

I made a knowing face. 'You work with him a lot?'

'Always.'

I looked over at the far end of the studio. He was standing with his back against the wall, one foot propped up on it. He had a telephone receiver tucked into his shoulder and he was rocking his upper body backwards and forwards slightly while he listened.

'The two still-life shoots. There are two, yes?'

'Yes.' I could feel myself starting to blush. 'Yes. Uh. One's a garden… um… thing.'

'Yes,' said Sylvie. 'Miniature gardens with accessories. Six pages.'

'Uh no. Four spreads. One for each season. Six pages for the other still life. Uh. As well.'

They didn't say anything. She leaned behind her and picked a bit of paper off the table. She read off it. 'Suits for the working woman.' She looked down at me with her one eye. 'Eight to ten pages.'

'I know. But that one is. I have to do it.' I peeled one leg off the chair. It made a sound like ripping a plaster off.

'So.' She put my fax down behind her again. 'The second still life we shoot underwater with diamond jewellery.' She clasped her hands. 'When I saw it on your fax I was so happy.'

So-appy. Soapy.

'Oh.'

'The way you describe it, I know it is all about the light.'

'You know that colour when you're snorkelling, when you go over the top of a coral reef and on the other side, it's the drop-off?' My hand did a slow dive. 'And suddenly underneath you it's that kind of really deep blue?'

'Black-blue. Like a sea under the sea.'

'You could say that yeah. You float across the top and it's beautiful. And then it's nothing right underneath you and you're terrified.'

'But you want to swim into it.'

I stared at her. 'Yeah obviously.'

Sylvie sighed. 'You like it Sergei?'

'Uh huh.' When he smiled his left eye half-closed.

'I've made contact with all the PRs over here for the jewellery. They're expecting me to collect the stuff mid-week.'

'Sergei will do that. He will arrange everything for everything. So for the gardens, maybe you want roses. I don't know. Red velvet roses, baby roses, green roses—'

'Green roses?'

She shrugged. 'He will drink too much chartreuse, breathe on the roses. Voilà. Green.'

Sergei leaned forward and opened his mouth. He mimed breathing on roses and hiccuped. I giggled.

'OK. Then when we finish the coffee, we start to plan the little décors for the gardens, no? You must guide us, Noy-me.'

2

The two boys at reception rushed to open the door. 'Bonsoir, mademoiselle. Did you have a good day?'

One of them went back behind the counter and reached into a pigeonhole. He handed me some telephone message slips. I leaned on the counter and fanned myself with a hotel brochure. 'It was OK. But it's hot, it's too hot.'

'Oh yes,' they said at the same time, 'it's hot.' One added: 'Even for this time of year.'

I went over and pressed the button for the tiny elevator. 'How was your day here?'

'Oh .' They looked at each other and held up their hands. 'Boring,' said one.

'But seeing you it's better,' said the other.

There was a ping. I waved at them and got into the lift. I could see my nose and lips distorted in the polished brass panel with the number buttons set in it. I watched my lips moving in the panel. Shar moh. Sharr. Moaaa. Moooaaaaah. What the French were. First time I'd ever got the chance to use it in French or in English.

The air in my room was like the wavy air coming off a barbecue. I pushed open the two sides of the window to let in some cool. Needle-pitch screams seething. I leaned out and looked round the sky. After a second I saw them looping and skirling high up. It was a nice way to eat your dinner. I put my head back in. I switched on the TV and got myself three Evians from the minibar and lined them up on the bedside table. I took off the rubberised lace skirt and the leotard and threw myself on the bed. I spread out my arms and legs to maximise my surface area. Russia. I rubbed the back of me against the bedcover to get any sweat off. People gathered outside a big official building. There were thousands of them. They didn't seem to be doing much. A voiceover in French saying something about les représentatives du peuple. Cut to close-up of windows in the big white building. Shadowy men at windows. I craned my neck up a bit to drink one of the Evians. What felt like a fly between my breasts but it was some sweat slipping down. I rubbed it away. A commentator appeared on the screen. I noticed he was wearing a raincoat. La situation something something something. Something appears almost inevitable. Some kind of effusion. Of his. Pan back over the crowd milling about. Cut to some tanks rolling up a motorway with normal cars going along on the inside lane. Effusion of blood. Effusion of blood appears almost inevitable. I looked at the telephone messages. One from the magazine, two from model agencies, one from Dan. I picked up the receiver and asked for the international code and the code for Great Britain. I hung up again and dialled our number. While I was listening to the ring tone I thought about what he might sound like from over here.

'Hello.' The line was crackly.

'It's me.'

'Hey. How's gay Paree?'

'I got to the studio and Ryan was really unfriendly and then there was this older woman with her assistant. She said she's a stylist. But I'm the stylist on this shoot.'

'Nay you've got to take control of the situation. If you don't want her there tell the photographer.'

The commentator held his mike out for a man in a suit.

'No I know.'

'Don't be a mouse.'

'I'm not a mouse. I've just got to figure it out. Can't I just talk to you so I can figure it out?'

'OK. Go on then.'

'You've spoilt it now. It's just. No listen it's just a weird situation. I'm much younger than her. So she can't just be there to help me right?

I just walked in and there she was. And I think that should have been discussed with me you know?'

'If you don't tell them you are unhappy, they're not gonna raise it.'

'Dan you don't understand how these things work. This is my first really big job as a proper stylist. I've got to work with these people.'

I heard him sighing at the other end. 'Right.'

'And it's not just that. She, the woman, Sylvie, *has* turned out to be really helpful. Which was a surprise.' I waited for him to be surprised.

'Good. So you're happy then.'

I closed my eyes. I opened them and looked at the TV screen. Boys clambering over a tank. A soldier coming out of the hole at the top of the tank and one of the boys laying into him. You idiot. They'll shoot you.

'Yeah. Really happy. How about you? Everything OK?' People pulling the boy off the top of the tank. The soldier ducking under the hatch and slamming it. Lightweight. I started to nibble along the edge of a fingernail with my teeth.

'Yeah, everything's fine.'

'What you been up to?'

'Oh. Working. Watching telly.'

There was a bit of silence.

'What's going on in Russia?'

'Old commies have ousted Gorby.'

A bunch of men in suits on top of another tank. One of them reading aloud off a couple of sheets of paper. Cut to Swan Lake. Wobbly and with lines travelling up it so you knew it was a telly picture of something on telly.

'Well I gotta go. I've got to get some dinner.' I sat up on the edge of the bed. 'I wish you were here.'

'Me too. I love you.'

The Milord only served breakfast so I showered and went out. The streets round the hotel were narrow with tiny strips of pavement. Couples were walking hand in hand and gaggles of backpackers were chattering and munching on crêpes rolled up in paper. I kept walking down one street after another looking into the windows of the brasseries and cafés. It was getting dark and the windows shone yellow and orange. I saw tables of two, four, five but nowhere with a woman eating alone. Come on I said to myself and I walked myself into the next brasserie. When I opened the inner door the damp heat of the place gusted out with the smell of ripe cheese and burnt sugar. Voices talking and laughing, the clatter of plates and cutlery. The noise swelled and dropped back. I tried to catch the eye of one of the waiters as they hurried past. One or two of them glanced at me but no one came forward to ask me what I wanted. I took another couple of steps into the room.

'Excusez-moi?'

A passing waiter half-stepped out of his trajectory and leaned towards me. I asked for a table overlooking the terrace if possible. Surveying I had to say. Surveillant the terrace. The waiter looked me up and down.

'You are waiting for someone, mademoiselle?'

'No it's just me.'

I'd forgotten the word for just. I didn't even know if there was one. C'est seulement moi. It's only me. He nodded and started moving through the tables. I stood there not sure if he meant me to follow him or not. He kept going almost to the back where there were swing doors through which waiters kept coming and going to the kitchen. Right in the corner there was a table with only one chair. The waiter looked over and jerked his head at me to show I should come in. I set off through the closely packed tables without looking to right and left and stood behind him while he spread a fresh white tablecloth and lit a candle from a matchbook he kept in his apron's deep pocket. Waiters brushed past me on their way from the swing doors, calling out: 'Show d'vaughan!' I looked above the diners' heads at the prints on the wall. The waiter pulled out my chair and at the last minute snatched a tea towel off his shoulder and snapped it on the padded seat. I sat down. I held the menu up to block out the tables. I read the name of each thing slowly to myself in French. I am in Paris. I looked at the small vase with a single rose in it. The waiter filled my glass with wine, offered me a roll. Steak frites salade. The sort of thing a Frenchwoman might ask for. He nodded as if he approved and whisked off. I let my eyes look across the restaurant to the reflections in the window, sipping at the wine, someone in a film.

3

A nothing feeling from the lift shaft. I pushed the plastic bags against the wall with my knee and pressed the button again. No whine, none of those internal noises from far down in the shaft. I knelt down and put two of the boxes of accessories across my arms and stood up with them balanced like that. I felt for the handles of the plastic bags and picked them up and walked along the corridor and down the stairs. On each half-landing a window opened onto the small courtyard behind the hotel. Patches of sunlight came in through them and lay on the walls and further down the stairs on the red stair carpet. If I paid attention I could hear them. Whee whee whee.

When I got to the last bend in the stair I saw the tiled reception area and one of the boys from the day before behind the reception desk.

'Ah Mademoiselle.' He shot out from behind the desk and halfway up the stairs. 'Permit me.' He took the boxes and went down the stairs ahead of me and put the boxes on the counter. 'The elevator is broken.'

I leant on the counter. 'I know. Why today I ask myself. I just have to go back up for the rest of my stuff.'

'You have more? Please. Permit me to get it for you.'

'No, it's OK.'

'No please I insist. It is in your room?'

In one stride he crossed the reception area to where two gilt and red plush chairs were pulled up on either side of a sort of table that was attached to the wall instead of standing on the ground. It had a mirror above it. He pulled one of the chairs away from the wall and stood behind it.

'Please sit a moment.'

I sat down and listened to the sound of him going up the stairs two at a time getting more and more muffled till I couldn't hear it any more. It was hot already and the doors onto the street on one side and onto the courtyard on the other had both been thrown open to encourage a breeze. There was the sound of a broom rasping over the pavement outside. A bluebottle buzzed round the reception counter. I leaned forward so I could see out into the courtyard. There was a big slanted line halfway up the back wall of it, shadow below and bright sunshine above.

The thump of the boy's feet getting louder and louder down the stairs.

'It is everything?'

His arms were full of bags and boxes and he moved them away a bit from his body to indicate what he meant by 'it is everything?'. I nodded. He piled them beside me and went behind the counter to call a taxi. Then he disappeared through a door painted to look like part of the wall. He came back with a tray which had a glass on it and a metal jug. He put it down on the semi-circle table attached to the wall. Those kind of tables had a name but I couldn't think what it was.

'Permit me.' He lifted the metal jug. There was a fur of water droplets on the neck of it. I could hear ice cubes clinking inside it while he poured water into the glass. 'You are hot mademoiselle.'

I took the glass and sipped at the cold water. Ma'moi'zelle. Ding-dingding. A peal of girlish bells. Remind me when I get back to England to change my name to ma'moi'zelle.

4

Sylvie was wearing a black pencil skirt and a black chiffon shirt that kept slipping down her shoulder. She had taken her shoes off so it was easy to sit on the floor. She loved the south of France. She had just said: 'I met him on a shoot in the Camargue. You know the Camargue, that smell of the maquis? Puissant.'

I tamped down a bit of turf with my fingers. I nodded.

'I adore it. So there I was one morning walking through the maquis. It was just as the sun was coming.'

The sky red at one side. The makee. Pweesawh. The plants greyish. Quiet.

'And there he was swimming in a river.'

I put my hands in my lap. 'Swimming in a river.'

'Yes in a river. He was riding before and then his horse was standing in the river drinking the water. I knew the moment I saw him walking out of the river that this was the man I wanted for my children. The little blue ones – there.'

She dabbled her fingers in the air in the direction of one of the boxes. Sergei scooped his hand in the box and it came out with forget-me-nots in it. I reached into the big flat box with the turf rolled up in finger-length rolls. I took a roll out out and spread it flat on the polystyrene base for the garden.

'So what happened?'

I tweaked the grass stalks along one edge of the new roll together with the stalks in the bit I had already laid to hide the join.

'He picked his shirt to dry himself. Then he saw me.'

'What did he say?'

'Oh something very nice.'

She had the forget-me-nots in her lap. The stems were only green for a couple of inches and then they went a skinny white. She leaned forward.

'Something like' – she put on a deep voice – 'Thank you God who brings such a gift.'

'He thanked God.'

'I explain before. He is Lebanese. All the time they thank God.'

I picked up another roll of turf. I pressed it open gently with my hands so as not to break the back of the roll.

'Was he naked?'

'Of course. He wasn't waiting for a girl to come.'

'It's so romantic.'

She put a hand out to the metal bucket where some flowers were standing in water. 'You said at the back no? For the big roses?'

'Yeah but I think we need to build the hedge at the back first, what do you think?'

'Yes I see what you say. Sergei, you got the hedge no?'

'It's here.'

'Can you be the one to make the hedge, chéri?'

'In a minute.'

He was half-kneeling. One shin along the ground the other bent up. He rested his cheek on the bent-up knee and with his hands untangled snarls of flowers laid on a few sheets of newspaper. A sour damp came up off the newspaper.

'And   Did you   did you swim?' I placed the new roll of turf next to the rest. I picked it up again to uncurl it more.

'Yes.'

'Huh.'

She laughed.

'Did he kiss you? In the water?'

'Yes.'

'Did you   uh   do anything else?'

She snatched a rose off the newspaper. 'Yes. Sergei, you damage that rose. Be careful maladroit.'

'God. It's just too romantic.'

'I feel it myself telling it to you.'

I sat back. I could smell the grass juice on my fingers and the raw green smell mixed with the different thicknesses of sweetness coming off the different kinds of flowers. His mouth was squashed against his knee and that made it open slightly near the corner.

'What happened then?'

'We were married at the end of three months. I was pregnant with Saïd.'

'What! That quickly?'

'I was crazy with love.'

'But was it a mistake?'

There was a popping sound as she stuck a rose stem through the polystyrene. It swayed over at an angle.

'I knew he was the man for my children.'

'What do you mean?'

'I suppose I was about the same age you are. Well maybe you are younger.'

'So why not just fall in love? Why have a baby and get married?'

'Sergei, attention. He is not listening to the flowers he is listening to us.'

I caught Sergei's eye. She started snipping a mound of moss with the clippers. She hadn't noticed the rose.

'What can I tell you? I was not thinking. When I saw him come from the river I could feel it.' She waved the front of the clippers back and forth above her groin. A French way of indicating humping? I looked at my piece of turf.

'What's the word for this?' she said to Sergei in French.

He went on rummaging in a cardboard box. 'I don't know.'

'I could feel it here. Children.'

'You must be madly in love.'

'Yes madly in love. Sergei' – tapping him with the clippers on the back of his hand – 'if you don't put mist on the violets they will die.'

I brushed the dirt off my dress and stood up. I walked backward still brushing. The garden was about the size of half a desk maybe less. I slitted my eyes. At the same time I could see Ryan to my right getting behind the big camera on its stand. He put the dark cloth over his head and crouched.

I could take out more accessories. Then you would see more green and that would unify it more. I heard the tock of the shutter cocking. I looked round. He was standing beside the camera holding the cable release. He pressed the button and stepped back. The assistant pulled out the polaroid holder, snapped the lever and ripped out the polaroid.

I put my hands up round my eyes to block out everything except the garden. The pink was good. Those horrible but cool salmon-pink flowers that Sergei had got and which we'd suddenly put in instead of the roses. She might not get it back in London no one might but it was good. It was different from what I had imagined but it was good. I took my hands down from my eyes. Ryan's assistant was peeling the polaroid apart. He handed it to him by its corner. Ryan pushed his glasses up on top of his head and took the polaroid with the other hand. Then he did a thing with his head so his glasses jumped back down on his nose. He handed the polaroid to Sylvie. I looked back at the garden. I was distracted by the thing Ryan did with his head so that I looked without thinking. I bit my lip.

'Your garden it is un rêve, mais c'est un rêve.'

She handed me the polaroid. The colours were always nicer in a polaroid than in real life somehow.

'Yeah a dream.'

'I love the salmon.' She pointed with her nail at the off-pink flowers. I noticed she bit them which I hadn't expected.

'Me too. I love that.' I looked at the polaroid.

'Something you don't like.'

' No. No, it's good.'

'No but tell me.'

I handed it back to her. A click and a low buzz then the bleeps from the power packs.

'Do you think there are too many accessories?'

She did a French thing. Squishing her head down between her shoulders and lifting up her palms at the same time. St Theresa. 'Every picture always look better if you take something away. It's so easy if you put more space uh?'

'Of course.' I looked at the garden, I tried to let it steal over me.

'But you know that.'

'Yes.' I chewed a nail.

'Yeah I can't do like just three accessories across a whole spread. I need to get a few advertisers in. Well. Maybe I could get away with it on one spread.'

'What can you take out?'

'The green purse? It's just a British brand. Maybe a bit of the Gucci, it's shit but they're major advertisers. And I suppose those ceramic flower hairclips.'

'Oh but they are the best.'

'I know. My friend brought them from Tokyo.'

'OK, lets shoot a couple.'

Ryan straightened up at the back of the camera. The dark cloth slid down onto his shoulders.

'Look it doesn't matter. It's just me.'

'Of course it's just you.'

I wasn't sure I understood her tone. I heard them fiddling with the camera. Sliding the film in.

'Noy-me?'

I stared at the garden. I felt myself starting to blush.

'Noy-me. That's what it is, it's you.'

'OK, I'm sorry. Lets just get on with it.'

She put her hand on my arm. 'But only if you are happy.'

'It's too late.'

'It must be how you want it to be.'

'But I don't know what's wrong.'

'The light perhaps.'

'Probably. It's probably that isn't it?'

'Probably.'

We turned towards the garden. I tried to empty my mind. I heard the buzzing and the light equipment bleeping to signal it was back at full power.

'So if you want a garden where nature and artifice grow together OK.'

I kept my eyes on the garden.

'If you want something that speaks more nature then we can change the light.'

I sucked a bit of hair. 'The light is a bit dead isn't it?'

'It's still too cold.'

'Yes.'

'What do you feel Ryan? Is it too cold?'

He nodded at where his assistant was rummaging in a box. 'I'm putting an 81A on it. Warm it up a bit.' He moved over to the softbox.

'Shadows,' I said to her.

She snapped her fingers. 'Ah! Like clouds passing. It needs clouds. But of course.'

I could only see one eye what with the shaggy fringe. Shiny and black. Really black.

'Can be beautiful no?'

'Yes really beautiful.'

She still looked at me like she was waiting for something.

I clapped my hands together. 'Yes. That's it. Cool.'

He was back under the cloth refocusing the camera.

'Ryan, a moment.' Her voice sounded deeper. I saw the lens move out a fraction then pull back in again. 'What about we put some little shadows of clouds on the garden? To give some feeling of nature.'

The lens moved out. In. 'Fucking bastard lens.' He stood up and put both hands at the back of his waist and leaned back over them. 'Sure.'

Sylvie walked over to me. 'Now, for tomorrow.' She touched my elbow and began to walk away. I followed her. 'I am thinking to ask Sergei to take you to the aquarium.'

'You mean to get some fish?'

'As a location.'

'But I thought we were going to do a tank here. Fill it with fish and things ourselves.'

'Of course we can do it but I think you must see the aquarium before you decide. It's special.'

We reached the kitchen area. She picked a glass off the draining-board and turned the tap on. She held the glass so it rested against her stomach while she let the water run into the sink to get cold.

'OK,' I said. 'If you think so.'

We both looked at the water while she let it run into the sink and then her hand moved out smoothly from her stomach and swivelled round till the glass was under the tap. The water plunged in. I turned and looked back over at the garden without meaning to. I imagined the cloud shadows in advance. It occurred to me how they could look like blonde highlights in middle-aged hair.

'In the morning then before you come to the studio.'

'OK.'

We spent the rest of the afternoon making the cloud shadows. It turned out to be something hard to do. Should they be angled from the left or the right or dead above? If they were curly like cauliflowers would that look even more fake than before even though real clouds were often like that? But then Sergei said something about how real clouds were so much higher off the ground and diffuse. Clouds were made of water not paper so the shadows they cast were fuzzier. He saw me looking at his lips. I turned to Sylvie and looked at her lips. If you just look at lips, anyone's lips, without looking at the rest of them they get stranger and stranger. Especially when they're talking or if they suddenly lick them.

We tried making clouds from different kinds of paper. We tried cut-up net curtain. Then Ryan brought in a light with a silver umbrella to cast a harder, more directional light with the big softbox as a filler. It was meant to look like early morning sun coming low through the stubby trees and bonsai hedges so that they would throw shadows across the whole composition and we wouldn't need clouds. But it ended up looking too contrasty and complicated on the polaroid and in the end we went back to just the big softbox, with the warm filter over the lens, and without cloud shadows or any special shadows.

I was hot and greasy. A spot was trying to break through near my nostril. Sylvie handed me a small box wrapped in blue paper as I was leaving.

'Medicine against the heat.'

5

The white shift dress was filthy down the front. Potting compost and bits of green from where I'd wiped my hands. That would never come off, the green. I pulled the dress over my head and there was a weird second or two when I was hooded in dirty white. I switched the telly on and threw the dress behind it. I opened the mini-bar and got out all the small bottles of water and held them with my arm against my belly while I got out more. My nipples pulled in on themselves.

I lay down on the bed and spread my legs and arms to maximise my surface area. Chanting, fists, barricades, umbrellas. Great-looking barricades. Close up on piled-up buses, smashed cars, bricks, hundreds of like rods, railings, poles, telegraph poles. I cracked open the seal on a water bottle. Side street, blurry. Thousands of people standing, tanks coming through. I reached over for Sylvie's present and turned it so I could see where the Sellotape was holding down the flap on one of the ends. How will they get through? The Sellotape coming away in tiny isoceles triangles. I picked at the next bit. People jostling in front of the camera and their hair lit up at the ends, backlit because of the glare behind and boys, wheat-haired boys with seventies kind of hair with deep fringes and the kind of hair no boy would have these days in the West. Inside was a white box with black writing. Yelling in Russkie. Scuffling. Inside that was a bottle of eau de toilette. Bits of fire, guns? No they're throwing Molotovs. Shit. It's going to kick off. The bottle slid out into my palm. It had an old-fashioned label with a black-and-white drawing of a girl burying her head in a tree. Tanks on fire. They shot anyone yet? The wheat-haired boys. Wouldn't they highlight that? Breaking news? News craquant? Probably flared jeans. There were circles all over the tree that must have been fruits. Roses were growing at her feet. The correspondent standing with the white municipal building lit up behind him and his own hair just catching fire at the ends. Depressing coat. Gestures behind him and says something the army. Something the army to begin the assault. If they could just get back to the boys I could check and I bet you anything it'd be flared jeans. I opened the bottle. Cut to an ambulance trying to drive through the crowd. Cut to Jean-Pierre in the studio. The situation in the Soviet Union gobbledy gobbledy extrêmement gobbledy. I put the bottle top on the bedside table. Drought. Famine. Back to John. Terrorist. Rapist. Back to John. Bomb. Bomb. Back to John. The perfume stung my eyes like raw onions. When I dabbed some on my wrist the smell changed to torn-up grass then it became a bit like roses. I splashed it on when I went out to the brasserie for my dinner.

6

The sound of a needle pocking the membrane and another one coming up out of cold white moss, and a puncture and it seethes through, a puncture and another one another one, the pressure pocks the membrane, sound seethes through the cut and cold white moss, birds puncturing never landing hunting morning till night looping in the sky but over Paris not over white sea. My eyes opened.

I took a shower. I put on my favourite T-shirt with the little strip of plastic between the breasts so the fabric rayed out over them and my green skirt and flip-flops. I did three big squirts of the bleeding grass perfume as medicine. The lift was still broken. I went down the stairs, stepping in and out of the patches of sun on the stair carpet. I ran down the last few steps and across the hallway to the reception desk. The two boys were behind it.

'Good morning!'

Together: 'Ah mademoiselle!' Ding-dingding. Girlish bells. 'Good morning.'

I smiled and they smiled. I leaned on the counter. A wodge of sunlight fell on me through one of the windows. I felt the heat of it on my left cheek.

'No boxes today?'

'No, no boxes. Just a taxi please. I'm going to the aquarium.'

'To sleep with the fishes?' said the tall one with glasses.

A sign: L'Aquarium Cousteau vous invite pour un plongeon au coeur des océans et des systèmes fluviales du monde. Sergei was already there leaning against the wall in the full sun. He got the tickets and we went through a pair of rubber swing doors. Immediately we were in a dark tunnel. It sloped down and at the bottom of the slope there was low blue light coming round the corner. When we got to the corner we saw tanks set in on either side of the walls. The only lighting was the blue seeping from the tanks like some kind of emanation of the water. There wasn't another soul in the place. We walked along, looking at the fish fanning themselves with their fins and hearing the gurgling of the oxygenating systems. When we reached the next corner we turned and there was another tunnel sloping down with the same low blue seeping from the tanks.

'Look at their heads.'

He was looking at some goldfish-type fish. What looked like brains bulged out of their heads and pushed down in frowns over goggle eyes.

'That's a crazy fish,' I said. 'What is it?'

'I don't know.'

'It's so ugly.'

'Yeah. Kind of ugly. It looks like brains.'

'Do you think it is their brains?'

'Could be.'

'Could you really have your brains on the outside?'

'I don't know. Life is strange in the ocean.'

We walked on. A muffled sound came from somewhere behind the walls like a grampus breathing and the constant bubbling and trickling of the oxygenating systems. When you looked away from the blue tanks it was so dark in the tunnel that you couldn't see anything. It took a while for your eyes to adjust. Once the floor ramped up momentarily and I tripped and took a quick extra step or two in the dark. I said sorry and Sergei said are you OK? We walked on hearing the bubbling and trickling as if water was escaping from the tanks into the tunnel and the breathing sound. I tried to see what was happening under the blue light, down at floor level, but it was too dark. We walked on. After a while the watery sounds and the way the fish drifted in their tanks made me forget again.

We came to a bit where the tunnel split into two different directions.

'Which way?'

'You choose.'

'The darkest tunnel.'

'OK The left one.'

We started into it. The only light was a faint reddish-black coming from one long tank meant to show the sea at night. Nocturnal fish slid in and out of shadows, visible only because of the sense of a movement or when their scales caught a red gleam. When I looked round Sergei was made up of black and grey blobs that split apart and moved together and splodges of dull red.

'You've been here before, haven't you?'

'Many times.'

We were whispering.

'Do you know what's down here?'

'I always get lost there are so many tunnels.'

We were standing side by side with our hands on the tank glass. I saw how close the spread-out fingers of his left hand were to my right hand. He had long fingers like I imagined a pianist would have. Behind his hand silver-red fish flipped all at once to face the other direction. I peeled my fingers off the glass and walked on. In the next tank purple fish merged with clumps of blackness. Sergei came up and stood beside me.

'So do you always work with Sylvie?'

'Yes.'

His lips were level with my eyes and reddish-black. I looked back at the fish.

'I came in to her office at Paloma one day to show her my sketches. You know how it is. I hoped they would put them in the magazine. She said she needed an assistant and I should come to work with her.'

'You were an illustrator?'

'I was studying to be a painter. So I left. That was almost a year ago.'

There was the sound of pressure being let off in a pipe somewhere.

'Was that the right thing to do?'

'I don't know.'

'But why did you leave?'

'I don't know.'

The fish watched us. Their lower jaws opened and closed as though they were chewing the water.

'Was it the right thing to do?'

'I don't know you know. I just don't know.'

The sigh of pressure being let off.

'So,' I said, 'you are really young then?'

'I left when I was nineteen.'

The jaws opened and closed, opened and closed. I felt the weight of my eyelids. We turned away from the tank and walked on.

'That's so young,' I said. 'Really that's very young.'

Our pace had slowed till we were hardly drifting.

'I know,' he said. 'It's really young.'

The tunnel went round a corner and without taking my eyes off the dark line of his profile I put out a hand to steady myself against the wall. It touched cold glass. I turned to see what it was.

Blue light. The tank was round like a large porthole. There was no landscaping, just blackish-blue water in which transparent jellyfish suspended. They moved like extensions of one semi-dissolved body. They floated up, trailing almost invisible tendrils. Then, spreading out their bodies, they began to descend. They went up and down in slow motion as though they were sighing. Tiny sparks flashed as they caught the light and patches of iridescence played arrhythmically over their surface. They were like some form of radiance. As I watched them I could feel Sergei's presence getting stronger beside me. I could sense the way his body expanded and contracted with each breath. He said something. I thought it was: They are so beautiful. I whispered yes. I could still hear the word after I'd said it. Yesss. I saw the way his hand was spread out on the glass. It was so close to my hand that if he moved his little finger just half a centimetre it would connect with my finger. I felt the jellyfish coalescing in the bottom of the tank. I looked at the gap between our fingers. I pressed my fingers more into the glass and saw how the gap between our fingers became smaller.

'Is this what you want?'

The jellyfish rose past my closing eyelids.

'Yes.'

'OK,' he said, 'but they cannot go from the aquarium. We will have to get permission to shoot here.'

I opened my eyes. 'Can you arrange it?'

'I think so.'

I heard myself say, 'So you really can get anything.'

'Well. Not anything.'

They hung above our heads. All at once they spread flesh veils and exhaled to the bottom. When they start to go up, I said to myself. A nerve throbbed in my little finger. I watched them sinking down. When they start to go up. The first one reached the bottom rim of the porthole and sank a little below it. A stream of bubbles. In one second. I breathed in. I unpressed the little finger nearest to his finger so it hardly touched the glass. The jellyfish huddled in a cloud of sky-mushrooms at the bottom of the tank. I felt them gathering. Any minute now. I exhaled. I pushed the glass away with my finger.

'Shall we go?' said Sergei.

'Yeah, we better get back.'

7

Ryan and his assistant had set up another still life at the far end of the studio. A different job altogether. I couldn't really see what it was because they had propped poly boards round it on three sides and on the fourth side the bulk of a big 10 x 8 camera obscured the view. Sergei straightened up from the fridge and handed me a bottle of water.

'Hot no?' He shook his head and blew air out of his lips to show how hot. His hair was black and went back from his forehead. I put the bottle into my lips and let cold water trickle in.

The dark eyebrow hairs came to an end about an inch and a half away from the hairline, but if you looked closely you could see that they didn't end completely. Close hair like light fur carried over the gap. At the hairline the same kind of thing was happening in reverse but with longer thicker fur extending into a border area between the head-hair and the fur running out from the tip of the eyebrow.

I pulled out the bottle. 'Where's Sylvie?'

'She has to work at the magazine today.'

I tried to think of the inch or two between Dan's eyebrow and the side of his hair above his ear. 'Is she coming later?'

'No. We are alone.'

He looked at me. It was the natural thing to do. A second of whiteness came over me that I knew would be followed by a backrush of blood. I walked away to where we had upturned a wooden box and covered it with a thick chopped-down poly board ready for the second garden to be laid out on top.

'Right,' I said. 'We should get started then.'

He came and stood next to me. The cuff of his old blue shirt was crushed where it was pushed back to just below the elbow. From under the cuff's edge emerged the inflated tube of an artery – or was it a vein? – that ran down the forearm and flattened back down into the flesh at his wrist. It was heat that made it do that, made it inflate like that so that I wondered what it would feel like if someone pressed it with their tongue, say, to see how high the pressure in it was. Would they be able to feel the blood resounding against the tip of their tongue?

'How to start?'

He half-turned to look at me as he said it. I could feel my ears now as separate hot things. I headed back towards the fridge. I shouted over my shoulder, 'Can you stick some music on? And maybe see if we can get some air?'

I opened the fridge and took out the boxes of flowers. The turf was in a coolbox in the cupboard where Ryan kept his brooms and squeezy-mop. I went to the cupboard, hoisted the coolbox in my arms, and started to walk over to the upturned box. His legs coming towards me.

'Let me please.'

I handed it to him. I stopped myself noticing how his fingers had to touch my arms for him to get the box out of them. There was a draught. I looked up. One of the skylights, two of them, were swinging open behind their cover of nailed-on cotton.

'That's better.'

Stupid to wear this skirt on a day like this. The lycra in it made it cling and it meant I couldn't sit cross-legged. I squatted. I drew circles on the polystyrene with a biro. His face was an almond, or a sculpture by that French sculptor who had done the very smooth graceful kind of faces. You didn't get them like that in Britain.

'You think I should leave a bigger gap between the trees?'

He looked at where I was drawing the circles. 'No it's good.'

'OK then could you maybe cut the holes for their pots to go here?' Ser-gei.

The word in the back of my mouth like a dancer waiting to leap on. Just in time I realised I couldn't say that word that I had begun pronouncing with a little gurrh in the middle like I was having the ghost of a fit.

'It's Appleland this one. The ancient British heaven.'

'Ah.'

'You know the ancient British people, a lot of them were Celts.'

'I know. The Irish and the Scottish, they are still not like the English.'

'That's right. We're totally different.'

'You are Irish?'

Each tiny crab-apple was packed in a single ply of pink tissue and set into a dimple in the shallow dark blue trays. They looked fake.

'Welsh.'

Sergei unwrapped an apple and polished it slowly with the tissue. It was smaller than the end of his thumb.

'So not like Irish. You sound English.'

'I wasn't brought up there. My grandparents live there.' I put the bonsai trees on the floor. 'My great-grannie spoke Welsh.'

'Say something in Welsh.'

'Um. Rwy'n dy garu di.'

'What does it mean?'

'Nothing. It's the only Welsh I know. Any idea where the scalpel is?'

He went over to the kitchen area and got the scalpel from the cutlery drawer and came back with it and stuck it into the polystyrene so neither of us could cut ourselves on the blade. He threaded an embroidery needle with brown thread, handed it to me and took another needle from the pack. I picked up the apple he had polished and inserted the needle in the bottom and through the core so it came out the top. I wrapped the thread round a branch of one of the trees and tied it.

'That's good.'

'I like Appleland.'

His fingers were working right under my nose. They had what people called spatula tips. I watched them tying an apple to the tree.

'So what does it mean, rruin dee cari chrhee?'

'What's your name.'

'Say it again.'

I looked up at the ceiling. 'Rwy'n dy garu di.'

'Sergei. Rruin duh garee dee?'

'Naomi.'

He misted the garden. A few minutes after he'd done it the smell of apples and grass sharpened as the evaporating water lifted the scent off the surface of the plants.

'I love it,' I said.

'Un rêve.'

We worked on in silence. When we'd inserted the last white floweret into the turf he got to his feet.

'OK. I must go. I meet the press guy at the aquarium in one hour.'

I watched his back till it went through the door and the door shut after him. I looked over at Ryan. He was standing on a camera case looking through the viewfinder at his other shoot. Sweat had gathered behind my knees. I got up. It ran down the back of my legs. I went over to the stereo and put the same record on, the one Sylvie's son had made. I went back over to the garden and looked at the accessories I'd laid out on a sheet of newspaper. It was easy just to place them among the trees and then take a couple back out. When I'd done I walked away then went back in and clipped the enamel bee earrings to a couple of branches. I wiped my forearm across my lip to rub off some sweat. I went over to Ryan.

'You ready?' he said as I got near.

'Just when you are.'

I went back to the garden and looked at it with my arms crossed. I went in and moved the metallic shoestring belt a bit. I took out the enamel bee earrings. Ryan took up a wide-legged position in front of the garden.

'This done?'

'I think so yes.'

He pushed his glasses up on his forehead. Then he did the thing that made the glasses come down onto his nose again.

'Nah. Not working.'

I felt the whiteness then the backrush of blood. 'What's wrong with it?'

'Dunno. I just know it's not working.'

He walked off to the far side of the studio and said something to his assistant and the assistant switched on the lights round the other job.

I went to the kitchen area and filled the stovetop coffeepot with water from the tap. I got the bag of beans out of the freezer and put a handful into the grinder. I glanced round at Ryan and switched the grinder on. Don't think about the garden yet. Put it out of your mind and screw the top bit of the pot on more firmly. I put the coffee pot on the stove. In front of me was one of the windows with the white cloth nailed over it. What I needed to do was just rest my eyes on the white window while the coffee heated. Then, when the coffee was ready, I needed to just drink the coffee, not thinking about anything in particular and not looking at anything in particular. When I was finished I would put the cup down and turn back around and see the garden with fresh eyes.

I watched the blue flame under the pot. I adjusted it so as not to waste heat, a common error. A car went along the street outside. I hadn't noticed if many cars did. I lifted the lid. Nothing in the top bit yet. I put on the tap and let the water get hot and then I washed all the mugs and a couple of tea plates and then I cleaned the soap dish and round where the soap dish sat. I flipped open the top of the coffee pot. Nothing. I got the dish towel down. I dried the cups. I went into the cupboard and saw some of the glasses lined up in it were clouded. I put the water on as hot as possible and started to soap up the glasses with the scrub pad. Hissing from the pot. I washed another couple of glasses. I tried to do it like the monk who had written a book about how when you wash the dishes you should do it mindfully thinking about nothing but the dishes as though this could save you. The coffee gurgled as well as hissed in the pot. I reached for it. I poured some into a white cup. It looked beautiful and poisonous. If I could just do the technical stuff with a camera I could get the most fantastic shot now just of coffee going into a cup and how happy that could make you feel.

I picked up the cup and drank the coffee. It almost hurt it was so hot. I made the sips very small. When I got to the last ten millimetres I put the cup down on the draining-board and turned round.

*

Fuck gardens. Fuck dinky little miniature gardens. Fuck this stupid job, meaningless stupid pretending job. I went over and started pulling everything out and chucking it on the floor: flowers, belts, purses, turf chunks, rings, ripped-off apples. Small clods of earth flew in the air and splattered the floor. I tore baby leaves and a couple of branches off the trees from tugging at tied-on apples. I started sticking things back together any old how, picking the tiredest-looking trees for the front, poking the damaged flowers in with a finger. I got the metal bucket with the other day's flowers. Some of the roses had wrinkled and turned brown. I plonked them in in the foreground, jabbing them hard through the polystyrene under the turf. They were so big they almost blocked everything else out. I stuck my hand in the plastic bag full of rejected accessories and pulled a few things out without looking like it was a lucky dip. I threw them in among the trees shouting: 'Ryan! I'm ready!'

He took his time ambling over from the other end of the room. He took up the same wide-legged position square-on. He pushed his glasses up onto the front of his head and stood there like that for a long time.

He jerked his head and the glasses dropped back down onto his nose. 'We'll call it a day.'

'No we won't. This is exactly what I want for the shoot.'

'I said.'

He walked over to the far corner, got his jacket, and left the studio.

8

The boy came out from behind the counter and held out his hands and I handed him the two carrier bags.

'You had a bad day mademoiselle?'

I must change my name to mademoiselle. 'Terrible day.'

He stood there with the bags.

'Is the lift working yet?'

'No I'm sorry. But I carry your bags for you.'

'It's OK.'

'Please, it's no problem.' He started up the stairs.

'Just nothing would go right. You know when that happens?'

'Oh, I know!' His voice came down the stair over his shoulder. 'It's terrible.'

'I know,' I said. 'I feel kind of terrible. I feel depressed.'

'Don't worry,' said the reception boy, 'because tomorrow it can suddenly be a lot better.'

'You think so?'

'I know it.'

'But why did I make it worse by going into shops?'

'Into shops?'

'Boutiques, little boutiques.'

His shoes trudged up the steps one after the other ahead of me. Brown shoes with paler brown wavy soles.

'I ask myself.'

'I got the taxi to stop on the other side of the river. I had nothing else to do anyway, I was early, and I thought I could get out and walk across the bridge.'

'It is a good idea.'

'Yeah it was good, it was lovely on the bridge and then I decided just to walk down the steps and go for a walk along the river as well.'

All the boyfriends and girlfriends on their holidays, their arms round each other, kissing each other down by the river or groups of young Europeans, unknowns, golden, sharing bottles of beer and actually playing guitars and singing like we were in a musical.

'And then I went back up to street level and I just went down a tiny street and there were all these boutiques. You don't get them like that in England you know, not that small and full of lovely, lovely things.'

He reached the landing. I watched his two feet moving across the red carpet ahead of me. There was no direct sun on this landing at this time of day when I was never here. I listened automatically behind the sound of his feet and the swishing of the bags against his legs. At first I thought they weren't there but then I heard them screaming up in the sky. You never heard them at street level. He was saying something.

'You buy something?'

'A top, an expensive top, une chemise. Bars of French soap for my boyfriend. Verveine and vetiver. Unbelievably expensive.' The way the woman in the shop said verveine. Her outfit like a French maid in black satin with a starched pinny and La Boudoir d'Odette embroidered across the front.

'Excuse me but you say it was too much money for you?'

We were both panting. I stopped and held onto the banister.

'Sorry. I shouldn't have said that. I'm not myself today.'

'No. Please. I understand. Why not buy something if you feel bad? It's OK if it is too much money.'

We reached the top landing.

'Do you really think so?'

'I know it.'

'You think it's OK?'

'It's OK. I do like that sometimes. Please don't regret nothing.'

It smelt like warm meat pies in the room. I went over and opened both sides of the window. There was the sound of one car following another down the busier street at the end of ours. Voices talking in German at the entrance to the hotel down below. I couldn't see them because of the way my window embrasure was set back into the roof tiles. I slumped on the edge of the bed and sat there listening to the mini-bar ticking. I looked down and saw that there were smears of grime up and down my legs. There was a tap on the door.

'Oui?'

'It's me, Eric from reception.'

He was standing there holding a tray with a paper doily on it and a bowl of chocolate ice-cream. He ducked his head and went off back down the stairs.

In Moscow the correspondent stood in front of the bland building. Between him and it a huge crowd of people that you knew extended far beyond the edges of the screen. I pulled off my top and undid my skirt. The usual tanks. Covered in some kind of rubbish. I crawled backwards up the bed so as not to disturb the tray on the bedcover and opened my legs wide apart. It was bouquets of cellophane-wrapped flowers. The tiniest breeze trailed up my leg. I concentrated on feeling it. He was wearing a thin beige-coloured raincoat like he was one of Smiley's people. no one really wore those raincoats except in films about the British secret service or maybe if they worked at the Bank of England. I put my spoon into the ice-cream. The top layer had liquefied in the time since he'd got it out of the fridge and it was glassy. Underneath it was rougher and thicker and I had to push my spoon in. Flashback, night. Tanks forcing through barricades. The people behind the barricades all moving at once like they were polyps unified in a flesh carpet below the level of the screen. I worked the spoonful of ice-cream across the roof of my mouth squidging it a bit. The polyps surging in a current towards oncoming tanks. The tanks keep coming. The camera moving in on people in the path of the first tank. I sat up straighter. The people turning their faces away from the tank and pushing against the people behind them. I worked it slowly backwards and forwards so it melted layer by layer. They surge back, all the polyps resolving from chaos to a unified movement away from the tank. It ran down onto my tongue and pooled. But they're met by the polyps from further back surging towards the tanks. Everyone yelling. I tried not to move my tongue. They might be great for a shoot those raincoats. Left field. There it was. A flattened clot of ice-cream stuck in the upturned spoon. All the girls in the same anonymous coat in every picture, several girls in every picture and maybe one or two of those nobody little civil service men in some of the pictures as well with the same coat on. I pulled the spoon down with more pressure onto the tongue and brought it forward and then angled it up as I worked it back over the arched tongue. The ice-cream started to dissolve into saliva. The tank on the screen swinging its gun from side to side. I tried to hold it in my mouth without swallowing it. You can see right up the hole in the middle of the gun the hole that big bullets come out of. Hold it on the tongue. Those people in front trapped against the tank and it still moving forward. The graininess of my tongue against the metal. They're going to be crushed but if they get the command inside the tank they're going to be ripped apart as well. I pressed another hump of ice-cream against the roof of my mouth. But if the tanks are going to start pumping ammo into the crowd this would have been the first item. I felt a trickle in my throat. Hold it. Unless this isn't a flashback. Hold it. Cut to a boy lying on the ground with a sheet over him but not right up over his face. I had to do it. I swallowed. Image jerking, cameraman being jostled. I put the telephone receiver into the crook of my shoulder and dialled with my free hand. My voice coming out small.

'I'm really missing you.'

'Is it that stylist woman?'

'No. It's just I miss you.'

'I miss you too.'

'Really?'

'Really. The moment you left it started to rain here.'

'What do you mean?' I moved from buttock to buttock to cool them off.

'Ain't no sunshine when you're gone.'

Focus in on someone crouching over the boy. She turns to camera and she's digging her fingers into her cheeks and dragging them down her face.

'What will we do when I get back?'

'I'll open the door and I'll put my arms round you and hold you really tight.' Slaps her own face. On her knees rocking up and down over the boy. Wearing a headscarf.

'Then we'll go into the bedroom and I'll take off your clothes one by one.'

I stuck my spoon into the chocolate ice-cream. The woman hysterical. 'Mmm hmm.'

'Then I'll kiss you in some special secret places no one else would think of.'

'Like where?'

'Like special secret places.'

I rubbed the ice-cream across the roof of my mouth. 'What will we do then?' Ice-cream trickled, pooled.

'I'll lie you down on the bed.'

'Uh huh.'

'And then I'll get in beside you.'

It was getting softer because of the heat.

'Will we pull the covers over our heads?'

'All the way.'

'Mmm. What will we do then?'

'All the things I've been thinking of every night since you've been gone.'

Rolling the boy onto a stretcher. Blood. People in the front linking arms like in a barn-dance and leaning back on the people behind.

'How long are we going to be under there?'

'Days. Maybe a week. We'll have to call in sick.'

'Yeah seriously ill, maybe chest infections.'

I tried to see if his face was covered. Too many people.

'Oh yeah, the chest. Seriously congested especially in your case.'

'Oh yeah in my case the chest will be like stuffy to say the least.'

I said the word chest and at the same time the woman makes a fist and beats it on her chest. She's doing all the classical things. Maybe she's going to rend her garments.

'I wish that was now.'

'Naynay you're in Paris.'

I ate all the snack foods in the mini bar: salted peanuts, hickory-smoked almonds, cheesy crackers, a Toblerone, coffee-flavoured caramels and a clear plastic box with four liqueur chocolates. I drank the small bottles of wine and sparkling and still and I opened the tiny bottle of Courvoisier. I had always liked the picture on a Courvoisier bottle. I leaned on the windowsill and swigged the brandy out of the bottle. It was cooler with my head out in the open air. The swifts were higher up than before, ruffling the air through their lyre-shaped wings. Maybe they slept on the wing like albatrosses. Blown a hundred miles in their sleep. I leaned out further and slid my hands down the golden pasties. They were roasting hot. If I let my body slide out a bit beyond the waist I could see straight down to the pavement underneath.

It was getting dark especially when I went inside again to look at the TV and then looked over at the window. I got out the tiny bottle of Johnny Walker Black Label. Peppery after the sweet brandy. I didn't like the guy on the bottle. Too show-pony. It was dark in Moscow too. You could see the white faces of the Russians standing in a huge square with grand old buildings behind. They were singing. The correspondent appeared in his mac and said something about now the Russian people have started to sing something cold summer night, songs something salvation hell. You've gone too far now mate, I said to myself. I sat on the edge of the bed facing the window but with my head turned to watch the telly. Stick to telling the news mate. Between one breath and the next thousands of people joined in the singing. The camera must have been up on a gantry. It panned over the crowd and the screen was a solid wall of upturned faces with their mouths opening and closing in Os of song. I sat on the bed with the whisky miniature and sang along in pretend Russian. Ovssky plovovov druskmeershky tumsky-tumsk! The camera went in for close-ups of the ones who had tears rolling down their cheeks. Tears rolled down my cheeks.

9

'And you are together how long?'

'Three years.'

'You hear that mon bébé? And she is away from him only three nights till now. You are missing him?'

I snapped off a side stem. 'Oh God yes. It's unbearable, especially at night. I'm not myself.' The oily yellow light.

'You meet him how? Oh that's un rêve with the big roses in front like that. Ryan' – over her shoulder – 'she is clever, n'est-ce pas? More disturbing now. So go on, tell me.'

'It's not that interesting. Not like you and the river and all that.'

'Love is always interesting.'

I pulled a fat rose out of the bucket. I placed it almost out of frame. 'Well I had a summer job working in, believe it or not, a refrigerated transportation depot in Birmingham.' I snorted.

'Of course! And you saw him covered with ice, and you kissed him and he was alive?'

'You got it.'

She stopped to light another Gitane. She was wearing a black silk wrap skirt and I kept looking down to see if it had fallen open and she was wearing the black ribbon tied round her thigh.

'No what happened was, he was at university, he was on a holiday job too. He'

'What was he studying?'

'Some kind of business degree. His job was helping one of the junior managers at the depot and I was a clerk, checking the dockets. You know, how many boxes of fish fingers have been delivered where. It was a summer job.'

'I cannot see you in thousands of fish fingers. Sergei, can you see it?'

'I have seen her with the fish.'

'And what happened?'

'Nothing really. He asked me out for a drink and I went, and one thing led to another and we fell in love. Really in love.' I picked up a beaded purse and placed it behind a tree in the garden. 'Rêve?'

'Ouf, more than rêve. So you were really in love.'

'Badly. I had to go back to my university and he had to go back to his and we had to keep meeting in train stations.'

'Oh but that's romantic.'

'It was really.' I took a bundle of blue flowers on hair-thin stalks onto my lap and started to thread my fingers through to separate them. 'I'd have to catch the early morning train in the dark. I had to be back for lectures. We would have to get up in the dark and go to the station and wait for the train. It was always freezing cold and then when you saw the train coming it was terrible. I wouldn't see him again for a week or more.' I wove the blue flowers between the fingers of my left hand like I was plaiting them.

'Then you were apart more than three nights.'

'What?'

He held up the nail scissors and gnashed the blades a couple of times to get the grass off them. 'You said you have not been apart for more than three nights.'

He bent over the turf again with the scissors. He was kneeling in the same way as before with one shin along the ground and the other knee propped up so his cheek could rest on it.

'I meant since we started to live together. After university. Not since then.'

He combed the grass with his left hand so it all stood up. I saw how his fingers swelled out a bit at the end like pads.

'What thing it was you love in him?' said Sylvie.

I thought for a minute. 'I don't know. That's too hard.'

'But you know the answer. We always know.'

'What about you?'

She indicated her pelvis. 'The way he dried his reins. If he did not do that I do not marry him.'

What were rrhan? 'No! It can't be true.' Kidneys?

'Why not?'

'You can't marry someone because of the way they dry themselves.' Loins.

'Pfff.' She took a drag. 'People do not like to confess about these things. They like to think, you know, I love him for his person-alit-eee. I love him for his – sooooul.' She clasped her hands and looked up at the ceiling. 'But why not the reins?'

I tried to pull the plait of blue flowers off my fingers by easing it gradually up one finger after another. 'It's not enough. Not for real love. I know you love him.' I looked up to check I hadn't offended her. 'But not for his loins.'

'Coming out of a river. The sun is rising. And just under a little animal.'

I started laughing. Sergei raised his eyebrows to ask me about placing a fern. I nodded. I was trying to think of the one thing.

'OK. One night, maybe the third night we were having a drink at the pub, I had my arm on the table and – we hadn't kissed or anything at this point – he started stroking the inside of my arm all the way up. Just with the tips of his fingers.'

I felt the colour draining out of my face. It came back red. Sylvie placed a rose.

'You see? It was the way he touches you.'

10

I went for a walk. It wasn't as dark outside as it looked from inside the restaurant. I walked along the river but on the side with houses and cafés not on the river side. I got past the cafés and then there were big stone buildings with important functions and I was more aware of the cars whizzing past to my right and the hardness of the street lights. I turned down a side street and it was empty. I walked up and down streets like that for a while and then there were inhabited streets and café streets and the corner with the market in the daytime that I knew and then I was back at the hotel. In the day the glass doors with the gold Hotel Milord were open to let a breeze through. Normally when I got back in the evening they were closed. But now the hotel was more closed than usual with an extra pair of wooden doors shutting it in. I saw an ancient-looking brass panel on the wall with a white ceramic nodule in the middle. I pressed it. After a while the door was opened by an old man with a comb-over. He shuffled back in through the glass doors and held one open for me. As I went past I saw dandruff on the shoulders of his jacket. There was the sound of a telly coming through from the room hidden behind a door made to look like part of the wall behind the reception counter.

I had forgotten to leave the window open. The first thing I noticed was how strong the meat pie smell was and separate from that a bakedness coming off everything else in the room. A bit of baked telly and baked chest of drawers and baked pillow and baked under-the-bed and other baked things. I opened the two sides of the window as wide as they would go and slithered half-out so I could put my hands on the edge of the roof where the wall went down vertically. Heat radiated off the roof tiles. The sky was the alien orangey-black it goes above cities at night. I hadn't noticed it before in Paris. I had thought maybe it was a bit different in Paris. I listened to hear if anyone was going down the narrow street the hotel was on. Nothing. People whooping for a few seconds where the street made a T-junction with a bigger street at the end. I strained my ears. Broken whooping and running as they carried on along the bigger street.

I took off my clothes and lay on the bed and watched replays of Gorby getting off a plane in a bomber jacket. Talking heads. People cheering and chanting. Why did I love Dan? The special thing was that he stroked the underside of my upper arm. no one had ever touched that bit of me before. Imagine. It's such an out there bit of you, it's not a forbidden bit with warning signs on it, skulls and crossbones and big red dangers, but all those years no one had noticed it. Smiley's person, his coat on, his tired eyes. Doing vox pop on the streets. Roses, flags, balalaikas. Flashback to the burly white-haired man standing on the tank. Yeltsin, some kind of saviour of the hour. Crusty Commie generals had failed. Hurrah for perestroika and glasnost. The underside of the upper arm. It hasn't really got a name and no one pays it any more attention than the outer side of the upper arm. But it's a completely different kind of skin, whiter, thinner and with virgin nerve endings that have never been fired by a touch.

More flashbacks. Tanks. Shadowy men in suits looking out of the white building. A motorcyclist parking next to a tank and taking a stack of pizza boxes off the back of his bike. Goes up to the white buildings. The tanks don't stop him. The enemies of the people's soviets are waiting for their last meal. Decadent capitalist junk fare. Maybe I loved him not because of the way he touched me, his fingers, but because of where. There in the virgin territory. He made me known to me by drawing my attention there with his fingers. Maybe it was me I was in love with. My underarms. It could have gone the other way. They could have arrested Yeltsin, assassinated Gorby, fired on the crowd, the army divided, civil war. Mad KGB types with big bushy eyebrows and tinpot medals. Their fingers on the button. If the USSR is going down, we'll take you with us! It could have gone that way just as easily. I could be lying here in bed worrying about the underside of my arm vis-à-vis someone else's fingers and we are about to be swept into global conflict or just nuked. London obliterated. I hear about it in the morning when I reach reception. Washington gone and while I slept, Leningrad and other grads zapped as well. Dan dead clearly. I can't get out of Paris, it's chaos. I am swept along in the tide of the resistance east with Sergei. Especially since Sergei must be Russian or something or why would he be called Sergei? All his family are in terrible danger, so we battle across Europe, fighting the reds and the whites and the pinky-whites and it's terrible. Pan back over the faces of wheat-haired Russian boys. You see it in their faces. They know they are about to die for something. Maybe they don't know what side they are on yet, all they know is, it's life and death. I switched off the TV and went to sleep.

A revving sound and a mechanical squeal coming over it then chomping. A shout. Revving. Chomp. I opened my eyes. Properly dark. Revving. Squeal. Chomp. The clink of metal bins against the truck's side. Beep beep beep beep. Revving, and the chomp on the rubbish followed by the revving. The binmen hollered and whistled to each other. They didn't hold back because it was the middle of the night. As it moved further down towards the T-junction another sound. Faint but nearer. Tiny squeak. What could have been a scratch. I scanned the room with the ear that wasn't in the pillow. I heard the truck turning the corner and the muffled sound of it revving and beeping in the next street. A binman whistled. Silence.

The net curtains lifted and fell back. I watched them. The breeze was getting stronger. The curtains were being half-sucked through the open window when they fell back. I closed my eyes. I could feel myself sliding over. I hovered on the edge slipping. Squeal. Behind me. Moving as quietly as I could, I propped my head on a hand so as to hear better. They had stopped. They must have heard me moving. I had to be patient because they are very patient, cautious. I let only my eyes move. They looked at the curtains filling with air and then straightening out and streaming into the room, faltering, falling back but no, coming on again, streaming, and then empty, beating against the window frame. A squeak and another squeak answering it. Something else. Whimpering.

There was a half-drunk glass of fizzy water on the bedside table, still a few grey bubbles visible in it. I swung my legs over the side of the bed and sat up. I picked up the glass and drank a few mouthfuls of the water. It tasted salty. As I swallowed it I heard tapping behind the headboard. I got up and pushed through the net curtains and leaned out on the windowsill. The wind was quite cool. I thought about slipping right out of the window and crouching on the roof tiles to feel it. I slithered forward till I could put my hands on the edge where the tiles gave way to the guttering. Back in the bedroom my feet were off the floor. In this position I could see right down. The streetlights were throwing cones of sodium on the pavement. I looked up and down the street. Empty. In the silence I heard a buzzing coming off the streetlight directly underneath. I turned my head. Each window on this floor was split vertically into two big panes that closed with a latch in the middle. The right pane of the next-door window was wide open. It was so close that if I walked my hands in a quarter-circle across the roof tiles without coming out any further I could just reach to shove it shut. Sacre bleu! What waz zat! I could see the opposite wall of their window embrasure, a mass of shadow. I wriggled my hips to get my feet back on the floor and slipped back inside my room. Different. The air close and the meat pie smell and an indoors quiet. Behind the headboard of my bed their headboard tapped smartly on the party wall. I knelt up on the bed and put my ear against the wall.

Everything amplified. The sharp intake of breath she made at the start of every yelp. As if she kept trying to push something heavy away. Yelping in rhythm with the squealing of bedsprings and the bump of the bedhead against the wall. The wall vibrated on my cheekbone as their bed thumped it. Every now and then the man – older, lumbering, half-bald – made a grudging sound in his throat, shaking off something that was annoying him. What could have been a paunch bouffing her belly. Fast wet churning. Yelp. Squeal. Yelp. Squeal. Slop. Slop. Yelp. Slop. I turned on the TV. The big white building swam wonkily into view. The stocky white-haired man called Yeltsin standing on top of a tank. A replay. He raises his fist. The crowd cheer. His voice hoarse over their heads. The headboard thudded harder against the back of my head. The crowd cheer again. The headboard thudded. I turned the volume up. Oui oui oui oui. She was probably faking it. The cheering dies away. Someone off-screen translating the speech into French. Now is. What could have been a massive gut-belch. The hour to stand for freedom. I muted the sound on the TV. At the window the net curtains blew into the room and fell back on the window frame.

11

I pushed open the rubber swing doors and walked down the blue-lit tunnels. Sergei was already there. He said hello and I went up and stood beside him. The jellyfish were gathered near the top of the tank. Bubbles revolved up through the fluctuating mass. Sparks and winks of light flashed up and down the tendrils. They seemed to be communicating like fibre optic cables. The gel that made up the rest of their bodies was marked with dissolving blots of hardly perceptible purple and blue. All at once the domes flattened out, drawing all the tendrils up and inwards at once. They sagged down through the water.

It seemed to take for ever. Then they reached the bottom of the porthole window. I felt the change in them just before they pulsed their flesh wide then gulped it in again, going up through blue light, their tentacles in saliva strings. The rhythm of his breathing beside me as though he were standing much closer than he was. The way the skin on his sides thinned as his chest made room for air. I felt the skin stretching and under it his blood flushing in stops and starts down tubules and his heart jerking. I closed my eyes. When I opened them I knew that he was looking at me. I stared at the tank. The jellyfish swooshed up past eye level. I looked around the tank but there was nothing else in it. I looked at the wall beside it. An information panel. Latérale cnidocytes pneumatophore existent neurotoxine peléagique. It was like his eyes were ionised and I was being forced by the power of electrons to turn my head. Pteropod. How did people read this stuff? I stuck my neck out to get closer to the panel. There was a button. I pressed it. The panel lit up and gave off the low hum of a poor quality electrical unit. De manière surprenante, les cnidaires pourraient avoir un génome plus proche du nôtre que la mouche drosophile. The light stuttered and went out. I turned my head. Moving points of light on his right eyeball reflected from the jellyfish. He must have said something.

'Sorry?'

'Here's Sylvie.'

High heels clicked in the tunnel. She was wearing a white dress with pintucks down the front. I'd never seen her in anything but black before. The dress glowed in the near-darkness.

'Sergei says the meduses are the most beautiful things in Paris.'

'The what?'

She nodded at the tank.

'Oh right. I wonder if they sting.'

'I don't know. Maybe someone should put the hand in and touch.'

'That's a good idea.' I looked at Sergei. Blue shadows moved over his face.

'Me?'

'Yeah.'

'It's a joke.'

'No.' I looked at Sylvie.

'No. We must find out.'

'When the aquarium guy gets here, he'll take us round the back. You'll be able to put your hand in.' I said.

'You're crazy.'

'Just put it in and see.'

She laughed and I started laughing as well. Sergei looked back at the tank. He laughed.

'I'm not so stupid, why don't you do it?'

'It's not stupid, we want you to find out if they sting.'

'I'm not stupid.'

There was the sound of a door opening further along the tunnel and an aquarium attendant came out. At the same time we heard Ryan and his assistant banging their way along the tunnel with the equipment. We all took bits of the equipment and followed the attendant through the door and into a corridor that ran round the back of the tanks. It smelt of fish food, the kind I remembered feeding my goldfish when I was small. We climbed some steps. We were in a metal-sided hangar with walkways suspended above the tank network. Blue light suffused up from the pools like werelights. There was the sound of water dripping and echoing.

'Here is the tank,' said the attendant.

Sylvie and I knelt down on the walkway and looked into the water. I moved my head about so as to change its angle. I couldn't see anything.

'Can you see them Sylvie?'

'No.'

'That's how most of them they function,' said the attendant. 'They float or they propel themselves depending on the species. Fish can't see them clearly. They enter an invisible poisoned forest. Paralysed.'

'But you could see them from down there quite well.'

'Yes you can see them according to the light.'

I looked round for Sergei. He was getting Sellotape, bulldog clips and rolls of plastic thread out of his bag and laying them out on a flat area.

'Sergei?'

He went on rummaging in the bag. Next to him Ryan's assistant talked to the attendant about lighting rigs. They began to walk off along the metal walkway with rolls of cable.

'Ryan put in your hand.'

She was leaning so far over that the points of her hair were touching the surface of the water and spreading out on it a little way. Ryan screwed up his eyes.

'What in there?'

'Yes. Touch one of them.'

He crouched next to us. I got up off my knees and stood back a bit from the edge.

'Didn't you hear what the guy said? Crazy chick.'

'It's not crazy. Most meduses are not poisonous to man.'

He walked off to where Sergei was arranging the stuff. She rocked back on her heels and stayed like that looking at the water. He came back.

'Aw fuck it.'

He squatted, rolled up his shirt cuff and plunged his arm in to above the elbow. He moved it back and forward in the water, looking up at the ceiling as though he were listening for something.

'There's nothing in there.'

'Wait.'

'There. Slippery little Wow!'

He yanked his arm out and turned up the palm. A red streak materialised, forming a snaky ridge. He bent double over it.

'Fuck! Fuck!' He hunched, squeezing the stung hand at the wrist with the other hand and rocking backwards and forwards.

'They sting,' said Sylvie.

The attendant ran up. 'It is not permissible to touch the animals.'

'Fuck!'

The word rang in the metal hangar and echoed.

'Quick, help him.' I recognized my own voice echoing.

The attendant wrapped a towel round his own hand. He grabbed Ryan's hand with the towelled hand and took the tweezers Sergei passed to him. He picked at the hurt hand with the tweezers, lifting off bits of jelly.

'Find me something,' he said to Sergei. 'A plate, a piece of cloth.'

'F-uck. F-uck.'

'Is it dangerous?' Sylvie asked the attendant.

He shook his head. He wiped a bit of jelly off on a cloth Sergei held out towards him.

'Be careful. Don't touch that. I'm sorry but if any of you do that again I'm going to have to stop this shoot. It's irresponsible.' He dropped Ryan's hand. 'Come to First Aid. I'll get you an injection.'

'How about a drink?' said Ryan. He managed a clenched grin.

'Vodka,' said Sylvie. 'Sergei?'

Sergei went over to his bag and pulled out a hip flask.

'You're like Mary Poppins with that bag,' I said.

Nothing on the telly. I finished drying myself with the towel. The big white building but no one outside it except the commentator, now in a kind of golf jumper. I got a Coke from the mini-bar. Sat on the bed. Sergei propping himself over the tank, suspending fishing-lines from bamboo canes. Sylvie saying be careful petit idiot or you'll fall in. Laughing like she wanted him to fall in. Me running down the stairs a hundred times and out into the tunnel to look through the tank glass at my picture. The diamonds pinsharp in the blue-black water. The jellyfish miasmas of glimmer. Sergei pulling on a pair of the surgical elbow-length gloves the aquarium guy gave to us. Me saying you're not really going to wear them are you? Sergei not saying anything, concentrating on getting the rubber right down into the space between each finger. Sylvie laughing into her hand, banging the heel of one shoe on the floor. Ryan calling Sergei the belle of the ball. Sergei leaning over the tank with his arms thrown out over the top and one foot on the adjacent walkway like a Daddy longlegs. Hold my belt at the back Naomi he says. Will you please? What for? I ask him. Just hold it he says and he sounds annoyed. I say sure and I hold it, rolling my eyes at Sylvie.

12

The American girls popped gum and said hey guys. They loved Sergei. Sergei Sergei Sergei morning till night they were hollering and screeching, their own words. We had two other girls as well, one Belgian and one Danish. Different in an immediately noticeable way from the Americans. More backward or else more sophisticated, it was hard to tell. Jaimie, Tina and Montana were the American girls' names. Jaimie was the one most in love with Sergei. The whole time she wasn't in a picture she was standing behind him with her arms over his shoulders and crossed loosely in front of his neck. One minute she'd whisper in his ear. He showed no expression. Then she'd yell Huh Huh Huh. They'd all join in HUH HUH HUH. Rap all day long. Sergei grabbed at the arms round his neck and tried to wrestle them off.

'Nooo, Sergei. Pleepleepleeplease.'

'Get off Jaimie your arms are too much.'

'You saying I got fat arms?'

'Heavy arms. Get off.'

Etc etc.

I sat with my feet up on the sofa in the kitchen area with Sylvie. We drank coffee and smoked cigarettes. The girls came in in the outfits one by one and we'd decide. The Dolce shoes. Not the top. Cut the bags. Sergei helped dress them in the little room where the make-up artist and the hair stylist had set up their shop. There were rails for the clothes in there and a clothes-steamer and an ironing board. All along one wall a mirror with naked lightbulbs round it like in a film about the theatre. The girls sat in chairs drawn up to the mirror and held up their faces to be made up. No windows and all the lightbulbs round the mirror, the steamer and the blow-dryers going. The hair stylist and the make-up artist babbling and bubbling in French. The models shouting Sergei! Sergei spraying everyone down the back and front of their T-shirts with the mister we had used on the plants. Jaimie made him do it down the front and back of her jeans as well. He showed no reaction. All the girls wanted it down the front and back of their jeans. He squirted. They squealed and clutched each other. He guffawed. He doubled over all lanky and dropped the mister. They jumped on him. Jaimie swung up on the counter that ran along under the theatre mirror. She was in her jeans and a vest. You could see her nipples sculpted in T-shirt cotton because there was a big damp stain on the front of her vest. She lifted her legs up and parted them in a high V.

'Spray me baby!'

'Fuck off.'

'SPRAY ME BABY!'

He sprayed. He was standing too far away and it barely touched her crotch.

'Harder!'

He moved in so the end of the mister was two inches from where the seams of her jeans made a cross. He kept pumping until the whole area was sopping wet while Montana and Tina screamed in the background. Sylvie came in and clapped her hands.

'Eh, Sergei I will have to install you in the bathroom. The shower here is not as good.'

He swivelled in cowboy pose and squirted water down the front of her blouse. I burst out laughing. She started shout-laughing at him in French too fast for me to catch and went out. He caught my eye. It was the first time he had caught my eye since the jellyfish shoot. I was holding a working woman suit. I held it up in front of my face.

'Don't even think about it.'

The inside of the jacket collar was right in front of my eyes. I read the label. Ralph Lauren. I waited. I could hear everyone talking at once on the other side of the suit but I couldn't see what was happening. Made in Mauritius. Fabriqué à l'Ile Maurice. My arm was starting to hurt. I lowered it. The girls were wiping each other off with paper towels and the make-up artist was helping them. Sergei had gone out of the room.

We shot the girls in their suits for the working woman on and around a derelict barge in the canal. The barge was further up the canal outside an abandoned warehouse whose door had been broken in. There were old loft doors at the back of the warehouse with the wood rotted along the bottom so you could see glints on the green water between the planks. Crowbarred the loft doors open and got Jaimie and Montana to sit in the dust of the doorway with their legs dangling down into the water reading Le Monde and a Financial Times we got from the English language bookshop on the rue de Rivoli. They sat cave-chested with long straggly hair. It was before that undone look went big and I felt anxious. I knew it wasn't what they wanted back in London for the suits for the working women story. Babs looking at me through the winged designer lenses. This one story more than any of the others has to be on-message Naomi. Clear and commercial, OK? It has to work for the readers, it has to work for the advertisers. I gave her the nod of someone who understands.

The light on the green water and the smell of the flowering bushes that grew out of the warehouse wall and trailed into the canal. Everyone was having such a blast. We shot from inside the building looking towards the barge and we shot from the barge itself looking back at the girls where they lounged in the doorway. Three of the girls sailing by in a rubber duck dinghy, squashed in together with their legs hanging over the fat sides. You couldn't really see the suits so I had the idea of making this shot shoes for the working woman. Their legs in the air all with ridiculous strappy heels on. We dragged a filthy old mattress squatters had left onto the barge and flung it in the rust with old beer cans. The girls lounged on it smoking and drinking beers with their jackets off and smudges of grime on their faces. Tina and Montana making paper doll chains out of the Financial Times. Jaimie in a Chanel suit over a grubby hoodie top wearing thick chain hung with dollar signs round her neck and leading a mongrel on a string. We shot them standing on top of the sunken barge using white blue and red shirts tied to a buddleia branch as a flag. At the end we shot them all five holding hands on the barge and one! two! three! wheeee! letting their cheapo Tati briefcases fly into the air and smack down into the yellow-green water. We did a shot of the briefcases and newspapers in the water. We went back to the studio to pack up.

The girls scrubbed at their made-up faces with Kleenex to get the stuff off. Sergei and me hung up the suits and brushed them off with clothes brushes. The make-up artist rolled up her sponges and brushes in cloth rolls and packed her foundations in her wheelie bag. A toot allure everyone said. We hugged each other. Sergei promised to make it one day to Ohio. He said he didn't think he could make it to Les Bains Douches on Saturday but he'd make it to Ohio. Slips of paper and model cards torn in half with telephone numbers on. Toot allure. Toot allure. The door closed. Sergei, Sylvie and me were left standing in the kitchen area. For a while we just stood there.

'Great. It was great,' I said.

I did a farewell look round the studio. The white cotton nailed over the windows. The oily yellow light.

'Really, it was great,' she said.

I couldn't look at the two of them. 'I better sort the clothes.'

I went into the dressing-room. Sergei came in. 'When do you go back to London?'

'Tomorrow.'

I clipped the stapler along the bottom of a clear plastic sheath covering a suit.

'Why don't you stay? Just a couple of days more.'

'I can't. I don't want to go but I can't.'

'But you're coming with us tonight right?'

'Where are you going?'

'Out with you.'

13

In the hotel bar the heat was lifting the odour of sat-on velvet into the air. A single overhead light made the air look hard. I picked a drinks menu off one of the tables and went through some French doors into the courtyard and sat down on a wrought iron two-seater with cushions on it. One of the reception boys came out.

'Good evening mademoiselle. Can I bring you something?'

'I'd like a glass of champagne please.'

'I am so sorry but I can give you only a bottle.'

He came round beside me and indicated on the drinks menu where it said champagne.

'OK. I'll have a bottle then.' I added, 'Very cold.'

He nodded, even kind of bowed, and in three big strides reached the French doors and went through into the hotel.

I slipped out of my shoes and curled my legs up on the two-seater. Pagrrhee. I looked along the rows of windows on the lower floor of the hotel. I wanted to see if anyone was going to pass in front of their window or push their window open and look up at the sky or down at me. I heard the voice of a woman saying something and laughing. I looked down at the blue silk dress. There were patches of darker blue where it had touched my body when it was still damp from the shower. It would dry.

The boy came back with a candle in a glass holder and the bottle of champagne in a silver bucket. He held the bottle in front of me and folded back the napkin so I could see the pinky-bronze label with the olde writing and the mysterious coat of arms that told how this was the drink of princes and hotels particuliers and girls in white dresses on the eve of wars.

'Oui ça va.'

He popped the cork. White froth seethed in the glass resolving from the bottom up into liquid. I tasted it. 'C'est parfait. Merci.'

I emphasised the see of merci. I went up at the end which would have sounded really stupid with thank *you.* It was completely different, French. I drank another mouthful. I looked up at the square of sky. It was that long drawn-out summer dusk. There were small high-up clouds and the sky was dark blue up there but somehow with light in it as well. I could see dots moving in it and then because I was concentrating I could hear them. The stinging sounds they made hunting for their dinner. Or maybe they were more like Jonathan Livingston Seagull. They weren't hunting at all. They were doing sky-ballet up there and the piercing sounds were screams of bird-joy.

The reception boy came out and said for you mademoiselle. He put a telephone slip on the table and went back into the hotel. I swallowed a big mouthful of champagne and felt it hurt all the way down. I picked up the slip. I liked the words En Votre Absence across the top and the icon of an old-fashioned telephone. I liked the dotted lines after M … and De … and N° de tél … for you to fill in and the shape of the slips. They were almost square. I might never see one like this ever again.

❑ vous a téléphoné ❑ demande que vous le rappeliez

❑ est venu pour vous voir ❑ vous rappellera

❑ désire un rendez-vous ❑ vous a rappelé

None of the choices had been filled in. It was always the same with multiple choices. The answer you wanted was never one of the choices. He hadn't bothered to fill in M., De, or N° de tél either. But that didn't mean the caller had had nothing to say. The rest of the slip was covered in writing. Small precise letters like those wedge-shaped early alphabets designed for pressing into wet clay. I had to read the first few lines a couple of times before I realised that the message was a poem. I put it down on the table. I looked at the back wall of the courtyard with the jasmine growing up it. Maybe they hadn't said the name and he'd just assumed it was for me. I picked it up. I tried to read it but there was a buzzing at the front of my mind that made it hard to take in especially since it was in a foreign language. Your gaze. Your smile. Your disparition. Like apparition but its opposite. I got to the end and I turned the slip over and there was more. I read down to the last stanza which began: Naomi. I put the slip on the table. He hadn't left his name, maybe he didn't want me to know. Wanted me to know but also wanted to be able to deny it if I laughed at it. Don't make a fool of yourself. That would be the terrible mistake. I drew in an audible breath at the thought of the terrible mistake. No he didn't mean it seriously it was some kind of joke. It was a way of apologising for something, some sort of French gesture of rapprochement. Rapprochement. I looked up at the square of sky. It was dark high up, but it looked as if there was a light still shining somewhere behind the flowing currents of dark. His left eye half closing when he smiled. The way his face and everything about him made me think of a peeled almond. A wonky muffled sound. I glanced up. Someone had put a telly on.

'Excusez-moi?'

There was no response.

'Excusez-moi!' I jumped up and ran through the French doors in my bare feet. I ran through the bar and out into reception. The boy was behind the counter scribbling in a ledger.

'Excuse me, are you sure this message is for me?'

I held out the slip. He looked at it.

'Yes it is for you mademoiselle.'

'But who left it? Didn't they give a name?'

He looked confused. 'I left it.'

'Ah   no I don't mean that. I mean   qui a téléphoné?'

'Personne n'a téléphoné.'

❑ vous a téléphoné/called you ❑ vous a rappelé/called you back
❑ personne n'a téléphoné/no one called

I slapped it down on the counter. 'Well then where did it come from?'

'It come from me.'

He dropped his pen. We stood staring at each other and then he turned, opened the door painted to look like part of the wall and lunged through it.

It could have been worse. It could have been so much worse. Imagine if I hadn't come through to reception. Imagine if when we were out I'd gone up to him when Sylvie was in the ladies and said, I got it. Imagine my face all open. Misty-eyed. Imagine if I had just gone straight to a phone a minute ago and rung him. Sergei? It's me. It's beautiful. I can't wait to see you alone. What? Sorry? I closed my eyes. I looked down at it again. The neat but almost indecipherable marks.

'Excusez-moi?'

The door was ajar but he wasn't visible in the gap.

'S'il vous plaît. Excusez-moi?'

I knew he was there just behind the door. 'Please. I need to talk to you.' I leaned my body sideways and slid my elbows along the counter to try and see round the door.

'S'il vous plaît. Can you come out for a minute?'

'Non.'

'Please, I just want to talk to you.'

He came out. He didn't meet my eyes.

'I'm so sorry. I didn't realise. You wrote this for me?'

He looked down at the floor tiles.

'It's,' I stood on tiptoe to lean further across the reception counter. 'Beautiful.'

His head sagged.

'Will you come and have a glass of champagne?'

'No. It's OK.'

I noticed how his Adam's apple jerked in his throat when he talked. Like having a penis in the neck.

'Please. I'd like to talk to you.'

'I cannot.'

He came out from behind the counter. He was tall and gangly with brown hair. It was the whiteness of his face that got me and the whites of his eyes behind his glasses. I gave him what I hoped was a sympathetic smile. He kept his eyes on the floor tiles.

'Come on. Please.'

I walked past him into the bar and out to the courtyard. He followed. Look, your lucky escape for one thing. You're in Paree. You're walking into a courtyard with a fountain. The air smells of jasmine and behind you is the French boy who has just written you a poem. I snuggled into the wrought iron two-seater. Be sensitive and gentle. Gentil. He stood by the table and then used the white napkin to pick up the champagne bottle and pour me a fresh glass.

'Merci, and maybe you could get a glass for yourself?'

He went into the bar and came back with another glass.

'Sit down. Please.' I pulled the bottle from the ice bucket and poured him some. 'To your beautiful poem.'

He met my eyes. His were dark blue. They widened when they looked into mine so you could see the whites all the way round.

'Really. It's very beautiful.' I smiled at him. Tender. Gentil and tender he's so fragile or exhausted or something.

'Is it by Baudelaire?'

'The poem?'

'Yes the poem.'

'You think it is like Baudelaire?'

'It kind of reminds me of Baudelaire.'

I did an inner search. I got things about hair like an incensoir and poems linked into chains with rhymes that crossed from one stanza into the next. The main things that came up: he lived in a garret and was constantly asking his mother for money; he believed in being decadent and taking loads of drugs and drink, probably absinthe; he may have been an opium addict – or was I getting him mixed up?; he wrote at night and slept by day; his mistress eyes were nothing like the sun, if snow be white why then her breasts are dun; he had written about her catty dancing and the perfume of her flesh, only poets say that, perfume of her flesh; he died destitute but magnificent and probably syphilitic. It's coming. Luxe, calme et volupté. Yes. Yes. Là tout n'est qu'ordre et beauté, Luxe, calme et volupté.

I said it out loud. Too neigh cord(ruh) was hard to say. Cor(drrr) is the hard bit if you are not French. He said something back in French.

'Say that again?'

'Mon enfant, ma sœur, Songe à la douceur d'aller là-bas vivre ensemble.'

'Is that Baudelaire?'

'Yes. It is him.'

'Right. So that's why I wondered: is it Baudelaire? Your poem has something the same about it.' Or could he read a shopping list in French and I would feel the same way? Six œufs, du lait, du beurre non-salé, une douzaine de bières, des bougies pas chères.

'Thank you.' He looked at the champagne glass on the table. He kept his hand round the stem. 'It's me who wrote it. I put your name in it.' Sad gentil. Tendre.

'Yes that's true.' Yes but you could have added my name to something by Baudelaire thinking she'll never know, she's English. 'How long did it take you?'

'It is difficult to know.'

'You haven't drunk any champagne.'

I had never seen a hand tremble before. I'd only read about it. I hadn't thought it could happen for real just because you were faced with the object of your poem. I put my head back to drain my glass. When it came right way up I caught him looking at me. He had the look people have in horror movies when they've just seen The Thing.

I nodded at his glass. 'Please drink some.'

He looked at the glass.

'What's your name?'

'Eric.'

'Well Eric. Are you a poet?'

'No I am student in philosophy.'

'Can you speak up a bit Eric?'

His head jerked up. The horror stare. 'When I see you I feel poetry in me.'

'So you are a poet.'

'No.'

'No you are. You are a poet.' The poem was lying on the table. I tapped it with my finger. 'You are a poet because you can write poems like this. What other qualification is there?'

He held the champagne glass tilted over his groin. I swallowed another mouthful. He was actually shaking.

'no one ever wrote me a poem before. I'm   Well   I really want to thank you.' I picked it up. I read a couple of the stanzas to myself more slowly. I couldn't quite figure out what it added up to. 'Are you sure you wrote it all by yourself?'

'Yes. To see you it is hard not to write poems.'

Shar moa.

'I hope you will keep writing poems for ever. There aren't enough poets.'

I lifted my glass. In the micro-second before I did it I realised in a vague way that I was going to look at him over the rim with mysterious eyes. I managed to stop myself. He yanked his glass up to his mouth and gulped down two-thirds of it. My eyes drifted to his Adam's apple. I watched it jerk under his throat skin while he drank. A breeze, the first that had made its way down here. It blew jasmine across the courtyard mixed with chlorine from the fountain. I refilled his glass and waited for him to say something. He stared at the tabletop. So, I said, which poets do you like? He pushed his glasses up to the bridge of his nose. Do you know so-and-so? No I said. So-and-so? Uh, no. So maybe so-and-so? I don't really know that many French poets, I did study some French writers but not any modern poets that I can remember. I think you will like Robert Desnos he said. The name's familiar, I said, and wrote it on the telephone slip. He pushed the glasses up. Maybe you know Rilke, but he's not French? I did a quick search. I got Rodin's secretary, something about love, how hard it was. I like the love poems I said, but I haven't really gone into him. Mallarmé? God yes, even in England we know about Mallarmé. Anyone else? Nerval? he said. I nodded thinking nutter, lobster on a lead. Rimbaud? Lice, filth, jubilant buggery. Apollinaire? Good name for a girl. Collection called Alcools. Thinker and drinker. I have a record with his voice on, I said aloud, reading his own poetry. I didn't add that it was unintelligible. Keep going I said, no one ever talks about poetry. He shrugged. Blaise Cendrars. Sounds like blazing cinders. I don't know if you must read Cendrars he said, but I like his name, he is good on names. Right I said, that's interesting, that's very interesting that you should say that. More, more. Berenguier de Palou? I scanned. It came up blank. He sounds old, aristocratic. Yes he said, he die many centuries ago but his music live on isn't it great? I don't know I said, I've never heard any. I smiled and he smiled. And Baudelaire he said, I am happy you love Baudelaire. No women? I said. You mean poets who are women? Yes, women poets. He shook his head. No I have to discover more women poets. It's my shame. He looked at me and I panicked in case he was going to ask me to come back with the women poets.

'Never mind the women, who do you think is a real genius?'

'For me it's not relevant. I love to read Dante.'

'Oh yes, amazing, and funny too isn't it? Inferno I mean. We did it in Comparative European Literature. Not in Italian though.'

Emily Brontë. She wrote a few. And Goblin Market, a woman definitely and probably the girl who modelled for the Pre-Raphaelite Ophelia.

'His sonnets to Beatrice, you know them?'

Ophelia glided on her back between us with her mouth open.

'No. I must take a look. But I find the whole idea of her a bit irritating.'

The Russian woman.

'You don't like Beatrice?'

'Well it's not that. I just can't imagine a woman writing that way about a man.'

Can't remember her name just her picture in profile on the front of the Penguin edition. Huge nose with two even three ripples in it. Insane nose carnival nose.

'I've got one. The poet with the big nose. The one who'

'Cyrano.'

'No no. Though his nose was a joke wasn't it? No a woman, Russian. Wonderful. You should read her. Shit, what's her name?'

He smiled which made me want to touch the back of his hand. 'It doesn't matter. What matter is to come nearer to things with words. To feel them pass your throat and in your head.' He put his hands on the chair-arms and looked over his shoulder into the hotel. 'Can you excuse me a moment?'

He ran in. I heard the ding ding of the old-fashioned bell on top of the reception counter being pressed and his voice saying, Je viens tout de suite. Them? I pulled the clip out of my hair and felt it damp on my shoulders. I ran my hands through to ease it out and leaned back and let my eyes look up at the square of sky. What I wanted to happen had happened. A big star. The sort of star that is so big and vibrating so slowly it could be a plane. Behind it the sky was black-blue with dim lightness hidden in it. I widened my nostrils to see if I could smell the jasmine. I heard someone coming. I licked my lips.

He stood in the entrance to the bar white-faced.

'You're back.'

He held up his hand and disappeared. I let the back of my head roll onto the chairback. I looked at the star. He came back carrying a new bottle of champagne.

'Allow me to offer you a glass.'

'I'll get drunk.'

He peeled off the bronze foil and untwisted the braided wires over the cork. 'That will be very nice.'

It was colder than before. He picked his glass up and knocked some back.

'You'll have to explain that last bit about poetry.'

'I don't know. Sometimes I just do as a dog do, but as I am not a dog I lick with words.'

I almost snapped my fingers. Sylvia Plath. Of course really famous and we did a couple of her poems at school. Daddy, Daddy. Bean-green (yuch) over blue. The brute brute heart of a brute like you. Head in the oven having left biscuits and milk out for the babies.

'Dogs don't just lick,' I said.

'I don't just lick also.' He laughed.

'So your theory of poetry, it's licking?'

We both laughed.

'I don't know what poetry is. It touch things but it also change the things it touch. I suppose a kind of métamorphose. But I don't want that. I fight it but I can't escape. I just want to touch it, really touch it without myself being there.' He was sitting forward with his elbows on the table. He brandished his glass of champagne. 'Maybe only God can touch things without changing them.'

'But he changes everything, whether he exists or not.'

Ringlets, recumbent position, pet spaniel, doe eyes, permanently half-dead. For fuck's sake let me count the ways.

'In one way yes.'

'And you said you want to feel things in your head.'

'Without feeling my head. I want to pass beyond the limit of my head.'

'Then you'd be dead.'

I shall but love thee better after death etc etc. Elizabeth something.

'In one way.'

'Everything's in one way with you!'

I tapped out a cigarette and he picked my lighter up off the table.

'How about you?' he said over the lighter flame. 'Where do you want to go?'

'Well, I've never thought about it that way before.' I took a drag. 'But hell yes. Beyond the limit.'

He had a sweet laugh. Gentil.

'Who knows about any of it? I speak only about desire. To write poetry is to be stupid.'

'In one way.'

'Of course! Stupid in one way, and crazy in the other way.'

Behind his head Sergei and Sylvie appeared in the doorway to the bar. Black suits and ripped-up T-shirts. Something flashed at ground level. Metallic boots under her trousers. She said, 'Ah you are drinking champagne.' Sergei reached his hand up and broke off a bit of the jasmine growing round the door. He stepped down into the courtyard and dropped it on my lap. I caught a flash from Eric's glasses. I looked down at the jasmine. I was going to do it. I kept looking at my lap. I heard scraping and banging and saw Eric's feet moving in shoes that could have been Hush Puppies. Blood hot in my cheeks. I heard Sylvie saying bonsoir and him mumbling something and I reached down and picked up my bag which was lying beside my chair. I rummaged in the bag for as long as I could. Then because I had no other good reason to keep looking down I stood up. I felt Sergei's arm go round me and pull me towards him. He did it in a messing-around way as though the next move was going to be a playful punch to the stomach. He kissed my cheek through my hair.

'Here you are,' he said.

I felt my body sink into his body without me meaning it to. He let me go.

'Would you like some champagne?'

Eric had gone.

'You like to drink?' said Sylvie.

'Lets have it at the club,' he said.

'Yes OK.'

I started after them into the bar. 'Oh. Just a minute.'

I ran back out to the courtyard and there it was next to my half-drunk glass. I put it in my bag and went back through to reception. There was no one behind the counter. We went down the stairs to a small basement carpark, Sylvie joking about her twenty-year-old Renault. There was some discussion about who should sit in the back. I wanted to because Sergei was tall and there was no room for his legs in the back, but he folded himself in and I sat next to Sylvie.

We roared up the ramp and round a corner to the exit.

'There is your friend,' said Sylvie.

Eric was running in front of the car. He held one hand up to his face to protect his eyes from the headlights. His face was even whiter in the glare.

'He's not my friend. He just works in the hotel.'

He reached the wall and squashed himself against it. He was doing something, feeling up the wall. We drove the couple of yards to the metal roller-door and stopped. I saw Sylvie looking for her window handle when the metal roller started to open from the bottom. I was aware of Sergei sitting behind me. I stared at the metal roller and counted off each corrugation as it disappeared ...3...4...5... Sylvie revved the engine and let the car nose forward. He crouched, coming up right next to the car. I willed the roller-door to move faster. 10...11...12... He was shading his eyes, trying to see where I was sitting. I kept my eyes straight ahead. 13...14...15... She pressed the accelerator and we coasted through before the door was all the way up. As we passed I saw with my peripheral vision his hand held up next to his white face with the glasses. We turned onto the street and bumped down the cobbles past the hotel entrance. At the T-junction we turned into the busier road and Sylvie put the car in third gear. I felt bad then for not having waved at him in the carpark. The Boy Who Wrote me A Poem In Paris. I stored the memory away in my 'experiences' deposit account.

14

We took a table by the balustrade up on a kind of mezzanine. There were candelabras all along it with wax dripping down the marble. People were playing chess and backgammon against the backdrop of a sixty-foot-high velvet curtain.

'You play?' said Sylvie.

'Not really.'

'Champagne?'

She snapped her fingers at a passing waiter. I looked over the room below. There was a huge chandelier in the shape of an upside down tree. People dancing. Some kind of terrible French hip hop but it was fantastic. The waiter came back with a bottle and a bucket on a stand.

'To us.'

'To us.'

'To us.'

'Cigarette?'

Sergei pulled out his blue pack, half-tapped out a fag and held the pack towards me. I was resting my arms on the balustrade and my chin on my arms to watch the dancers. I parted my lips. You're drunk. Yeah so? He pulled the cigarette from the pack with finger and thumb and brought it across to my lips. I watched as the finger that was crooked across the top of the cigarette came closer and closer until it was a blur. The jaws relaxed so the lips almost closed again and the cigarette had to push through to get in. As the mouth adjusted to hold the cigarette the finger, which smelt of the rubber at the end of a pencil, came within millimetres of the top lip. By cocking my head just slightly I could move his fingertip to the far left corner where the top lip met the bottom lip and because the pressure of the finger right on the corner would push the lips wider it would take only a tiny adjustment of my head at that moment for the finger to slide into the mouth and along the inside of the left cheek before, dropping the Gitane, I could ease it round with the tongue and suck it. I breathed out. The heat of my breath came back at my skin from the nearness of the finger and the lips pulsed so that they came for a fraction into contact with the finger before they pulled back like the insides of an oyster.

The finger whooshed away. A few seconds later he held the burning match out to the end of the cigarette. His left eye half-closed. I inhaled, snatched the cigarette out of my mouth and Oing my lips, blew out the match. Naomi you are drunk. And?

Keeping my eyes off his face I turned my head to look over the balustrade. 'Hey Sergei, I've always meant to ask you where you got that name.'

There was no answer. I looked round.

'He is Russian.' She was smoking as well, leaning back with one metallic boot up on the balustrade.

'I'm French. I was born in the Soviet Union.'

'So how did you end up here?'

'My parents.'

'But I thought you couldn't get out?'

He raised his eyebrows.

'His father was a conservator at a museum. There was an exhibition of some of the treasures of the museum here in Paris and Sergei's father accompany them. He pass to the West.'

'Lets drink,' said Sergei. He raised his glass. Sylvie put her boot on the ground and picked up her glass.

'Vive la France,' he said.

'Vive la France.'

They upended their glasses. I did the same. I had to turn away to look over the balustrade so I could burp without them seeing. When I turned back Sergei was refilling the glasses.

'Like Rudolf Nureyev or something?' I said.

'Exacte. Sergei's father must be the Rudolf Nureyev of mechanisms of seventeenth century. Many cultural people come to the West I think because they are the ones who have an opportunity.'

He gestured towards the bar below us with his head.

'It's Françoise. With Jacques.'

'No. Where?'

'By the bar. See her?'

Sylvie moved her head to look between the uprights of the balustrade.

'But Sergei how did you get out when your dad defected?'

'It was a bureaucratic thing. A kind of error. My mother and me left from Bulgaria and join my father here.'

'Bulgaria?'

Sylvie said something.

'Yeah Bulgaria. No I don't want to see them,' he said in French. 'Not now.'

'Did you have to hide in a laundry basket or anything?'

'Sack of potatoes.'

'Seriously?'

He smiled.

'Do you still speak Russian?'

He shook his head.

'Oh come on. Say something. I said something in Welsh.'

'How about backgammon?' he said.

Sylvie clicked her fingers at the waiter and he shot out from his post then busied off. She picked up her glass and let it dangle from her fingers. 'Sergei's papa is a specialist in a kind of Russian clocks and toys with lots of little automates. You know the kind of little men who ring the bells, open the doors, ride the mechanical horses?'

It seemed natural to look every now and then at the person she was talking about. He had propped his feet up on the balustrade making a V shape and he was watching the dancefloor through the V.

'But these ones can do more things. Dance. Play at the piano. The much later ones make a little discourse of philosophy.'

The waiter came up. In one hand he had a backgammon set and in the other a plate with bar snacks.

'And the authorities did not know what to do with him here. You know how it is. You are a king in your country but in another country you drive a taxi. So one of the conservators at Versailles got him a job as Maître des Grandes Eaux.'

I was free to examine his profile. I did it mathematically so as to memorise it. The distance from his hairline to where the eyebrows started. The length of his nose vis-à-vis the width of his cheeks. Exactly how far below his nose his lips were. Stronger than pink but not red.

'Sergei you are dreaming. Do you want to play a game?'

He brought his feet down. 'I'll play with Naomi.'

'What is a master of grand waters?'

'Do you know Versailles?' she said.

Sergei refilled our glasses. He looked round for the waiter.

'I know where you mean. Where the Sun King lived. It's supposed to be spectacular.'

'Yes spectacular, and also it have many grottoes, fountains, water chutes, canals, reservoirs, aqueducs, lakes, everything you can do with water. And they work by seventeenth-century hydraulique still now. When Sergei arrive from the East Bloc all the hydraulique was in bad condition. Sergei's father repair everything.'

'Wow Sergei, that's incredible.'

He was laying the counters out on the pointy triangles on either side of the backgammon board. 'Do you want to be white or red ?'

'White.'

He turned the board round.

'OK, it was not so exciting for Sergei's father but better than a taxi, no?'

'I think it sounds fantastic. Better than working in an office like most dads.'

He passed me the leather cup with the dice. I looked down at his other hand resting on the edge of the board while I shook the cup. I threw the dice on the board. A three and a six.

'But what is nice is that once a month they put on all these many fountains and water chutes. On that day Sergei's father is the one who runs from grotto to grotto and he turns on the fountains with a special key that fit into a secret hole. Maybe behind the breast of a nymph or under the spear of a Triton.' She pronounced it tree toh.

The waiter brought another bottle of champagne.

'And when he was a little boy Sergei run after his father and help him to turn the secret key and voilà, the water comes from the mouth of a hippocampe or from the points of giant breasts.'

He indicated his two fives with the leather cup. 'Bad luck.'

'I wish my childhood had been like that. It's like a fairy story.'

He threw the dice and moved his counters. 'You don't know the water that comes out. It smells like hell.'

I picked up the cup and shook it. 'Maybe you can go back to Russia now. It's on the news.'

He stood up. His left eye half-closed. 'I don't want to go back there. I want to go back here.'

He walked along the red curtain hitting it with his hand until he found the place where it parted. He went through.

'What did I say?'

'Not you. Me. He is very conformist in some ways. He don't like his father to be like a mechanic. He wants his father to be a lawyer, a doctor, a professor. Like a lot of fathers want their son to be a lawyer, a doctor. You know, not a stylist.'

'It's a shame he sees it that way.' But what if he'd been a painter not a stylist?

'He don't like his own story. A lot of people are like that. Other people love too much their own story.'

'But it's such a good story.'

'For you yes.'

'What about going back to Russia? He must have relatives.'

'It don't exist for him. And he don't talk about the family there. If someone pass to the West they make life hard for the ones who are left. Come on. Lets go with him. You'll like it on the other side.'

She indicated to the waiter to bring the champagne and I followed her behind the red velvet curtain.

15

I pressed the ceramic nodule in the middle of the brass panel. I heard the inner doors opening then the sound of keys shuffling and one of the outer wooden doors swung out.

The white face, the heavy black frames of the glasses. Something else.

'Hallo Naomi.'

I frowned. 'What are you doing here?'

He moved his mouth without words coming out. I walked past him into the reception area.

'This means you've been on' I pressed the button for the lift 'almost twenty-four hours. In fact' – He was standing beside the half-glass doors with Hotel Milord written in gold across the glass. Only I couldn't read the words properly. I blinked and re-focused. Couldn't read it at all – 'twenty-four minus four and a half hours.'

The lift pinged.

'Please. I must talk with you.'

'I'd love to, but I have to be up in a few hours. I have to catch a plane.'

'Please!'

Idiot, it's because it's written back to front from inside.

'I wanna thank you for the poem. Really it was amazing. Please go home.'

I got into the lift and bumped against the brass panel with the floor numbers on it.

'Naomi I beg you. I have something to say.'

His voice all hunched. Should never have invited him for that glass of champagne. The big mistake is being nice to them. Then you never get rid of them. The doors closed and I went up to the top floor.

The air in the room moved in and out of my nostrils with the consistency of snot. Opened the window. Air. Spinny. Opened minibar. Really spinny. Got out all six of the mini-size Evian and the two Perrier. Took them to bedside table. Had to remove stuff from bedside table first so threw teeny-tiny bottles on bed. Something on bedside table. Piece paper. Writing on it. Small incised handwriting.

Two questions:
1. how to live without love?
2. why to love if to love is to suffer?
Eric

I put it on the bed next to the Evian bottles. I picked up the pen and the telephone memo pad and the bracelet and coins and dropped them on the chair. I moved the telephone as far to the edge next to the bedside lamp as possible. Of course there would be a master key at reception. I picked up the mini-bottles two by two and grouped them on the bedside table. He could have been in here for ages. He could have been looking through all my things. Masturbating on my panties. I sat on the bed. Maybe some panties were missing. Must have been a disappointing bunch, my panties. No lace. No silk. And if I learn anything from all this it is: style starts at the panties.

I picked up one of the mini-bottles of Evian and cracked the seal. A pure sound filled the room. I put the Evian bottle down on the bedside table. I looked at the phone. It was ringing. I watched it. It kept on ringing.

'Hello?'

'Naomi.'

'It's three in the morning.'

'May I talk with you for a moment?'

'I am sleeping.'

'Please.'

'OK well hurry up.'

'I cannot do it on the phone. I must see you just for a moment.'

Should never have invited him for that glass of champagne. That was the dumb thing. You're too soft it's not a sign of genuine compassion.

'I'm sorry Eric I'm leaving in a few hours. This is goodbye.'

Some kind of forties Hollywood sign-off. Fine.

I threw the blue dress onto the chair and kicked my way out of my panties. Sweat-damp. I picked up one Evian bottle and drained it. Threw it in the wastepaper basket. Two Evian bottle. Drained it. Wastepaper basket. Three Evian bottle. Four. I couldn't do any more. I snapped off the light, pulled back the covers and fell into the bed. I let the pillows puff up round my cheek and my nose but leaving a cool channel through the cotton where my breath could come and go. Spinny. Roomrocking. But if I just breathe and hold onto a centre position between the in and the out it will be OK. Don't panic at spinny don't moan at spinny don't pay attention spinny. Just stay at the centre point between an in and an out breath and let each of them sort of arc out from that point like signals you are sending out across a radar screen. You stay in the middle. You the blip. They the sweep. You the blip. They the sweep. You the blip.

Three sharp strikes. I froze under the bedcover. All my awareness in my ears like a dog or a deer. I opened my eyes. I'd left the curtains open. A faint orange glow was purling and streaming on the ceiling. He sighed. It was as if he were sighing right next to my bed. I lifted my head off the pillow, turned it in mid-air, and placed it back on the pillow as softly as possible. I was now facing the door. I could see the door handle. I could see the little button in the middle of the door handle that you pressed to double-lock the door. It was still pressed in. I had done that. That's good. He has a master key. That was how he left the note about how to live without love. Can a master key unlock a double-locked door? I stared precisely at the pushed-in button on the door. I listened. The silence listened back at me. Then.

'Naomi.'

My eyes widened when I heard him say my name. I sensed him

standing a few feet away on the other side of the door. I felt something rhythmic like breathing coming through the thin lit-up lines between the door and the door-frame. He must know I was awake in here. He had knocked so loudly. He must know I was listening. Maybe he had put his head against one of the door panels so he could hear any slight movement I made.

I parted my lips. It made a sound of plastic unsticking. I made my breath shallow and light. I stared at the door handle. If I heard a key, if I saw the door handle turning now I would scream my head off. Or would only a croak come out?

A breeze got up. I let my eyes roll around the room as much as possible without moving my head. The furniture looked calm. I saw my clothes for the morning laid over the back of the chair. My suitcase all ready and my washbag still sitting on top of the suitcase. I heard the net curtains filling with air, streaming out, falling back and batting against the window frame. They filled, streamed out for a few moments. I half-turned my head, very very quietly so I could see them. The grey of them was ghosted through with the faint orange glow. I watched them fill, stream and fall back. I must have fallen asleep then, because I came to with a jerk like when you think you are falling in your sleep. Immediately I knew where I was. He had waited on the other side of the door until he calculated I had fallen asleep. Then he put his key in the lock and entered. I tried to whip round in the bed but the movement was feeble like a sick person's.

I sat up in the bed and stared into every corner of the room. My heart was thumping in my chest and my throat. I reached for the fifth bottle of Evian on the bedside table. Ridiculous. He just wants to talk to you. He's pathetic, some French boy, a romantic, a wannabe poet. You're drunk. I finished the Evian and threw the bottle at the waste-paper basket. I got up and walked across the room. A moment of blindness when I yanked open the door. Then I took in the corridor yellow with electric light. I could see down it to where it turned in for the lift area and past that to the stairs. I looked the other way and saw a few room doors and then where it turned the corner for the other side of the building. He wasn't there. There was something on the carpet in front of the door. A packet wrapped in brown paper. I shunted it in with my foot and shut the door again. I double-locked it. I propped a chair against the doorknob the way I'd seen them do in the movies.

I got into bed and pulled the phone down onto the pillow. The cord was caught on something, I had to reach behind the bedside table and move one of its legs to get a coil of cord out from under it. It rang and rang. When he picked up I heard his breathing first.

''Lo.'

'Dan.'

'Wha'?'

'I love you.'

I heard him moving about in the bedclothes where I would be tomorrow. No, today.

'What time is it?'

'Late. I just needed to hear your voice.'

'What's up?' He yawned.

'Nothing. You have no idea how good it is to hear your voice. Say something.'

'Love you.'

'Do you?'

'Mm-hmm. You OK?'

'Yeah. You know. Just spooks. Bad dreams.'

'Aw babe. That's too bad.' He yawned again. 'I missed you.'

'Dan will you tell me a story? Please? I can't sleep.'

'Not now babe. Just go back to sleep.'

'I need you to tell me a story. Please I'm scared.'

'What's wrong Naynay?'

'Nothing.'

I looked at the orange light streaming slightly on the ceiling. The wavy old panes of glass were vibrating in their frames causing the refracted light to stream and purl.

'Really nothing. I just got a bit drunk. Bad dreams. Snakes. And I have to sleep or I'll miss my plane. Please baby.'

'OK.'

I heard sounds that must have been him sitting up in bed. I heard him drinking something.

'OK. You ready?'

'Yeah.'

I put the receiver down right next to my head. I snuggled into the pillows. I closed my eyes and listened to his voice coming out in an unintelligible stream of tinny sounds.

16

Bang bang.

'Mademoiselle?'

Bang bang.

'Mademoiselle? It's eight o'clock.'

Pale light. The heavy round ball of the receiver-end beside me on the pillow. I struggled to grab it but my arm had gone to sleep. I half-turned and picked it up with the other arm. The line was dead.

'Mademoiselle?'

Bang bang.

'Oh. OK. Thank you.'

Not him. The other reception boy. I pulled the cover over my shoulder.

'Mademoiselle, you forget to hang the phone.'

'OK.'

My eyes closed. Whee whee whee. They were so close I could hear the flick-knife sound of their wings cutting the air. Hunting or just happy. I sat up and swung my legs out in one go. I grabbed my washbag and ran into the tiny shower-room with its skylight set into the slant of the roof. I turned the shower on full and stood under it looking up at the sky. Black Ms cutting the blue. The sun baking the golden pasties. In the cafés people would be drinking cafés crèmes and eating tartines.

When I came out I saw the brown paper parcel lying on the floor next to the door. I opened it. It was a book small enough to fit in a pocket. Cyrano de Bergerac by Edmond Rostand. I turned it over. Le nez de Cyrano s'est mis en travers de son cœur. Cyrano's nose put itself across his heart. What a nose! I opened the book. The small incised handwriting. In English: to make you smile. I put it in my pocket.

The lift doors opened. Ray de show say. I prepared myself. But it was the other boy who smiled from the reception desk and asked me if he should prepare the bill now. I went through into the breakfast room and ordered a coffee from the Filipina in charge of breakfast and picked up a croissant and a plate of cut melon from the buffet table. Always a bit sad-looking the buffet table. You can't array cornflakes and cocoa pops. You can't make them look feasty. Thank God. Thank God he'd buggered off. Well, it was a story. I sipped the café crème and flicked through the book. Mon cœur ne vous quitta jamais une second. From Cyranochristian's last letter written as he lay dying. My heart will never leave you even for a second. Oh here it comes. A slow builder. The slow builder hangovers are the worse. I pushed a bit of croissant in my mouth. I flicked backwards through the play.

> Cyrano: Aimez-vous le gâteau qu'on nomme petit chou?
> La Duègne, avec dignité: Monsieur, j'en fais état, lorsque il est à la crème.

Cyrano: Do you like the cake that one names petit chou. Little cabbage. Do you like the cake that one names little cabbage? The Duègne, with dignity: Sir. Jzzoh fay ay tah when it's made of cream/comes with cream. Jzzoh fay ay tah. I make the state? I make room. I get in a real state when it's made with/comes with cream!

I broke off another bit of croissant. And then he says – slurp of coffee – j'en plonge six pour vous dans le sein d'un po – ahhh – ème. That's good that's really good. I plunge six for you in the breast of a poem. I got up. I wiped my mouth with the napkin. I picked up the cup again and drank another mouthful. Another mouthful. Monsieur j'en fais état, lorsque il est à la crème. J'en plonge six pour vous dans le sein d'un poème. I put the cup down I plunge six for you in the breast of a poem and stuck the book in my back pocket I plunge six for you in the breast and went through quickly to reception I plunge six I plunge.

*

Him.

'Bonjour Naomi.'

I felt myself go stiff. 'Bonjour. Is my taxi coming?'

'Just a moment.' He picked up the phone. I smiled at the other boy. I wondered how much he knew.

'Your bill is ready mademoiselle.'

'He will be here in five minutes,' said Eric. White really white. Kind of disgustingly white.

'Fine. Would you be very kind and bring down my luggage?'

He stared at me with the horror movie eyes. I looked away and went up to the reception desk and leaned my elbows on it. I heard him get into the lift. The other boy slid the bill across the counter to me.

'Ah Mademoiselle, would you please like to check?'

I looked at pages one, two and three without reading.

'Here and here.'

I signed.

'Thank you Mademoiselle. It has been a pleasure for us to welcome you here at the Milord.'

'Thank you. You've been really nice.' A tip. Or would it be patronising?

'No no, it has been a pleasure every day.'

I walked through to the back where the French doors were open onto the courtyard. They had been watering the plants and the paving stones were all wet. The fountain was off and there was a coil of hose attached to a tap just under the cherub. I looked round and saw the wrought iron table and the two-seater chair. I went back through to reception. There was the tiny lift. And there next to the lift doors was the first flight of stairs that went up and round a corner and up. The day I'd come back upset with my shopping. One of them, it must have been Eric, had carried up my stuff. Brought me that plate of ice-cream. That was a kind thing to do. Gentil.

'Your taxi mademoiselle.'

I must change my name. Ding-a-ling ding. Mad-ah moi-zelle! I went out and into the taxi.

The other boy stood in the entrance and waved and then looked over his shoulder and went in and I saw Eric coming out with three bags slung round his body and carrying my suitcases. He went back in and came back with two boxes. I looked ahead up the road. The driver got out and went round the back with Eric. J'en plonge six pour vous dans le sein d'un poème. A slow builder. The driver got in.

'Ça va, mademoiselle?'

'Oui. Allons-y.'

I didn't want to but I looked round one last time at the hotel. I rolled down the window.

'Eric can you come here a minute?'

He squatted by the window and his face came level with mine. I tried not to look at it, it was upsetting. I looked at his hand resting on the rolled-down window.

'Naomi, I'm sorry I disturb you. I just want to say you something.'

'It's OK. I'm not angry. I've got the book. Thank you for the poem. I'll always keep it.'

I started to roll up the window. A noise came out of his throat. I flinched.

'Will you come back?'

I raised my voice to carry through the closing gap. 'No I'll never come back. A l'aeroport s'il vous plaît.'

The taxi jerked forward.

PART 2

17

I closed the front door so it would make just a light click. A wedge of grey-brown light where the kitchen door was open at the end. To my right the bedroom door. Futher along the living room door. I slipped out of my shoes and left them on the doormat with the cases and bags and walked carefully up the passage. Sounds of the telly coming through the wall. As I passed the living room door a telly voice said 'ooz issat then?' He made a gobble noise like a marsh bird. I smiled. I looked at the door handle but I went on towards the kitchen.

I fortified myself almost immediately but I'd forgotten to remind myself while I was away so it hit me anyway. The old dirt that had fossilised where the metal rim round each electric ring met the white enamel. The sticky dirt under the fridge where we never went. The countertop with the formica of it eaten away at the corner. Blackened damp wood underneath the formica. Some gigantic insect that comes in at night and feeds on formica.

Or formica dissolving atom by atom into the air the way rocks go.

I took the kettle to the sink. There were two pots in it stacked one on top of the other and filled with water. Film of grease droplets on the water. A drip fell from the tap into the top pot and tendrils of a dried-on orange skin that was stuck to the side of the pot eddied in the water. I leaned over the sink holding the kettle. A new drop was starting to form on the end of the tap. It swelled and hung, swelled and hung. I let my eyes rest on the grey membrane of the drip that seemed to hold in lighter, more liquid water in the middle. The drop was hanging in an unbelievably big bag from the tap. It didn't act like water it clung on, shaking when a tube train rumbled in the ground under the house. I breathed in, out. It swelled a bit more, trembled. I inhaled. It swelled. I did a long inhalation from the bottom of the lungs. It fell like a body from a building and crashed into the water in the pan. The tendrils of tegument wobbled in the disturbed water. I looked at the tap. The next bump of water was forming. Drop by drop, the water was loosening the gel of baked bean sauce from the side of the pan. In time, how much time? In say, five days time, the whole sheet of gelled sauce would come away at some unspecified hour of the night when no one would see. Next day it would be found lying half-folded under the water at the bottom of the pan.

I filled the kettle and put it on one of the rings. The electric ring flushed from dark grey to dark rose. A lovely colour the dark rose of an 'on' electric ring. At least it was on the old cookers like this one. They had this advantage. I felt the warmth on my face. The television voices got louder. I looked up out of the window at the patio garden.

'Nay you're back.'

I smiled at the window and brought my head round. There he was. He was wearing the cords his mother had given him for his birthday.

'Yeah.' I smiled more. 'Hello.'

'OK. Right. You're in a bad mood.'

'No I'm not.' Smile.

'Well why did you sneak in stead of saying hello?'

'I was going to surprise you with a cup of tea.'

We looked at each other without blinking. He snapped his eyes off mine and went back out through the kitchen door. I felt words come up through my throat and go after him.

'Couldn't you even wash the dishes for fuck's sake?'

'Aw for fuck's sake!'

The living room door slammed shut.

I put a teabag in a mug and poured the hot water in on top. I stood with my back to the countertop and looked out of the window at the patio area. It was a small paved area with a few plant pots and then a wall and starting on top of the wall the proper garden where the basement flat lessees were not allowed to go.

18

The editorial department was in an L-shaped room with everyone in the long part of the L except fashion. We were in the short part of the L. I was almost at the crook of the L and if I leaned right back I could see all the way to the back of the long bit. There was no one just the features assistant putting her coat over the back of her chair at the other end. I turned back to the receiver.

'I don't know what came over me,' I said.

'You're always weird coming back from somewhere,' he said.

'Like where?'

'Anywhere. You're always weird when you come back from your mum's.'

'That's because Solihull makes people weird. It's the normalcy.'

'Normalcy?'

'I think it's American.'

'Oh definitely Yank. Maybe a Yank girl's name.'

'We could get a dog called Normalcy.'

'I feel it's more a bunny's name.'

'Lets get a bunny! Two bunnies. Baby bunnies.'

'Grow up fast to be fat arse rabbits. Maybe a good thing. Maybe we could set up a little bunny butcher's.'

'No.'

'We'd give them a nice life before the chop. What more can a companion animal ask for?'

'Dan?'

'Mm-hmm.'

'Dyou forgive me?'

'If you say you love me.'

'I love you.'

'OK then I forgive you.'

'Do you want to meet me at lunchtime?'

'Strangely I've got a job interview.'

'That's good. Is it a'

'Need to know basis.'

'God, you're such a grown-up.'

'You may not have noticed but I'm getting quite big now.'

'It is very noticeable.'

'I better get off and do some big man type things then.'

'When will you be home?'

'Lets go out.'

'But I'm broke. You're broke.'

'Naturally.'

'Can you get money out? No I can get some.'

'It's on me babe. Got my ways and means.'

'But aren't you on at the bar tonight?'

'I love you.'

'I love you much much more, I'm going to prove it, I'm going to show you.'

'How?'

'Physically. Realism.'

'For example?'

I craned my head to see round the corner. The features assistant was opening her post.

'Are you sitting comfortably?' I said.

'Should I be? Or should I perhaps be sitting uncomfortably?'

'Well if you put it like that Mr?'

'Mr Normalcy. Mr Nigel Normalcy.'

'What a coincidence, you know we have a Bunny Normalcy here at the Centre?'

'Ah Bunny. Distantly related. She's a very furry little girl.'

'Furriness is something of a speciality for Bunny. As well as speed and efficiency.'

I glanced through the L.

'And you Miss'

'Slatterly.'

'Miss Slatterly. What's your speciality?'

'Ah well. It's uh lingual.'

'Sorry?'

'Lapsus linguae.' A laugh got out of me. 'Sorry.'

'Really Miss uh.'

'Slatterly.'

'Really I don't want any tongue business, lapsed or otherwise. I am interested in normalcy. Do you understand me?'

'Well may I call you Nigel? You see, normalcy is a dirty word here at the Centre. You may find that the price you have to pay for it is high, extremely high. You may find the practitioners of normalcy are little more than familiar strangers bearing sad surprises.'

'Aha, now you are talking in the necromancy of normalcy.'

'Well as it's a black art masquerading as barely a modus vivendi.'

'Oh I like it Miss Slatterly, this casual tossing off of a foreen phrase that you go in for.'

'Believe me it is entirely ex animal.'

'Deo gratias.'

'I'm running out of Latin, Nigel.'

'Habeas corpus.'

'It was there last time I looked.'

'When do I get a look?'

'You'll have full opportunity to look at leisure.'

'I'll embrace it. Better go off to big man business.'

'Very well, Mr Normalcy. Good lu-'

'Seven at the pub Miss Slatterly.'

'I'll be waiting.'

My post was in a huge pile that had collapsed and slid across to where Becca's desk backed onto mine. I prised open the lid of my cappuccino with a finger and stirred the foam and chocolate powder together with the end of a pencil. I swept the big A4 envelopes back off her desk onto mine and opened the top one. I sipped. Too hot. Pulled out a glossy black press release folder. CHANEL in white sans serif. I opened it. Sip. Sheets of expensive paper that smelt of photochemical announced the winter cruise collection. The double C logo. The interlocked back to back semi-circles, facing forward and back. Snort. Links in the chain of being chic. Sip. I reached the coffee under the foam blanket. Still hot. A5 prints of the outfits. Too boorg. Sip. They should just sell the logo itself, like on the make-up le maquillage. All we want is one perfect full logo. Sip. Black sundress white piping. Black mini-trench. Black cloth camellia. White straw hat black ribbon. Black flyeye sunglasses. Sip. White piqué sundress. Bin.

Rip. Sip. Calvin. Christmas bra and pants sets in selection boxes. Saddo grey T-shirting masquerading as American sportwear chic. Snort. Bin. Sip. Small envelope creamy laid paper. Card inside. 5mm thick. Sip. My name written with a calligraphy pen. Underneath tiny red metallic letters that bit into the card: *I'm in London and I have a secret I simply must share with you. Meet me in Suite 221 at Claridges on September 12th between 10 a.m. and 4 p.m. And I'll tell you everything over tea!* Sip. Bottom right corner flowing script Cartier. No jewellery pics. Probably a perfume launch. Cashing in. They were all doing it now. I glanced at Ellie's desk just at the beginning of the long bit of the L. Beauty a bridge between long L, Features and short L, Fashion. She probably already had one. But in case dork at PR agency had made a mistake. I half-stood and frisbeed the invitation across.

Becca walked in. 'You're back. God it's been so-o-o boring.'

I took her in anew. Ordinary clothes. Generic clothes like jeans jacket, cotton skirt, espadrilles, T-shirt, and not noticeably designery. But just the right little jeans jacket. The perfect length cotton skirt and in a special dusky pink. It was vintage designer found at Almighty to Save the Salvation Army shop. I'd been with her. The T-shirt was Aertex it fitted her body. The legs pale brown ceramic blemish-free. Shiny brown head hair sexmussed.

'Did you go to the little café?'

'Yeah I had the croque monsieur. I went into the church in the square.'

'Good good. How did the shoots go?'

'I think they went well. We went out on a limb a bit.'

'Good good.'

'Yeah I think we've got something different especially for the diamonds.'

'Cool.' She poked through the things on her desk.

'So what's been happening here?'

'Nothing. Just trying to get this shoot together. Babs being a bitch.' She smiled then looked back down at some model cards.

'Do you want to have a sandwich later?'

'Can't. I've got to go to Jed's. My two first options for this shoot have both dropped out. Bit stressed.'

'Can I do anything?'

'Yeah, you could do me a favour and go to the God of Love launch. Kim wants a presence there and I've got to go to Jed's and see girls.'

'Sure.'

Her phone was ringing. She reached behind her and pulled a paper cutout of a dove from her pinboard and handed it across the desks to me while she talked into the phone.

Sip. Rip. Thick gold lines Medusa head. Good, not as good as double C. Still, clever Gianni. A big V would have been shit. He wanted classical old Rome not noov. So he gets an old mythical thing. But no snakes. Her piled up hair sketched in gold foil waves not proper snakes. Chicken. Sip. Don't scare off the Americans. Sip. I opened the folder. New watch collection. Must be careful. Must not become the one who always gets made to do the jewellery shoots. Watches the total pits. Nobody good wants to do them. Sip. *Destined to repeat previous triumph thanks to the touch of the Medusa.* The logo embossed onto the card in foil so thick and shiny I could see patches of self reflected in pupilless eyes. Big advertisers. Keep.

19

Babs looking down at someone's copy through her glasses. Her right hand in the air holding a red felt tip. At her left, her PA, Emma, holding a bunch of papers and looking down at what Babs is doing. Babs made a noise. Her pen darted down and scratched the paper. Her forearm swung up again. I held onto the sides of the seat with my hands and tapped underneath with my fingers. The sound of her pen rasping over the paper.

'I can live with that, what else?'

Emma showed her the other papers. 'And you've got a cover meeting now.'

'OK. Leave those there. In a minute. Naomi.'

I adjusted in the chair. 'Hi Babs.'

She didn't say anything.

'What it's about is one of my Paris shoots.'

She looked at me through the glasses.

'It's the diamond story. I saw the layouts just now and they've cut it back to four pages.'

She said nothing.

'But I thought we said six. And the thing is, it doesn't even work with six. This is the best of the stories by a long way.'

She didn't acknowledge whether it was or it wasn't.

'And somehow it has the least pages.'

Big glassed eyes scanned my face. I felt a blush. Suppressed it.

'It's scheduled for December?'

'Yes. Suit alors! and Gardens of Earthly Delights, November. And this one is held over.'

'Mm.'

'Because the reason is – can I just explain? – the reason is that it's the one story that doesn't work over four pages. It needs a minimum' I made my voice deeper, firmer, 'of eight.'

Babs did a show-blink.

'Because what's important is the rhythm of it. It sounds naff but what I mean is that it's all about the movement up and down through this kind of nothingness.' The blush coming. She saw. 'That's the other thing because Simon – sorry to say it like this – but he's laid them out so it doesn't work. I mean they look elegant but it's not the story. He's cropped in on them so the jellyfish are right in the middle of each page and that's, well it makes it boring. I see why, if he was going to crop in, he only wanted to use four. And he's put a white border round each picture which ruins it, because it's the abyss. It has to be full bleed. Look at this.'

I got half-up and dragged the chair over under my bent knees towards her desk. 'Do you mind?' I got a bit of paper off the top of the pile in the smoked perspex open-top box. I found a pencil. I started drawing a series of rectangles and scribbling jellyfish in them.

Babs opened her mouth. 'Nay oh'

'Like this, dark full bleed so you enter the world of it. The jellyfish just'

'It's not'

'Can I just. I know you're in a rush. Facing page we're closer in we see them coming down through the page, I would still keep them off centre though I'

'No I'

Voice higher. 'But the fourth spread left hand page here. It would be far far better to have more but due to commercial concerns eight pages could give a rough idea. Shame though. And then the last spread you see just something rising off the top of the left page. What you see is just a track. Bubbles. But you can see a bit of a necklace you can see the shininess of it anyway maybe not what it's made of, that would be naff. And it's Tiffany. Major advertisers. And the last page should be just nothing. No bubbles, no diamonds. Because sacrificing this one page to pure nothing will underwrite the strangeness of their being there. It'll make the others stronger. For the advertisers.'

I pushed the piece of paper towards her.

Closed her eyes. Opened her eyes.

'Naomi this is not a story about nothing. It's a story about jewellery.'

I noticed how loud even her one-on-one talking voice was. 'I know that.'

'If Simon did what you said the jewellery would be hardly visible on most of the pages. The reason he has cropped in so close is because this is a story about diamonds.' Tapping my drawing with her felt tip.

'Yes.'

'You went out there on a major chunk of our budget and you shot two-thirds of these pictures so far away that we can't use them at all.'

I looked at the desk.

'Thank God they were shot on a 6 x 7 so we can crop in close on them. I told you very clearly before you left for Paris that this is the one big real jewellery story we do each year and I was giving it to you. You said it was going to be sunken treasure.'

'Yes but'

'I know. Fine. Except you haven't done the one thing I asked you to do which was to show the jewellery.' Tap. The. Tap.

My whole head red.

'What's wrong with you Naomi? I let you out of my sight and you go completely up your own.'

I pressed my fingers against the bottom of the chairseat.

'And God knows what happened to you on Suits for the Working Woman. Your point seems to be to snigger at professional women, not help them plan a winter wardrobe with seductive, creative pictures.'

I looked at her feet under the desk. Manolos.

'You are starting out as a stylist and you have.' Tap. 'To show me you can keep.' Tap. 'The photographer.' Tap. 'Under.' Tap. 'Control.' Tap.

I swallowed.

She sighed. 'As it happens, the suit pictures do have something and I get it.' She moved my drawings away from her. 'The hair and make-up are atrocious. I don't know what the working woman is going to make of it.'

'But we're working women.' My voice vibrating.

'We are working women who work in fashion.' Tap. 'They are working women who look to fashion for something more than pretentious silliness.'

I pressed my nails into my bottom through the leather slats of the chairseat.

'The jewellery shoot will have to do. Simon has had to work hard to get what we need out of it. Do you understand?'

'Sorry Barbara.'

'Fine. Now what's your story for January, have you talked it through with Kim?'

'She wants me to do the black and white story.'

'Are you happy with that?'

'Yes.'

'OK. Well, remember. It's a fine balance.' She got up. 'We do think you are very talented.'

Baby blues.

I went out.

20

The trees in the square shivered and threw bits and bobs of light over the table and over Becca's face and hands where she was using them to lift the paper cup to her lips. A pause. A deeper rush of wind and all the branches were in motion behind her head so that for a minute I felt I was on a merry-go-round and it was me and Becca rushing past the trees.

'Your jellyfish pictures are awesome,' said Ellie.

'They're ruined now.'

She sat down and unstacked two tuna salads and a green salad in their clear plastic containers and got the knives and forks out of the plastic bag. 'I think they're still cool.'

I opened my tuna salad. 'They're not. They're rubbish. You want your pictures to get at something, Babs wants you to keep the advertisers happy.'

'You know she actually told Kim to keep a chart of how often we use something from each advertiser?' said Ellie.

'All art needs sponsorship,' said Becca.

'Don't kid yourself,' said Ellie.

'I should have gone into advertising. At least you get top whack.' I said.

Becca pushed the bacon bits to one side of her green salad. 'You're living in the past you two. Magazines are the art galleries of now. High art – dead, elitist shite. Fashion photography is populist and abstruse fantasy at the same time. Like church art in the renaissance.'

'At least the church wasn't about shopping,' I said.

The wind rushed across from the other side of the square and made the opened flaps on the plastic containers yaw up and down.

'Futures market. The church. At least we're just flogging shoes. Shoes and frocks and bags, that's the manifest content for people who can't read pictures. Plodding bourgeois shoppers, fine. Let them eat shoes. We're interested in dreams and subversion. We're the frontline of culture. Museum art is arse-eaten, dead.'

'You should be someone's speechwriter,' I said.

'Beauty's worse. I shoot lipsticks. That's dead,' said Ellie.

'But you get amazing press junkets. You're always on Concorde or checking out some luxury spa,' I said.

'Spa spa spa. It's a fucking gulag archipelago of spas stretching round the globe,' said Ellie.

Becca closed her eyes and turned her face up to the light coming through the trees.

'Well how was it? The spa?' I said.

'A week out of my short and brutish in suspended animation.'

'You mean you were made to do nothing for a week?'

'Fuck no. They don't just leave you on a lounger. You've paid thousands – unless you're a media whore like me. You got cardio box, spinning, salsercise, watsu, chakra balancing, daily massage in your room.'

'Sounds like hell,' I said.

'Pedicures, manicures, cranio-sacral, peach peel body scrub, sea salt body scrub, "the ultimate" back and butt scrub, seaweed detox, liposphere wraps, Yoga Box, Yogalates, Yogayama, Yoga Bingo.' The branches above her head were pressed down so low the leaves almost brushed her hair. 'Aromatherapy Steam Room, enzyme wrap, rehydration body cappucino, and I signed up for the Labyrinth Mindfulness Programme as well.'

'You're a sucker for punishment,' said Becca.

'Up at five.'

'No,' I said.

'They come and get you in the dark. Then you all hike up the side of a mountain to see the dawn. It's a silent meditation hike. You're scrambling up these rocks in the dark thinking, rattlesnakes? But no it's all the oldster Hollywood wives trying to breathe.'

'Breakfast?' said Becca. She kept her face turned up to the trees.

'When you come down the mountain. Fruit. One slice of wheat-free toast. After two hours of climbing – fucking tisane.'

'No coffee!' I said.

'It's a toxin innit?'

'Poor little rich girls.'

'You'd be better off on a sink estate, honest, peddling crack out of a pram. The spa-bunnies believe in the perfectible. They are always striving in the face of time's rockwall and the fates' genetic handout. They're idealists, but the possible ideal has shrunk for each of them to the circumference of their own bodies. It would be tragic if it weren't so stupid.'

Becca sat up for a second and whisked a morsel of tuna off Ellie's salad.

'You'd think they'd just let themselves go a little bit,' I said.

'Well they do but then they feel remorse. It's the new morality. That's the subplot of the piece I'm writing on it anyway. You gotta push the material. Punish the material.'

'Sinners have always mortified the flesh,' said Becca.

'At least they used to have sins to be proud of, not just not being sexy enough,' I said.

'Nothing wrong with doing your best. You're such a puritan,' said Becca.

'And then they make you think you've graduated to the metaphysical after all by getting you to make Native American prayer arrows. You eating the bacon bits, Becca?' Ellie winked at me.

'You can have them.' The twig pattern on Becca's face trembled. The leaves were drying out, slowly turning the colour of old blonde hair.

'Is Prayer Arrows where you bind your secret prayer into the arrow with coloured embroidery threads?' I said.

'Yeah, though I bet nobody in the class was praying for like, a resolution to the conflict in Yugoslavia.'

'Most Americans don't know where it is,' said Becca.

'I don't know where it is. Exactly,' said Ellie.

Two girls lying on the grass in the middle of the square were rolling their tights down over their shoes. The tights mustard. The legs the colour of raw haddock. I shivered.

'So did you save your soul then?' I said.

'Oh that's old skool. I made mine at the Now I Must Make My Soul workshop. Basically they get you into a room full of scraps, old mags, kids' craft kits, and they tell you to build a model of your soul in half an hour.'

'Fantastic. Was it hard?' I said.

'Piece a piss.'

'What did you use for yours?'

'Red mohair, middle of a toilet roll, cutouts from a couple of old Vogues, blue feathers, fake dollar bills pinned together for a tail, and some Kinder egg toys – my inner monsters.'

'Which Vogue?' said Becca without opening her eyes.

'What?'

'Which Vogue? French? Italian?'

'Fuck. I don't know. Maybe it wasn't even Vogue, maybe I've only got a Marie-Claire soul.'

Becca looked down at her half-empty salad container. She snapped it shut.

'What would you make your soul from Becca?' I said.

'Diamonds, ice cubes, panther skin.'

'Wow bet it keeps you awake at night singing Big Spender,' said Ellie.

'Why those three things?'

'You know Joseph Cornell? The artist who collected things into boxes? Oh he's brilliant, you'd love him Nay. I'll lend you the book. He'd be brilliant inspiration for jewellery and watch shoots. You must check him out.'

'Yeah. Thanks.'

'This one box he did is a wooden jewellery box and when you open it there's a diamond necklace and a dozen ice cubes in a dozen little compartments all lined with velvet. And inside the box he's written the story of this Russian ballerina. She was going along one snowy night in her carriage and she was stopped by a highwayman and she was terrified that he was going to rob and kill her. But what he did was he spread a panther skin on the snow and he got her to come out and dance on it for him under the stars. Then he let her go.'

'Wow.'

'And when she got home to St Petersburg she started keeping ice cubes with her diamonds in her jewellery box.'

'I wonder why?'

'So do you feel happy having a soul that's someone else's work of art?' said Ellie.

Becca shook her head. The twig pattern broke up, reformed on her skin. 'No no, I just love the image that's all.'

'Right, so your actual soul would be a lot different.'

Becca widened her eyes at Ellie.

'What did you get after breakfast?' I said.

'What?' said Ellie.

'The rest of the spa cuisine.'

Becca closed her eyes, shaking her head up at the leaves.

'Unfucking believable. I was on the point of eating my own soul, or at least going back to the workshop room to see where they stashed the Kinder eggs.'

'Lunch?'

'A knob of tofu and two crystallised butterfly wings.'

'God, no bread.'

'Not allowed except that so-called bit of toast at breakfast. Dinner is at six-thirty. You can eat all the salad you like. You can fill a washing-up bowl with salad and stick your head in it and moo. But no dressing nothing. On the third day I went to the kitchen and I said look I'm here to write about it, I'm not here to lose weight, if I lose any more weight they'll hospitalise me.'

'I thought you looked really thin when you got back,' said Becca without opening her eyes.

Ellie and me looked at each other. 'Not completely wasted then,' said Ellie.

'So you went to the kitchen,' I said.

'Yeah so the head chef, right? He had to get special permission from the spa director for me to go to the kitchen at elevenses and teatime so they could give me toast with butter – butter! – and honey on it. The chef gave it to me at the back door of the kitchen in a napkin and he said, one thing, do not let anyone else see you eating this or there will be hell to pay. So I kind of hid the napkin under my tracksuit top and I slunk off into the Mindfulness Labyrinth and I was going along between the hedges shoving it into my gob, the best food I've ever tasted I swear, I felt if I could just go on shoving this heaven into my gob I'd be happy, I'd never ask for anything else I swear, and suddenly I hear this howling and stomp stomp stomp and all these Hollywood wives and gym-bunny CEOs are running up and down the labyrinth screaming "Toast! Toast!". They'd smelt it like animals.'

Becca started biting bits off round her nails.

'Did they get you?' I said.

'Yeah but it was too late, I was just shoving the last bit in. They went fucking crazy. I got in trouble. Some of them got toast too in the end.'

'Hey fat is a feminist issue.'

'Most of them don't need more butter in their lives.' She yawned.

'At least it's funny all this, at least we have a laugh,' I said.

21

Small cappuccino extra shot no chocolate. Pop cap off. Styrofoam *The new black but more so – blue, blue, blue* gives a smell to coffee. Weirdy-nice like sniffing glue. *Lines that at first glance seem deceptively simple are actually determined by the idealised* Crane neck. See into long part of the L *physique of a contemporary* Features ed, features assistant and the one Ellie called the Pilsbury Doughgirl *demi-sungoddess counter-pointed by the richness of detail* No sign of Babs *featured in the seductive double act of* Sip. She shouldn't really have called her that the Pilsbury Dough *knitwear and shirts* girl. But it was *biker blousons interstitching and interplay of opulent patching* yeah catchy and sweet in a *patent intarsio* way. Sip. I had started calling her *winter garden filled with trangenic flowers* that too I guess we all had. Bin. Sip. Rip. *Egg-citing Easter Accessories! Malkin's ethnic design philosophy has a fresh take on spring's co-ordinates.* Flick through loose pics tucked into press release folder *Crochet foot thongs n' things are* What? Look carefully look closely *inspired by traditional Jain decorations from the heart of India*

Girl under banyan tree gazes off-camera.

Flick.

Girl in early morning sea with driftwood.

Flick.

Girl squats, smiles at little Indian girl in sari.

Sip. Flick.

Little Indian girl in sari yes? They're in India yes?

Sip. Flick back.

And the girl's the girl on Kim's Indian trip.

Same. From Select.

The trip Becca went on, to assist Kim.

Flick.

Becca getting allowed to do her own shoot on the side, and for Push.

The carrot.

India though, to get to India.

Who needs carrot?

Flick back.

Bin.

She must have done these as well on the side. White sky through window. And? And nothing, and really clever, using the money she must have got from naff accessories line Egg-citing Malkin to fund her freelance shoot for Push mag. The Push pictures. Sip. Rip. Where she put the season's coats and dresses over shalwar kameez trousers. Rip. Or spliced with shell suits. Sip. Trainers or cripple stilettoes with spaghetti straps bound up the ankle over trousers and trackies. Ah that was one I'll not forget *in the Prestige line and features unusual hand-stitched details on the vamp.* I knew the moment I saw the first page of the story in Push. *The elegant loafer makes its debut appearance* Not on the models they'd taken for our mag. Sip. Local Indian girls. Obvious in one way but genius *Available in Pewter, Chocolate, Eau de Nil and Manila* because of the look in their eyes. *Reflecting an increasing demand for elegant summer wear for both casual and smart occasions* Black and white. Rip. No make-up except own kohl. On the Delhi streets not the beach resort where the pics for our mag were done. Our mag for the wannabe-edgy but in reality real woman and her banal catalogue of bourgeois desires. Bin. Sip. *Have It Off! Hunky Hairdresser Calendar* They must have gone out early one morning around dawn *12 of the hunkiest hairdressers bare all* and just found the girls on the street *Picture This* her and Tonio Petersen's assistant and *12 stylish styling hunks naked and gorgeous* wasn't he supposed to be a hunk? *in your living room!* Sip. That n all. Him gorgeous and talented and now *there's no need to just daydream because here they are flashing for the camera* him and her both recognised as well as ones to watch.

Kim came in, waved. Sat on her desk in corner by window. Picked up phone talked into phone toying with hair *for Beauty Benign, the UK beauty industry's No.1 charity.* Everyone acts like they don't remember that it was supposed to be me *Each hairdresser comes pictured with a personal touch* everyone acts like *from shears to Cheers!* it was only a vague idea going round *to hammer and tongs* that I might be the one to go *to a Waterfield brush encrusted with Swarovski crystals* on that trip to India. Everyone acts like that now ever since. Look away. Sip. *All proceeds to fund training for young Bangladeshi women at the nation's top beauty academy.* Sigh. White glare sky.

That day back in November. When Babs called me in to her office and said Naomi sit down. Babs never said sit down she was always doing something else and then she'd notice you like a fly had come in and landed on the chair opposite. Naomi sit down. Leafing through a copy of the November issue. Your Gardens of Earthly Delights story, very nice. She looked up from the issue. She looked back down at the page. You were coming along nicely then I pushed you too fast. Rested a fingernail on a page of the mag. I could see from where I was sitting the way the page was laid out and how near it was to the front that it was the masthead. Her nail reading off the names from the fashion department. Fashion Director Kim Hoggard. Fashion Editors Rebecca Ball, Naomi Price. Fashion Assistants Melynie Green, Janie Wu. She said and it's not fair on Becca. Becca has been here quite a bit longer than you. More experienced more mature. I shouldn't have given you the same title on the masthead. Do you think that's fair honestly? A funny feeling. Oh I said, I don't know I suppose it's not fair. I think you're right, she said, and anyway you're not quite ready to be honest. So all in all. But in time. For now how do they put it over there? Reculer pour mieux sauter? Oh gosh I said, I don't know. Gosh, like one of the characters in my mum's old Bunty albums. You know she said. Step back so as to leap forward? Oh, I said, is that what it means.

Glance at Kim. Sitting on her desk, back to me. Opening her post with phone jammed into shoulder low hum of voice. Sip. Coldish. The *Have It Off* calendar included with the press release. Thick card, spiral binding.

JANUARY. Arms crossed over gymbody. Hammer in one hand. Curling tongs in the other.
MARCH Leather chaps with holsters. Blow-driers in holsters. He reaches for the driers, fingers itching. Body twisted at an angle. No cock. Cheat.
12 stylish styling hunks naked and gorgeous in your living room!
JUNE, JULY No cock in any of them.
AUGUST Straight to camera stark naked yes. But holding Swarovski crystal-studded brush at groin. Crystal flash out of groin conceals bits. Cheat. Write Bagsy August on calendar. Frisbee calendar onto Ellie's desk. Rip. Sip.

So we've got a new title for you, Babs had gone on. Junior Fashion Editor. You will still do your own stories. Your salary is safe. Any questions. No I said. Stupid self-immolating thing to say. Jump. Babs' voice behind me now. Crane neck into long part of L. There she goes. Striding through long part of L in the kind of super-bourg but beautiful suit that makes covetous and nauseous at same time. Into her glass box. Pause. Emma running after with armful of papers. White sky. Stupid and self-immolating. No, no questions I had said. Focused on getting out dry-eyed. On getting out and taking in. Right then, I'm glad that's sorted. She picked up her phone. I got up and left. Walked through the desks with other people sitting at them and straight up the corridor to the toilet.

Heavily beaten wool makes no reference to geography, personalities or history

I'd gone into the end loo with the frosted window. Relief for a minute observing the cellulite pattern of the frosting. Then it came over me whoof. Cried into toilet paper pulling more and more off the roll as I went along. The jellyfish? She hadn't liked them. Or was it because I shot the suits for the working women story not like they wanted to be in the office more like the loonies in One Flew Over the Cuckoo's Nest? Someone entered. Echoey. Banged into the cubicle at the other end nearest the door. Sniff. Her zip undoing. Pause. She started. I opened the frosted glass window and let the sounds of the traffic in. A warm full sound. Flushed loo to blow nose undercover. It had dawned on me that she realised I was no good at it in general. She'd come to realise it but she was too decent to fire me, she wanted to let me down gently. Staring out of the window with my mouth open and tears running into it. I'm the crap one. *Colour yourself happy in Acapulco with its feminine touch to rock chic trends in a neatly detailed bag.* How I'd gone out for a cappuccino and then rang in to say I wasn't well. Needed to take the morning off. Just the morning mind. When I came back in Becca at her desk opposite mine. Are you all right Naomi? You're really pale. My face held in. Cup of tea? She would be so upset for me if she knew. Don't look at her big soft eyes or you cry she cries. I breathed said, I'm not fashion editor any more. What do you mean? Frowning, puzzled. Looked away, managed dopey smile. I'm being relegated. Junior Division Fashion Editor. Clearing up stuff on desk but tears right there like they were being pushed from behind. Maybe I should resign, this is the kind of thing you resign about isn't it? Holding them in but thinking, all the PRs will know, all the photographers will know in this gossipy bitchy business. They'll know that I was let go coz I was crap and no one will ever touch me with a bargepole coz I'm shit. Collecting model cards scattered and putting in intray. Everyone laughing, she thought she was something, she really thought she was going somewhere. And do you know something? She just didn't have it. Dead wood.

Say Aloha to Sexy Swimwear! Get a one-way ticket to paradise this summer with Sweetface show-stopping swimsuits Becca had come round to my desk and crouched by the side of it. *Make a statement in a revealing sexy one-piece while topping up your tan.* She had held my hand *With a strong Hawaiian influence* said, Naomi that would be silly you *crazee gingham and pineapple prints on zinging fluo colours* are very special *leave boys hot hot hot!* You just need more time.

Rip. *The blades of the fan beat to the rhythm of the heart.* Then the Christmas party in a new office building down by the river that wasn't yet fully let. Expensive but they had invited all the London designers, the key PRs and media buyers for the big advertisers. Us career-geishas sent out to charm in our borrowed clothes. *Fragments of unknown rapture.* A split-level glass box at the top of the building with a white piano in it and hushed lighting. Below us sweetie-coloured stars. *The essence of desire takes flight on wings of languid reverie.* I went up the spiral staircase to the top level of the glass box and stood looking down. Glass to my feet. The sweetie stars on the water and the bridge hung with strings of them. You got drunk at office parties that's what you did but not very drunk because of all the important people who had to be made to realise subconsciously that the mag had a glamorous enigma to it. *Mario Eckenburg films Natalia in the house of glass.* An enigma that only a very few could embody but that each one of us who had been taken in under the portal must carry a gene fragment of. Emma had come up, drunker than me. *Intoxication, dizziness, pleasure.* Giggling about someone on the floor below. We went over to the spiral stair so she could point him out. I giggled with her in the way you do, snuggling into a jumble of floaty dresses and kinetic breasts. Laughing into each other's faces and skittering off so he couldn't see. Back to the glass wall. Us gargantuan reflections in body-conscious dresses. City constellating through insubstantial bodies. *Great perfumes are those that take us on the most beautiful voyages.* I shouldn't really tell you this. Really quite a lot drunker than me. What? I said. About what happened when Babs told you you'd have to take that demotion. *Transgression, Initiation.* What Babs didn't tell you was how. She looked over her shoulder. No I shouldn't really but I feel bad about it. *Awakening.* You don't have to I said, if you don't want to. The guy at the piano started Fly me to the moon and let me play among the stars. Thing is, she went on, a few days before you were called in Becca asked to see Babs. *Mystery.* She was upset that you had been given the same title as her. *Inner Turmoil.* She said it wasn't fair and she wasn't going to stand for it. *Elixir Bewitching.* She wanted you made back to assistant or she was going to leave. I looked at the lights bleeding through our abdomens. *Narcotic dissolution.* That can't be right I said. No it is right. Emma shook her head. What Becca said was how she'd tried to put up with it, only she couldn't because it wasn't fair on her. *Exaltation of the senses.* Either that or she wanted to be made Senior Fashion Editor. Emma lifted her flute glass to her mouth and drained off the champagne. So a couple of days later Babs calls Becca back in and said what she could do was create this new junior position for you. Would Becca consider that adequate? *Voluptuous crystallisation.* Emma put her hand over her mouth. I'm so sorry. I shouldn't have told you. But I feel bad, I feel it's not right. God Emma, no. *Abandonment. Ennervation.* I'm glad you told me. Don't tell a soul she said or I'll get in trouble. No, not a soul. A waiter came up behind us. She held out her hand for a new glass of champagne. I picked one off too. *Always and For ever.*

Talk of the devil.

'Morning!'

'Morning. Nice weekend?'

Makes a face. 'Nothing much. Cocktail party. Movie. You?'

Rip. Rip. Bin. Bin.

'Nothing much.'

She over to Babs' office, head in the door. Laughing with Babs.

Only the plain narrow envelopes left. Envelopes for folded pieces of A4 paper. Cheapo press releases. The downtrodden of the fashion folk. Little homeless brands, little street people labels shuffling sadly round Oxford Street. *Each piece, beautifully constructed using the finest materials.* Bin. Extrathin white envelope through which see outline of folded-up A4. Rip. Les Déchets. Look up. Her coming back. Switching on her computer. Look down. Extrathin paper. Onionskin paper. Cheapo. Hiding behind my computer. Slow down.

I laid the thin piece of paper over the keyboard and smoothed out the creases so it lay flatter over the keys. Crossed my arms over my body so I could hug my sides. The strange authority of foreign words. I let them chime in my head first then went back in. Felt around certain ones for the meaning. Paupières. Paupers. Puppies. Papery things. But soft papery things, the more cupped sound of paup rather than pap. The longer more caressing ières compared with the short ier of papier. Papier was crisp, thin. Paupières was something rounded, a pastry casing, a chrysalis. The word hung there wavering back and forward over the edge. I stuck my head round the side of the screen.

'You don't have a French dictionary do you?'

'No.'

I hunched over the keyboard and scanned the poem again. Her voice from behind the two screens.

'I speak French if that's a help.'

'Paupières.'

'Eyelids.'

'Thanks.'

It would be my hands that closed his eyelids.

22

Dan said, 'You finished with the review section?'

I passed it to him. He turned a page, another page.

'What would you like to do now?' I said.

'Get another cup of coffee.'

My eyes moved over things on the table. White napkin roughly folded. Butter in a white china dish. Slim rods of metal. Egg smear on plate. Scrambled egg similar colour to butter, different texture.

'Dyou love me?'

I thought he hadn't heard.

'Sure as eggs is eggs.' After a bit. 'You OK?'

'Mmm.'

He turned over a page of the newspaper. 'What is it?'

'Don't know. My job.'

'The bitch?'

'It's not Becca. I like Becca.'

'She's an idiot, all she cares about is shoes and being too cool for school.'

'That's a stupid view of a job you don't understand. She's good at it.'

'So are you. You're brilliant at it and she undermines you. That's all I mean.'

'I don't seem to care about it any more.'

He picked up my hands and kissed them. 'You're just a bit blue.' He looked round the restaurant. 'What do you have to do to get a coffee in here?'

'Dan, you're lovely.'

'At last you see sense.'

'It's not just the mag, it's my life.'

'You're off life?'

'Our life.'

'Ah. So are you sick of the job or sick of me?'

I looked out at the road. A red bus, the swoosh sound its brakes made as if it was tired lugging things. He was looking at me waiting for an answer.

'I don't know. Sorry I know that's a crap thing to say.'

'Why not have it both ways? Sick of the job and sick of me.'

'That's an idea.'

'Right, no holds barred then.'

'Oh no, I'm barring holds.'

'Well what is it? What, as they say, have I done?'

'Nothing. You're the dream boyfriend.'

'Let me guess. It's not me it's you.' He was smiling.

'I love you. I just'

'Need more space?'

'Can you stop doing that?'

'Sorry.'

'It's OK. It's just'

'Money.'

'No it's not money. Why do you always think it's money?'

'I don't. I just know that if we had more money life would be easier and more fun that's all.'

'OK. I'd like more money but that's not what I'm talking about.'

'It can't help that nobody seems to want to employ me.'

I felt hot.

'You will get a job, a great job. But then, you know, so what if you do? Oh I don't know.'

'Start at the beginning. What do you want?'

'What do you want?'

He made a face. 'Well another cup of coffee is fucking hard to get in this place.'

'You will never just talk about things.'

'Well why won't you say what it is you want first?'

'You just won't face up to it will you?'

'It? What is it?'

'Stop it Dan.'

'What is the matter with you? You coming on?'

'Fuck off. I wish you were out of my life. I wish you were dead.'

I got up and started walking.

'Nay!'

Three-quarters of the way across the restaurant I changed trajectory. I had to be mature not spoil a day, a Sunday. Not spoil the rare special treat of the brasserie so with a bit of an effort I curved round and into the Ladies. It was nicer than my own living room. The lighting softer. no one had farted or crapped or maybe even peed in it yet that day. And if they had it had all been flushed away far far away and not a speck not a microscopic speck left on a toilet bowl or drying to yellow-brown under a cracked seat. Nothing like that in here. In here the white plastic seats were moulded in curves like snowfall. Just the smell of recently-wiped ceramic surfaces and three white-breasted soaps nesting in three shallow depressions beside the taps on the three wash-basins sunk into marble. I saw something waver in the mirror. Me. Not now. I turned on the tap. Looked down at my hands, the white-breasted soaps. I washed my hands, splashed water on my face. Looked up. Me only I mustn't let that be me. I moved my eyes over other things in the mirror. Three half-opened doors. A fern. xətoꓘ. I looked away from the mirror. There was a big basket with a lid under the basins and you were supposed to take one of the mini-towels, real towels folded up in a pile on the marble surface, dry your hands on it, and throw it in this basket. When I opened it it smelt of damp linen and the milky biscuit smell of wickerwork.

'Sorry.' I put my hand on the table. He picked it up and kissed it. I started to cry.

'I don't mean it, I love you. I don't know what made me say that.'

'C'mere.'

'I hate myself.'

He stroked the side of my face. He whispered stuff.

23

Ellie in headphones nodding to dance music. Reading

PUMP UP THE TAN

Take salon quality self-tan home with you. Thanks to Pump n' Tan!

Becca behind her computer screen reading

> cocooning mini-capelet, £745, by Jil Sander; poplin skirt with gathered peplum and ribbon tie, £470, by Jean-Paul Gaultier;

Me reading my name.

Naomi. Nom caché. L'etrangère. Instaurant. Oculaire. Words that tolled as they sank away. Souffrant. Oscillant. S'épanouit. S'efface. Glaces flottantes. Words I knew or half-knew or thought I did.

S'épanouir. To spread itself around, to generously throw itself around like stuff being scattered out of a panier.

Nom caché. Hidden name.

L'etrangère. Female stranger.

Oculaire. Ocular (to do with eyes).

Souffrant. Suffering.

S'efface. He/she/it effaces itself.

Oscillant. Oscillating.

Glaces flottantes. Floating sheet-glass, mirrors, ice.

Instaurant. Instoring? Instarring? Noun must be instauration, which feels like a starry form of restauration, French for restoration. Maybe a cross between instating and restoring.

Even vers was hard because he kept using it slightly differently. Vers was towards, like I go towards you. But les vers, the towardses? A ver, an old-fashioned unit of distance, something you covered when you were going vers somewhere, like when in Russia they go twenty versts over the snow to Moscow? Or could it be poetry, verse? Les vers, the lines of poetry.

I bought my own French dictionary and kept it in my filing-cabinet. I looked up s'épanouir. To blossom to light up to curve outwards.

I looked up *vers.*

vers[1] / vɛʀ / PRÉP a *(direction)* toward(s), to

vers[2] / vɛʀ / NM a *(sg=ligne)* line b *(pl = poésie)* verse

ver / vɛʀ / NM (for noun masculine) *(gén)* worm; *(= larve)* grub; *[de viande, fruits, fromage]* maggot

Instaurer was to instaurate which Dan's big English dictionary said was 1. The action of restoring; renovation, renewal. 2. Institution, founding.

A lot of the time I didn't look the words up for ages. I'd keep one with me all morning or even till I got home and play around with it when I was in the bath or waiting for the kettle to boil. **Sanguinaire**. Sanguine, hopeful, happy as blood. **Les poumons**. It had to be lungs because of the rest of the bit it was in, linked with breaths that were irrétrécissables a word which clashed and hissed like tinfoil. And of course the connection to pulmonary in English. A texture deep down in poumons, a sort of pomme pourri. Sweet browning sawdust-spongy lungs. His lungs were rotting, decaying inside. Irrétrécissable. He was being clenched up like scrap metal in a compactor.

Sometimes I'd read the whole entry wondering which bit of it he was after.

déchet / deʃɛ / NM a *(= reste) [de viande, tissu, métal]* scrap b *(gén, Comm = perte)* waste, loss ◆ **il y a du** ~ *(dans une marchandise)* there is some waste *ou* wastage; *(dans un examen)* there are [some] failures, there is [some] wastage [of students] *(Brit)*; *(viande)* there's a lot of waste ◆ ~ **de route** loss in transit ◆ **les ~s de l'humanité** the dregs *ou* scum of the earth NMPL **déchets** *(= restes, residus) [de viande, métal, tissu]* scraps; *(= épluchures)* peelings; *(= ordures)* waste *(NonC)*, refuse *(NonC)*, rubbish *(NonC)* (Brit); *(Physiol)* waste *(NonC)*

Sometimes the definitions included opposites.

hôte / ot / NM *(= maître de maison)* host; *(Bio)* host; NMF *(= invité)* guest

irrétrécissable / iʀetʀesisabl / ADJ preshrunk; unshrinkable

instaurer VT restoring; founding.

Kind of opposites.

Sometimes they missed the essential of a word, what stained it. The metal clash in irrétrécissable missing in preshrunk unshrinkable. Other times the definitions disappointed me in a way I couldn't pinpoint.

cible / sibl / NF *(Mil, Écon)* target ◆ **prendre qch pour** ~ *(lit, fig)* to take sth as one's target; → **langue**

24

A postcard arrived from the Maldives. Ma chère Naomi, How is spring in London? Sylvie and me are having the cool time making a shoot for Paloma. We miss only diamonds and you. Grosses bises, Sergei.

Big loops high and low, a masculine hand, generous but strong, a thin pen, a biro, probably a pen he found in a drawer in his hotel room, a cheap pen with the hotel's name written on it. I looked to see if there was a name of a hotel on the postcard. I looked at his writing again. Written fast he hadn't thought about it too much. He'd been in some little shop. He went in to try and get a French newspaper. There had been a rack of postcards. He'd looked through them casually. Better send one to Maman. He stopped turning the rack. Looked closer. Smiled. He took the postcard to the counter and bought it with the newspaper. Got a stamp. Posted it there and then outside the shop. Put his sunglasses back on and went to the café.

Les déchets. Liver dome. Half-brown half-bluish rags dangling off. Some of them almost invisible in the water others the colour of blood serum. Darker area towards the centre. Dried blood colour. You could see how it was oozing away at the edges into the water. A spark in the flux. I got up. I took the postcard into the art room and switched on a lightbox. I put it flat on the lit surface and got a loupe and placed the bigger end against the postcard and the lens against my eye. A silver fish jumped into focus, its eye a black speck surrounded by a white circle. It had been swimming along when it saw a rotting lump so it darted up to take a bite. As it got closer, a hanging garden of flesh so passive so slumping in the current that it didn't think for a second that the thing was alive. As if teeth had already chopped into it. Flopping like something dead till the squiggle of a small quick body fired its nerves, setting off triggers that shot hairs filled with poison into the fish. It would have felt like fire and then nothing.

I picked up the postcard and went back down the long part of the L. What I didn't understand was how you ended up being eaten by the thing. Did the jelly shreds somehow finesse the prey deeper and deeper into the centre for it to be pulped by some gummy mouth? I sat down at my desk and looked out of the window. White sky. I pulled the rest of the post towards me. Rip. Or were you liquefied by a rhythmic caress of the tendrils millimetre by millimetre into a kind of passata that soaked into the thing by osmosis? Bin. Rip. Little puffs of blood sifting off your edges and flecks of flesh loosening and eddying away into the water? How long did you stay alive in there? Rip.

Forget money
Forget power

Become free

A door opening
A future unfolds

The unknown breaks upon us

An ocean

A dawn

Your dreams
Your desires

Are pure
Are precious

Relinquish false idols

Fashion
Convention
Manufactured
Media culture

Something
Within you
Is calling
Is yearning

No more trappings
No more labels
No more exile

From
essence

Luxury is liberty
Or it is

emptiness

Abandon celebrity

The paparazzi
The public
The gossip
The glitter

The mirror
A traitor

Truth lies

Elsewhere

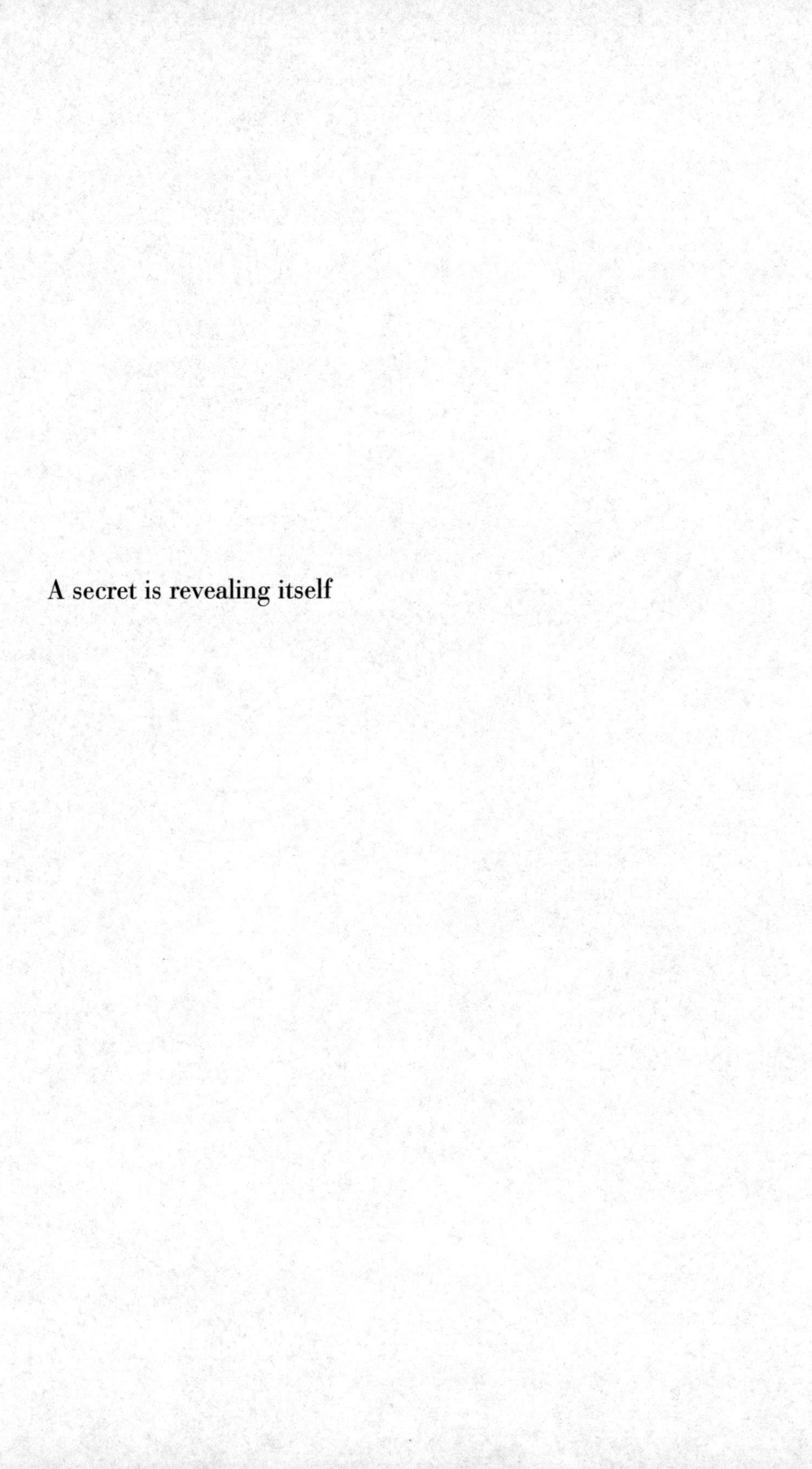

A secret is revealing itself

A woman is being born

See her
Inhale her
Circumnavigate
Enigma

Vers la femme qui

. . .

Jennifer Ronda is a star
Who negates

Our idea of star

For *Vers* she
reveals
a splint
er of her
Truth

in an
encounter
with a legend
in modern fashion

More than the fusion
Of a fragrance and a star

Infusion

of woman

Images that move
Beyond
The commercial
Becoming
A manifesto
For luxury
For liberty

Designer Christian Kelly
And star Jennifer Ronda
Share a belief
In the sublime

Jennifer inspires Christian
Christian glorifies Jennifer

Vers

… infusion de femme …

Sun on the building opposite. I threw the press release in the bin and went over to the window. Since I'd been sitting there opening the post it had moved across the white face dividing it into golden soft and ashy soft. I could spend a thousand years watching the splitting of the building into golden soft and ashy soft, watching the building become old, decrepit, becoming boarded-up, becoming abandoned, the city becoming abandoned, civilisation becoming abandoned. Three years of working here, a thousand days, and I'd never been into the building opposite. I'd never ventured in there. I wanted the door to open. I wanted to see the chartreuse carpet. Wood-panelled walls. It was cosy in there with a hush. Trendless suspension. People sat at desks that originated in no discernible period. They left the building at 5:30 precisely to go to homes that were neither in London nor commuter belt nor in areas that anyone could designate 'suburb'. They found gardens waiting for them and husbands who were also peaceful deep ponds. The husbands let them curl up in their laps in big armchairs on their lefthand sides. The husbands kissed the tops of their heads and said, you smell of floor polish from a higher floor level.

'Pregnant picnic' right in my ear.

I half-turned. Becca standing just behind me talking across the desks to Ellie.

'Every single model in the story pregnant. Dejeuner sur l'herbe with the men formally dressed, like modern formal. Roast chicken, wine, apricots, summer flies, the girls naked and pregnant.'

'*Naked* and pregnant?' said Ellie.

I went out to get a sandwich.

25

For a long time I hadn't been able to cut up magazines. Sanctuaries of white space and saturated colour. Graphic capitals soaring across a page. Flats of fathomless glossy secrets. OK there were too many ads. The front-of-book pedestrian but sometimes with a tiny picture you needed. (French soldiers bathing in a river during World War I. Tiny pic. B/w on an arts news page. The soldiers in the water walking up the river between leafy banks, away from me.) Then the Well with its typical structure of four big stories. Grand; semi-functional; sexy; edgy. Magazines have a musical structure. How cut? But then I discovered that it was only when you cut them that you could get in.

Edgy. B/w pics. Wasted girl, wasted boys, hair in eyes. 20 pp. Lots of kohl. They're a rock band, she's a groupie or a girlfriend. It's all about thin black jersey and low-slung jeans and beat-up heavy metal Ts. One pic shot through a half-open hotel door. He lies back in jeans on the bed she sits naked on his thighs. Too skinny to have sex. I opened the scissors at the bottom of a page. I closed them *schrum* and opened then and closed them *schrum* till I'd got what I needed. She fell on the bed. Not with the boy. I just needed her. She looked a bit like me. Not a lot but in the ballpark around the cheeks and if you were pushing it round the mouth.

Grand. Early morning beach. Supermodels in fairytale dresses with the light coming through. Supermodels dancing and getting salt water on the hems of dresses that cost. I checked. The one I wanted. The sky blue with pearl drops and the word *wonder* embroidered in silver across it. Four months salary. *Schrum. Schrum. Schrum.* Not bad for that dress. What I needed for The Game. That dress. This hair. That expression. That place. And that place. Finland. Lots of snow. A whole page of a path through the birch trees going somewhere. Whole other page of jumbly glass roofs. Inside, lit stove, old reindeer pelts, a leather armchair. Blue oilcloth on the table, pink roses. And snow falling on the glass roofs above the roses. *Schrum.* The Palais Bubbles. Bubble shaped windows by the sea. The Med. Round bed in round room. Pink room. Lunette of sea. *Schrum.* Gertrude Stein's wallpaper with giant doves. *Schrum.* Black horse against a white wall. That girl on its back in red ruffled skirt and old cowboy boots. *Schrum.* That smile. That hair of hers caught flying past his face. *Schrum.* This house. This house is where today's Game really takes off. House by the sea made of driftwood. Instead of furniture figureheads hanging out from the walls with snaky hair their mouths open singing. *Schrum.* Shells. Spanish brandy. The sound of the sea. It's out there in the world, it's a real place, they didn't make it up. *Schrum.* Who cares if in order to show me this, to get this past the gatekeepers, they have to do a feature on poxy advertisers' furniture? Designer coffee tables. I scanned for the one if pushed. This one with blip-shaped white legs and a thick sheet of glass on top. I checked. After tax a year's salary would get me one of these tables and a spare blip-shaped leg. Nothing to eat, nowhere to live the year I buy the coffee table. I have to strap my coffee table to my back and choose a different park each night to sleep in. I'll get under my coffee table with the blip-shaped white legs and the glass top will protect me from the elements and I'll be able to lie with my face close up to the glass top and the rain will land right on top of me. It will sound beautiful smell beautiful and look beautiful and I won't get wet because the annual income coffee table is as long as my body. I can use the extra blip-leg as a weapon.

Schrum schrum. Schrum.

I got out of bed. Hacking cough. It was almost dark in the bedroom where the window looked out across the basement area to a wall. On top of wall, railings and through the railings the legs of passers-by going past. *Schrum. Schrum. Schrum.* I went into the kitchen and got another Lemsip and a fresh length of loo roll. Got back into bed and pushed the pile of cut mags to one side and went through my cuttings.

1. Wasted girl with fringe
2. Path through birch forest
3. Wonder fairy dress
4. Pablo Neruda's driftwood house
5. Black stallion/red skirt
6. Roses on blue with snow
7. Gertrude Stein's dove wallpaper
8. Frenchwoman in futurist shoes
9. O bedroom at the Palais Bubbles
10. Non-fashion girl in wasteland
11. Spanish nuns with wimples
12. Francis Bacon with beef wings
13. Dogs far away in snow
14. Lips chewing glass
15. Gladiator Red lipstick
16. Film noir trenchcoat
17. Demeter fragrances: Old Money; New Money

Wasted girl with fringe. All I have to do is cut my hair off and get a little wasted. I wrote on the picture *tonight.*

Path through birch forest. A trip to Finland out of the question until Dan gets a proper job. I wrote on the picture *next year.*

Wonder fairy dress. I wrote on the picture *sample sale?* Even then. Even at 50% off insane. I wrote on the picture *sthg. similar in second-hand shops, doable this year.*

Black stallion/red skirt. I wrote on the picture *Marry bullfighter. Five years.*

Pablo Neruda's driftwood house. *Style Ralph Lauren campaign/ marry South American bullfighter. Five years.*

Gertrude Stein's dove wallpaper. *Tissue paper cutouts. This week.*

Holiday at the Palais Bubbles. I sucked the pen. *Second marriage: European industrialist. Ten years.*

Roses on blue oilcloth. *Roses: this week. Oilcloth: this month.*

Non-fashion girl in wasteland. *To Silvertown with Dan. Weekend.*

Frenchwoman in futurist shoes. *Get job at Vogue. Two years.*

Spanish nuns wimples Francis Bacon with beef wings dogs far away in snow. *Done.* (I just needed the pictures.)

Lips chewing glass. *Fucked-up end to European industrialist marriage. Eleven years.*

Gladiator Red lipstick. *Off Ellie, this week.*

Film noir trenchcoat. *Search street markets for old one. Three months.*

Demeter's New Money, Old Money. *Beauty sample sale: two months.*

It was all possible starting with the wasted fringe tonight and working my way through the roses and the lipstick to Pablo's house. I pushed the magazines off the bed and turned over under the duvet. I started on the beach just outside Pablo's house with the sounds of breakers and the ship's figureheads that hung from the ceiling creaking in the wind blowing through the open door. But then I looked up the beach from under the duvet and saw a black horse galloping along the waterline and it was the bullfighter not in a suit of lights, I realised as he got closer, but in jeans and a beat-up death metal T-shirt. The Game always took its own course and that was what I loved about the Game as the bullfighter hauled me onto the black horse's back with my wasted fringe and my futurist shoes and my ironic smell of old money and new money and lines of poetry and bits of glass on my lips and my future of silver wonder and wimples and beef wings.

26

'Did you get it, yeah? The Prada one, yeah? With the three straps yeah? No over the top. Like over the top of the bag. Front closure. Yeah. Yeah that's the one. The grey. Yeah. How much? That's good man, that's really good.'

'She got the bag.'

'Sounds like it,' said Becca. Clatter of her keyboard.

'Can I ask you something?'

'Yeah.'

'French question.'

'Yeah go on.'

'Se frôler.'

'To frolic? Would have to be to frolic with oneself or each other though because of the se.'

'Oh right.'

QWERTY QWERTY QWERTY. 'What's the context?'

'It doesn't help the word.'

'No but just give it to me.'

'No it's all right.'

She put her head round the side of her screen. 'Is the whole sentence in French?'

'Yeah.'

'Lets hear it.'

'It's not really a sentence.'

'A caption?'

'It's more of a poem.'

Her head went back behind the monitor. QWERTY QWERTY

QWERTY. A little laugh. 'What, are you reading French poetry?'

'Yeah.' I laughed.

'Instead of working?'

'Yeah.'

'You are a funny one. Who is it?'

'no one you know.'

'Try me.'

Her head came round the side of the monitor. She looked down at my hand. I was holding a sheet of the onionskin paper in it.

'What's that?'

'A poem in French, obviously.' I rolled my eyes jokily.

'Yes but who by?'

'no one. Not a real poet.'

'A friend?'

'Not really. Just someone who likes to send me poems.'

'Just sends you poems or writes you poems?'

Ellie came over. 'She got it! And for an amazing price.'

'Fantastic. Are you going to get one?' I said.

She blew out her lips. 'Tempting but.'

'Well?' said Becca.

'Writes.'

'What are they about?'

'They vary.'

'Helloing?' said Ellie.

'Helloing. Someone's writing Nay poems.'

'Tell.' Ellie sat on my desk.

I held the poem against my chest.

'Nothing to tell. Someone sends me poems, that's pretty much it.'

'Gawd.' Ellie swung her legs.

'But who is he? Is he published?' said Becca.

'I don't know. Probably not.'

'Sweet.' QWERTY. 'Quaint really.'

'Is he in love with you?' said Ellie.

'I think he thinks he is.'

'So where did you meet this guy?' said Ellie.

'When I was in Paris, last year.'

'God how romantic.'

'Well not really.'

'But how did you meet him?'

'Well he was working at reception in the hotel.'

QWERTY. 'The receptionist?'

'A summer job. He's a student.'

'Lets have a look.' Her hand held out across the line between our desks.

'So you are his muse?' said Ellie.

'I wouldn't go that far.'

'But you are. That's so cool. no one's a muse any more.'

'Fashion designers have muses the whole time,' said Becca. 'Whatever that means.'

'Well exactly,' I said.

'Are they sexy?' said Ellie.

'I don't think you'd use that word.' I looked out of the window. 'It's all so. I don't know.'

'Read it out,' said Ellie.

'No way.'

Becca snapped the fingers of her outstretched hand. 'Lets have a look.'

I held out the poem. She put her fingers on the paper. I snatched the paper back like in a reflex.

'Hey.'

'Sorry don't know why I did that.' I held the piece of paper.

'Read out one of the sexy bits,' said Ellie.

'I don't think this is a sexy one.' I scanned it.

'You're like his Dora Maar,' said Ellie. 'She was great-looking.'

'Give it here. I speak French,' said Becca.

'I don't really want to. Lets leave it.'

She wiggled the fingers. 'Come on. I'll tell you what it's all about. Come on.'

She smiled.

I put it in her hand. She held it up for a minute and then she laid it out on her desk. I looked at Ellie. 'He's just some student,' I said. 'Honestly they're probably rubbish.'

'He could be an undiscovered genius,' said Ellie.

'I only saw him once. It's stupid really.'

I looked at Becca. 'Can I have it back?'

She kept reading.

'Becca. Can you give it back? I don't want to know what it means.'

'Maybe he's the new Lord Byron and you can be   who was his muse, was it Lady Caroline Lamb and wasn't she served up to him inside a giant silver dish and had to dance naked up and down the table?'

'I hope so. Becca?'

She didn't say anything.

'It's not the best one,' I said. 'I was thinking that when I asked you about se frôler. It's not a good word.'

'Brush with death. That's what it means.'

'Becca.'

'Sssh.'

'What does Dan say about it?' said Ellie.

'Nothing. He says I shouldn't encourage him. But I don't encourage him. There's no address, nothing. He just keeps sending them.'

'Fuck it's romantic. Mysterious.'

Becca handed it back.

'Well what's it say?' said Ellie.

Becca's voice came round the monitor. 'You should chuck them.'

'Why?'

Her face round the side of the monitor. She tucked a strand of hair behind her ear.

'There's something strange about it. Something I don't like. Do you have any more?'

I opened the desk drawer. 'I've got a few here.'

'OK, quick. I haven't got much time.'

I passed them across.

'But what's it say?' Ellie picked up the first poem.

Becca's disembodied voice. 'First of all, this muse stuff. Don't let yourself be put in that position. It's dangerous.'

Ellie looked at me. She rolled her eyes. 'Dangerous how? He sees something in Nay you don't see. Love works that way.'

'What can I do? I can't stop them coming.'

'Burn them.'

'I raise up what? Where your pas lead me,' said Ellie. 'Doesn't pas mean not?'

'Yes but it's footstep as well, you know, pas, pace.'

Her head round the monitor. 'Pretentious.' Head back behind the screen.

Ellie picked up a biro and wrote on a press release: she jealous coz not her.

I bit my lip. Shook my head.

'No wait. No this is beautiful,' said Ellie. She winked at me. 'This is awesome.'

'Ssssh.'

'So let me guess. He's gifted but of course mad,' said Ellie. She bent back over the first poem.

'Unstable certainly.' Becca's voice.

I looked at my keyboard. I noticed for the hundredth time that it was the exact same colour as Cream of Mushroom soup.

Ellie put the poem down on my keyboard. 'God.'

'Do you get any of it?' I said.

'Well in a way I get most of it. But I don't know. It's kind of out there.'

'You think it's avant-garde?' I said.

'No I mean it's like out of nowhere. I don't know if he's avant-garde or rear-garde. Arrière-garde? Anyway, my French.'

Becca's hand round the monitor with the poems. I took them back.

'So what do you make of them?' I said.

She stood up. She got her jacket off the back of her chair. 'It's you that worries me.' Her eyes anxious, soft. 'You're not taking this seriously?' she said.

'No. No I'm not.'

She examined me. 'I hope you're telling the truth.'

'You make it sound like it's some kind of spell,' said Ellie.

'I don't like what he's doing in these poems. You should rise above this.'

'Why worry? It's just poems,' said Ellie.

'I think they're disturbing. And probably quite pathetic. Who is this person?'

'I don't really know. I spoke to him once.'

'I see. And he's been sending them how long you say?' She buttoned the jacket.

'About nine months now.'

'It's a free world,' said Ellie.

'You're leading him on. Can't you see? Call the hotel and complain. You've got to be pro-active in shutting this down. It's creepy.' She picked up her bag and walked out.

'I wouldn't worry, he's French,' said Ellie.

27

I raise up altars where your pas lead me

I picked up the phone with one hand and put my subbed caption copy on the desk with the other. I glanced into the wastepaper basket. The poem had slid down a press release folder to where the bottom edge of the release touched a few sheets of typing paper that had been half-crumpled and thrown into the bottom. Slag from an emptied ashtray lay mostly on a blue plastic water bottle.

When I chucked the poem in there it was a tight ball. Onionskin paper is thin it scrunches well. I scrunched and scrunched. I used both hands. When I threw it it bounced like a real ball off the side of the bin and rolled on its way down to its final resting place.

I had seen it take in a bit of air almost the moment it landed. While I was in the meeting it had extended a spur and when I got back from lunch it had developed gorges and rift valleys down which trails of words led. Now I looked at it while I held for Storm Models. It had been knocked round by someone throwing in a styrofoam cup that spilled milky coffee down one side. Perhaps no shape like this had ever been in the history of the world. It was possible. From here it looked as if it had opened up like a pair of jaws but that was only anthropomorphising. Really it was an abstract polyhedron. A nature culture juncture where words met freeforms too complex and riven for man to comprehend. The poem was responding to air pressure, temperature and the momentary impact of other objects thrown into the bin. Jig jagged. Crumples within crumples. Blurry bluey-black patches of damp where the coffee had partially dissolved the ink of some of the letters. Le v**gl*s. Ton ***a*e. It was moving slowly in time. Taking on accretions of coffee and ash and mineral water like something creating itself, wide open to change, something moving towards opening but also effacing.

'Lo. Janine.'
'Janine it's Naomi.'
'Hiiii Naomi how you doin'?'
'Oh cool you?'
'Yeah not too bad. You wanna check your options?'
'If you don't mind.'
'K jus a mo.'

The other bits of paper thrown in by others, less energetically crumpled, made engineered planes where blue shadow and grey-toned whites played inside the bubble environment of the bin. A styrofoam cup went past my line of vision. It hit the glossy scarp of a surface photo-image and rolled down against the poem. The cup had been crushed in a hand before being thrown. Now it popped out in staccato bursts accompanied by a general smooth rapid extension of the whole.

'Naomi? You've got first option.'
'Oh fantastic. I'll confirm her then.'
'Cool. OK.'
'OK. Bye.'

pas[1] / pa / **NM** **a** *(gén)* step; *(= bruit)* footstep; *(= trace)* footprint
b *(= distance)* pace ◆ **c'est a deux ~ d'ici** it's only a minute away
c *(= vitesse)* pace ◆ **'roulez au pas'** 'dead slow' **d** *(= démarche)* tread
d *(Danse)* step **f** *(Géog = passage) [de montagne]* pass; *[de mer]* strait
g *(Tech) [de vis, écrou]* thread *[d'hélice]* pitch > **le pas de Calais** the Straits of Dover > **pas de clerc** *(littér)* blunder > **pas de deux** *(Danse)* pas de deux

I looked up. Jules from the art room.

If I were an artist I would take a series of crumpled onionskin pages like this and have them made up enormous in bronze. Or if there was a white metal, a white long-lasting substance maybe a kind of resin I'd have enormous sculptures done in that. I would have them rolled into position in random spots round the city. Then office workers would come out of their offices and sit on the curved edges of the gigantic scrumples and crawl inside, drawn into exploring the mindfulness labyrinth of shaded and sunlit spaces like insects crawling further and further into a bin. Better. If I could get them to be made of some futurist probably Japanese new substance. They would be crumpled every night at midnight and declench into unforeseeables by dawn. Sun would set them so they would stay in some random shape until darkness fell and then that particular form would soften till it was gone for ever to be recrumpled night after night or until we got fed up with them and left giant sheets of substance to crack and blow round the city streets gathering cartons, leaves, dust.

I went into the art room. When I came back Becca, I think it was Becca, had thrown a clear plastic salad container with some oily leaves and a few bacon bits in the bin. Wooden fork half dressing-stained. I took in how it changed things. I picked up the phone. Dialled Dan. I picked at a brownie. I didn't want it all. I threw it in, the moist crumbs scattering over the poem. I saw a fly I preferred bluebottle mastering the space of the bin. It maneouvred onto a brownie crumb blocking a crevice of the poem. Depositing traces of liquefied cat shit or whatever they also liked to eat on the poem. I got up and put my jacket on and went out to a posh restaurant for the launch of Matilda Matilda a range of leather goods accessories from Australia and when I got back I leaned over to see into the bin. Another styrofoam cup, intact, two plastic coffee cup lids, dead biro leaking, a Kleenex crumpled into an origami swan held together at the centre by by mucus jam. The poem underneath. I moved my head about till I could see what I was pretty sure was a bit of it down in the shadow. I wondered if any of the mucus had touched it. I opened my notebook. I wrote Luxury Lovers. I underlined it. I wrote down the names and numbers of the five luxury lovers I had agreed to contact.

The words cat shit candied on the back legs of bluebottles came to me. First liquefied then candied. I picked up the phone. I looked at the notebook for the number and dialled Luxury Lover No.1. That's how bluebottles fed. They snorted mucus onto a substance. They had no teeth see. Then they sort of pulped the mucus and substance together with their legs like trampling grapes. The paste stuck to their legs and later when they were just hanging out buzzing on windowsills or the back of your hand while you dozed they held out a leg like a lollipop and licked the candied shit off it.

> **pas²** / pa / ADV **a** *(avec ne: formant nég verbale)* not ◆ **ne me parle ~ sur ce ton** don't speak to me like that, do NOT speak to me like that **b** *(indiquant or renforçant opposition)* **vient-il ou (ne vient t'il) ~ ?** is he coming or not?, is he coming or isn't he? **c** *(dans réponses négatifs)* not ◆ **~ de sucre, merci!** no sugar, thanks! **d** *(devant adj, n, dans excl: *)* COMP > **pas grand-chose** *(péj)* **NMF INV** good-for-nothing

Dial tone then click. A flash as a voice said Ilona Yurchik in upward-moving Americanese. I said where I was from. I asked for Ilona. The flash: that it's exactly in places like that, places of rubbish and shit that artists look for material, inspiration etc.

Hi Ilona, it's Naomi Price here. I don't know if you remember

Not that everyone modern doesn't know about rubbish and art. Everyone knows that, I know that.

Good. How about you?

But being told that or reading it, and then having the flash whoom in a stream of ionised particles just as someone says Ilona Yurchik

Yeah almost too hot.

through an invisible plane that has always bisected your body unknown to you now vibrate as all the atoms in it charge and every one of the billions upon billions of them

Really we have no air-conditioning.

flips and starts to sing the same charged note like an electron choir singing into awareness a plane that had been invisible, a plane that like an extra dimension has been passing through your body

Actually it's about my own personal favourite subject. Luxury.

all this time but only now comes alive and starts to hurt. That's different.

Huhuhuhu. Second favourite subject.

So if I were a modern artist today I would make a special study of wastepaper baskets.

Well we're doing a major piece about luxury, modern luxury as defined by key luxury leaders

I would go through every wastepaper basket in this room at the end of every day for a month and I'd do a couple of projects on it.

and I was just wondering what your luxuries were.

One project I'd take them to a studio and empty each bin onto a big roll of background paper and photograph what was in there.

Yeah. Luxury as defined by you.

Not sure if I'd arrange each bin-set or just tip. Probably just tip. I'm a wild crazy artist I'd just tip let life come at me.

No not disappointed that's a sweet luxury.

Second project would be word-based. I'd catalogue what was in each bin at the end of each day.

No no children but if I had dancing barefoot with them would probably be top of my list. Any other luxuries?

Day One
Ionithermie press release partly torn
3 invitations to spring/summer shows
Chanel hardback perfume press release, art book size
5 envelopes various sizes, 2 white, 3 brown
2 styrofoam coffee cups
2 plastic coffee cup lids
Traces cappuccino
Grounds
Ash smears
Crumpled fag packet
13 used staples

Mmm that's nice but I was hoping for something really wild and mega. Like am I right in saying you have your own plane?

No I realize that's an essential.

No of course with your kind of life I didn't think the number 37 bus was really going to do the job.

Day Two
Tiny ball aluminium foil
Gum wad
3 paper clips
Squashed scraps foil
4 sheets typing paper with 4 versions of Portrait of a Lady
Day before's horoscope torn from Evening Standard, stained (Scorpio)
3 styrofoam coffee cups
2 coffee cup lids (third lid absent)
Zig-zag, gloss-trimmed semi-circles of pencil shavings

Pair of tights, 10 denier nude, laddered
6 standard envelopes, 3 with cellophane windows
Torn paper scraps

Dreamy. Oh that's lovely that's really lovely.

Mmm. Mmm.

Day Three
Quarter croissant
Croissant flakes
4 paper clips, 1 pulled out to a wobbly line
5 standard envelopes, 2 with cellophane windows
3 board-backed A4 brown envelopes
Shaper yoghurt pot with spooned swirls of pale orange
Versace press release in gloss card folder
Partly scrunched Detox Dressing contact sheet
Pale blue plastic water bottle w/lid
Lancôme mascara wand, brown-black
Two cotton buds smeared milky-orange
Gum wad

Huh! Oh that's amazing. That would definitely be my luxury.

Ellie sat down on the corner of my desk. She upended a Jiffy bag and packets of Chanel compacts and lipsticks fell out on my intray.

And can you think of anyone else who has a unique take on luxury that I should call?

She swung a leg. She started ripping open the gloss black packaging and chucking it in the bin.

Oh fantastic. I'll call her. Yup OK. Thanks bye.

I dialled the new number. Craned my neck to see in the bin. Gloss black blocks of lipstick packets and the pulled-open rectangles of card packs off compacts, gloss black on one side, matt black on the other. They piled up over the mainly white and clear contents of the wastepaper basket.

Oh hello. It's Naomi Price here from

She was taking the lids off the lipsticks.

Yes yes that's right. Hi.

She twisted the bottom of each lipstick two and three-quarter turns

Actually Ilona suggested I call you about this piece we're doing on luxury.

(the optimum number of turns for a lipstick, she'd done a piece).

And she sort of implied – and I was so excited – that you have your underwear hand-sewn by Carmelite nuns.

She sat the lipsticks in a row along the join between my desk and Becca's.

Oh Ursuline nuns. Huh! Oh much better.

She pressed each of the black lacquer compacts so it made a swallowing sound and sprang open. Placed them open in front of the lipsticks.

Seriously? Oh this is amazing.

I craned over the edge of the desk and saw the overlapping Janus Cs of the Chanel logo in white on gloss black repeated everywhere in the bin. A hole between a fat pair of thighs. An eye with the corners torn off. A set of manacles waiting to snap shut on your wrists

Oh gosh. Embroidery.

or your lips

Mmm. Mmm.

or your eyes.

Tiny feminine stitches yes, no one but nuns have the time.

Red streak flashed.

Captive workforce. Haha.

I got it. She was editing the props for her shoot.

Lost couture skills absolutely.

Rouge à Lèvres Allure. The lipstick slashed a red stroke down a grey-white piece of paper. A berry stain. A ruby red. A yellow-red thrown so hard it clanked on the bin side and broke in two.

And prisoners. I hear Lacroix is teaching female prisoners how to use ancien regime looms.

Bright fragments in the ash and coffee. Scarlet crumbs sinking into the pearly succulence of mucus. The Kleenex so fine they should make nuns sew panties out of Kleenexes.

Pre-Soviet?

Ellie scrawled me a message across the top of my notepad. I nodded. I wrapped up Ilona Yurchik's friend and looked at the next name on my list. Dialled.

Day Four
Pale blue plastic water bottle
6 standard envelopes, 1 with cellophane window
Calvin Klein press release, loose
Christian Dior press release in blue and gold glossy folder
4 styrofoam coffee cups
4 plastic coffee cup lids
3 board-backed A4 brown envelopes
Gum wad
Clear plastic salad container with bacon bits, salad dressing
Tiny ball aluminium foil
Fag ash
Coffee puddle
Dregs

I got the quotes from all the Luxury Lovers. I wrote it up. I was almost the last to leave. I put on my jacket and swung my bag over my shoulder. As I went past the wastepaper basket I squatted without thinking and felt my hand rustle deep in and instinctively cradle a scrunched-up ball of paper. I pulled it out and stuck it in my pocket.

On the bus I got the ball out. Even before I pulled it open on my knees I knew it wasn't it so I got off at the next stop and ran back to the office to get there before they closed it up for the night and got down on my knees by the bin and went through everything until I found it pushed almost to the bottom and stained with coffee, lipstick, ash, mucus, biro and candied remains of half-digested cat shit. I smoothed the page out there on the office carpet and looked at the altered words.

pace step strait footprint dance-step thread pitch pass
(*nég verbale*) not
(*indiquant ou renforçant opposition*)
not print not dance not pace not step not
pitch not thread not
pass/not
raise up altars where your nots lead me

raise up altars where your [not] steps lead me
raise up altars where your pass-nots lead me
raise up altars where your non-passes lead me
raise up altars where your ~~prints~~ lead me

28

Parghree. Pacchurrhee. J'ai deux amours. Palais-Royal, September. Sitting in a café, sitting outside because it's warm for September though actually what do I know about the normal September temperature in Paris?

Begin again. Began again. Sitting outside a café in the Palais-Royal in Paris in September. Dan's birthday, a long weekend in Paris. I told Dan that I was going to meet the people I'd done that shoot with. Just for a coffee. You're welcome to come. We'll probably talk about fashion and stuff but still, come. He said he'd go to the Rodin museum to look at Iris and her split beaver. He hadn't been there, he said, for years. Tired in his way of Iris but, you know, still fond.

I was early. I entered the Palais-Royal, an indoors outdoors place that also managed to be in at least two centuries at once. I felt different right away. I walked in the arcade feeling myself walking just slightly, very slightly, like someone who could have gone out with a Musketeer. Maybe like the one Cyrano loved. Roxane was her name. I looked into Pascal Arnaud's vintage clothes shop full of old ladies' cast-off couture. Pascal Arnaud was in it. I recognised him from Kim's description. His shop was tiny the racks double height and stuffed with gear. He had dark limp hair. A toupé? He asked me if there were any way in which he could help me at the same time letting me realise that regretfully not only could he not help me, not only was it crystal-clear that I could not afford a single item – maybe the individual buttons each priced the same as a High Street coat – in his boutique but that I didn't know un volant from un gallon. I handled the buttons. I asked the price of some plain sixties plastic ones. He mentioned a sum approximate to the price of a cashmere jumper. I said I'd have to think about it. He put his head on one side and closed his eyes.

Further along the arcade there was an even tinier shop with a scrolled tin sign swinging outside the window. Au Duc de Chartres. Ordres Français et Etrangers. Inside was a woman and trays and trays of velvet stuck with badges and ribbons, military decorations and orders of merit. The woman had painted her eyebrows on with brown paint. She pulled the drawers with the velvet trays out of the glass cabinet one by one for me to see and ran on in a French I knew was full of flourishes but that washed over me unread. I held the medal of the chevaliers de Notre Dame de Mont Carmel de Lazare draped over my hand on its purple ribbon. I asked for the price of a ring of tin scallop shells on faded moiré with the words Immensi tremor Oceani on them. It was sad that I had already bought Dan his present. I wanted him to have Immensi tremor Oceani pinned on him. There was a small round badge enamelled blue and white with a sort of Eiffel Tower piercing through the circle of it. The insignia of a radio engineer corps or corporation I couldn't tell. The woman attached it to a piece of velour-covered card and slipped it into a white box that opened like a large matchbox with an Au Duc de Chartres shield-shaped sticker on it.

I stepped out from under the arcade and walked on the dust paths between the rosebeds. The paths smelt of cake crumbs. The sky was white and the dust on the paths was beige. The stone arches of the arcade were darker beige. Blackbirds ran about under the shrubs and pigeons pecked on the paths. Old men sat on the benches. One old man was feeding the birds out of a paper bag with crumbs and a toddler ran towards the birds and picked up some of the crumbs in his fist and shoved crumbs and dust in his mouth.

The café was at the far end. I got a table outside and ordered a café noisette. I could taste the sweetness of milk and the bitterness of coffee as two different things at the same time. I'd never noticed that about a café noisette before. I closed my eyes. I heard a pigeon wooing on the dust in front of me and the toddler piping Maman maman like another bird. I felt something push into the hair at the side of my head and nuzzle against my ear. Not just touching not just kissing but taking in the edge of my ear and, as he pressed his lips together with my ear in between them to make the noise with his lips that means kiss, tugging slightly on the soft edge in a way that I could feel through my whole ear. Feel through my whole ear and all through my body.

It was a moment that went on for a lot longer than the average moment. Maybe because it unfolded more dimensions than ordinary moments. Wasn't the universe all folded up? There was hidden time concertinaed into the ordinary moments of the universe, ordinary moments we moved over without unfolding them, without even thinking there were creases in time that a practiced flick of the mind could unfurl, rippling time out with a snap into twenty times its length or more so your consciousness could run free up and down the flattened pleats.

He came round to the front. I couldn't take him all in at once. I was getting up briskly pushing a cheek forward and the other cheek. His smell was still on my cheek and caught in my nostril hairs. He held my upper arms to steady me while he dropped quick dabs that I willed myself not to feel. He handed me a bunch of flowers.

The bunch of flowers. I was in the act of sitting down my bottom hadn't touched the metal seat but then it did and he was still standing which meant that the bunch of flowers came towards me from above with the white sky round them and some of Sergei. If I could have lunged forward and grabbed him and flown up at speed into the white sky with Sergei and the bunch of flowers. A couple of sheets of damp newspaper and a bit of string round roses with buds on some and the nubs left when roses shuffle off and some with greenfly on the sepals and cut-outs where caterpillars had crunched and swollen blossoms asking to be rumpled squeezed and crushed to release their scent which was lemony as well as flowery and they smelt of rain. Lilac. Cream with grey scrolled-back edges. Buff. An almost black crimson. There wasn't a bunch of flowers like it. I started laughing then I stopped in case he interpreted it as inanity, or worse, happiness.

He ordered tea. I got another noisette.

'You know when I see you I realise even more how much I miss you.'

Keep eyes on the flowers. Jerk a few glances so as not to seem strange.

'Oh God well. I just wish I'd been coming when Sylvie was going to be in Paris too. How is she?'

'She's working on some of her own projects which is good.'

'How is your new job? I mean wow.'

You're being goofy. You're taking on some kind of American teen mantle as if it will stop you blushing. What will stop you blushing is not separating from yourself like this. Stir coffee. Get sugar. No. Appear as though listening. Listen a bit. Genuinely try to listen. Don't get lost in bits of him like that. Keep the eyes moving. Don't look at the wrist. Don't look at the fingers.

I ruffled my hand over the top of the roses. He got out his cigarettes, offered me one. I took it. The way he did it. The way I took it. It was one of life's big wastes that a French auteur director wasn't standing right there filming it.

'I got them at Versailles. Of course it's forbidden so I must go around in the night with the secateur.'

'You still live there then?'

'For the moment.'

'With your parents.'

'Yes but I am looking for my own apartment here in Paris. This morning I saw one in Belleville.'

'Was it nice?'

'I'm thinking maybe I will take it. How about you Naomi?'

I heard my voice coming out a bit harshly talking about London, the magazine, British fashion for God's sake. My boyfriend was really well yes. Yes he is in Paris but he had to go and meet an old friend. Actually you know they hadn't, can you believe, really liked the pictures with the jellyfish. When he looked down like that he was like something by Brancusi. Sometimes people can't understand what's beautiful because they don't speak that language. I know I said. It's like there are thousands maybe millions more languages in the world than we know. Yes I said, she doesn't speak our language. I looked more at my coffee, his tea, the pigeons, my hands, his hands, than his eyes. The longer we sat there the worse it got so that I had to tighten the muscles in my stomach to try and hold on. Every so often I made myself look at him so as to seem natural. Now. And I'd force my eyes across or up to his. Even before our eyes connected I'd start to blush. Sometimes I'd manage to get over it by quickly moving on to another subject. Sometimes I'd cover it up with a laugh or by propping my face between my hands so the cheeks were covered by my fingers.

'Tell me more about Sylvie.'

'She is working pretty much only with Ryan now. He is becoming a star. Everyone says he will get a contract with Vogue and she will go there to work with him.'

'French Vogue.'

'Yes the magazine is making a strong voice now.'

'Sylvie is such an amazing woman.'

'Everything I know she teach me. Really she give me everything with a generous heart.'

'You must miss working with her.'

'I can't be the assistant for ever.'

'And I guess you are such close friends.'

'I don't get the chance to see her so much now. They do a lot of shoots on location. She always love to travel.'

'What about her kids?'

'Saïd fly from the nest. He is in America making a record. Little Dominique started at the lycée.'

'But if her mother is away so much?'

'There is the grandmother.'

'And are you in love?'

We looked at each other. I shook my head, upset. He put his cup down on the white-painted metal table.

'A lot has changed in my life.'

I brightened my voice. 'Aha. So you are in love.'

He didn't say anything.

'Come on tell me about her.'

'Naomi something has happened to me. I don't know how to tell you.'

I blessed his forehead and his eyelids. 'You don't have to tell me if you don't want to.'

'It's a boy.'

Sergei has given birth to a boy.

'Congratulations.'

It's a boy. Of course you stupid bitch of course it's a boy it was obvious the whole time that it's a boy. You knew you must have known working in this industry where the only straight men are taking the pictures or delivering the sandwiches. What straight man becomes a stylist for fuck's sake? What straight man wants to choose skirts and play with lipsticks? Look how slim he is, for God's sake, how he knows the best colours for roses, how he even asked you who your lace shorts were by that day remember? You're so naïve. If you hadn't just been thinking about me me me all the time it might have dawned on you. He lives with his mum for goodness sake. It's why girls love him it's why you love him if only you had the whatever it takes to realise. Women feel safe with him, puppyish, remember the models? They couldn't get enough of him. That's why he loves girls, why he's nice to you. He wants to be your girlfriend.

'Don't say it.'

'Cheer up. This is amazing news. You are in love with him right?'

'I am in love.'

I am een leoev. Looking down at the chips in the white-painted metal. Bring on the French auteur.

'Obviously.'

'Obviously?'

'Obviously you are in love with a man.'

'No.'

'What do you mean no? You didn't know you were gay till now?'

'I don't like that word.'

'It's a lovely word, it means happy charming, which you are.' I signalled to the waiter for another coffee.

'I don't know if I am gay. I only know I love this boy.'

'What's his name?'

'Jean-Marie.'

Oh very good for a fag, that girlie Marie at the end. I teased a cigarette out of his packet and lit it.

'So go on. How much are you in love?'

'Very much.'

A male pigeon strutted in front of a female pigeon on the path beside us. She turned her back and pecked at the dust. He plopped himself in front of her frilling his neck feathers and calling woo woo. She turned aside, pecking. He fluttered over in front of her woo.

I heard my voice. 'Oh Sergei.' Sympathetic. I tapped his hand with the matchbox. 'How did you meet him?'

'Oh a few months ago.'

I'd left my cigarette burning in the ashtray. He started to roll it from side to side. 'I had to get some thirties furniture for a shoot and I found this one place and he was there. I talk to him, I borrow some things. It's not his shop but he is running it for the guy and then I take the stuff back myself. You know I don't think anything I just find I am in that shop a few times.'

He picked up the cigarette and took a drag. 'One day I bought a vase from him and we discuss things for a long time. You know, art, fashion, design, and then he say hey why don't we go for a drink.'

'And?'

'I don't know.' He took a drag. He looked up at the sky. I stared at his throat. 'We just talk. For two months.'

I saw myself leaning across the table and putting my mouth on his throat. 'And then what?'

'I kissed him.'

'*You* kissed *him*? Is he gay?'

'Naomi you don't understand.'

'I'm just asking. Was it your first man?'

'Naomi.'

'Sergei this is wonderful news. You are in love. It happens to be a man. Don't be so old-fashioned come on.' I touched the back of his hand. So natural.

'I love him.' Our eyes met. 'I don't know why I told you. Almost nobody knows. There's something special about you Naomi. Something I notice the very first moment I saw you. You can see it in your eyes.'

Yeah yeah le regard doux.

'What did Sylvie say?'

'She doesn't know.'

'Sergei it's OK. She's not going to be upset. This is nowadays. You work in fashion.'

'Please. I want to tell people at the right time. Please if you talk with her anytime, don't say anything.'

'OK.'

There was a queue at the taxi-stand so we walked down to the rue de Rivoli. It started to rain and he bought a fold-down umbrella from a news-stand. The drops of rain released the dust up from the ground with the Paris smell of cake crumbs and old urine mixed together. He put the umbrella up and I leaned in under it and slipped my hand through his arm. He seemed to pull me in closer to him.

He handed me into a cab and tossed the folded-down umbrella onto the seat beside me. The taxi driver had an Alsatian in the front of the cab. When the cab didn't drive off right away the dog half got up and put his paws on the front seat to look at us. Sergei squatted down by the open door of the cab to kiss my cheeks. Then he grabbed my hands and turned them over. He kissed my palms and then held them up to his face while he rocked back and forwards on his heels. I could have pulled his face closer and kissed the mouth between my hands held under his hands. I could have slid through his lips my whole body turning inside out as it went down. He placed the hands back in my lap.

'Lets be friends for ever.'

The cab drove off. I twisted round right away so I could look through the back window. First I could see his eyes and then just the smudge of his face. He kept being blotted out by other people walking on the pavement and then we turned the corner to go down the side of the Louvre. As we started across the bridge I remembered I had left the bunch of flowers on the chair at the café.

29

He was lying on the bed with the telly on. European football. Crisp crumbs lined the seams on the bedcover. I hung up my coat on the door.

'Nay.'

'Hi.'

'Hey you've been crying.'

'Why would I have been crying? How was Rodin?'

He did that thing of pausing so I would know he knew. 'Iris is being cleaned.'

'I should think so.'

I squeezed into the box-size bathroom. I flushed the toilet and ran the water quietly in the basin under the flush noise and splashed my face with water. I found eye drops. Tinted moisturiser. Interestingly it was a new tinted moisturiser that Ellie had asked me to try out for her. I examined my face in it. I needed more coverage. That was the word, coverage. I went out of the bathroom. I moved round the room sorting things.

'What're you sighing for?'

'Nothing. Just leave me alone.'

'Fine.'

There was a rustling sound as he reached into the packet of crisps.

'Stop doing that!'

'What?'

'Pigging.'

'I'm not pigging, I'm starving.'

I said something too low to hear.

'What's it to you?' he said.

'I have to sit here and watch you that's what.'

'No you don't. Fuck off downstairs if you don't like it.'

'Fuck you you're so fucking *selfish*.' Half-scream half-spit of selfish. I opend the suitcase, grabbed a brown paper bag. I snatched my bag and coat off the hook.

'Where you going?'

'Fucking off downstairs.'

I banged the door. He called my name. It hurt me to hear his voice say it like that. I ran more quickly down the stairs and out onto the street. On the street I felt better. Also sadder. I looked for somewhere I could go to cry without anyone looking at me. There wasn't anywhere. There wasn't anywhere in the whole city. They ought to provide dark holes free of charge. It should be a marker of civilisation. Democracy, opera, the rule of law, and free dark holes.

There was a taxi-stand with a taxi waiting. I told him the name of the street.

'Eh mademoiselle, it's just a few hundred metres from here. You can walk.'

'But it's more than that. I would like you to wait for me and bring me back here.'

He looked me up and down through the side window of the cab. 'The one-way systems round here. To go from here to there I would have to go up there' – he started waving his arm around – 'right back round along the quai then blah blah blah and blah blah blah...'

'Excuse me sir but I don't care how much it costs. Please take me.'

He humpfed. 'If you are that crazy I know you are a woman. Hop in.'

In the back of the cab I opened the paper bag and took out the hardback book. I flicked to the title page.

To Eric
Thank you for the poems. I hope you will carry on writing poetry and never stop. But I must ask that you stop sending them to me. I hope you understand. I wish you well.
Naomi.

It had the feeling of a caption you had gone over too many times. It would do. I still liked stop stop one minute and hated it the next. I couldn't move on from loving hating the stop stop thing. I put the book back in the paper bag. I tried to reseal the Sellotape. It was a lot shorter than the first few versions I'd written but I didn't want to encourage him. I only wanted to encourage him as a poet. I mustn't put a stop to poetry. That would be a terrible thing to do. I must send him away without making it stop.

The taxi went down the long street that made a T-junction with the street the hotel was on. It reached the corner. It slowed down and turned. I sat up. Behind me the director and the crew were watching from the end of the road. The big camera trained on me.

I watched the Milord halfway down on the right. I felt them at my back. I wet my lips and let them fall slightly apart. I was panting a bit. I pressed on the old Sellotape again. The underside of it was furred brown with stuck-on brown parcel paper. I had a pen in my handbag. I used it to write his name on the package.

Of course he wouldn't be there. I wasn't expecting that. He must be off doing philosophy at the Sorbonne or whatever any other university was called in Paris. Université de Paris. The Sellotape lifted slowly away from the paper. I smoothed my finger along its length. Although he could still be on his summer break. When did they go back in France? The taxi pulled up. Shit it was possible. He might be standing there a few feet away behind the reception counter. The big camera swung to the side and zoomed. Maybe he was dreaming up a poem right now to send to Naomi in another country. Dreaming of her a few feet away.

'This is it.'

The glass doors of the hotel. The way the light was hitting them they reflected the building opposite and a bit of sky. I could only see patches that could be the reception area behind. I handed the driver the package. He made a noise like he was going to cough something up. I got out a decent-sized note. I flapped it over his shoulder. He droned nons. He clicked his tongue. S'il vous plaît. S'il vous plaît monsieur. The camera coming right in for a close up. Her creased forehead. Her damp eyes. Muttering stuff he creaks his bulk out of the seat and lumbers up the steps to the hotel. He pushes open one side of the half-glass doors. He goes in. Slowly the half-glass door swings shut behind him and swings back and forward in tight arcs a few times. The images on the glass swoosh, slop and vibrate. Everything goes still.

I heard my breathing and the ticking sound of the meter. If he was in there either he'd take the package and not understand, maybe even open it later. He was away with the fairies. He was writing a poem. No he wouldn't. He'd know immediately. He wouldn't even pick the package up he'd run out from behind the counter and push past the taxi driver and come bursting out of the glass doors. The reflection of the building opposite wobbled like it was starting to run down the glass of the doors. I watched it settle back. Maybe he was just standing there behind the doors hidden by the reflection. She looks away. She shakes her hair back out of her eyes and frowns slightly.

But if he was in the room behind the door painted to look like part of the wall and someone else was on reception, or if he was doing something in some other part of the hotel, then the driver would leave the package there on the counter and come back out and get into the cab. The driver's seat made a sound as the foam in it came back up to neutral position. I tapped my fingers against the window. What was he doing in there?

Only then would the door burst open and it would be him and I'd yell at the driver Drive! Drive! I'd look for the thing to lock my door. Quick! Quick! Click just in time. The taxi pulling away. I'd hear him running down the street after us banging on the roof of the car with his hands. I didn't want any of that to happen. I didn't want to see him ever again. I just wanted to do the right thing. To say thank you for what he had done. To show him that I had heard. Because what he had done was, well someone like me didn't have the word. But what he had done was something already out of a book. Something well I could say out of this world. I wanted him to get the present. To read the note. To follow the instructions even though it would hurt him.

The reflections on the half-glass doors shook smeared and dissolved. A black gap opened up. The doors were opening. Someone came out onto the top step. I gasped. This person with the chequered paunch and the brown nylon trousers was the taxi-driver. He shambled down the steps looking left and right up the street. He opened the driver's door said something in what I imagined was argot a word I always associated with ingot. Muttering. Fidgeting.

'S'il vous plaît. S'il vous plaît, si on peut' I made a rolling movement with one hand to help me remember. 'Go away quickly? Dépêchons-nous.'

He wheezed. He rocked his bulk from side to side against the fake fur cushion at the small of his back. 'Calmez-vous mademoiselle, eh?'

He sat still. He clicked his tongue. Vague front seat commotion. He was trying to swing his whole body round so as to see the beaded back-roller behind the cushion.

'Please.'

'Du calme. Du calme.' He craned forward and reached an arm behind his back and tugged at the beaded backroller.

'Monsieur we have to go very quickly.'

He stopped. Faced out of the windscreen as if he had been turned to stone. Then I realised he was easing back slowly against the seat, rocking his weight minutely from buttock to buttock as he inched backwards. He stopped. Assessed. Groaned. He grabbed the steering-wheel and came forward on the seat again.

'Monsieur. I will pay double. S'il vous plaît. Dépêchez-vous.'

Something compelling me. The camera was tracking slowly up the street behind me on its dolly. I look round at the glass doors. The reflections undulated. The camera on tiptoes. Time on tiptoes. I slid down in the back seat as far as I could. I looked for the lock.

'Where to?'

'Back where we came from. Lets go.'

'OK, OK. We will get there just the same.'

He put the taxi into gear and waddled his backside a last time before glancing over his shoulder and pulling out. The car dandered up the street. I blew air between my teeth. I sensed the camera was off me. It was pointing at the entrance to the Hotel Milord for the shot where the reflections on the doors tremble, split into fragments and are blown away. He bursts out from behind the exploding fragments like something out of this world bursting through the panes of normalcy. He sees the taxi carrying her about to turn the corner. Close up of his face. Unforgettable. He starts to run slo-mo down the street. We hear his breathing loud over the blurred motion of his body. The strain on his face like on the face of an Olympic athlete. His face is made out of rubber, flubber, blubber. It expands and contracts in big effortful waves as he urges his body up the street towards her. His eyes. As if someone was going to shoot him from behind. This moment. This moment. This moment. As he reaches the end of the street the film speeds up to real-time and his momentum takes him round the corner onto the longer busier street as the taxi accelerates away.

30

A letter. Different paper. Two days before I went to the Milord he had been there to see Georges, the other boy on reception the year before and who was still working there. The thought that we had passed so close was terrible for him. He had trembled to read words written with my own hand in the book I had given him. He had read them again and again. It was as though I had been beside him watching him calmly and for a long time. For a year he had sent poems without leaving his address. He didn't want to trouble me in my life. Would I permit him to keep sending them? I was the source of the poems he couldn't write them without me. When they were written he needed to know that I would receive them. Even if I only traced the shapes of the words with my eyes. This was all he asked with the deepest respect. Some French sign-off. Eric. A return address maybe a Paris suburb.

I wrote back in French intending to say:

Dear Eric,

Thank you for your letter. I don't know much about you and your life. All I really know are your poems. You knew me basically for an hour. So it seems quite extreme that a year later you are still writing me all these poems and talking about how you tremble when you see my writing.

I would not want to stop the poems coming into being. If you need to think about me somehow to write, I suppose my part is I have to accept that. But I wish you didn't have to send them to me. I feel disturbed when I receive them. I can't explain. They feel onerous. (I looked up this word in the French–English dictionary and it said pénible. Then I went to pénible in the French part of the dictionary and it said pénible means hard as in fatiguing or difficult; tiresome; painful. No mention of onerous at all, which is typical. But what I want to say is onerous which doesn't mean fatiguing or difficult or anything like that.)

I think the poems are [...] (can't find the word). I've written them down in English, sometimes several different ways. But although I studied literature at university, I'm not familiar with modern French poetry, as you know (remember our discussion?). You should show them to someone who knows. You're special, Eric. You've got this rare talent, even though I'm not sure exactly what it's for.

Remember this is not reality. You don't know me even if you think you do. I have my life here and you have yours there. Mine (in case you didn't notice from the telephone messages when I was staying at the Milord) includes a boyfriend. I don't want to cause you pain but I think you need to know that I love him very much and I live with him. I don't know what you finally intend by your poems, so excuse me if I mention this fact unnecessarily. I wish you well. I will not respond to any future letters because I want to make it clear that we don't have a relationship other than this one that only happens in poems.

Look after yourself,
Naomi

PS I just looked up onerous in an old dictionary and it says it's from a French word onereux! So maybe you know it anyway. 'An exiled person, absent out of necessity, retains all things onerous to himself, as a punishment for his crime.' That's a quote it gives as an example. Please don't abandon your poems.

31

Feeling round égerie with my tongue:

– girlish eagle
– shadow of tracery
– good name for a French perfume
– a box at the theatre
– canary cage
– edgery
– nervy movement like shying
– trickle of water

I got out the big French/English English/French dictionary.

> **égerie** /ezeRi/ NF **a** *[de poète]* muse ◆ **c'est la nouvelle ~ de Chanel** *(= mannequin)* she's Chanel's new icon ◆ **une ~ du cinéma américain** an American movie queen ◆ **elle est l'~ du président** the president looks to her for inspiration ◆ **la police a arrêté l'~ de la bande** the police have arrested the woman who was the brains behind the gang **b** ◆ **Egérie** *(Hist)* Egeria

I got out Dan's encyclopedia.

Asteroid 13 Egeria
a genus of aquatic plants
a 4th-century pilgrim, a Spanish nun, a mountaineer

a figure of Roman mythology
Mountains: Sinai, Tabor, the Beatitudes, Carmel, Egeria, Quarantana

In my lunch hour I went to Westminster library.

The **Peregrinatio Aetheriae** or **Itinerarium Egeriae** might be the earliest prose work written by a woman

the water nymph who gave wise counsel to the ancient king Numa Pompilius
they used to meet in a sacred grove in the midst of which a spring gushed
the name is still commonly used in France to designate the female inspirator of a political man

King Numa's spiritual adviser
also regarded by some as his wife
when King Numa died she withdrew to a grove and couldn't stop crying so Phoebe changed her into a spring
or well

one of the Camenae or Casmenae, ancient Roman goddesses of wells and springs later identified with the Greek muses

ancient pre-Roman goddess of springs

PART 3

32

Horizontal plane of green laser.

Crump. Crump.

A siren building.

Crump.

Sheet of green light coming down. Green arms burst through feellessly.

Nothing. Just a high-pitched eery on and on and on and it can't keep on and it will never end it will never on and on and on happen and it happens.

Implosion of the underpass. Laughs.

Closing its eyes coming in waves of nauseavibration and fuckout aquasound. Just a feeling lose control and I don't know time. Lost and crossing vast prairies of time and space on a wind of warp speed and I don't know just a feeling am moving in time to no ahead of a beat so hot and fuzzy it's making the wires in my head glow in time to no ahead of a beat so hot and fuggy it making the synapses inside my pop from kernels into clouds one after the other gogogogoo gggggggggggg insides of a computer lighting up binary node by binary node as one tripswitch trips another and the message zips to the millionth node in the inkling of an eye and the message is Up and the message is Love.

Got to get to the inside of the back of beyond chugging through dark on a choochoo train and *it's all about love.* And beats boom and expand like those Chinese paper flowers that start out tight knots just a feeling just a feeling and burst out big and slow in the blood and *it's all about love.*

Glass shattering and re-constituting shattering and re-constituting.

Metal rods dragged down a row of railings.

Boards booming in and out membranes of a giant heart.

Earth dumping on earth.

Voice of the devil breathing *ecstasy.*

Voice of the washing-machine at the centre of the universe.

Beats thumping emergency cardiac resuscitation.

Sound of gravel poured down a metal conveyor belt.

Sound of factory bellows.

Scraping of chairs while a beast pounds its tail on the gate.

An is all bout lerv.

And now here come sparkly succubus noises.

Thunder torques through and is withdrawn.

And the sparkly noises synch up again and the thunder torques through and is withdrawn.

And the succubus comes up again and oh no it's a building beat that comes from nowhere mounting until it's drilling with a pneumatic duh … duh … duh … duh … duh. duh. duh. duh. duh. duhduhduh duh duhduh duhduhduh duhduh duhduhhhhhhhhhhh.

Flup. Flup.

Behind the speaker a young boy doubled over with his jeans round his knees. Something folding into a pile of rising dough and *is all bo lur.* Baby and a he pulls me into him and grinds hips into hipbones and laugh and spin away a sunburst of energy irradiates barking sounds at the ceiling tracer fire of red laser tracking across head and *ess erl buh luv.*

And the clear calls of a woman roving over my head in a glassy wave. And the faces round me laughing and blurring out as they travel at speed. And Ellie smiling into my face and just a feeling falls and we hug and close our eyes and stroke each hair cuz *illell but luh.*

And a mechanical arm banging on a rubbish bin lid while a rinky-dinky baton breaks up into peals breaks up into shoals breaks up into pennies churning out in a penny arcade and a Nazi drag queen enunciates *Pull.* She says it again *Pull.* And a hearty bo'sun saying Oooh-aarr. Oooh-aarr. A wet chocolate beat nosing between my thighs. A hearty bosun Ooh-aarr. Ooh-aarr. A wet chocolate beat just a feeling take me away. Throbbing zum-zum-zum and a lift going up a lift shaft vertebra by vertebra. Something rising vertebra by vertebra and it's laughing that laugh that's not very funny and it's inching up the spine and it shoots out the top of my head and it shoots my head and arms fly up and touch the sky. *An iss all bit lahv.*

Can't speak can't move nerves of the sediment and wade to a ledge round dancefloor with a railing above it and I wanna say *cuz is ol bi leh.* Sitting on the ledge with railings behind me and lean back breathing fast can't breathe and I close and I open and the light drags across the room in big long flash and makes a noise fffwoom. Uh do it na-choo-ra-lee. Uh do it na-choo-ra-lee. Sag and the light ffwwoooom. Uh do it na-choo-ra-lee. Can't breathe. Just a feeling. And someone holding a bottle of water to my lips. It's a boy it's a boy ees sliding isands down ssssssidessss of ssss naked torso an golden parallelograms accelerating off of him sT hanging from waistband of ssjeans ana beautiful boy breaking and nearly touching the ground with his arse and popping an clapping to call me back *unisul.* Throw my head back and suck in oxygen ana man leaning over the railings and pustulated face snaps into a weird smile and the music says *it's all bout love.* An the boy reaches up and starts to kissuck the pustulated man and I see melting glass coming down down for vast prairies of time so clear shining and it falls on my face and slides down my cheek and I lick it from the corner of my mouth and the boy breaks back and I see glass on his chin and I say it out loud. *Love.*

She is there and she radiate eels of energy and pulls me onto the dancefloor and boom. Squelch squelch squelch squelch squelch squelch squelch squelch. Ellie puts her face in my hair and her eyes funny bluewhites screams and the scream is

Ay –erv –ooh.

Because it's all about love.

Crystals of painful clarity cut out of my chest and fly and I break into a trance dance stamping away in my 20 hole Docs under the DJ booth where it's hot and fuggy. A bank of speakers and the beats moving out like weather fronts making all the hairs vibrate making all the flesh fluctuate making all the bones susurrate and feel sick if you want to know alone on the elevation and it's getting darker and I'm spinning at in the centre of industrial battering when a fucked voice says *Hocus* *Pocus.*

The crowd yowls. And the man behind the wheels means business. He's laying down steel girders over megawatt power drills while fascist jackboots invade the air in succeeding waves. A plane takes off across the room and a piston backfires over and over *coz it's all bat luff.* People are grey and strung out. People are leaning on each other. People can't dance. They can't stand. I have to get away but I can't get away. *Dominator!* *Dominator!* Mutants with red pusholes puncturing monster faces are coming out the walls. *Dominator! Dominator!* The sirens' singing punched and punched and the hole generates fast-mutating forms and I crouch the floor and the sweat falls and the fucking dominatrix sends out cohorts of fuckbeats to frogmarch over my face with evil smacking noise. The walls are sucking in and out with the vacuum of the boomboxes The dark is alive. I can't get out. A scream starts in my brain and builds and builds an *iz ow bow wuuuuuuuuuuuuuuuuuuuuuuuuuuuuuuuuuh*

33

Warm lips.

'Naomi.'

It's a fag. Open lips. Close them on fag.

'Naomi?'

Release fag.

Turned.

Her hair was fucked. Her cheeks were spotted red and they were sucking in on a cigarette. Now her hand came up off her collarbone took the fag out of her lips and carried it across to mine. I sucked. Flare.

'That was awesome.'

'Incredible.'

'You OK?'

'Yeah. You?'

'Bit sick. I could be sick.'

'D'you want a bucket?'

'I think it's OK.'

I sighed. 'Can't sleep.'

'Ghost bass.'

'Yeah.'

'Spanking my eardrums.'

'Yeah. Me too.'

'Fuck though.'

Ellie pushed the cigarette against my lips. They parted. I inhaled. Fag so sweet. Like a wonder.

'That was awesome.'

'Yeah.'

*

I opened my eyes. Alarms in eardrums. Discordant with the light in the room. The light was a bit redder but it was still pink a pinkish grey. It touched things unsurely.

'Wow. Dawn.'

'Yeah.'

'Never seen dawn much.'

'What?'

'In my life.'

'I know.'

'Could change though.'

'Yeah.' Massive sigh. 'That was'

'Was it like when Dorothy opens the door and everything's in colour?'

'Yeah.' I closed my eyes.

Things pouring and shifting in my head. Alarms sounding in my head. Quiet in the room. Feel how quiet it is outside my head as opposed to inside my head. Wish I could go out there with the wardrobe and the chair with its back to the wall and the sweaty top lying on the seatpad.

'You know what?'

'What?' Things shifting and pouring. Alarms.

'I felt I could have died down there and it wouldn't have mattered.'

Just before dawn. It will be dawn soon or is this dawn? A dead mouse smell in the room.

'Did you feel that? That you could have died and it would have been OK?'

She's looking at me. I turned my head. There tucked in to her fucked hair. Serious worried even. Pupils open holes.

'Yeah. Yeah.' She turned her profile. Stuck her fag in.

My eyes opened. My head was still turned at an angle to her. The top near corner of the wardrobe the things on top of the wardrobe. Blankets. A storage box with a swirly pattern. Broken bedside lamp.

Dust making a mat on the blankets and the lid of the box. The light going from pink to red. But it wasn't red yet. It was going to red. Outside the light would still be grey coming out of dark. A pill you could dissolve into dark to dilute it.

34

Mornings at Ellie's I lived in my fashion freelance outfit, a synthetic pink dressing-gown and a pair of Daffy Duck slippers. Underneath I had a giant T-shirt with a number on it that an old boyfriend of Ellie's had left at the flat. Number 47.

The living room was where I was supposed to write up little fashion news stories that just popped into my head and sell them to the style sections of Sunday newspapers. Ellie's idea. What else could I do? I was trained in nothing. Well, Comparative European Literature, I was supposedly trained in that. But I hadn't bothered to read most of the texts. I wasn't even trained in that. I could read, I could write, I could shop professionally. I could find the photographer to make the shopping look like the passport to over the rainbow. I just needed to survive for a bit. I took the odd styling job. I dragged myself to the odd fashion PR event so people would see my face. I tried the writing gig.

I'd bought a computer with the money I had when I left the mag. It lived on the big wooden table that ran along one side of the living room. On the opposite side was the two-bar fire with a narrow shelf above it. There was a pine sofabed and a comfy chair with a Mexican blanket thrown over it and opposite the sofa by the window a telly. Wooden chairs were drawn up round the big wooden table. I usually sat in the one at the end with the computer on the table and the window behind me. I'd turn round so I could look out of the window while I was drinking my coffee.

While I was drinking the coffee I looked down at the patch of municipal grass that grew outside the mansion block and the road running parallel to the block beyond the grass. On the other side of the road a row of terraced houses. Behind the houses the tower block and the estate. Three trees grew in the municipal patch of grass. I looked at the trees so much I noticed the gradations within the seasons not just spring summer winter like before.

I arrived when the trees had been dead for months. You'd have thought they were a goner but if you looked closely you could see nubs all over them where new leaves were going to come. The trees looked death but inside some secret sugarwater was stuffing the buds. They started to split on the tree furthest away from the mansion block more out in the sun first. Then inner buds slithered out of the split black casings, silvery-green. I'd never noticed how sexual trees were before. How the live stuff coming out looked like organs matted with sticky white. A couple of days and it had all changed and they were sunless embryos all crinkled pathos and innards folded within innards. Each day the furls would shoot further out in inches. Now the trees were covered with breech birth lambs, sticky legs and blunt hooves hanging out of the prune vulvas of aged ewes. After a bit of languishing the hooves exploded into wings, yellow-green, the sun coming through each one. They looked young and happy flapping in the wind. Then there was a more boring time when over ages the leaves got bigger and more turgid until by August they were coarse and ugly.

I'd start to cry. I'd get up and walk around the room. Sometimes I'd crouch in a weird corner maybe behind the TV or on the floor next to the fridge. Sometimes I'd wander from room to room crying. After a while I got so I could carry on looking at the trees and thinking about them while tears dripped down my face. I got so I could even read the paper and cry. You just blink really rapidly and the words reappear for a minute through the wateriness. I got so as I paid attention to tears only to wipe them away like wiping away sweat. I sniffed back the snot in my nose like someone putting up with a cold. Sometimes I'd be walking round the flat snivelling and I'd start to laugh. Other times I slapped myself on the cheek and said aloud 'Shut the fuck up.'

35

Sometimes we flogged a whack of beauty stuff at a car boot sale along with old copies of fashion mags which sold surprisingly well to the Filipina carers and from-elsewhere catering workers. Then we'd have bonanza nights where we'd play one kind of pill or tab off against another. Ellie gave them the names of beauty brands in homage. Estees. Yves. Shanelles. Body Shop was a real wrecker. Plenitudes which we thought described a certain mongy kind of tab especially well. Before we went out we'd hang out on the sofas at the back of The Light Rums of Puerto Rico. We'd wear pick n' mix eyes and fruits of the forest lips to use up the unsellable samples. On other nights I'd sometimes pop into The Light Rums early on just to get out of the flat. I'd sit at the bar and order Mo the Moroccan barman's speciality, tea with mint. I'd sip and read. I'd read anything I found round the flat except magazines; the paper, the odd novel, Doughgirl's pass-on biogs of rock stars, tomes of spa wisdom like You Can Heal Your Life and every now and then the Eric poems.

Mo helped me out with poems. He spoke French. I'd ask him what he thought of a particular phrase, he'd ask to see it. I didn't mind Mo. I'd turn the poem round so he could figure out what it meant in context and he'd get the pencil out from behind his ear and scribble the answer on the paper. If it wasn't clear if it was one thing or the other, he'd ring up his French girlfriend and they'd discuss it on the phone. I never got him to do a whole poem, I liked to do them myself, it just took time. But once the letters started arriving, I did a deal with him. I'd bring him a goodie bag bath products and hair gunk for him, moisturisers and fragrance for the girlfriend. He'd take a letter away and sort it. There was something about getting a letter right away in English that I liked. It felt more straightforwardly Eric than if I'd had a hand in it.

He was cool, Mo. He never said anything about what the letters said. Just winked and handed over their his 'n' hers version next time I was in. Usually a free drink as well.

Dear Naomi,

You asked me, no you insisted, that I must not write you letters. But sometimes I badly want to ask How are you? Even if you do not reply, even if you throw this letter away. Just to ask how are you? just to write to you as I'm doing now without thinking, without crossings-out, quickly without stopping to think what I will say which naturally leads me to let escape the words I love you. I don't deny it's strange that I still do, but it's as if you struck me and left poison in me. I tried to forget you with someone else but something stopped me. I tried to continue my studies but I couldn't concentrate any more. I can't talk to my friends any more. They ask me what's wrong, why I don't have a girlfriend, why I don't want to spend so much time with them any more. No, I don't want to give you the impression I am a recluse. I see people, I go out, I talk to them, but not like before. My real life happens in solitude when you saturate me with the desire to write. I write a lot at night. Night is also when I must at times leave the house. I have gone back to live with my parents. I climb out of the window at night so that I don't disturb them. Below is the flat roof of the kitchen and from here I can go down by the drainpipe till my feet find a bench in the garden, more like a small yard. I feel better outside. I walk for hours without choosing my direction. You might walk towards me round a corner. I might catch a glimpse of you opening the door of a bar or an apartment building. It's just a fantasy, I am not crazy. I know you are not here. But I feel you surrounding me like music. Sometimes I find a good place to sit and write a poem. Sometimes I write by the river, sometimes in Buttes-Chaumont. Do you know it? I make you another body since I don't have the one you call your own with me. Why should you not be both? Humans are more limited than they have to be. I come back home before anyone is awake and it's good to sleep until the afternoon because when I am asleep I don't feel the hurt of being apart from you. When I wake up, sometimes I'm not aware of you for five minutes or more. Then I feel it and it's like you struck me again. For five waking minutes I was free of this hurt that has an exact location in my body. I have discovered that love is a stomach-ache! You say you will never be with me and I respect your feelings. All I ask is that you also respect mine. I didn't wish for this but I am going to be truthful and live truthfully. I know that you only reluctantly accept your obscure link to me. You say you do not recognise yourself in the poems. But why would you recognise yourself in poetry since you live outside poetry though it does not live outside you? Things are formed in obscure ways. The prints which are the inscription of our identity are formed on the blank fingers of the child in the womb by the waves of amniotic fluid moving over the flesh. When the fluid in the mother's belly is turbulent, whirpools form on the fingertips. When the fluid is calm, smooth waves form. What drives the rhythms no one knows. But they are engraved on the fingers of each child in a singular way. I kiss you goodnight, the kind of kiss you will not have to refuse since it exists only on the page. Sleep well my beloved Naomi, sleep beauty and dream of sleep.

Eric

PS I include four poems

36

I had been staying at Ellie's a few weeks when she came in and found me crying in the kitchen up against the fridge. She got the vodka out of the freezer and poured two large vodka and tonics and dragged me into the living room and onto the sofa. She took the Mexican blanket off the chair and put it over my shoulders and chucked the toilet roll I'd been using into the cushions beside me. I tried to get up and go into the bedroom. She stopped me. I put my face in the cushions. She lit a cigarette and tapped me on the back. I took it. After a few drags the crying came down a notch or two then after a bit longer it went down to jerky in-breaths. I lit another cigarette and stared at the two-bar fire.

'What happened?'

'I went round because I wanted to get this one box. It's nothing just photographs from when I was a kid, letters from my Dad, lucky charms, teen diaries. You know the type.'

She nodded.

'I rang the bell. He wasn't there so I tried to open the door. And, this is really stupid but it didn't occur to me he might have changed the lock. Why would he do that? We were talking. He said I could keep my stuff there till I found my own place, remember? I kept putting the key in and rattling it around and this nosy neighbour, Mrs Viner, comes out of the main house and says is there something wrong with your key Naomi? I said I thought I'd brought the wrong one. Then I said didn't she have a spare one? and she said she'd lost it, and the way she looked at me I knew she knew exactly where it was. It was horrible. So I came back here and I called him at work. He said you take away me my future I take away your past.'

'What had he done with it?' She passed me another lit cigarette.

'Thrown away. Long gone he said. It's too late.'

'Bastard.'

'He says I've hurt him so much it will last for ever.' I controlled myself.

'Bastard. That was a bastard thing to do.'

'Yes but I was the one who did it. I left.'

We watched Casablanca. Ellie cuddled into the Mexican blanket on the chair. Me on the sofa with the cushions round me. Telly on low, Ingrid Bergman's black lips in the shadows. We were almost through the wine. I sipped the last inch from the tumbler. Ellie got up went in the kitchen. I heard a soft bam. Scraping clinking. Bam. She came in with two saucers of ice-cream. I took one. They're at the airport. Black and white fog. Lots of eyes sliding about behind other eyes. Hers to Rick's behind Laszlo's. The policeman's to Rick's behind hers. Rick's to hers behind the policeman's. Laszlo's to Rick's.

'No don't do it.'

'Stay with Reeck. Stay with the man you love.'

'Don't let him tell you what to do.'

'Don't say it!'

We'll always have Paris.

'No no no!'

Then the lights of the plane whoosh past in the fog and she is gone for ever.

Ellie looked round. Her face was funny. I thought it was a joke but I saw her eyes were full.

'Why does she go off to spend the rest of her life with a man she doesn't love?'

'Like she says, she's part of his work, the thing that keeps him going.'

'The thing. You couldn't make this movie today.' She wiped at her eyes.

'They all think they're doing the right thing instead of the selfish thing,' I said.

'Based on a lie. She's just some unit of exchange between them.'

'I suppose these kind of movies have got to be sad. Still, that ending.'

'Maybe it's us.'

'Probably. Or maybe Rick's being sensible.'

'In what way?'

'He's a drunk. Wouldn't work.'

'Yeah but Laszlo is sexless. He's twice her age as well. She's being sacrificed to some obscure cause.'

'Have you looked at Rick? He's ancient.'

'Apparently Humf was only forty-five when he made it. People looked ancient then.'

She put the video on rewind.

'No more wine?' I said.

'Tiny bit vodka though.'

She went to get it. Bam. Clinking. Bam. She had two shot glasses in one hand, bottle in the other. She poured. Oily, vapours coming off.

'How do you know when it's The One?' she said.

'You're just supposed to know aren't you?'

'Was Dan The One?'

I knew she'd asked me by surprise like that to help the real answer surface. It didn't.

'Ye-es. And no.'

'So is that a no? Classically speaking?'

'Welll classically speaking. I mean I was the one who left him and I don't even know why. I know I love him.'

'You'll always have Balham,' she said.

Tears ran down my cheeks.

'Oh I didn't mean that,' she said.

'No that was really funny.'

37

She was a size-12 woman with a heart-shaped face. She was wearing a black jumper and trousers that made me aware somehow of the meaninglessness of existence.

'Thanks for coming in to see us,' she said. I couldn't remember if she'd said on the phone what her position was. 'Shall we pop round the corner for a coffee?'

'Yes.' It sounded not enough. I added, 'That's a good idea.'

She scanned me without wanting to seem to.

I followed her out onto the street. In every direction the roads and pavements were grey and on either side were grey buildings. The sky was blinding grey.

'Excuse me if I'm a bit doolally, I've just had a glass of wine. At lunch!'

I made the noise a hen makes to her chicks, an almost soundless clucking that is meant as a kind of laugh. She sorted her hair over her shoulder with her hand.

'Honestly at the moment my job is nothing but entertaining. Breakfast, coffee, lunch, coffee, tea, coffee, cocktails, coffee. I've had so many coffees today already I'm buzzing like some kind of junkie and then I'll have to do drinks after work.'

As long as you don't do another coffee. Hey too much of a good thing never did anyone any harm. God lets swap lives I could do with that kind of nothing. You must be desperate to hang up your coffee mug and sit down at a desk.

'Lucky you.'

She pushed open the glass door of a café. 'Will this do? You can't smoke in here though it's organic.'

'Fine by me.' A good phrase.

She ordered a cappuccino and I said same again. She groaned as she led the way towards a table. 'Another coffee. I'll probably get a migraine.' She rolled her eyes to heaven.

I pressed an internal search button but nothing came up in the window. I had to make do with another hen noise.

We sat down opposite each other. Immediately I sensed myself sinking into lethargy. I felt it showed in my face which she looked at with an expression I couldn't work out.

'Matthew speaks so highly of you,' she said.

'Oh yes he's brilliant.' I worried that it sounded like a backhanded compliment to myself.

'Before we go any further, the secrecy agreement. Sorry but the powers-that-be are very strict on this one. Can you just take a look and sign before I tell you any state secrets?'

'No problem.' Too deadpan. I brightened my features. 'I love a state secret it makes me feel like'

Like who? Who does a state secret make me feel like? Who had state secrets? Who kept state secrets, for example, during the War? Or during say recent political scandals? Or films. Were there any well-known films in popular culture that involved, that centred on, the keeping of state secrets? She's waiting. Watching. Time running out. I need a state secret role model *now*.

'A Bond girl.'

She made a polite noise and passed a few sheets of closely typed paper across the table. I let myself slip away into The Recipient will be responsible for any breach of any of the terms of this Deed by the Recipient or any of his/her/its employees and the Recipient shall be liable to indemnify and hold the Company harmless against any losses, costs, claims, damages or expenses incurrred by either the Company or its Group Companies either as a result of the unauthorised disclosure by the Recipient of any of the Information or as a result of the breach of any of the terms of this Deed. What was making life good at this moment was the way the heat came at just the right temperature through the china of the mug and into my hands cupped round it. The aroma of coffee. Not from my mug which smelt of scalding. But in the café air. Things like these were the hooks and eyes. The warmth of the coffee mug against the grey pavements and the hard radiance of the grey sky outside and the burgundy bent metal chairs and the small round tabletops that had been covered in sticky-backed plastic printed with a brownish marble effect. The soft batons of sugar in a bowl of no particular anything. The marks of other people's coffee mugs on the brownish marble effect. The sticky dirt where the flat table surface met the rim of metal round the edge.

Her eyes taking in information that leaked from some waste outlet of my being.

'It's a magazine for a discerning reader. ABC1, C2.'

'That's quite a big catchment.' Nothing gets past me.

'Yes but that's what's different about us. We're about an attitude not a demographic. That's our USP. And it's not just fashion. This is a broad vision of women's lives. We're not reducing women to fashion victims. Sorry because fashion *is* important and of course that's where you come in.'

Lamb eyes asking me something.

'No I know what you mean. Fashion can be shallow sometimes. Well most of the time. Well no it depends on what else. On the environment of the magazine.' I held the coffee mug between my hands.

'I couldn't agree more. The environment of the magazine is the thing. That's where we've really taken the shoot the puppy approach.' She looked at the ceiling and laughed a puppy-killer's laugh. The warmth coming out of the mug passed into my hands. She wants me to ask.

'Shoot the puppy?'

'You know. Think the unthinkable. Blow the time-honoured structure of the magazine out of the water.'

I looked down so I could blink quickly a few times. 'Wow, sounds radical. Great.'

She shone her eyes on me.

'Tell me more.'

'It's section-led. There's no well.'

I kept my head low. You shouldn't have said great. Too arse-licky. I reached for a sugar baton. 'Is that strictly wise?'

'Welll, if wise means conventional, no. We're talking about a radical restructuring but all the research shows' – she shook the long dark hair from her shoulder – 'women are ready for it.'

Her hand on the table small and soft. The blunt round ends of two fingers touching a dried-in ring of milky coffee. The way she'd gone and had her nails done. The way they'd snipped off the cuticles so the new nail coming out at the bottom was exposed to the forays of air. She'd asked for clear polish.

She was waiting for me to say something.

'So no beginning, middle and end.'

'Well, differently done.'

'No but I mean the way they usually start you off gently with the front-of-book and build to that big crescendo of pictures and major features in the middle. You're not doing that?'

'No. Each section is as vital as the next. Each has its own beginning, middle and end. It's a portfolio magazine for the modern portfolio lifestyle.'

'Wow.'

The cut from a cheese knife on the side of my right hand ring finger. I'd held the blade instead of the wooden handle. Hadn't realised it was sharp enough to cut flesh. Badly bitten nails. I looked up. Lamb eyes. Pleading somehow, but watching.

'Uh. Sections? Fantastic. How does it break down?'

'Sorry?'

'Sorry, I mean what does each section cover?'

'At the front there's Life Wife which is what a woman's life would be like if she had a life. I mean a wife!'

We laughed.

'Kind of a positive solutions section. We actually want to identify women's concerns and help them address them.'

'Oh good so you're actually going to help women not just the advertisers.'

The dry cuticles with white tags at the sides. The nails stopped well below the finger ends. The irregular white keratin line along the tops. I should have had a manicure.

'Yes we're really keen on that. Two, there's Style Life which is where you come in. We've got sixteen pages on average of fashion a month. Then Face Life, which is beauty, Life Guard, which is the working title for soft health, a couple of pages on fitness and diet news, Sex Life, which is relationships, Inner Life which is kind of'

I felt in my bag for a notebook, nodding every once in a while as she talked about hard health and soft health, about the modern woman's desire to be diagnosed, about not taking the typical pictures but pictures that would be relevant to women's real lives. I found a packet of Handy Andies and took one out. I unfolded it and wrote Mag X at the top with a biro. I searched for a relevant question. On the ball.

'What kind of designer will you cover on the fashion pages?'

Her panicky lambs while her voice said quickly, 'It's more High Street, with, you know, carefully edited designer pieces thrown in. You know, good High Street stuff.'

She extended her hands on the table. She moved them around in a little dance. I lowered my head over the hankie and wrote edited designer pieces. I noticed how the biro tip was hard and kept snagging on the tissue. I tried to make the biro's touch lighter like soft health but without losing clarity.

'We haven't necessarily identified the really excellent stuff that lurks out there yet, but I guess that would be part of where you come in, and then throwing in maybe   you know   a really beautiful Armani coat   or a Donna Karan jacket   or lets see   Gucci maybe, you know, just one really sexy but wearable pair of trousers for the season. Classic with a twist. People just don't understand the meaning of classic any more.'

I put the end of the biro in my mouth. Mulling it over. 'What you mean is the pages are going to work the way women really shop,' I emphasised really.

'You've got it. None of that fashion pretentiousness. Of course we'll have to address the advertisers, but you know everyone has to do that, it's the rules of the game.'

Les yeux d'agneau. I thought only I was allowed to have them.

'Oh absolutely.' I put my hands round the coffee mug. I would have liked to hold the coffee mug against my chest for a second.

'So designers like maybe Nicole Farhi and maybe   that sort of level?'

'Yes but good really top stuff every now and then. You know, edited pieces.'

'Like maybe a really clever piece by Dolce & Gabbana.'

'More like maybe Moschino.'

'Well if you prefer Moschino yes. He had some great stuff in his last show.'

'You saw the show?'

I felt a blush coming. 'No I saw the video though. I don't do Milan.' Or Paris or New York. 'But there are some amazing young British designers coming through.'

'We have to be careful. We don't want anything too "out there". It's not relevant to real lives. What photographers do you work with?'

'My method is not to favour any one photographer. I keep it varied. But you've seen my book.' Seven months since I'd resigned and almost nothing new in the book since then. I lifted the mug with both hands.

'And when was it you left?'

'Almost five months ago now. God it seems like yesterday.'

'I can imagine. There have been a lot of changes there.'

'Yeah well in the fashion department first Becca and then me leaving. Kim is still going strong though.'

'Such a nice woman.'

'Lovely to work for. I loved it there but I wanted to stretch my wings. And try lots of different things which I've been doing since I left.'

Her eyes were out of place. Lamb's eyes isolated in a Petri dish. Exposed. Kept alive. I looked down at the mug. 'Doing jobs that won't necessarily thrill the bank manager but will you know stretch you creatively. And I've been writing the odd small fashion news thing here and there as well. You know give it a go.' I rolled my eyes in a give it a go way.

'Ooh that's good very few people can do both. Can you come up with some ideas for the dummy?'

'No problem.'

She looked at her watch. 'And a list of photographers you like to work with.'

'We haven't discussed a fee.'

'It's a dummy. We haven't got set fees yet. I'll have to ask.'

'I'll send you some ideas in the morning. How about that?'

'Great. Well I've got to run.'

'God not another coffee.'

We shook hands outside. The strength of the sky above the buildings was something shocking. I could tell I wasn't going to get the job.

38

Dearest Naomi,

Right now, in a now that is in the future for me as I write this, you are reading this letter. My words enter through your eyes and go where? They go through you, maybe leaving their mark or not. Maybe they pass through like neutrinos which are able to pass through you and the Earth undisturbed, which makes them hard to detect though it doesn't mean they haven't been there. My words and neutrinos passing through you all the time undetected. They are only able to be detected very faintly and occasionally as they pass through reservoirs of heavy water thousands of feet underground. These are strange particles, and maybe they are not even particles, just names plus something barely detected which no one knows what it is. Passing through you all the time even when you are sleeping and don't think about words. My words together with the words in the newspaper, the words on the milk carton. Open here. Display until. The words on a shop sign. The names of destinations. Piccadilly. Elephant & Castle. The word traced in the dust on a car bonnet. The message on a box of matches. Strike softly away from body. The graffiti on a wall. The words you write yourself. One hundred and ten pounds and twenty-five pence. Your signature. If you would send me just one word. Just if you sign your name. Dear Naomi, I love you in spite of your silence. I include five poems.

Eric

39

Coming up out of cold white moss, something hunts through net curtains blowing without a sound, moving up through cold white, its chill, hunting through the stockpiles, discarding, looking for something. Quite a long way above me is the ceiling. That colour they call magnolia. A patch of damp. Paint peeling off and underneath matt grey and where that's rubbed away Germolene pink. So magnolia is actually an evolutionary step on the ladder of decorating. And why they always have to just paint over the Victorian cornices without taking off the old paint underneath so that what were once bunches of fruit and leaves thicken to excrements. A team of nice decorating men in old-fashioned overalls. Mornin! Mornin! They put big white sheets down. On top go their ladders and they go up with little blowtorches which they use to burn off the very top layers without damaging the forms hidden under magnolia guano. Like Michelangelo said he's only trying to get the sculpture out from inside the marble guv.

You don't know where you are. I turned my head and saw someone else in the bed beside me who was not Ellie at the same moment that it went from hazy to sharp that we don't have cornices. We live in a thirties block. Or fifties? Don't know. Low ceilings. Very low. No cornices. And in Ellie's bedroom painted pale pink.

The stranger was asleep. I think because his head's not turned this way. It's OK don't panic keep looking at things round the room and the longer you lie here the more it will come back to you. It's quite funny really. You don't know where you are. Quite funny. Moving my eyes without moving my head much so I didn't disturb this stranger with his head turned away. We're in an old house. My face is freezing. The tip of my nose is especially freezing. We are on a mattress on the floor. The smell coming off the carpet: mould. It's a terrible carpet they've laid it really badly so it's up in bumps and you can see yellow layers of old newspaper round the sides where the carpet has rucked up and there's a big hole. Floorboards through the hole. No. A hole through the hole. I wanted to raise my head up and look to see what was in the hole, how far down the hole went but I'd better not. Chair which is flesh in French. Clothes on the chair. My clothes which are a rag of silver tissue to wrap round your breasts and a pair of army trousers. Israeli I think. Wicked camo man. Someone said that to me where? Desert camo. Raise up altars where your tracks lead me. And next to the fleshchair a pile of stuff like its been there for years, clothes and sheets magazines gone wavy with damp. Old jumpers dirty filthy dirty jeans his jeans? Bits of T-shirts showing and shirts and there's grubby old trainers in the pile as well and a jacket leather with paint on it purple and pink patches of paint. I can smell a smell coming off the pile it's a mixture of weed and some other drug I think and staleness and sweat and damp. Everything's damp in here. The wall. I'm looking at huge patches of damp and opposite the bed someone's graffittied Dawn is Shit on the wall as well.

I turned my head slowly the other way. Back of the stranger's head. Greasy dreadlocks. White. Male. A bay window. The length of it can only mean we're on the ground floor which is good for exit. Boarded-up but light is coming through some holes. It's coming through in shafts that cross the room like light in a Charlton Heston film. The shafts pool a bit on the carpet making it look dreamy in those places. A noise. Loud. It's not in this room it's above and someone is moving about up there. I have to lift my head to see the door is it shut? It's not fully shut and the way it opens I can't see through I can only see the door which opens in with its back towards me. It might wake him up the noise. I stare at him with my head held stiffly up. Nothing. I put my head down carefully.

Go back to the last thing. Don't panic little girl. You're not a little girl. It's quite funny this. It's a crustie rave in East London way out beyond East London it's Far East London and 7-Eleven took us there yes. Some houses, the last in a row of condemned houses, the rest of which they'd bulldozed into piles of rubble. That looked strange in the night with the one still-standing lamp-post, all these piles of rubble and bottles and bent metal rods sticking out of the rubble like quills. A road, some sort of motorway they were doing an extension to yes. It was going to pass through where the houses had been and some still were. But the police couldn't get them out they were too clever. It had gone on for months with a system of tunnels between various houses and some of their positions had fallen to the police but a war of attrition and now these last four houses crawling with The Oaks of Punk. That's right The Oaks of Punk that's what they called themselves. These four condemned houses beautiful old houses and then one that wasn't a house it was a coachhouse with stable doors and a hayloft, no hay. A garage from the 1950s connecting the Georgian coachhouse to the Victorian houses that made up most of their gaff. You didn't come in the door that would have been stupid. The doors were heavily fortified. You came in through an old outside toilet in a jumble of sheds and stuff at the end of one of the gardens. That was one way in. You went and you went underground down through what must have been old layers of Victorian cess, God yeah going through that tunnel with a candle. This beardy bloke really sweet leading you through. The thumping of the bass coming along the tunnel walls. Is this safe? she kept saying. I can't believe Doughgirl came. She who hates all this chose to come to this one instead of just the West End or up behind King's Cross which would have been fine for her. Doughgirl holding the sides of her skirt away from the walls which were wet. This could collapse on us she said. Seven do you hear me? I don't like this she said. A second later we were in the coal cellar under one of the houses, still with black on the walls from coal and a candle stuck on the floor. Wooooo. We jumped. 7-Eleven trying to be funny. The people in the cellar see 7-Eleven and it's all high fives and yeah awrights, everyone loves Seven. Of course these were his mates that he got the gear off. His colleagues I suppose.

A warren of rooms upstairs. Lots of the doors to the rooms are barricaded or blocked with rubble so you get from room to room through holes they've punched in the walls. The windows boarded up with sheet metal. Some rooms nothing just music and candles stuck on the floor or the mantelpiece and writing sprayed on the walls. One room with sawdust to the ankles. People trance dancing in the sawdust and it coming in puffs round their legs and dazzling higher up in the air where it caught the strobes. Rooms with lots of old sofas and chairs and people and dogs everywhere, drinking from crates of beer stacked in the corners even the dogs got beer and this little imp of a man sitting on top of a stack almost at the ceiling and playing his harmonica. Dancing for hours and hours in two rooms joined by a huge hole in the middle. The music dubby and some of it more Eurokid nutter stuff. The drugs like fuzz in your blood really dirty. 7-Eleven walking through everywhere holding Doughgirl and Ellie by the hand. Doughgirl begging him to take her home then going off somewhere in the huff. I go to look for Dough on my own. Ellie out of it in a corner and 7-Eleven doing business in what must have been a kitchen. Lost in the dark. Some rooms dark as holes in the ground. A voice. A cigarette end. I trip on something. A person. You awright mate? I wandered and wandered. Off my head. Ellie! But I'll find her. I was going along for a while with a guy with ginger hair holding my hand. Not him. He must have gone off at some point. Him massaging my head for a bit squatting on the floor in a room full of lit-up plastic Santas. How it feels like spearmint spiking up and down your veins and bifurcating and unfurling when youre trashed, the massage.

I'm on the roof there's a few of us and a dog. I've got the dog's head in my lap. Skinny dog with a thumpy tail, then he goes prancing along the guttering looking for scraps. He puts his front paws up on the low parapet wall. He puts his muzzle up and he howls. It's dawn. Dark red behind some warehouses but no sun yet and we sit with our backs on the frozen slates and smoke spliff and smoke fags and drink water from old cans someone's filled. It's freezing. The dog howls. Shuup says a crustie. Shuup mutt. Everything iced up. The whole world airbrushed diamond. Now he barks at something down there. His woofs coming out visible the shape of sounds. I'm cuddled into someone with a huge coat. I'm trying to get under the coat without giving him any ideas.

Two coats and fingerless gloves. I want the gloves. It's all frosty up here. God we could have died. I laugh now against the duvet. Careful darling he says. Want a puff? My head wet strands round my face which I know will be mottled red and white from dancing and now the cold. Them looking at me giving me the big wave. Just for a coffee he says. But there's no coffee here in the magnolia room. When we got back here fuck. That bit when I thought I was turning round and round in the bed like the girl's head in The Exorcist. I closed my eyes again thinking about it. I pushed it all out of my head. Clonk clonk. It registered. Someone's coming down the stairs. Someone in heavy boots. Oaks of Punk boots. I looked at the back of his head. It moved a little bit. Clonk clonk clonk. Getting nearer. Echoing. My eyes moved to my clothes.

It's happening they're outside the door. In a second someone is going to come round the edge of that door and they're going to see me. The stranger coughs. God people make so much noise even just coughing even just shifting volumes of air. The door swinging open. A bald woman comes in. Like super 3-D. Like she's more than there. Maybe I'm still fucked. Combat boots. Serious piercings. I mean top marks. The aim has been to look half-man half-machine with ball bearings, spikes, thick industrial rings that do things inside engines and swags of greaseshop chain across the face. Spots. She's lucky to have so many spots and bluey scars of old spots given the look she's going for because she's not sturdy. Blue blue eyes.

She stared at me with the blue blues doing the thing cats do of not blinking.

'Lo Lorraine.' He's awake. Facing her, back to me.

'You're in my bed Bison.'

Goldilocks!

He's got a hacking cough. He's looking for a cigarette on the floor. She just stood there. He struck a match. Coughed. Inhaled.

'Thought you was away. You said I could stay here while you was away.'

'Not in my bed. Upstairs.'

'Awright.' A manlaugh phlegmy and slow. She came in a step or two.

'Get up.'

'OK, OK.'

'Get fucking out my cunting bed!'

'Awright. Let me come to. Been out.'

'What's that piece of shit doing in my bed?'

'She ain't done you nothing.'

'Get it out. Now.'

'Awright.'

'I don't like shit like that in my cunting bed!'

Like what?

'Awright give us a minute OK?'

He scratched his head. Took a puff. Lorraine coming through the shafts of light. She leaned over. Roared at him. He flinched.

'Get out my fucking bed or I'll kick shit out of you!' When she said the word kick she kicked the mattress.

'Fuck off bitch,' he said.

She yanked the duvet off of us.

Our bodies huddled into the same zigzag shape but not touching at any point like we're in a chorus line. He still had his socks on. He hunched over his cock.

'What the fuck do you call that you abject fucking object?'

She's almost on top of us screaming. I rolled out of the bed to the other side. Ice cold. She yelled. Echoing. Start to put my clothes on fast. They don't go on right. Just don't let her notice me. Forget knickers. Let her concentrate on him. This no time to look for knickers. I looked down to find the Israeli army combats and for a second I didn't understand. Have I been shot? Stabbed? I looked back at the bed. He was sitting on the edge of it now with his head in his hands. His knees up round his ears. Lorraine in front of him with her legs apart holding an edge of duvet. Behind him a big patch of blood soaked into the bottom sheet. Into the mattress it must be. Got to get out of here.

'Dunno,' he's saying. 'Dunno.'

Lorraine twisting into pointy shapes that darted at him with each yell. 'What you fucking done to her? You motherfucking bastard!'

They both looked at me pulling the combats up bloodied legs. I tried to break my eyes off quick. Fight with the wisp of silver tissue stuff get it over one arm. Leave it. Jacket.

'I didn't do nothing,' he kept saying. Didn't do nothing. I looked at the purple and pink painted leather jacket in the pile but Lorraine will kill me. Beside the pile there was an enormous old book lying open and half-burnt. The writing was big with big gold capitals every now and then. I cuffed my feet into my boots sockless. It's a Bible open on page. She hit him. I shoved a heel half down into a boot. He put a hand up to shield his face. Punching sound. Under cover of the noise I grabbed a jumper from near the bottom and started across the room yanking it on. I passed the bed still fighting the jumper. The sheet a murder.

'Fucking doing you cunt you fucking womanhater you filth you!' She looked round at me. She's going to do it. She's going to hit me. 'Look at her!'

I felt her hand grabbing my arm pulling me round to face him. I cringed. One boot not on properly. Righted myself against Lorraine. I am much bigger than Lorraine. She held my arm tight.

'Look at her.' Shook me at him. I looked at him. No not with him not with that. Lorraine's face in front of me licking her fingers. I tried to pull away. She swiped her fingers across my cheek hard. Not a slap. I made a sound. She licked them again.

'Poor darling.' The fingers burned my cold cheeks. 'You've fucked her up inside you filth!'

She dropped me, twirled round and thwacked him. I heard him bellow. I ran dragging the half-on boot. Please God don't let the front door be locked.

'Hey. Cmere love!'

Please please! I put on a burst of speed, out into the hall, yanked at the latch and I'm out and it's been snowing. Everything's white the sky the street and the cars. I run down the steps and I've still only got one boot on properly and no laces done up and I fall and roll down the steps and get up and stumblerun down the street my boots the first to step on this snow.

40

She was in the easy chair wrapped in the Mexican blanket. She kept her head turned towards the telly. 'Hello.' Unnaturally high voice. I knew what it meant.

I went into the bathroom and looked at myself in the bathroom mirror. White as teeth with black rubbing off round the eyes and smudged down the cheeks. What she was wiping at I suppose. Pupils I-have-seen-visions size. Red whites. Hair in scribbles. Blotches. Tremblings. A hag hag-ridden. I was impressed. She came in and stood next to me.

'Nice.'

We stared at each other in the mirror. I couldn't stop my teeth chattering. She turned away and put the plug in the bath. She started to run it.

'Nice jumper.'

I looked down. It had a pattern of red reindeer and something yellowish staining the chest. It was comfortable looking down at the jumper so I kept in that position resting. She was touching me. 'You're like ice.'

I kept looking down at the jumper. 'I'm sorry.'

She stormed out of the bathroom. 'And so you fucking should be!'

From the living room: 'Marching off   7-Eleven   hours and hours.'

She re-appeared. 'I was exhausted, in the middle of fucking nowhere and you were nowhere to be found. We looked everywhere we asked everyone and then someone said, they said right – that you'd gone up to the roof. The roof! It was ten degrees of frost. Do you know a dog was up there and it fell off? Or maybe it was thrown off. It's dead.'

She bent over the bath and swirled the water about. She put the cold tap on low and went to the bathroom cabinet. 'Lavender or neroli?' Before I could say anything: 'Both.'

It came on me in a wave. I put my hands over my face. I snivelled.

'Don't give me that,' she said.

It stopped.

'Get out of that disgusting jumper. No. The bin. The kitchen bin!'

I had it half over my head. She yanked it off and went off with it into the kitchen. 'So selfish! Didn't you think we might be worried? We didn't know where you were. You don't get minicabs there. You don't get buses there. No tube. How would you get home without 7-Eleven? Why would you ever leave me there like that I thought that was our deal?'

She checked the bathwater. She sprinkled more neroli from the tiny brown bottle. The opposite of snow filled the bathroom. 'I look after you you look after me we never leave the other one. Ever.' She stood in front of me hands on hips. 'Take them off. Get in go on. Stupid idiot.'

The dog.

'Can you go out for a minute?' I said. 'I need to pee.' My voice like I hadn't used it for years.

'Well pee. I don't care.'

'I need to   I've got my period.'

'So?' She opened the cabinet got out a bumper box of tampons and flung them next to the loo.

'Just can I have a few minutes on my own?'

She stared at me like this was the final insult. She got out. I undid the trousers and let them fall round my ankles. I sat on the edge of the bath so I could work off the boots. It was hard with no socks.

'You OK?'

She was talking from outside the door it was ajar. I saw her through the slit which meant she could see me too sitting on the side of the bath. She came in. 'Fucking Jesus.'

I put my hands over my face. 'Leave me alone.'

'Jesus Naomi.' She crouched in front of me. She touched my thighs with both her hands for a moment. 'What happened?' Different frightened.

'It's OK. It's fine.'

I got up. I stepped into the bath. It was agony. I was too cold. I ran more cold in. 'It doesn't hurt.'

'But where's it coming from?' She was squatting on the tiles peering up. I laughed.

'Are you trying to see up my?'

She dropped her bum down on the floor. She stroked my leg. We smiled at each other. I got in very slowly all the way with small ouches as the warmth hurt different bits of me. Under the water the blood began to bloom orange and swill up off my legs. I reached down and rubbed the still dried-in bits. It came off easily. I put my hand in my crotch. It was bloody there but it felt normal. I rubbed soap around a bit to get it off all the hair.

'I'm going to get you to a doctor.'

'I said. It's my period.'

'I know when your period is.'

The bath didn't even change colour really. It was all gone. Ellie sat on the edge of the bath. We were always running baths for each other. She for me. Me for she. One would get in and the other would sit on the edge and listen to the story. The one in the bath was the one with the story and the other one did things like put in the essential oils, think up thrilling questions, pass the towel and light the cigarettes. She lit two, handed me one. Nectar. Don't knock the cigarette.

I closed my eyes feeling survival.

'So lets shoot the breeze,' she said. 'Wh'appen man?' Leaning back on the wall arms crossed. Dimpling.

'I woke up this morning. Well.' It was dark outside now. 'Must have been around two o'clock and I didn't know where I was. I looked round and I was in this squat somewhere and there was someone next to me in the bed. A stranger. It turned out to be South London as I then discovered when I left.'

'So how did you get there?'

'I don't know. No I remember. OK this is how it started. I went off to find Doughgirl coz I was worried about her and you were in a corner completely out of it. But I don't know I just got drawn deeper and deeper into that place. I was looking for her so I'd ask people and get talking and dancing and having little smokes and little chats and I think someone gave me some more drugs.'

'What'd you get?'

'Rhubarb and Custard. Yeah. And, you know, just a corner off someone's trip. You know how the night seems to go on for ever like lives and lives could have passed outside and in here just the music and weird little scenes that come and go and all the little moments?' I looked round for an ashtray. 'Then I was talking I think to this bloke who was well in with the Oaks of Punk.'

'The Oaks of Punk,' said Ellie. I understood. It was like years ago and now she was tasting it again.

'He was lovely. A traveller mostly in Ireland going on about the police and his time with the Biology sound system and then Chemistry and probably Physics, is there one called Physics?'

She smiled a bit more.

'Etcetera. Then when he heard I was a kind of journalist he went ballistic.'

'Why didn't you make something up?'

'I can never think of anything but the truth when I'm at the sharp end. I tried to explain just shoes not politics. But somehow he'd got them mixed up and someone had to get him off me. Verbally I mean. It was quite scary me on my own with all the oakies in the candlelight all beardie and in jester trousers and on acid and me saying no no I just write about Giorgio Armani.'

'How did you get out of it?'

'I said down with the pig system basically. But hey.' I took the fresh fag. 'What can I say they think I'm in with the pigs, bigging up the pigs. So this guy who rescued me just hauled me up by my hand and we danced and we ended up on the roof don't get mad!'

'I'm not mad. Go on.'

'You're going to get mad, you're pretending to be fine so you can hear everything and then get really mad.'

'No I promise.'

'No but really. If you do that.'

She sighed. 'So you're up on the roof.'

'Up to the roof. Oh my God I wish you'd been up there with us. I'll never forget it. The sky was lovely, dark blue and dark red. All the roofs of the place twinkling with frost and the roofs of the factories and warehouses and the cars, and all the bulldozers round about and the wrecking equipment all sparkly. And there was thick see-through ice up there in the guttering bit but someone had litten'

'Lit.'

'Yeah a fire in the guttery bit where the water runs along. There was a low wall by the way before the drop, we were quite safe.'

She laughed.

'And we sat round the fire and people were using the slates as a slide and someone had a bottle of   Cointreau! Can you believe Cointreau.'

'I love life,' she said.

I felt at ease then. 'Yeah so you know chatting and snuggling into this bloke from somewhere. A big bloke. They called him Bison. Ah the dog, the dog.' I put my hands over my eyes.

'Don't.'

'But it was sad as well up there because soon it was going to be proper daylight and then the other world. So after a bit I said I had to go.'

'Yes?'

'Well we went down and we did look for you. I was out of my box so what I did was I looked for you in some places and I asked him to go and find you in other places.'

'As if he was going to find me so he could lose you for the night? Did you really think?'

'Well yeah because he was a really nice bloke. He'd rescued me. He wanted me to come home with him I said no I wanted to go home-home. Then he couldn't find you and his mate was leaving with his van and it was light and it was the middle of nowhere and the fact was I got in the back of the van with him and that was that.'

That long drive back in the van. I would never forget it though I wanted to forget it as I put my chin into the hot water and looked along the weak-coloured surface with me blurry underneath. But then I told myself I would forget because sex, the important thing about it is you can't really remember how it felt, just where you were and who with, and that's its secret strength as well.

'And the blood?'

I did my grampus thing. Under the water with big noisy bubbles blobbing up from my lips. Everything swaying and blurring, Ellie's shape and colours swaying and blurring at a distance. Down here I thought about later in the bed and the blood. I replayed edits slowly and without sound. I surfaced blowing. She handed me the towel.

'That's better.'

She crossed one leg flat across the top of the other so she could lean an elbow on it and put her chin in her hand.

'You're in pyjamas,' I said. 'Huh! You've ironed them.'

She said maybe one of the best things she's ever said. 'I ironed a pair for you too. The Dopey pyjamas. They're on the bed.'

'Ahhh.'

She looked at me over the hand, waiting.

'So the blood. Well look the truth is. I'm not sure. I asked them to drop me at Elephant and Castle but apparently when we were passing Elephant and Castle I was kind of inconvenienced in the back of the van.'

'Inconvenienced how?'

'I was   not feeling myself. They didn't want to chuck me out to find my way home alone. So they drove me on. I said I'll get out here but someone said it was Catford and I thought I didn't know there was a Catford. I wondered if it was in London or out of London. So I thought well I'll sit tight and everyone said look you can have a coffee where we're going but it didn't work out like that. We, me and Bison, were dropped off at some derelict building and they went off in the van to morningtime and we went back into nighttime.'

I stubbed out the cigarette in a soapdish.

'He said we could have coffee at his but we didn't. He didn't seem to know where the kettle was. I should have known when he didn't go in the front door but instead we went down the basement steps and there was this box attached to the wall the kind that's got the gas meter in it. The gas meter had been ripped out. There was just a bit of hardboard at the back of the box and we knocked it out and crawled through and we were in. So not really his gaff right? I said I'd love a cup of coffee but it didn't work out. It was freezing so all the time we were right under this disgusting duvet. God it was disgusting.'

'How was the sex?'

'Druggy. Brilliant technically speaking. I suppose. Anyway after hours and hours we must have fallen asleep you forget that bit it's all a kerfuddle. I do remember it being very damp and sticky but I thought you know.'

'He was wearing one right?'

'I don't know.'

'Naomi.'

'Well let me think for a minute.'

She watched over the side of her palm.

'No.'

'No condom.'

'No.'

'Why not.'

'He refused. He got mad. I just let it go.'

Her eyes shrank to frozen peas.

'I see. He got mad and you just let it go. He didn't wear a condom and you had some kind of sex where you got covered in blood. Covered.' She got up and went out of the bathroom. Her voice from the kitchen high-pitched. 'Coffee?'

'Yes please.'

I did that thing of slipping down almost to the lips and then opening the lips and letting them taste the bath water. A letdown taste. I heard the click as the kettle went off. I heard her opening the jar of instant coffee. I heard the spoon inside the mugs then the water going in and her stirring it tinkling the spoon on the side of the mugs. She hit the spoon a couple of times on a mug rim.

'Sugar? Or milk?' We always had either or.

'Uh. Milk. No, sugar.'

She got it down. The big jar thudded on the counter. I could hear the spoon going into the weight of it. The spoon clattering again in the cups. She came in with them. I hated those dreary mugs. I wanted a white porcelain cup as thin as shell with freshly brewed Ethiopian berries giving off a thick black odour. Number one in my catalogue of bourgeois desires. I put the mug on the corner of the bath.

'Thanks.'

She sat back down in the cross-legged pose at the other end near the toilet. She blew on her coffee. 'So if you die what shall I tell your mum?'

'I won't *die*.'

'It's called AIDS, honey,' she said like we were in a bad American movie.

'You do it without a condom.'

'Never. Ever.'

Well then I thought, so you cheat. 'OK well you're smart and I'm stupid.'

She drank some in with some air to cool it.

'A bit more than stupid Naomi. You had unprotected sex. You bled like a pig or was it him? Your sexual partner is a stranger. Maybe he's gay. Maybe he's a straight guy who fucks around. Maybe he's an injector. I bet he's an injector.'

'Oh God.'

'And you have to wait a month a whole month before you can test did you know that? Or are you not going to test?'

'Can we not talk about this?'

'OK lets just pretend like it never happened.'

'Look I feel really drained. I will never do it again never.' I wiped my hand across my forehead. 'If God will just give me this one break.'

'God is it? People get their arms chopped off in Africa, boys get run over at age seventeen when they're the apple of their mother's eye, women – unspeakable things so what makes you think you're special he'll save you? Naynay his little favourite.'

She left the bathroom with her mug. Her voice from the living room. 'I'll let this little Iraqi toddler girl die of starvation. Sorry! Rules of the game. And that young mother trapped with her baby in an earthquake praying to me, please God just save my child. Sorry guys! Gotta go. Rules of the universe. But Naomi who just wants this one break? Saved! Big tick! Nothing can ever hurt *her*. Oh and by the way she'll never die. Not till she's ninety and gagging for it.'

I did the grampus thing. I blew the air out loudly and watched the big scallops of colour and shape made by the disturbed surface of the water. I shouted through: 'He sees the smallest sparrow fall.'

Her voice: 'He sees the smallest sparrow fall. He doesn't pick it up again. He just sees it.'

I washed my hair. When I was running the water out she came in and threw the Dopey pyjamas on the toiletseat lid.

'Thanks.'

'Don't thank me, thank Mr Disney.'

We didn't look at each other.

'OK.'

I went into the living room. She was watching a Disney cartoon maybe that's why she'd said that. Jungle Book. As I climbed onto the sofa Baloo was just going into Bear Necessities. I started to sing along under my breath.

Look for the bare necessities
The simple bare necessities
Forget about your worries and your strife
I mean the bare necessities
Old Mother Nature's recipes
That brings the bare necessities of life.

She joined in:

Wherever I wander, wherever I roam
I something fonder
Of my big home…

41

Naomi,

I have to calm myself. I have to find a way to go on. I feel as if I don't have any weight. I don't understand anything, Could you write me one short line? Could you send me a blank postcard? I don't want to disturb you but I need a gesture from you which will give me the strength. My body is being penetrated by soft bullets which move through my flesh by consuming it. I wake up sweating, very afraid. Certainly I should not write a letter in this state, I must stop. I have not one night of freedom from your absence and your mocking presence which remains unrealisable. I stood on the outside of the bridge one night and looked down. It was your arm that held me back. I go to the page. I stare at it and I feel a stupid pain. I don't know if you can understand how it disorientates me. I can't write anything on a page like that. I can't do it. Then somehow, maybe in the way milk comes without the mother doing anything except wanting it to come, she feels it coming from inside her, sometimes so much it overpours, at other times a few slobbers dribble and deposit a dried-out stain. No relief. I include the poems.

Eric

42

I prepared the desk. The computer centred at the top end of the table with the keyboard towards the window. The chair pulled back to show the comfy leather seat pad (fake). That the printer is 'on': check. That the printer is connected to the machine: check. I took the paper from the printer, I fanned it, I restacked it. A fat wad made out of thin layers. Same with words. A few thin ones stacked together soon added up to a piece of heft. Phone at one side, not too near the mouse hand. Pen. Pencil. Is is sharpened? No. It can be sorted but it will take some time. I had to go through kitchen drawers, bedside table drawers and underwear drawers. I looked under the table, on top of the telly. It was on the shelf above the fire half behind the clock. Then the sound of wood being shorn and the smell of it homelier than bread. Don't get carried away. Pencil by pen in line. Notepad for rough jottings. Not the same one as for phone messages. And finally – not finally because the coffee was still brewing in the new stovetop espresso thing – Ethiopian beans roasted to a high French cackiness – ground by me even – both bits of kit bought as it were with the money from the thing that was now going to be placed on the table in front of the computer and raised on a stack of magazines aka catalogues of bourgeois desires: This Week's Must Have.

Not that I was quids in exactly. But This Week's Must Have, although not exalted every week by me, was still a lifesaver. This was my sixth. I wasn't quite up with the rent but Ellie said coffee was important.

My hair. It had to be back. It had to be combed so that it didn't slump out of the hairclasp it had to be combed smartly and pulled gym-mistressly into a smartly snapping clasp so that not a single hair was left on the loose. My fantasy and your hair. I raise up altars. That done, coffee can be collected en route since it's making that noise and producing a smell of roasted stones. The spoon can be quickly rinsed and the coffee taken into the living room which is coloured London drab though it's spring.

The coffee cup – and saucer – went down on the wooden table. To the carrier bag which this week is the orange Hermès bag, the most orange anything in existence. Just as the Tiffany blue bag is the bluest thing in existence, bluer than the sky the sea or kingfishers, the Hermès bag is far more orange than oranges and what else is orange? Goldfish. They have done something almost Promethean. Orang-utans sort of. Stolen the essence of colours and used the great secret to shift merchandise. The Gods will have blood! Marigolds. Fire.

Inside the Hermès bag: an Hermès box. Can I send This Week's Must Have back without the box? Say the box was damaged? Eaten by the cat? A semi-wild thing we'd only just rescued from under the arches. We'll call it Hermès as a kind of apology.

So orange it's Haliborange which can make you hallucinate when you're under-five. Slick brown lines framing the plane of the lid. The regular bumpiness of the cardboard like baby crocodile skin. Can this be mere cardboard? You could build palaces from this stuff. A specialist board prepared to a regional formula in the heart of the old Austro-Hungarian empire, some secret Polska village of boardmaking skills that is now available only to the honchos at Hermès. So much orange concentrate in the grey day. You can probably get these boxes on prescription.

The flatness of the box as opposed to the thickness the weight the heaviness you feel in your hand. Whatever is in here is a slip of a thing minor extravagant and by definition completely unnecessary to even the most neurotic existence. It's outside norms of desirability in a non-desirability so extreme that it creates a famished desire for desire itself.

That would flummox them as a lead-in on the style page. Would I lose them their Hermès advertising or the opposite? The opposite! Hermès take their first double page spread in the paper. Everyone is ecstatic and a memo goes round: don't hire that girl again. Clever of them and of Hermès.

I slid onto the fake leather seat pad, a seat pad which no Hermès shopper (client, clientèle) would dream of brushing with a subtly-suctioned bottom. Interesting how lipo rhymes with hippo. And of course I haven't mentioned the grandeur the glory of Hermès, the logo. I've saved that till last.

The Hermès logo. At a stroke it stops you having to read Jane Austen, Vanity Fair (the book *and* the mag), Georgette Heyer, Liaisons Dangereuses, and Black Beauty. Maybe even Eugene Onegin.

I opened the box and it was another wonka exploder to the psyche. The brown felt with the pinking-sheared edges that the Must Have is folded in. If everything in life came folded in that meek brown felt. A luxury felt that will never nubble or fuzz but showing that even here inside the orange an almost Zen humility of craftsmanship together with a sense of *storage* has its expression.

The motion of the Must Have evacuating from the folds of felt. Thinking nothing, the other hand outstretched to receive it. Down the felt slipway and out onto the other hand:

A . We don't have a name for it but the Americans call it a billfold. You clip paper money into it. Then you put it in your pocket and when you want paper money you get it out and open it and there are your banknotes held in place by a gold-plated springloaded clip. Your bills in protective brown leather the kind called grain de poudre/powder grain which is better than the whole billfold for a start.

Oh a billfold. A billfold! A flap of leather. Inside, a gold-plated clip. What am I going to say? Billfold In a Flap It's the Money Money Matters Notes to Self Style Stash Chic Clip Penny Pincher Pocket Pleasure Get a Grip! Isn't it men who carry billfolds? Messenger of the Wads.

I got up and went back over to the orange bag. I got the press release out. A subtly superb press release comprising an orange thick card folder with same calèche logo etc. and inside several sheets of laid paper, each headed with a delicate rendition of the logo and with very little writing on each page. Still, page after page on the billfold and the heritage of the billfold. Typeface old school slab serif. Grain de poudre is definitely going in. Words like craftsmen hand-made double-stitching unparalleled summer colourways. Chic not mentioned but it would work its way in as usual. Fresh I had to stop using. Also key. Here's a key product for the chic spring pocket! As sung by a noodle in a boater in a Gene Kelly movie. They say chik in Glasgow. I like chik. Or bag. You add two words if you add or bag. I looked at this week's word count. 395. 395 words on the billfold that leaves you famished with desire for desire itself.

I looked out of the window. Trees in full fresh leaf in spite of the grey air. The young leaves ripe and flexible parting their ribs. Evolution a fucking joke otherwise why aren't there winged cows hovering round trees to munch these delicious morsels? Lightweight cows certainly, maybe miniature cows. Or huge wings. Imagine the wingspread.

I opened the Miffy notebook.

1. Why do you need a billfold? To carry your ~~bills~~ banknotes. Why use a purse, that staid~~ly~~ item of the old lady's handbag when you could slip a slim chik billfold stuffed with crackly new bills into your pocket and carry your change loose in the other pocket ~~jangling and free~~?
2. Why do you need a billfold? To carry your ~~bills~~ banknotes. Why use a purse ~~that staidly item of the old lady's handbag~~ when you could slip a slim chic billfold ~~stuffed with crackly new bills~~ in~~to~~ your pocket~~-and carry your change loose in the other pocket~~?
3. Why need a billfold? The short answer is ~~to carry your banknotes~~ for a chic, simple way to carry wads of cash without having to ~~carry without having to transport lug heave bring with take along~~ weigh yourself down with (4 wds) a whole handbag. Handbags, ~~especially~~ of the ~~turbo-charged-~~logo-~~heavy~~ variety, are so last decade. ~~34~~ 45 wds.
4. Needs? No, no one needs, forget needs. Get brand in. Must be brand-appeasement on part of paper otherwise why such fucky object?
5. ~~Hermès, those purveyors of the finest luxury leather items~~ For Hermès, purveyors of luxuries in leather, no item is too big

or too small to be ~~made as perfect and desirable as a leather item can.~~ considered worthy of ~~it's craftmens atentions~~ perfecting. 21 wds. No to big. ~~Hand-crafted –~~ no, lo-grade gifty – Crafted by these French specialists by these quintessentially French specialists an object as throwaway as a billfold becomes chic, key! In a word, a must-have. 43 w/out big. Quintessentially count as 2?

6. Bring in this season. Ref: streamlining. The streamlined look of the season, as seen in [ref: endless other high-end designers]. Idea hidden luxury not overt labelled look. Streamline your silhouette and keep it ~~chic~~ modern. Slip a billfold, that essential item beloved of the mavens of American sportwear into your pocket or a ~~small~~ dinky [allowed?] dainty – yuch – ~~pocket-sized~~ down-sized evening bag and you're ready to go /run out the door.
Go = 1 wd
Ready to run out the door = 6 wds

Billfold, billfold,
Wherefore dost thou
Scold the silly cow,
With banknotes few,
Who sits here getting old?
And pondering o'er
Her copy cold which later
On they'll make her rehew
To their hackneyed tune
And wizened rune
Of mirthless luxe and
Needless mindfulness.
She vomits forth the spew
Of masturbatory vocab you
Leery, knowing none of it's
True. Tis a cup of coldest
Sick expunged at noon
That must be drunk again

And brought forth anew
Oh ghastly foul and expiatory brew!

The coffee was cold which was very disappointing. I took the cup and saucer into the kitchen. I washed them. I stood leaning against the sink pressing the front of the pink fuzzballed dressing-gown against it. The gloom of the kitchen. Ellie always switched on the light but I hated fluorescent strips. You knew people were tortured under fluorescent strips never under table lamps. I preferred to face it dingy like this and the sound of the fridge and the view out the narrow window which was of a hellish architectural space. They're called wells. Round the sides go the backwalls of toilets, systems of waste pipes, furred heating ventilators, side by side the almost slit-sized kitchen windows, the effluent smells from the toilets mixing with spicy fry-ups and boiling potatoes. At the bottom of the well years of filth and bits of rubbish people have thrown out, bird droppings. There is no access to the well except by flying down or exit from the windows (hard for an adult).

I went out of the kitchen and up to the airing cupboard. It stood directly opposite the front door. I would have liked to live in here on one of the slatted shelves where towels and sheets lived, pillowslips, bedlinen. The concept bedlinen made me feel OK. The boiler big and jacketed in orange. Hey? No. Not as good an orange, not as saturated, as satiated with the secret. Copper pipes and very little dust on them. A humming clicking from the boiler. Sometimes big old tummy sounds from the boiler. Behind the boiler thicker dust the wadding kind which acted as protection for my red binder. I poked it out. It was warm from when we'd had baths that morning.

I could have gone back in to the living room but this was a good spot especially if you didn't think about it too much. I sat half in the cupboard with my legs poking out. The Daffys are mobile airing cupboards. Wish I could wear them out. I opened the binder. I flicked through reading a stanza here and there and stopped on the one about my eyes, or my regard. If it was me, because although a lot of them were about you, he never actually said which you, he never said that you was definitely me, not since the first one. Your/my eyes are holes out of which comes un regard doux. It's not les yeux which are doux, not the gentle eyes the soft eyes the sweet eyes; it's le regard doux. The eyes exit holes for le regard, the look, the gaze, the guard though that wasn't all that came out of the eyes, a ray of safekeeping, no. The eyes are holes which generate fast-mutating forms. The eyes ouis ouïes yesses ssses eyesses through which come lames des couteaux which is knife blades.

> **ouïe**[2] / wi / NF hearing *(NonC)*
> **ouïes** / wi / NFPL *(Zool)* gill; *(Mus)* sound hole

My eyes sound holes that amplify, reinforcing certain notes, muting others. My eyes echo chambers for words that are not said though I hear them with an inner ear, a ghost ear, guarding and reguarding. And/or gills. I am a creature skank and slimy with gills slitted into my face ventilating something that lies far down. The gills open and close by day and twitch by night, oxygenating amphibiously. Oxygenating l'âme du câble optique which turns out to be the core of the optic cable. **Ame** is NF *(gén, Philos, Rel)* soul. But also *(Tech) [d'aimant, de cable]* core. L'âme. Lames. Blades of knives/souls of knives. I rest my eyes on words for an instant and with one lash flick tear incisions that bless. Ame also *[de violon]* soundpost. My eyes soundposts that amplify, mute, enrich or heighten, alter.

And doux? I don't want my regard to be doux, just soft pappy doux. But oeil, the French for an eye, a single eye, is quite pappy, oily, the feeling you get in your head your mouth when you make it is what an oeil would do on your tongue if you sucked it out. I need to flick tear into it more. The dictionary says **Doux, douce** / du, dus / ADJ **a** *(= lisse, souple) [peau, tissu]* soft, smooth; *[matelas, suspension, brosse]* soft; → **fer, lime b** *[eau] (= non calcaire)* soft; *(non salé)* fresh **c** *(= clément) [temps, climat, temperature]* mild; *[brise, chaleur]* gentle **d** *(au goût) (= sucre) [fruit, saveur, liqueur]* sweet; *(= pas fort) [moutarde, fromage, tabac, piment]* mild ◆ ~ **comme le miel** as sweet as honey; → **orange, patate e** *(à l'ouïe, la vue) [son, musique, accents]* sweet, gentle; *[voix]* soft, gentle; *[lumière, couleur]* soft, mellow, subdued ◆ **un nom aux consonances douces** a mellifluous *ou* sweet-sounding name **f** *(= non brutal, gentil) [caractère, manières, reproche]* mild, gentle *[personne, sourire]* gentle;

[punition] mild ◆ **il a l'air** ~ he looks gentle ◆ **elle a eu une mort douce** she died peacefully ◆ **il est** ~ **comme un agneau** he's as gentle *ou* meek (Brit) as a lamb ◆ **d'un geste très** ~ very gently → **œil** And the more I tear into doux and not just into doux but at where it comes in the line, the towards, the more it bulges like lava in a lava lamp, always lava but always moving, squidging and blobbing into shapes that won't stay still and the more I incise into doux and forwards and backwards from doux the more I see how it's like the nine levels of a drinks mat. Not the thick card beermats you get in pubs, the fine quite absorbent paper coasters you get for cocktails in bars. Most people can only divide them into seven layers, a few can split them into eight but actually there are nine, I can always get nine, it's my thing at a bar, and sometimes I suspect that for the real coastermasters it might be ten or eleven layers to a mat, and now as I tear bless incise doux, douce it/they begin to bifurcate and multiply and it's like someone splitting an atom and thinking they've got to the elemental particles, the fundament, but then they realise they haven't because every time they flick the detectors onto the newly discovered elemental, or at what it affects or displaces, it splits and they see that it is made up of yet more fundamental fundament, and this throws them at first then they are happy that they have finally got down to the indivisible, the real, only under sharp eyes the new fundament peels apart again, and again, receding away and away in an ever more micro cosmos, giving off spasms of energy and slipping in and out of being. Doux splitting and doubling under my smooth blades as I amplify his air and make his gentle death resound. I am his piment comme le miel and a pas fort and the matelas non calcaire. With un geste très oeil I go down a l'ouïe and give sucre and saveur with sweet son and my dus du, my lisse and supple nom, my peau de musique and climat of couleur. I am his mustard and his tobacco, his fromage non salé, the punition of skin, reproach of his smile, a brosse soft fer, as a fruit fresh (orange); (potato) meek; he looks at me non brutal; subdued soft sweet-sounding or meek (Brit) as a lamb. Suspension → **oeil**

43

Sylvie and Ryan came to London for French Vogue and hired me. I was to do some production, find locations, get the permissions, etc. before they arrived in week one. Be their woman in London in week two. Good pay, great pay. I was still behind with the rent. I galvanised myself. Out of the Daffies, out of the door. I earmarked twelve locations. When they arrived, Sylvie whittled it down to three with an optional fourth, all in the East End.

We started shooting down on the marshes where they shot Full Metal Jacket. Sylvie liked it a lot, a few toppling factories, Canary Wharf in the distance westwards. She said there was nothing like it in Paris. I said OK you can have the Louvre we'll have this. She laughed. She was being nice. She looked older. She still had the shaggy fringe over one eye. The other eye in its scribbly sooty casing had quite a few wrinkles. I wondered if she dyed her hair to make it so black. She had an assistant, I didn't have to iron or anything which was sensitive of her. She didn't ask for the details of who I was working for these days, who I was working with. She asked me about the ice man. Oh you mean Dan, we split up. She asked if I was happy. I said never happier. You don't look healthy Noy-me she said, are you OK? A cold I said. She kept looking at me one-eyed which made me nervous.

'I've been watching what you and Ryan are doing in French Vogue. Brilliant.'

'Fashion is boring,' she said.

'You're over fashion?'

'I have never loved fashion.'

'I didn't realise. You want to get out of it?'

'And you?'

'Well yes. I keep asking myself how I fell into it.'

'Because sometimes pictures are good.'

The location van rocked in the wind. The make-up artist came in and got his wet wipes and went out. We smoked.

'Everyone says Ryan is a genius.'

She considered. 'He is having his good moment.'

'And you want to stop now?'

'I want to make films.'

'Costumes you mean?'

'No I want to make them, realise them.'

I cleared my throat. I thought but they don't let stylists become film directors not good ones anyway.

'You look at me as if I wish something impossible.'

And you're quite old actually, to be starting a career as an auteur.

'Not for you. You can do anything Sylvie.'

'What about you Noy-me?'

'I don't know. I'd like to be a marine biologist.'

We both laughed. Frail, that was how I felt. Wasn't that the old hard-boiled word for a woman? Like a quail, but more breakable, a cut-glass quail.

The third day we parked the van on a street I'd found passed over in the middle of industrial parks. It was a cobbled street of terraced houses with washing hanging out. Expecting women in shell suits. The street had a big wall at the end but the cobbled road went through a gap in the wall and up a hump. When the van topped the hump for a minute it was just sky. A ramp continued down the other side and disappeared into the river. The river was crazy here. At high tide the water was a mass of churns and smooth places that bulged in the middle with interference patterns round the edges.

There were children huddled in sections of old sewage pipe next to the wall. They were sniffing glue or dropping acid. They yelled insults and sexual come-ons at the models from their hidey-holes. Then they started running into shot and trying to touch them.

'Stop that or I'll get the filth,' I said.

'C'mover here. I'll give you one.'

'Shouldn't you be at school?' said the make-up artist. He was soft-spoken, American. He had a ponytail.

'Fuck off poofter,' they said.

'Yeah fuck off poofter.'

'Oi, oi! Nice juicy arsehole.' The boy crawled out half out of the pipe and mooned. 'Yours for a monkey.' He leered and gave the make-up artist the finger.

The make-up artist walked slowly away wiping powder off his brush on the back of his hand. 'Boys, boys, you've got what I wanna do to you all wrong.'

Ryan went to the top of the hump in the road and called the boys over. A couple went after him, looking over their shoulders at their mates, sniggering and pushing each other. Ryan said something to them, pointed down the ramp and back along the cobbled road. The two boys ran back to the other boys and they all went away. We all looked at Ryan.

'How you do that?' said Sylvie.

'Luck. Lets take a break.'

We went to the van and made some tea. A howl and a rattling sound outside. The boys coming back. They were going fast on bikes and skateboards. They shot up the cobbles to the hump with their heads juddering and at the top they spun and jumped and vanished down the other side of the ramp. The tide was out, it was just sand and mud at the other end. Ryan took pictures of them for an hour. He gave them cigarettes and cans of Coke and said he'd send them prints.

After that we went down on the mud. It was deep. We had to use old bits of board to cross it. We stood around in the wind looking up and down the desolation.

'This is another thing we don't have in Paris,' said Sylvie.

'Why don't we shoot another story down here?' I said.

'Then we must get more clothes.'

'French Vogue, no problem. Half-buried in mud. That would be cool. Clothes'd get ruined though.'

'Hmm.' She rolled up one leg of her trousers and and put her naked foot on the mud.

'Sylvie!'

She held onto my arm.

'Icky!' said the Polish model, Krysta.

Sylvie balanced, let go off my hand. 'It's OK,' she said. 'This is the bottom of where the foot goes. They can stand to the knee in mud and the hem of the clothes will be just above or going inside the mud. It's good.'

I called in the clothes while they were doing the other story on the street, and the next day we came back just before sunrise to do the mud story. At first light me and the assistant and hair and make-up each took a camera-ready girl by the hand and walked her along the boards to the spot. We had to get down into the mud first so the girls could hold onto us and not fall in right away. The mud sucked at your feet as they went in and squelched between the toes. The cold of it made me gasp. I had Krysta. I had pinned her skirt up round her waist just in case. She stepped in after me holding tight and screamed.

'Something's there.'

I felt something whip over my foot. I grabbed at Krysta and almost pushed her in. 'You're imagining it. It's just movements of the mud.'

'Ya ah ah ah! It's a thing!'

'It's not a thing.'

She wobbled and stood firm. The other girls got into position with a lot of squealing and squelching and the rest of us squidged the holes we'd made together and backed off the mud lifting the boards behind us.

I went back into the location van and wiped off the mud with a towel. I made tea. The van rocked in the wind. I hunkered down and started sewing some buttons on a jacket. I drank some tea. I started to pretend I was an old man whose life was over bar the tea-drinking and the gazing out with mucous eyes at gulls water wind. I looked out of the window with my cup in my hand. The wind made an eee sound blowing the voices from over the wall. I began to get a kind of landscape stupidity like an old man would get not thinking over his memories not thinking about anything just feeling the weather through the sides of the van and hearing the gulls and other birds he didn't know the name of and not so much taking in the browns and greys and the sky white a lot of the time as letting them pass through him with a kind of sadness that is maybe the ancient man's version of sex.

The van door burst open. Ryan came in, then Sylvie, talking. 'Ryan trust me the other girl is the one for that shot.'

'I don't like her.' He went to the back and opened the fridge door.

'She may not be so now but she's more unconscious than the other girl.'

'I said.' He got a beer out, pulled the ring on the can.

Some of Sylie's kohl had smudged at the side of her eye.

'Noy-me what do you think? For the shot of the girl alone.'

'The one where she comes back like the boxer coming back to the ghetto?'

'No for this story. The mud, the almost-naked girl. The one who belongs to the mud.'

'Oh that shot.' I looked at her wondering which girl she was talking about, thinking it must be Boukje but maybe it was Nati. I wished she'd just mouth a Boo or a Nah while Ryan was looking out of the window.

'Uh it depends but I'd definitely go for'

She looked at my mouth. I felt it making a shape.

'Boukje.'

She faced Ryan. 'It has to be. Maybe it's not so clear to a man.'

Ryan pushed past her and crumpled the can.

'Please trust me Ryan. I understand these things.'

He chucked the can at a seat. 'You take the fucking picture then you who understands these things.'

'Ryan.' She touched his arm. He flapped it away.

'Ryan.' A tiny voice. Bleating.

I got up to leave the van. Ryan shouted, 'Stop trying to manipulate me all the time! Don't you think I see what you're doing?' He went out and slammed the door. The van rocked. We both looked at the shut door.

'Hey Sylvie have some tea.'

'But do you know what I mean?'

I poured tea into a mug for her and filled mine. 'I know exactly what you mean. Krysta is'

'Posing all the time. Looking at herself in the camera.'

'Yeah too model.'

She sat in the driver's seat and I got into the seat next to her. She offered me a Gitane.

'No thanks, it's like putting a gun in your mouth. I'll have one of these.'

She made a noise through her nose to show she knew that was meant to be funny. We looked out at the flats of grey light.

'I wish Sergei was here,' I said.

'Me too. I miss him.'

'Have you met the boyfriend?' Just on the b of the word boyfriend I remembered but it was too late. 'I mean I don't know. I'm just assuming. Hasn't he got one?'

'Don't tell me lies.' She kept her face facing the window.

'Oh no, I'm sorry.'

She smoked.

'Is it a big deal?' I said. 'I mean?'

'No.'

'He told me he wanted to tell you himself. A year ago. I just assumed that by now'

'What's he like?'

'I haven't met him. I don't even know if they're still together.'

'What did he say?'

'He's madly in love. Don't tell him I said will you?'

'No.'

'And the boyfriend works in some kind of grand antique shop.'

'Ah.'

'Jean-Marie.'

She stubbed out her cigarette.

44

Good morning Naomi,

You the one who does not answer me but who does not reject me. You the one who accepted the first poem. You didn't ridicule me. You invited me. Forgive my last letter, I regret sending it. That was a night when I felt at an extreme point. Now I am fine, I am happy to be able to write these poems flying between us like homing pigeons with two homes. The state I am in is difficult to bear. Happiness is difficult to bear. I accept what has happened to me as a disaster that I nevertheless want more than anything else. I wish I could see your face across a street, in a window. Sometimes I feel so lost that to lose what remains would be to lose almost nothing. Sometimes I feel I could unlock the mathematics of the universe not with a formula but with a word. There are words that have died, leaving just bones. I will bring them back, or, if I can bring back just one, let it be rose, that too sweet flower of our forefathers, which I will resurrect and throw into the world as a firebomb to incinerate the cynics and the poseurs.

Eric

PS Three poems

45

'And you're in what hotel?'

'The one halfway down Holland Park. The pink one. A lot of rock stars stay there.'

'And you'd been talking how long?'

'Say three quarters of an hour.'

'Ages.'

'Not for this mag, not a music mag. That's why I like this job better. This is a cover line. I'd been promised a two-hour slot. And I thought My Life My Life. I am sitting in a champagne bar with a rock god and he's singing to me. And I've got it on tape. And I'm working. This is work! And then he broke off singing. He did this.' She banged her forearm on the low table in front of the sofa. 'And he said Donelle I need to make a couple of calls. How about we finish this off in my room.'

Ellie laughed.

'No listen. I thought I get to see his room, more colour for the story. What luggage, is his bed unmade, that crossed my mind, just casual conversation I might overhear on the phone that might add a line or two, something different from the same old same old biog he's spouted in every interview. Does he wear pyjamas? I mean the readers would want to know that yeah, he wears blue Sea Island cotton pyjamas with the name of his first album across the top pocket. And – wait a minute – he was looking at me dead straight and I thought why would he bother? Don't flatter yourself girl because lets face it, it would have been flattering.'

'Would it?' I said.

'To be fancied by the saviour of pop noir?' She shrugged which made her breasts go up about an inch and when they settled back they swayed. 'Might not do it for you girl.'

'But was he fancying you or just thinking I can do her easy?'

'What's the difference?'

'I suppose he wasn't gonna propose.'

'Same again?' said Ellie.

'What was that?' said Doughgirl.

'A rum cocktail, that's what they do here rum.'

'Yeah fine same.'

Ellie turned on the sofa and tried to catch Mo's attention behind the bar. He was talking to three girls getting onto barstools. She did a big wave, signalled three of the same. He did a thumbs up.

'So I went up right. He had this fantastic suite on the top floor. He said make yourself comfortable and he went to the phone and I heard him order a bottle of champagne.'

'Yeah I just got to make a couple of calls,' said Ellie.

'Hang on. Vintage Ruinart. It's the most expensive one in the Claridges Bar.'

'Did that worry you?'

'More than if he'd ordered a cheap one? Then he propped the pillows and threw himself on the bed and started making calls. So I just wandered round the room taking things in.'

'What kind of things? Anything cheeky?' said Ellie.

'What like sex toys?'

'Yeah any sex toys?'

Ellie kicked off her shoes and curled her feet up beside her on the sofa facing me and Doughgirl. Rob came up and slid a silver tray onto the low table. He lifted three red cocktails with slices of watermelon and cherries on sticks stuck on the sides and put them on the table.

'Cheers!' We clinked glasses.

'Yeah so any sex toys?' said Ellie.

'Nothing visible. I would have loved to dive into his bedside cabinet.'

'No qualms?' I said.

'About what?'

'I dunno. Privacy, media ethics?'

'No more than him using the media to the max. It's not a qualms game. There was just anonymous stuff around I can't even remember. Oh guitars. I remember he had like three guitars propped against the wall one was yellow with a black wolf on it. His suitcase was open but I didn't really feel I could get down on the floor with him there and start rummaging for the leopard print jockeys.'

'Did you come on to him at all?' said Ellie with a little smile.

'Well. I just dragged my bait a little through the water. You know, while he was blabbing I'd kind of go over to the window and look over London. Hands on the back of the chair there so my arse stuck out a bit towards him. Then I'd do that thing of lifting up your arms to rearrange your hair.' She did it to show us. Her back kinked in, her breasts lifted like snouts scenting faraway food. She mussed the hair on top of her head and reclipped it into her hairclip. 'I mean I didn't slouch round the room with my belly stuck out picking my nose.'

We hooted.

'So then the champagne arrived and I sipped some and he put his hand over the receiver and said hey babe.'

'Hey babe?'

'Hey babe there's a line for you in the john I'll be with you in five.'

Ellie and me looked at each other.

'So I thought. Uh. OK. Do coke with a rock star. I mean. Oh kay.'

'They're so predictable.'

'Sure I'd have liked it if he'd got out his little Amazonian frog at that point and suggest we get off on licking its back but hey. You play it as it lays. Would you have said no?'

I fiddled with my straw. Ellie shrugged.

'Like hell,' said Doughgirl. 'And you know it. It would have felt really prissy saying no thank you like one of those kneejerk good girls who only ever have just the one glass and ooh! dwugs? No no. And if you ask them why no drugs? they can't really explain.'

'Coz mummy said so,' said Ellie.

'Scared of life,' I said.

'They don't want anyone to see them messy. Normally they're the ones who like you to get messy and then they can laugh at you and disapprove at the same time.' She sipped La Sangre de la Santa Caterina.

'You tell them Miss Thing,' said Ellie.

'Bag a chips,' I said.

'So I went in and I saw the line chopped out all nice and fresh and I thought, Fuck it.' She sighed. 'I wasn't going to tell you this right? But hey. I work an honest programme. I looked at it and I thought Nah. I made the noises. I picked up the fifty-quid note and rolled it and everything and then I swept the line into the toilet sat on it and peed.'

'No!'

'Yeah.'

'Quite right you shouldn't feel you have to.'

'Yeah it's the way he just assumed.'

'I just felt somehow no. Then when I stood up I got the crumbs still lying on top of the loo and rubbed them on my gums. Fuck knows what was going on. I flushed the loo and I went over to wash my hands. I was looking in the mirror. Actually I was looking in the mirror and putting on his cologne, Creed's Silver Mountain Water – it's in the piece – and I saw the door open in the mirror and he came in.'

Ellie squealed.

'To do the other line?' I said.

'Yeah I'm just here to do the other line thanks very much,' said Ellie, 'and then I'll leave you to it. Babe.'

'No but imagine,' said Donelle. 'You see him coming in in the mirror. You close your eyes you turn round and part your lips and you hear these snorting sounds and you look round and he's holding the fifty quid and looking at you like, You think I came in here for you Miss Nobody?'

'So what did he do? Come on come on,' said Ellie.

I grabbed a cushion. I held it against my stomach.

'He came up behind me and he put his arms round me and cupped my breasts.'

We squealed.

'Cupped your breasts!' For some reason we both added 'Ugh.'

'He's got a front on him,' said Ellie.

'Course he's got a front on him. The job is having a front on you.'

'What'd he do then?'

'He kind of rubbed the flats of his palms on the ends of them.'

'Like what?'

'Like this.' She swivelled sideways on the sofa beside me and put her hands flat against the ends of her breasts and started pushing them about. We squealed.

'I froze to the spot. Look, I know you two think I'm a total slapper.'

'No!'

'But I'm honest and if you're honest you'll know what I mean when I say I thought Donelle. You are standing in the hotel suite of one of the major rock stars of our time, of all time, and he is pressing his cock into your butt and'

'Hard on?'

'Rock hard. And massaging your breasts and This is My Life.' She mashed the bits of watermelon and cherry in her cocktail with the end of the straw. 'This is good. I like it in here. It's your local yeah?'

'Yeah. It's got a nice vibe. Fancy another one?'

'All right just the one.'

I looked at the door. No sign.

'Shall we do something different? How about ice shots?'

'Rum shots?'

'Yeah they've got special vintage rums here. We always have this one, Don Fernandes Làgrimas Argentes.' Ellie pointed to it on the bar menu.

'C'mon then.'

Ellie yoed Mo, made 'small drink' with a finger and thumb, pointed at the melting ice in her glass and wiped imaginary tears from her eyes. He gave her the thumbs up.

'Go on Miss Thing.'

'So there I am, breasts being manhandled by a modern god, looking at myself and him in the mirror and thinking if I had a camera, and then he does this thing. He gives this primeval groan and he puts his head into my shoulder and he says'

'Oh no it's a Wonderbra.'

'How do you like my penis extension?'

'Aw baby you make a man so horny,' she cooed.

We groaned.

'Where do they get the lines?'

'Look it's the American accent. He could have said I don't know what to do and I'm always in the dark, We're living in a powder keg and giving off sparks, and I'd have turned to custard.'

'The Bonnie Tyler song, yeah. He covered it. Awesome,' said Ellie.

'Right so he was bumping me and kissing my neck and undoing my shirt and I could see the whole thing in the mirror. I could see me watching me and the sexiest man in pop lost in my body. It was unbelievable.' She gargled up the last of the cocktail. 'Then he flipped me round and leaned me back against the sink and we started snogging.'

'So this whole thing wasn't a total surprise to you?' I said.

'The moment he said can we finish this off upstairs it crossed my mind, OK, but only as one possibility among many. And when he actually got on the phone I thought well anything could happen now. He'll make calls, we'll drink champagne. I'll interview him more, I'll go. He'll make calls, we'll drink champagne. His mates'll call and I'll end up having dinner with him, Courtney Love and Keith Richards.' She shrugged and the breasts sniffed.

'He'll make calls, we'll drink champagne. I'll end up having sex with him, Courtney and Keith Richards,' said Ellie.

'Would you have done it?' I said.

'Me and Courtney in a double-decker with him and Keith? Them up for it and me not? I'm teasing you Nay. I don't know. Life comes at me I catch the ball. So there I was with my arms round his neck snogging the biggest rock star in the world and then I heard something wet.'

Our eyes widened.

She nodded. 'Glugging.'

'Glugging!'

'It was the bottle of Silver Mountain Water. I was pouring it all down his back onto the bathroom tiles.' She banged the arm of the chair. I rocked back and forward over my cushion. 'He reached round grabbed it out of my hand and chucked it in the bath and it smashed. Then he bit me and said you sexy little bitch.'

'The lines! The lines!'

'Well think of it as a sacrament. The lines are always the same and in a way that makes them more powerful.'

She kinked her back, unsprung her hairclip, and put it in her mouth while she regathered her hair. Mo came up with the silver tray stamped with snorting bulls. Three glasses sat on it full to the brim with ice and half full of clear liquid. We picked them up off the tray.

Doughgirl smiled. 'What an evening eh?'

'One for the grandchildren,' I said.

She swirled the rum round the ice.

'Don't stop there, Dough,' said Ellie.

She smiled and swirled the rum. I looked up at the door. Still no sign.

'Did you go through with it?' I said.

'Oh yeah.' She picked up the glass, drank some.

'Did you want to?' I said.

She made a face. 'Ye-ah. You know how it is. I'll be honest with you. When he did the aftershave thing I got a bit of a shock. Then he laughed and I laughed and it was like something clicked and I was ready to go back into the bedroom switch on the tape recorder and finish the interview.'

'You didn't feel sexed-up any more.'

'I did and I didn't. I mean fair cop. I'd let him go that far.'

'What, you mean it would have been rude to stop him?' I said.

'I acted like I was up for it and then suddenly I wasn't.'

'Fine it's allowed,' said Ellie.

'Yeah but I still had to get the interview didn't I? I didn't want to piss him off. He was really horny. He had to get off.'

We all picked up our drinks. Donelle shook the ice cubes in her glass.

'So how was it?' said Ellie. 'Was it good for you?'

She shrugged. 'Not as good as he looked I suppose but that's not his fault.'

'No.'

We sipped.

'Cock?'

'Hardly saw it really. Respectable.'

'Did you do the interview?' I said.

'Bastard said he had a dinner date. He had to run. I'd distracted him.'

'For fuck's sake!'

'Yeah well you know.' She undid the hairclip and shook out her hair. 'I could have told you a story. I bet lots of girls would have told you a story. I Shagged a Rock God and He Couldn't Get Enough of Me. Sex Flowers Champagne Dinner Phone Number.'

I saw the bar door open.

'At least you weren't scared. You had the guts.'

'Yeah I guess so.'

'Yeah.'

Sylvie was walking down the bar towards us.

'You know what?' Ellie said, 'If what happened to you had happened to a man he would laugh it off. Yeah she got her rocks off sent me packing. He'd still get bigger balls from that.'

'Yeah whatever.'

'Here she is,' I said, standing up.

I made the introductions. Sylvie sat down next to Ellie. She was wearing old torn jeans and a thin cashmere rollneck sweater that kept slipping off one shoulder.

'It's not your first time in London?' said Ellie.

'No but it has been a long time.'

'Well I've been longing to meet you. Oh that's another thing. Naomi, I think Becca might be coming.'

'Becca?'

'She phoned me and I said you know, Sylvie and Ryan Jackson were here and.' She turned to Sylvie. 'Our friend Becca, she's like a really hot stylist and your biggest fan. She wants to say hello.'

'That is nice,' said Sylvie.

Donelle leaned across the low table and said something to Sylvie.

'Where shall we take her?' I said to Ellie.

'I thought we were going to The Kebab Shop That Cares with 7-Eleven?'

'I know but I've been thinking, it's not right for her.'

'Well she's old, it's true.'

'I want to take her somewhere fabulous.'

'The Kebab Shop That Cares. She'll love it. The Czar of Rock 'n' Roll's playing.'

'My God here's Becca.'

Becca in a series of vintage T-shirts full of rips and holes, so you could see one or the other of the underneath ones layered archaeologically. She kissed me, found a chair, and dragged it over by Sylvie.

'Is your friend having an affair with her photographer?' said Ellie in a low voice.

'Ssh.'

'Yes or no,' she whispered loudly.

'No.'

'Got the most incredible pictures out of it. So real' Becca was saying.

'What makes you think no?' said Ellie.

'What are you two saying?' said Doughgirl.

'She's happily married,' I said to Ellie. 'Sylvie would you like a drink?'

'All the more reason,' said Ellie.

'Shut up.' I waved at Mo. He came over.

'New York to work with him. I was nervous but with me it was different,' Becca was saying.

'She's the only person he'll work with. They go all over the world,' said Ellie.

Sylvie tapping out a Gitane. A vague smile on her face.

'Shut *up*,' I said.

'Gives his pictures such melancholy,' said Becca.

'No but think about it,' said Ellie.

'You're probably right,' I said to shut her up.

'Diet Pepsi,' said Becca.

'Cuba Libre,' said Sylvie.

Ellie sat back in the sofa and turned to Sylvie. 'But is it true you only work with Ryan?' she said.

'Now yes.'

'Really? no one else ever?' said Ellie.

'It's quite common in fashion. Maybe not in beauty,' said Becca.

'Maybe it would be good for us sometimes to work with other people,' said Sylvie.

'I guess you are his muse,' said Doughgirl.

'She's a co-creator,' said Becca. 'Muses are more models. They're like a lucky charm. You know how photographers get a feeling for a girl and for a while their pictures only take off when that girl's in it?'

'Can't you be a muse and a stylist?' said Ellie.

'How can you be the artist and the muse? It's a power thing.'

'Georgia O'Keefe. There must be more,' said Doughgirl.

'Naomi's a muse,' said Ellie.

'Your receptionist?' said Becca. 'He's still sending them?'

Ellie turned her back a bit more towards Becca and faced Sylvie on the sofa. 'He writes poetry. Do you know him? She met him on that trip to Paris where she met you. How long ago was that?'

'Let me see. Now is June, the shoot was in August two, no three years ago,' said Sylvie.

'This is turning into OCD,' said Becca.

'Maybe but the poems are really something,' said Ellie.

'When did you read the poems?'

'I read them all the time. I'm the one who brings them from the office.'

'But you don't open them.'

'You keep them in the airing cupboard. I can't help it. The man's a fucking' She looked at the ceiling 'A fucking' She looked at Becca 'Genius.'

'Why don't you give them to Sylvie to read? She's French,' said Becca.

Sylvie caught my eye. 'That night at the hotel? The boy with champagne?'

I nodded.

'Maybe they're private, like a diary,' said Doughgirl.

'It's sex,' said Becca. 'He can't get laid.'

'Oh come on, lets not talk about Eric.'

I saw the bar door swing open. 7-Eleven came in and sauntered up to the bar. He said something to Mo. It must have been really funny. I could tell by the way Mo hunched his shoulders while he was getting a bottle off the back wall.

'Hold on a minute,' said Donelle. 'You're telling me a French writer'

'Receptionist,' said Becca.

'Look whatever he does for a day job, this guy has been writing poems to you for years. Have you seen him in all this time?'

'No.'

'This is love, amazing true love. My God I'd have been over there months ago. Why are you resisting?'

'Oh Dough you're such a sucker for romance,' said Ellie.

'I'm not in love with him.'

'But you haven't given him the benefit of the doubt. You're scared of love,' said Doughgirl.

'And she's right to be scared. We're talking about a sicko,' said Becca.

'A genius,' said Ellie.

'Look I just don't want to stop poetry coming into the world,' I said.

'Why not?' said Becca. 'no one reads it any more except fogeys. It's like not wanting to stop cave painting coming into the world.'

Sylvie laughed. 'You are funny,' she said to Becca.

'But why not give him a chance? Get on a plane. If it doesn't work out you can say bugger that for a game of soldiers and come back,' said Donelle.

'He's obviously not the brightest. Poetry is dead. Why doesn't he write a novel?' said Becca.

'Well it's true you can't really sell poetry. no one wants it,' said Donelle. She undid her hairclip, gathered hair, refastened it. 'Poor thing.'

'What's so great about sellable? I'm sick of sellable.' I started to feel hot.

'Yeah, it's strictly worthless. That's why it's genius,' said Ellie.

'Rubbish,' said Becca. 'The point is, why string him along?'

'Yes you should either go to Paris or cut all ties,' said Donelle.

'No because I think he needs me to do exactly what I'm doing. I've just realised that.'

'What are you doing?'

'Well just being there. Letting him send them, reading them. Sometimes when I get a poem I feel. No I can't explain. It's embarrassing to talk about in public.' I reached for my glass. 'Sometimes it does feel like it's getting to me. I don't know.'

'Listen to your inner voice,' said Becca. 'Don't be put upon. He's a nobody.'

Ellie faced her. 'How do you know?'

I saw Sylvie smile into her Cuba Libre.

'Imagine if he stops because she tells him she's not there for him any more and years from now it comes out he was a genius only Naomi shut him down because she was too shallow to realise.'

Becca shook her head. She spoke to me.

'He'll drop you when it stops working for him. It happens to all those girls. One day they don't do it for them any more and they're nobody. I always feel sorry for them.'

I glanced at the bar. 7-Eleven was standing next to the three girls on barstools. 'I bet Beatrice didn't have to have these conversations,' I said.

'This is not about some other girl. This is about you,' said Doughgirl.

He had draped his arm over one of the girls. She turned to the girl next to her and I could see her face all lit up. Behind her back Seven sucked up some of her drink through the straw. The other girl stretched out and slapped him on the hand.

'It's not healthy. For him or you,' said Becca.

Doughgirl frowned. 'What do you think? Is this healthy?' she said to Sylvie.

'No it is not healthy.'

I looked at Sylvie. 'Well what am I going to do?'

'Do you think he's just projecting a fantasy onto her?' said Doughgirl.

Sylvie laughed.

'I think what Donelle's trying to say is what if he doesn't love *me*.'

'Oh *me*,' said Sylvie. 'Everyone always worries, does he love *me*?' She pushed her fringe back and I saw her other eye. A shock like she had secret eyes she could open all over her body if she wanted to.

'But don't you see that's the only reason you don't stop him? Because it is you. It's all about you.' Becca stuck her neck out elegantly and sucked up some Diet Pepsi.

I heard Sylvie laughing again. Her head thrown back on the sofa.

'Here comes 7-Eleven,' said Doughgirl.

Ellie licked her lips and looked over the back of the sofa. Seven leaned on the back of it. 'Hello ladies and who's the new lady?'

46

'You were gone,' I said, 'on top of the speakers. You must remember.'

She opened her eyes.

'The evil televisions remember? You said I had to protect you from the evil televisions.'

'Oh. Oh yes.'

She opened her mouth and I slipped the cigarette in. She took a drag. I let the cigarette hover in the vicinity. She exhaled.

'What did you do?'

'I kicked them away with my boots one by one remember?'

I put the cigarette between her lips. She inhaled. She was raising her eyebrows.

She blew out the smoke.

'That's right. They were staring and I couldn't switch them off. People were fucked on the speakers.'

'You looked terrified.' I took a drag.

'God it was fantastic.'

'So,' I said, 'and you haven't said. When you went off with 7-Eleven.'

She sighed.

I looked up at the ceiling. I noticed because I'd been looking away that it was changing and that the pink light was getting greyer and shadows were getting thicker at the near corners of the ceiling.

'He was amazing.' She sighed again. 'So sweet. And raunchy.'

'And raunchy. God.'

'Oh dear.'

47

Naomi,

I have written many letters that I didn't send with the poems. I tried to stick to your demand and now I am afraid I have enraged you with my letters so you don't receive the poems any more. I am tired. Every hour, every day, for days, months, now it's years. And you don't say anything, nothing for years. If you could just let me know that you still accept the poems. I just want to hear your voice. To hear your laugh, even down on the street. If I could hear your laugh, even passing and disappearing before I can climb down. I run after you down the streets. I erect roses to your laugh all over the city. Has this changed you? I don't want you to change, but it has changed me to a degree that is becoming intolerable and I ask myself if you can remain untouched. There are too many words already. I don't want to add to what is already surplus. I write as little as I can and there are many poems which never reach you. The bottom of the river here is covered in the poems you don't receive. Maybe the fish swim over, take a look, a nibble. Maybe they are the kind of fish who are happy to chew up paper salted with ink. Do I make you laugh just a little bit? No. I have crossed a line. I am committing a sin that I don't understand, like when you are a child and they let you know you have done something and you feel afraid because you don't know what exactly was wrong about it, and you don't know how to measure how wrong and if you will be marked out by it for ever. My father is angry with me because I gave up my studies. My mother worries about me. I tried to reassure her. I explain that I am working on the most important work of my life. But I can't tell her exactly what, since she would not understand. To them it seems as if I have lost my mind or that I have fallen into a medical depression. And you don't say anything and you aren't here and the only thing I can do is put a sheet of paper on the table and stare at it. I stare at it. I stare at it. I get up. I walk around the room, I leave the room, I leave the house or I sit and immediately move my pen over the paper. I have to contain the whiteness. I use a fountain pen so I can feel the ink slippery under the nib. It shines wet for a moment before it sinks into the paper. If only it would stay like this till it reaches you. Then you would have me full on the end of your fingers, what a dream!

Eric

48

We both screamed and clutched at each other. It was him standing there in the dark hugely tall.

'Who's been sleeping in my bed? Heh heh heh.' He always had a big lazy laugh.

I sat on the side.

'Why didn't you say you were coming over?' said Ellie. 'You can't expect Naomi to get up now.'

'No no it's OK.' I walked towards the door.

'Nah don't get up' he said rubbing his hands together. Stoned. 'Jiggy jig the both of you.'

I was out the bedroom. Woozy. I put the light on in the living room. She must have given him a key. I screwed up my eyes. I went into the boiler cupboard and got a couple of sheets and some blankets. They were the old yellowish beige ones with black lines at each end. War stock.

'Naomi let me help you.'

'No no go on. It's fine. My fault.'

'In what way?'

'Lets talk in the morning.'

'You know what he's like.'

She went back into the bedroom and I went into the living room and pulled out the sofabed.

The living room faced the road that came down the hill parallel to the mansion block. I had left the curtains open. Everything felt exposed. I could see the tower block lit up like a cruiseliner crossing the sky. Every few minutes there was the drone of a car coming down the hill and then the loud slushy sound as it went by under the window and the change in the sound to a purr as it went on down the hill. Even before I heard them there was a ghost of light on the far right corner of the ceiling and then the light came down the wall and vanished. The building of the pressurised sound till it expanded under the window and dropped to a purr. I heard loud bass and how it changed as he drove by and away. I assumed it was a he. After it had gone the silence came back. I lay looking at the ceiling. From behind me now, from inside the flat, a squealy creaking. Quavery at first no-ho-ho no-ho-ho. It built to a confident rhythm. To pass the time till it was over I did a visualisation: a handyman sawing through a tough bit of wood on his workbench.

The silence came back. Not all at once. At first it buzzed with the departure of conscientious workmen, the air full of shimmering specks of presence. It took a while for the air to clear completely. Then the different vibration of the night came back. I sat up. This was a room where the dark was orange. I wrapped the yellowish blanket round me and went over to the window. There was no wind at all. The clouds round the tower block were not moving. I put my head against the glass and felt it cool. Below was the patch of municipal grass a shadowy grey. On it the three trees in full summer leaf. After a while one of the trees stirred and became motionless. A few seconds later one of the others took it up in a vague way as if it were moving in its dreams. A car came down the hill.

I heard the bedroom door open. It was him. He went into the bathroom. He peed like he was sand-blasting the toilet. He didn't flush. I saw the living room door open and the top half of his body appeared round it. When he saw I was up he came in and put the light on.

'Awright?' he said.

'Yeah. Can't sleep.'

'I'm buzzing.'

He sat on the foot of the sofabed and it sagged so he moved to the corner. He rolled a spliff. Whistling under his breath. He lay back and put his arm behind his head on the pillow and took a puff.

'I want a talk with you.'

'OK.'

He checked the roach for bits of tobacco. 'You two leslies?'

'Oh shit you found my dildo.'

'Should have got a bigger one.' He did that lazy laugh.

'Men, you just don't get it. Play your cards right I'll teach you a thing or two.'

He held out the spliff. I shook my head.

'Nah, nah. I'm gonna play teacher. Lesson one, find another bunk little girl where you can go play with yourself.'

'Can we leave my sex life out of this?'

The lazy laugh. 'What about Bison?' he said. 'Int you seeing him?'

'There's a few people I'm seeing.'

'Bison innit?'

I looked out of the window. The long shape of 7-Eleven stretched away and up his head smeared with a light from the tower block.

'So if you're seeing him wh'aren't you seeing him. Know what I'm saying?'

'What's it to you?'

''Stead of hanging round here.'

'I live here.'

He laughed again. I tried to shade my eyes so I could see out the window.

49

I said to her next day I should leave, I had to leave and it would be much nicer for them to have the place to themselves. She insisted that she wanted me to stay. If only there was another bedroom, I said. Oh come on, she said, you can come in with me and we can lie smoking and talking about everything the way we always do and then if he comes in you can just nip out to the sofabed. Is that OK? We could keep it made up, all folded like bachelors used to have their beds in the fifties.

But in the end it was less upsetting to start in the living room with the sofabed and not be chucked out the bed in the middle of the night. Three or four nights a week I'd hear him coming in between 2 and 6. I realised I was listening out for the sound of his trainers coming down the corridor. They almost yeowled on the lino. Sometimes I even heard the lift ping or thought I did from my bed in the living room. Then I went tense. Sometimes he went straight in to her. Serious carpentry. After a while the sand-blasting. Back to bed. He banged about no consideration. Other times he'd throw open the living room door and squeeze round the bottom corner of the sofabed to switch on the telly. He'd go into the kitchen and I'd hear him putting on the kettle. If I hadn't already done it I'd get right over to the far side of the sofabed while he was in there. I'd wrap myself in the yellow blanket so he wouldn't be able to see that my eyes were open looking at the near wall. He'd come back into the living room whistling under his breath. He'd sit on the easy chair and sometimes he'd prop his feet on the bottom corner of the sofabed. He'd plonk them down. He had huge feet. The whole sofabed bounced while he squirmed them around to get comfy. He watched anything; old movies, seventies cop shows, MTV, cookery, porn. He'd roll a spliff, slurp his tea and mutter and laugh at the screen. Blood clart! I'd watch the flickering grey shadows projected from the TV playing over the wall in front of me. The smell of his sinsemilla would hang over the yellow blanket. Sometimes I'd drop off for short bursts between Kojak saying who loves ya baby? rutting Roumanians, Rick saying we'll always have Paris, some woman going pour in a thin stream, a horse galloping dully across New Mexico, that bobbins Madonna video etc etc.

It got so as I'd wake up even when he didn't come. After a bit I'd sit up. It was dark in the room but with the orange dark from the street lights reflected off the cloud cover. Sometimes I sat there for a while not doing anything. Sometimes I wrapped the yellow blanket round me and went over to the window right away. I liked to look down at the trees. Sometimes they were completely still, sometimes they moved in the wind for hours. I liked it when they gave off a muffled roar. On some nights they cast moon-shadows onto the patch of grass and I could spend an hour watching the way the shadows moved slowly across the grass. After I'd looked at the trees for a bit I got in the habit of scanning the tower block looking for lighted windows apart from the stairwell windows where the light was always on. No matter how late it was I could usually count several lighted windows. There was always at least one.

In the mornings, 7-Eleven was quite chatty. She'd long gone by the time he got up. I'd be in front of the computer staring at the screen. He'd ask me did I want an egg sandwich, did I want a toke on his spliff? Sometimes he made me laugh. He had the laugh of someone born to laugh. Other mornings he'd come in and throw himself down on the sofabed made back into a sofa. I'd be sitting there in the Daffies calling in stuff on the phone for some shitty styling job or with This Week's Must Have propped on the table. He'd put on the telly. When he was good and ready he'd jump up and fry himself some eggs and stick them in between two slabs of sliced white and eat them standing up by the stove. The yellow running out the back of the bread and dripping on the countertop or one of the electric rings. He left for the garage where he worked odd hours without cleaning the frying pan.

50

'Now this,' I said out loud, 'is a Must Have you really must have. These are gorgeous, gorgeous.'

Everything. The pale pink box the black tissue paper the tags. Breast to Impress. Oh for God's sake. Think silk, satin, sexy, slinky, nice, naughty. Naughty Bits Nice. For fuck. Sugar and Spice. Simply the Vest. Where did that? Damn coz it's quite good but they are never going to choose a vest, not even a Prada vest, for the Must Have. Maybe a Prada vest. I touched the bra. Was that silk? Slip Into Something Way Cooler. Were they called plunge bras? And this little gap at the back of the panties, with pink bows above and below it. Was this? Did they really mean to put this in the paper? Touch Bottom. I picked up the panties. You could see through the material if you held them up. Rear Window. This must be for some other mag. I tuned in to a faint thump thump. They've mixed up the samples. I've got the stuff for an edgy style mag or a smut mag. The domp domp getting closer. Sweet Nothings. Past the Irish boys' door, that meant one thing. Nights in Pink Satin. I pressed Save. I pushed my chair back as the doorbell rang.

He still had his helmet and gauntlets on. It was a muggy day and stale body odour was coming from under his leather biker jacket. He was holding a bunch of flowers. A cellophane goblet and inside that a smaller brown paper goblet. He tipped the bunch towards me. There had to be two dozen, all white. I tucked them under my left arm and signed his pad. He stomped away down the lino. I watched him go all the way to where the corridor bent to the left and you could see the shadow of the opening to the lift area on the right. He went round to the right and disappeared. I fancied I could see his separate shadow extending back in the corridor. Radio blurt. A ping. Then faintly, the lift doors opening. The lift doors closing. A pause and the gulping sound it made going down. I shut the door and took the roses into the kitchen and laid them on the draining board.

The knot was too tight I had to cut it. I pushed through the cellophane. It made a showy crackling, arching up when I kept pressing it down on the draining-board so I could get at the brown paper. It was the kind of old-fashioned brown paper that is slightly gleamy on one side and absorbent on the other. The roses lay on it giving off damp. I read the card. Happy Birthday, love Dan.

There wasn't a vase big enough in the kitchen. I remembered a huge jar in the boiler cupboard that looked like it had once held fish 'n' chip shop pickled onions. How long'd it take her to eat those in some other life? I half-filled it with water. There was something nice about the jar just half-filled with water. The stems snagged on each other when I tried to disentangle them a bit. I lifted off the top rose. I tried not to snap the side-stems the leaves were growing off. I cut the stiff stem with the big kitchen scissors and placed it in the jar. The rose drooped over the side. I pulled another rose from the pile. The stems were tough with huge thorns. I changed to a big knife. I placed the second rose on the other side of the vase so the stems crossed under the water. The white heads were heavy. They needed water. I felt a desire to crush one in my mouth for a second. Sift the layers of petals with my tongue. I pulled another rose from the pile on the draining board and felt a sharp stab.

There was a pause like when a conductor lifts his arms before signalling to the orchestra. Then blood in a bright note that swelled longer than seemed possible before it burst and ran easily down my finger. It kept coming out and running down the finger and splashing onto the mound of roses lying on the draining board. I held the finger out straight between the finger and thumb of the other hand. I moved it away from the roses and a drop fell into the water in the pickle jar and curled like a separate thing in the water slowly clouding at the edges. I'd forgotten how red blood was. There was so much of it running down the finger. The strength of the colour. Outside we were beige or dun. Inside splendour. By what law of nature was it hidden away? So that animals lusted to rip open bodies and lap chindeep in it. I put the finger in my mouth. I started to cry. I put my hands up over my face and hunched over the flowers. I said his name inside my head. Dan. It felt like a stranger's. I knew blood was running out between my fingers with the tears as well and splashing on the white roses. There should have been someone, music. It was too good to waste even while it hurt. I washed almost all the blood off them and put them in the pickle jar. I put it on the table in the living room and put the stovetop coffee pot on to boil. I moved the computer out of the way and placed the notebook square on to the chair. I looked in at the kitchen. It hadn't started the noise. I went into my suitcase under the bed. Various bits and bobs, some nice shoes I'd forgotten about and the notebook with a blue cover and a fleur-de-lys.

hi-quality

MOST ADVANCED QUALITY

GIVES BEST WRITING FEATURES

& GIVES SATISFACTION TO YOU

I took it into the living room and put it in the place of the other notebook. There was only a blue biro which was a shame because those Paris notebooks had an incredibly smooth feeling under the point of a rotring pen. I opened a packet of cigarettes and pulled the central cigarette so it stuck out ready to be taken out. I placed the matches at an angle next to the cigarette packet. Right on time the coffee pot started making the noise.

My eyes narrowed at the page. Creamy white not like the roses which were sharp white. Very smooth paper. I ran the side of my hand across it to feel just how smooth. I needed keywords just like for This Week's Must Have, in a way you need a list of keywords to get you going. I ran the side of my palm across the empty page back and forth. Keywords. It was a method Ellie had taught me seeing as she was the more expert writer. You felt stupid when you started out doing it but it worked. I glanced over my shoulder. White sky. A couple of leaves being taken off by the wind. I wrote

red
white
blood
petals
scraps
pure
pickle
furl
tear
bless
prick
spell
seven
sleep

I drank some of the coffee. It had happened again. Almost against the law of physics it was tepid before I had drunk the first sip. My hand moved across the facing page from the keywords.

When it was done I closed the notebook and went into the kitchen to make fresh coffee. I looked at the windows of the other kitchens and the toilets giving on to the well and the system of drainpipes and ventilators. Pigeonshit. When it began to make the noise I got a clean cup out of the unit and a saucer. I got a spoon out of the drawer. I got the big glass jar of sugar out of the other unit. I looked at the stovetop pot. I lifted it off and poured the coffee into the cup. I put in a heaped teaspoon of sugar, because this was a special event. I took it back into the living room. A spray of rain against the window. Just for a minute. I sat down on the leatherlook seat pad and put the cup of coffee beside the notebook. I placed it on a copy of Italian Vogue which happened to be sitting there because it was a good chunky size for a cup for example to sit on. I lit a cigarette. Once again I opened the blue cover of the hi-quality notebook and pressed it down with the side of my hand. I turned the page and let my eyes fall on the creamy right hand page and read the poem. When I was finished I closed the notebook. I smoked another cigarette. Then I took the precaution of throwing the notebook away.

51

No moon. I dragged the blanket round me and went over to the window. I checked the tower block. This was the dead hour when the ones who stayed up late were giving up and when the ones who got up early hadn't got up yet. Two flats had lights on. The fifth floor and the nineteenth floor. This nineteenth-floor light was on a lot late at night. Never that special kind of light that meant telly. Lamps not the overhead. Maybe they were reading or studying. Maybe just an insomniac. Maybe doing something soothing like knitting. A pair of old ladies who shared a flat. They got up at night to do knitting together and have cups of tea. Why not? They didn't have jobs. Each one had customised her rocking-chair one with a Western saddle and one with an English. They played records, they'd had enough telly. Sometimes they just clacked needles in silence. They were knitting for peace.

I crept through to the kitchen as quietly as I could. Under the sink where the cleaning fluids and cloths were there was a bottle of brandy. I'd found it a couple of weeks ago right at the back two-thirds full. Now it was a quarter full. I poured some into a glass and put the bottle back behind the bucket with the cloths in it and went back into the living room. Cars at the lights twenty-five yards down the hill. One was going to turn right into the road that went past the tower block. The indicator light clicked slowly on and off. One was going to continue straight up the hill. I lit up. I put my cheek and my bare shoulder and the side of my breast against the glass. After a minute I started to shiver. They revved, one much more than the other. I listened till their wakes washed out completely in the silence and while I was listening I saw myself fifty years from now an old lady. I was wearing a beautifully cut tweed jacket and jeans, why not jeans? And I was walking along in Mayfair near the cinema where they show a lot of French films. I tried for a minute to see my face but it was too hard though I could see my hair in a white plait down my back because it hadn't got thinner like some old ladies' hair if anything it had got thicker like I might be an old Cherokee lady. The teeth started to chatter. I pressed closer to the cold drawing it into me. It's a Wednesday afternoon as I walk down the street and on impulse go into the cinema because a film is just about to start and because I've had a full life, been married to a wonderful, unexpected man, and had children, now grown but very special children who I loved in a good and healthy way, and I was still asked to talk and write papers about my speciality because I'd gone back to university and re-trained as a marine biologist and I'd spent a lot of the last forty years helping to clean up the seas and bring about a stabilisation in whale numbers round Sakhalin Island where the Russian grey whales had their last breeding ground, and now, on this Wednesday afternoon in a month like April I can rest from my labours and wander into a cinema and see a film by myself.

I find my way in the dark to a seat near the back just as the titles are coming up. A film with subtitles. It starts with an old man writing. You see his pen moving over a sheet of paper. He looks out of the window and his inner voice, this rugged French man's voice, speaks over the image. He smiles and he bends back over the page and writes some more. He folds up the piece of paper and puts it in an envelope. Then he goes down some stairs and out onto the pavement. The local boulangère is standing in the doorway of her shop next to a window full of loaves. He says a few words to her and you understand that they have been exchanging more or less the same words for years. He goes to the postbox. Just as he is about to put the letter in the screen goes misty and we are in a sunny room and an American girl sitting up in bed in a broderie anglaise nightdress calls Come in! There's something about her though she's not beautiful in the conventional way. A young man comes in delivering breakfast. Dark, rumpled hair, very French. You can see that he is completely disabled with love. He leaves and she butters the toast and looks out of the window and you look out the window through her eyes and you see she's in Paris.

Shots of the old man are intercut with shots from his great love affair back then, an affair that lasted a total of seven and a fifth days. In most of those days there are just a few moments that the young man has any contact with the girl but they mean everything to him so sometimes they are replayed in slo-mo and then bits are replayed in super slo-mo. Then we see her go past him into the courtyard at evening and he writes her a poem and bravely dashes out and hands it to her. Then he goes back behind the reception counter, biting his nails, pacing. She appears. She encourages him out she pours him a glass of champagne. They talk. The camera moves over her face, his face, the champagne in the glasses, the jasmine, a nightingale, the stars. The young man gathers courage. He closes his eyes. Their lips touch. They draw back. Their lips touch again in super-slo-mo. At that moment people burst into the courtyard wearing masquerade outfits and sweep the young girl away and the young man is left standing there. The only sound is the bird singing on a bit of jasmine. In between we see shots of the old man writing at the table and posting the letters. We see him going out and saying the same words to the boulangère and then going to do the shopping and chatting to the man with the vegetable stall and the nice young man in the bookshop who really likes the old man, you can tell.

Then in a flashback we see the girl is leaving the hotel. Her taxi sets off and the young man breaks into a run and runs faster and faster down the street after the taxi with huge high steps. The camera cuts from his eyes to her eyes, back to his eyes, and at the end of the street she waves and the taxi turns and she's gone. He's left standing there panting and he drops a piece of paper and the camera focuses in on the paper and it's a poem.

We see his life from then on in snatches, how he gives up his place at the university, how he almost starts relationships with various women then can't go through with it, how he writes poem after poem that he sends to the girl's address in America. We see him in the night crying at the edge of the bed or walking the streets to the sound of old blues songs.

Then the old man seals an envelope and slides it inside his jacket, not in the pocket, but inside the breast of his jacket, the way people sometimes do in films. He goes out and he says a few words to the boulangère and just as he sees the postbox in front of him he doubles over and falls down on the pavement. He grips himself there for a moment and goes still.

The boulangère runs out of the door of her shop calling Monsieur Bertillon! Monsieur Bertillon! She listens at Monsieur Bertillon's chest and starts pounding on it with her two fists. The ambulance comes and M. Bertillon is put in the back and the ambulance drives away with its siren blaring.

The boulangère is standing on the pavement wiping her eyes and the crowd begins to disperse and a small boy is left standing there. He says, 'Look Madame, your friend has dropped something.' He picks up the letter and hands it to the boulangère. We look at it through her. We see Etats Unis and a Par Avion sticker. She is about to put it in the postbox but her hand hesitates just as half the letter is inside the slot. She withdraws the letter and goes back into the bakery and serves people baguettes and brioches and the cakes they call petits choux. At 5 p.m. she pulls the shutter down on the shopfront and puts the kettle on. She gets the letter out of the pocket of her pinafore and holds the flap of the envelope in the kettle steam until it unsticks. She reads the poem.

The screen dissolves and then we see the boulangère going into the bookshop. She walks between the high shelves and the people reading look austerely at her. She finds the young bookseller and hands him the poem. He reads it and they talk. Then the young man goes to the hospital to see M. Bertillon. He is alive but he can't speak. He is hooked up to a bag of plasma and he's wearing an oxygen mask. There are pads on his chest from which wires go to a computer screen where the trace of his heart travels across the screen. The bookseller asks the old man if there is anyone who does not know he is here who should know. The old man shakes his head with great effort. But anyone? says the bookseller. Maybe someone who is abroad or someone you haven't spoken to for years whom maybe now you would like to say something to? The old man turns his head away and refuses to look at the bookseller any more.

The bookseller is back at his shop. He paces up and down the rows of books disturbing the austere people trying to read. He goes out to the café and stands at the zinc and knocks back two Armagnacs. He goes to a phone in the back of the shop and makes a call. He looks at his watch.

We see a plane arriving at an airport and the steps are driven up to the plane and people start coming down them. One of them is the bookseller still in the same clothes. We hear the American twang of the voice coming over the information system and see fat kids running around drinking with straws out of paper cups the size of donkey buckets. He gets into a taxi and we see him drive towards a crystal outcrop of skyscrapers in a flat landscape. The taxi pulls up outside an old apartment block and the young man gets out. He looks up at the building and takes a deep breath. He takes the lift up and rings a doorbell.

The door is answered by an old lady. The young man takes in every inch of her. He puts his hand on his chest as if to apologise for his presence. He pulls the letter out of his pocket and hands it across to the old lady. When the old lady sees the letter her face changes. She invites the young man in. She takes him to a scullery behind the kitchen and opens a cupboard door. He sees a boiler in its orange lagging and round its base, sacks of letters. He gasps. He reaches forward and picks one up. It's the same writing on the envelope. He picks up another envelope, the same writing. Another, the same. He turns to the old lady. Has she never opened them? No she says because they are not addressed to me.

Together the young man and the old lady drag out the sacks and start to open the letters. They are all full of poems. Way into the night they read poem after poem. They pace up and down, reading them aloud to each other. Sometimes they laugh at what they are reading, sometimes one or the other of them cries. Sometimes they argue about a poem, sometimes one has to go over and put their arms round the other. Then it's morning and the young man stands up. He gives an address to the old lady and leaves a pile of banknotes which she tries to refuse. He takes a taxi to the airport.

Now we see the young man, very tired, enter the hospital. He speaks to a nurse and she shakes her head sadly and points him towards the door of the old man's room. The waves of the heart across the screen are smaller and less even. The old man's eyes are closed. The young man sits down beside him and after a moment he picks up the old man's hand and holds it in his. He starts to tell the old man how he had taken the liberty of going to America. He explains how he went up to the door number written on the letter and it was opened by the most radiant old lady he had ever seen. Here the young man starts to describe the old woman using some of the lines from the poems. He describes her eyes and her gestures, how she had a small mysterious smile. He explains how he told the old lady that he had come as an emissary from the old man to assure her, now and always, that she was surrounded by the 2,700 streams of his love. She had asked lots of questions about the old man which the young man tried his best to answer. She showed him the binders of poems and she recited many poems to him. But she didn't need to read from the pages in the binders since she has all the poems by heart.

The young man has started to cry. He strokes the poet's hand and the hand moves slightly on the bedclothes. Then he hears a loud alarm and he looks up and the trace on the screen is a horizontal line. Nurses run in and then a doctor comes and they rush round the old man and attach bits of equipment to him but it's too late. He's dead.

We see packages arriving for the young man at the bookshop and then we see him taking the packages to various publishers. The publishers shake their heads and hand the packages back to him across their desks. Some of them laugh at him. Then we see him preparing the galley proofs of a book. The book opens and the pages turn by themselves on the screen and we see that it is a collection of the old man's poems.

The screen fades to black. A paragraph appears on it saying that this film is based on the true story of Eric Lalanne the French poet who died five years ago leaving hundreds of unpublished poems. The film like the poems is dedicated to. Dedicated to. A la Muse Inconnue To the Unknown Muse

The old lady gets up from her seat and goes out into the afternoon.

52

Switch switch of a whip snap-crackling and the baby elephant lost in outer space mwaw-mwawing through its trunk. It's so sad! It's so beautiful and the big scary queen in goggles popping and jerking in front of Space Master and munchkins trying to feed him honey yelling Give it up! Skipping freedom for love whirling and sweating and catch an eye as someone leers up and whooosh, the light drags in slow motion and I see someone for what seems like a long long breath turning and staring into my hole with his dead hole.

And we dance away under the speakers where the big beats sick you and you rising to a puffball that fills and fills you can't take you really cannot take *Spay* Smaster *Spay* Smaster saying stop saying please dragging to the *Spay* Smaster dragging a half-lump of fucked-up beat-fucked *Spay* Smaster that saturates in the panoply and I rebound on the membrane and two girls ullulating right next to me under the ground on a Sunday afternoon and it's *freedom for love*!

Ellie gives me a dollyeye smile and I try to laugh but sand. Whirligigs intersecting bifurcating and sand sand and now the lonely elephant at the edge of the universe and my nine in my speaker and I open my eyes and it's too late it's way too late coz now I'm going up aw please and up on a big please breaking wave going up and up looming and fulminating it wants to break me apart and I will just break up. I am going to break. The wall just for a second lean just for a second and the music breaks through the holding wall of the munitions factory cataracting. And voices roar and waft roar and waft. Someone you OK? Can't speak can't move. Someone Is she OK? Can't move can't speak telling inside you can ride it baybay while racing foam fucks through the munitions

factory ridden by scaryfoam American chipmunks cute and evil with no pity screaming
lays *into* me lays *into* me lays *into* me lays *into* me lays *into* me lays *into* me lays *into* me lays *into* me lays *into* me lays *into* me lays *into* me lays *into* me lays *into* me lays *into* me lays *into* me lays *into* me lays

Gone in. Staring at muck smack thinks in a minute I'll move my head in a minute thinks soon it will be a minute a minute will pass in a minute feeling waves building and fulminating and it wants to break me apart down here on the muck breaking scaryfoam.
laysintome laysintome laysintome laysintome laysintome laysintome laysintome laysintome laysintome laysintome laysintome laysintome laysintome laysintome laysintome laysintome laysintome laysintome

Very still between nose and wall seeing floor flash onoff onoff sick-fast. See wet and dirt and silverwhite paper out of fag packets onoff onoff. Beer bottle by wall. Onoff onoff. See can't speak.
laysintomelaysintomelaysintomelaysintomelaysintomelaysintome laysintomelaysintomelaysintomelaysintomelaysintomelaysintome laysintomelaysintomelaysintomelaysintomelaysintomelaysintomelays

Sweat forming. Big drop

les sin to me *les* sin to me *les* sin to me *les* sin to me *les* sin to me *les* sin to me *les* sin to me *les* sin to me *les* sin to me *les* sin to me *les* sin to me *les* sin to me *les* sin to me *les* sin to me *les* sin to me *les* sin to me *les* sin to me *les* sin

forming, coming. Big drop

les sin to me *les* sin to me *les* sin to me *les* zinto me *les* zinto me *les* zinto me *les* zinto me *les* zinto me *les* zinto me *les* zinto me *les* zinto me *les* zinto me *les* zinto me *les* zinto me *les* zinto me *les* zinto me *les* zinto

eking forming. On the forehead. Can't move

les zen tomé *les* zen tomé *les* zen tomé *les* zen tomé *les* zen tomé *les* zen tomé *les* zen tomé *les* zen tomé *les* zen tomé *les* zen tomé *les* zen

Will pass. Time. All you have to do

les zen tomé *les* zen tomé *les* zen tomé *les* zen tomé *les* zen tomé *les* zen tomé *les* zen tomé *les* zen tomé *les* zen tomé *les* zen tomé *les* zen tomé

ride it bay.

Lei Zeng Tong May Lei Zeng Tong May Lei Zeng Tong May Lei Zeng Tong May Lei Zeng Tong May Lei Zeng Tong May Lei Zeng Tong May

Forming. Pass

they enter me they enter me they enter me they enter me they enter me they enter me they enter me they enter me they enter me they enter me they enter me they enter me they enter me they enter me they enter me

in a minute.

She OK?

Feel touching my head with minty fingers release cold nebulas of fire. Caverna. Die away and it's dark. Time creaks in here between nose and wall. Forming, forming. And outside fulminating cresting breaking. Speak! Can't speak. Don't let. Rising breaking with awesome force and they rise and they peak and they break

they end to me they end to me they en*d* me they en*d* me they en*d* me they en*d* me they en*d* me they en*d* me they en*d* me to n to me to n to me to n to me to n to me to n to me to n to me n to me n to me n t n t ntntntntntntntntntntntntntntntntntntntntntntntntntntntntntntntnt ntnt ntntntntntntntntntntntntntntntntntntntntntntntntntntntntntntntntnt

and I break.

Black dust. Under my feet. Stinging in the air. Fine as soot. I look up and see blackness and blackness into the distance. Dread. I walk. Soot drags on my feet and chokes my throat. I look left and right as I walk. I look over my shoulder. Blackness. I keep walking. Try to clear my throat. Dust too thick. Dust up to my ankles. I drag legs through. I drag air into my lungs. Soot into my lungs. Dread. I wade through dust and through nothing. Some kind of light flickering. I lose it but it comes back again. I go on. Then suddenly it is near so near I can almost touch it. The sound of flames roaring softly. Giant letters of fire. I stare at them and the letters melt in drops of flame. I come closer. The letters are forming words of burning power. I concentrate but on the brink of comprehension they move away, opening, and I pass through the fiery doors and see someone walking away from me. Try to call out. Dust cloaks my throat. He walks on. I walk after him. Drag my ankles in the dust. I mustn't lose him. I move my legs after him one in front of the other. Dust thick and heavy. Try to call out but choking. Legs getting weaker. I can't go on but the stranger walks on. Dust to the horizon but there is no horizon. Dust in my eyes. The figure stops. Try to run, catch up. Try to speak. Dust under my tongue. He stands there faint in the dark. I come closer. I can almost touch the back of his head. I am filled with terrible fear. He turns round. I see that it's him, he's here.

The drop falls and shatters in biomorphic tinkle.

I'm back.

Right by my head fingernails with hoops pierced into the ends of them. I look up the arm. A face sneers down at me. I look round and see Ellie sitting on the floor beside me smoking and looking bored. I move my lips.

'Wha'appen?'

'You spaced for hours.' She gives my arm a little pat to show me it's OK.

And nothing's changed. The clonk clonk clonk goes on as if it never stops day or night for the unconquerable Nazi war machine. Men and some women flapping their arms and staring at nothing. Cmon says Ellie. I get to my feet. I wipe my hands one by one over my buttocks.

Balls of gum, streaks of ash, smudges of oily dirt and a sweet wrapper are clinging to my white trousers. We head for the door past guys so fucked they've grown antlers and their nipples have extended in fingles. We climb up stairs slimy with sweat and gaysmuck and old bottles. We say hello to Pete the doorman and we go through and we're outside.

53

Bison had moved into his friend's flat way beyond the North Circular. I went into the kitchen. I opened the fridge and crouched down in front of it. A few things each separate in its space like in a gallery where you had to open a big heavy door to get in and it was colder and brighter than outside. Tub of margarine. Phileas Fogg taco dip. Two eggs. Carton of semi-skimmed. Veggie frankfurters. Half lemon cut side down on a saucer. Jar of capers.

I picked up each thing one after the other. Everything was past its sell-by date. The underside of the lemon was mouldy. I left the fridge and looked in the bread bin. A bag of bagels and a bit of a brownie with teethmarks in it. I took out the bagels and got the margarine from the fridge and the taco dip. I took the mould off the dip with a teaspoon. I checked the unit over the countertop. One tin. Button mushrooms. I hadn't known they came in tins. I was opening the can when the phone rang in the hall.

It was Ellie. 'Your French boyfriend rang.'

'But how could he find me?'

'Not the bard the other one, the big homo.'

'Sergei?'

'Yeah he sounded really nice. Says he wants you to style a show in Paris. He's working for some cool kind of fashion designer.'

'Brigitte Binet.'

'Whoever. But I think you better ring him back. He needs you like now.'

I looked at the button mushrooms bobbing in what could have been formaldehyde.

'So do you want the number?'
'What now?'
'Welll you haven't been home for days. You'd better call him.'
'No it's OK. I'm coming home now.'

54

'Man wants her to be charnelle, her beauty to participate in that of flowers and fruits; but she must also be smooth, hard, eternal as a pebble. The role of ornament is at the same time to make her participate more intimately in nature and to tear her from it, it is to lend to palpitating life the necessity figé of artifice. Simone de Beauvoir.'

I looked down at the sheets of information each of us had been given and translated the quote to myself while she was reading it aloud. I moved my hand over and wrote on Sergei's sheet, charnel? His pencil was motionless for a second or two above the paper. He scribbled sexual. I wrote carnal above the word charnelle on my top page.

'I asked you all before to think about this idea of women and fashion. Did anyone find it difficult?' Brigitte looked round the table. 'Good then we are going to have a big success. Sergei? Will you explain to everyone what we decided for the art direction?'

I looked down at the piece of paper. Beyond the edge of the paper I could see out-of-focus faces facing this way. His voice right next to me.

'I thought about this carnal beauty and about how fashion is to make a woman close to nature. She should be enjoyable by the senses like a fruit or a flower. OK. At the same time fashion must somehow make her more artificial.'

Brigitte tapped her nails on the tabletop. 'Yes because fashion must address our two conflicting desires. First to be something with a body. You have all see Wings of Desire? OK.'

I picked up my pencil. Under the quote I wrote Wings of Desire.

'And secondly to go beyond the carnal which must die. To be eternal.'

I wrote

1. To be in a body/nature
2. To be out of body/eternal

Sergei's voice beside me. 'So the beauty of fruits, flowers, women, and also the desire for some kind of shell beyond palpitating life. I found the idea of butterflies.'

I wrote palpitant papillons papiers paupières. On the edge of my field of vision I saw Sergei make his hands into a steeple. I began to draw small squares on the corner of the page and colour them in.

'I was thinking about Simone de Beauvoir but I was also thinking about the fabrics Brigitte has chosen to work with for this collection. She has a lot of light fabrics, quite a lot of long, loose sleeves and there is some pattern. Dieter what did you and Brigitte finally decide about the colours?'

'Black, emerald, white, metallic and there is some lapis blue now.'

'OK the blue now is even better.'

A glass half-filled with water had been placed in front of every seat at the table. He reached for his and drank some. I could hear the suppressed sound his throat made accepting each swallow. He put the glass back down on the table.

'Butterflies. It's a cliché of woman, isn't it? Little fairies dancing around pretty pretty. They don't bite or sting they just fly from flower to flower. But the more I researched butterflies the more I found butterflies have another side. Some butterflies don't drink nectar from flowers. They drink little gorgefuls from rotting bodies. Other butterflies are predators. They hunt aphids and use their trompes to pierce them and drink their internal liquids. They do it while the aphids are alive.'

'Cool!'

'Gross.' In English. It was the American girl, the intern.

'Nice butterflies huh?' Sergei smiling at her.

He opened a folder in front of him. I looked down at his hands. Long clean fingers with spatula tips. I'd forgotten about his fingers. I saw myself picking one up and putting it in my mouth. It would taste of the pencil he was holding and the stub of rubber at the end. I closed my eyes. I made myself think of a plain of grass extending for miles. His voice describing other things about butterflies. I opened my eyes. I saw the fingers pulling sheets of transparencies and sheets of paper from a folder and passing them round the table.

'So the more you learned about butterflies the more they reminded you of women?' said Dieter.

On the edge of my eye I saw Sergei's left eyelid drooping and I knew he was smiling. 'I don't know if I want to be the one to say that.'

Some of the boys giggled. I giggled.

Dieter fluttered his eyelashes sarcastically. He had traces of kohl round his eyes. I looked at Brigitte to see if she was giggling. She was holding a sheet of transparencies up to the light.

'Huh!' A boy whose name I'd forgotten. He had a big nose with nostrils pinched in like he was permanently inhaling. 'Have you read what it says here?'

'Read it out Paul.'

'The ancient Greek for soul is butterfly.' He looked up mournfully.

'Of course, because resurrection,' said a boy further up the table. 'The chrysalis. You go inside fat and stupid, you turn to boilings, you come out like wow!' He made wow with a hand through the air, following it with his eyes.

'It's interesting that you say that,' said Sergei to the boy. 'Because it says something to me. One of the strangest things I discovered in my research was about an Aztec goddess. Her name is on the sheet. Here. I don't know how to say it.' I looked at where his finger was pointing on the piece of paper. Xochiquetzal. 'On the day when young Aztec men go to battle she comes to them and makes love to them holding a living butterfly between her lips. A kiss from her lips is the promise that if they die on that day they will be born again. Though I put it here because once again, I was thinking about woman and soul.'

All the eyes at the table including Brigitte's were looking just slightly to one side of me.

'Can I say something?' It was the American girl. She spoke in

English. 'I mean can I just ask, which lips did she hold the living butterfly between? I would just think about that for a second? The living butterfly being born from the human chrysalis, the mother?' She looked from Sergei to Brigitte. 'Because you know that promise she made, was it resurrection or reincarnation? If it was reincarnation, which is by far the more sophisticated idea and I think more probable of a non-Judeo-Christian religion right? then of course she would have sex with them. Sacred sex? Because she would take them into herself and reincarnate them from the essence she took in, their DNA codes. Her promise was a little loaded? But also very beautiful. I mean the myth is probably symbolic of the love gift of their young wives.'

My pencil scratched over the paper. There was no other sound from the table. I tried to make the pencil very light. I drew tiny wispy lines.

Someone blew a raspberry. From the other side of the table someone said: 'Fine but how does this relate to fashion?' I recognised Dieter's voice.

'Well Dieter I'm majoring in comparative religions and fashion so I guess they must link somewhere.'

Dieter gave out a fragment of ironic laugh.

'What she says is fantastic.' I glanced up. Brigitte was looking at Sergei.

'Yeah it's great,' he said. 'Thank you Jude.'

'Maybe at the end what do you think?' said Brigitte. 'Or is it too much already?'

'Why not talk about what we found for now in terms of the art direction and then see if we can make more later? So the idea on the transparencies comes from seeing a moth inside the abat-jour at night. When the moth is backlit from the light it throws a big shadow on the abat-jour. And it's simple to make the projected shadows immense.'

'How big?' said someone.

'Well for the show I want to make them big enough so that crawling on a giant lightbox behind the girls the butterflies look like their predators.'

'Great.'

'May I suggest something?' said Dieter. 'I really think this idea is great and we should work it through on the clothes. You talk about the rigidity of artifice.' He looked at Brigitte. I wrote rigid above figé on the piece of paper. 'Could we bring this out with some hard shell jackets over some of the floaty pieces? I love your sculptural pieces. I think you do those incredible and we don't have any in this show.'

Dieter glanced round the table. I found myself nodding. Brigitte put her pencil against her lips.

'You mean for these jackets to be the chrysalis?'

'Yeah. I love that chrysalis of death thing.'

'Yeah it's really cool,' said a boy with a jet-black quiff a bit like Dieter's.

'Yeah can you just see all these women walking round Paris wearing the chrysalis of death?' Another boy.

Everyone started talking. I caught Jude's eye. We smiled. I bent my head back over the sheet of paper and let my pencil wander into another drawing. As my arm moved it brushed Sergei's sleeve now and then.

'I'll have to think about it.' Brigitte's loud voice. 'Chrysalis. Butterfly. Hard. Soft. Maybe it's a bit obvious. Butterfly should be the inspiration not blueprint. OK?'

'Absolutely,' said Dieter.

'Tell them about the sound element,' she said.

'Yes, Thierry,' said Sergei, 'I need to talk to you about this. At the beginning I want the audience in complete darkness. Keep it going for a bit too long. Then they begin to hear a sound. At first it's faint. It should grow from something you ignore like humming of machinery. Then it becomes a bit more intrusive and at a certain point you yourself you have to say What is this? It gets louder and louder till it's uncomfortable. It's their wings and their antennae scratching each other. It will make people feel like things are crawling over them.'

'Nice,' said Thierry. 'Maybe I can also work some of those sounds into the tracks later on.'

'Good,' said Brigitte.

'Yeah that would be great. So here's the plan. Just something simple. Because the idea as I understand it from Brigitte is that you take a concept and use it to make the images work. It's not about showing a concept or generating more concepts. It's finally about kicking the concept away and the image stands alone. OK?'

I felt him look round the table. I kept my head low doodling and feeling almost woozy as his voice fluctuated next to me and I brushed his sleeve every now and then.

'So here's the plan. First, dark. Then, sounds in the dark. Then the lightbox at the back of the catwalk lights up slowly. I'm talking about a lightbox metres long and metres high. At first the lightbox is dim so you can't see what's happening on it just shadows. Then it gets clearer and you can see that the shadows are gigantic butterflies. You realise that what looks and sounds horrific is butterflies. Then the girls start to come out onto the catwalk from either side of the lightbox. We take the lightbox up to pure white – sustain it – and cut. The girls proceed.'

A guy was waving his pencil in the air. 'Can I say? The girls will be backlit by the lightbox. We need to light them at the front for the photographers.'

'Sure. That's a good point. We can work it out.' Sergei looked round the table. 'What does everyone think?'

I half-raised my eyes so I was looking at a patch of melamine in the middle of the table. I could see a blurry Dieter agitating his chin up and down in the glossy surface. Brigitte brought both her palms down. I felt it under my elbow.

'It has fear, it has beauty, it has motion, it has this important new sound element. I love it.'

There was a pause, then talking burst out. I let the French act as white noise. I wrote motion/sound. Sergei's voice next to me louder. The talking stopped.

'these five traps at different points. Until now all the models will have avoided stepping on the traps.'

'Oh yeah?' said someone. 'For models it is already difficult to walk straight.' Everyone laughed and I made gentle laughing motions with my upper body.

'Yeah we will have to rehearse them more than usual. I mean it's a serious point. Maybe we could have red crosses on the traps, they will be above the eye level of the audience. Or something more infallible. Paul?'

'Yeah I will work something out.'

'So there it is, the last five girls coming along the catwalk and then, at spaces along it, each one knocks her foot on a trapdoor to release a burst of butterflies. Hundreds of butterflies. One colour from each trap. Emerald, white, metallic, blue. I'm not sure about black.'

Someone started to clap and in ones and twos everyone joined in. I put down my pencil and clapped. I looked at Sergei. He was saying something to Dieter. I bet Dieter fancies him. The clapping stopped and the talking began again. I let my pencil scribble over the rest of the paper. It made a regular scratchy noise across the surface making another butterfly. The wings were scratching on each other dislodging the scales like tiny fingernails that covered their surface. Scales falling on me and things scratching and scraping. A close-furred body under my arm. I jump. A sharp thing scraping across my throat. A bang and a burst of light. I panic. I try to move. Red butterflies beating their wings around me. We bang into each other, raising microclouds of dust as we try to get away. A volume of cool air. A loud whooshing noise. I look towards the source of the sound and see a gigantic brown column swinging up towards me. I push down harder into the wings but I'm slow. The column powers through. Butterflies plunge forward on the pressure wave coming off it. Some fall and lie on the ground. Others right themselves and stagger away across a dark tent. Blurred faces below, open mouths. Flying intently, flying fast, hitting heavy canvas, beating against it, looking for a gap. I fall down onto the floor. I try hard but I beat feebly. The noise of the audience getting to their feet. The reverberation of stilettoes striking the floor. I flinch something off. The crunching sound they make as they step on

'Naomi?'

I flinch it off.

'Naomi.'

I looked up and for a fraction of a second I didn't recognise him.

'Brigitte wants to know what you think for the styling.' He was talking to me in English.

All eyes at the table on me. I kept looking at Sergei. 'I just got here.'

'Just start with something general.' Quietly in English.

'Uh.' I looked down at the sheet of paper. I saw a girl I'd drawn with a butterfly on her throat sticking its proboscis into her. 'Vampire butterflies,' I said. 'No. No. Let me just start by apologising for my poor French. Um.' I cleared my throat. 'You know how butterflies uh.' I turned to Sergei and said in English, 'Land on? Atterrir?'

'Se posent.'

'I'm going to start by imagining the girls as branches that the butterflies suppose on like flowers.' I tried not to catch Brigitte's eye but without avoiding her.

'Living flowers which takes us back to Simone de Beauvoir's idea about women and uh fashion. So we attach butterflies to accessories. A choker, a hairclip, what's buckles? Yup OK of their shoes. I really like the idea of living butterflies at foot level. And maybe some on their socks, they could wear little socks but I'd have to see the clothes in more detail um'

A snapping sound. A small squeal. I followed the sound with my eyes. Someone was unscrewing the top of a Perrier bottle. He lifted the bottle and poured water into his glass. It hissed.

Dieter did a high-pitched offkey 'Mmmm?' Then he did singsong. 'Pretty-pretty, girl-girl.'

'Yes. No. I completely agree. And this is why I need to think it out more.' Someone sighed. 'But I was interested in what Jude had to say. The idea of carrying a live accessory that is so fragile and that contains in itself the promise of rebirth. But also' – I tried to ignore the sets of eyes – 'death. The butterflies should be sinister. And I think maybe they could go from sinister at the beginning to to the opposite of sinister at the end, joy maybe, so when the girls liberate these butterflies from inside the catwalk it's rebirth.'

I glanced down at the paper. 'So at the beginning maybe nets round the girls' heads with butterflies inside them. Suffocating. Or even inside space hats. The things astronauts. Well maybe not. Butterflies could cover a décolleté like a of bees. Butterflies actually coming out of their mouths towards the end. So each girl will have to have some kind of apparatus in her mouth to protect them.'

Brigitte's clear voice. 'No we don't need that.'

'No. But basically I am attracted to the idea of accessorising the girls with palpitating life. Since they already have the rigidity of artifice.'

'How already the rigidity of artifice?' Her voice strong.

'From the clothes, the make-up, everything about fashion.'

'Well.' I could see she was searching for my name. 'We already have real butterflies in the show. Where is the styling?'

Sergei's voice. 'Her idea of using real butterflies as accessories has narrative potential.'

Narrative potential. I wanted to write the words down next to palpitant.

Brigitte's nails tapping the tabletop. 'Maybe it has narrative but will it detract from the butterflies at the finale?'

'You could run the styling butterflies in the two earlier passages.' The one with light brown hair.

'Yes but the catharsis,' said Dieter. He shook his head.

'I don't know, the show is quite long and there is a gap between the lightbox at the opening and then the finale,' said Sergei. 'We have to keep the butterfly idea going in some way.'

Her fingernails clattered. 'But this is too literal. You know a butterfly on the *sock*.' She made a French kind of a noise.

I sat as still as possible. It was only now that I didn't have to make the effort to talk that I realised how sore my cheeks were. They all started talking at once. I felt a hand on my lower back tracing my spine.

55

We went to the Moroccan café round the corner. I ripped open a sachet of brown sugar and stirred it into my coffee while Sergei chatted to the owner. You are desperate for cash. Cash. All you want is cash. OK you get shit cash doing this but it's supposed to give you some kind of prestige. You use the prestige to get more cash. You need cash to pay off the rent you owe Ellie. You use the knock-on cash to get your own place. Without cash 7-Eleven. You're doing this for cash and it's not much to do for cash. It's what you're trained in. It's life. Do it. Take it. Get the cash.

He sat down.

'I don't think she's crazy about me.' Tried to laugh.

'No I don't know it's just maybe she likes to be the only woman. She thinks it gives her a kind of special vision.'

'That was horrible. And I don't even speak French.'

'You speak enough. And it's so sweet you know the way you do it.' My left hand was lying on the table. He picked it up and kissed the palm. He rubbed my fingers' ends on his cheek.

'Lets not go back. Lets go for a walk or go and see a movie.'

'We can't now. Maybe tomorrow night. Would you like to meet Jean-Marie?'

I opened my eyes wider. 'I'd love to. Would it be OK?'

'He really wants to meet you.'

'Why don't we get Sylvie along as well?'

'She's not in Paris. Anyway I would like it to be just us.'

'OK. Lets do it then. Excuse me a minute.' I got up. The tables had been crammed in to the café and I had to squeeze between our table and the next table and then move a chair to get out. While I was moving the chair I said: 'I you know told her about you and Jean-Marie when she was in London. It just came out.'

'It's OK. She told me.'

'You're not angry?' I tipped the chair at the next furthest along table.

'No I'm not angry. Actually you did me a favour. I love this.' He tappped the back pocket of my jeans. I looked over my shoulder.

'Oh yeah.'

'What is it?'

'Part of a poem.'

'It's French.'

'Yeah. I just wrote it in biro. It might come off.' I carried on manoeuvring between the tables.

'You wrote it?'

I was trying to think of something to say but before I could get any words together my trajectory carried me down the narrow stairs to the toilet.

56

I met them in the bar of an old cinema that showed arty films. They were both wearing trenchcoats. Sergei's was the classic colour and Jean-Marie's was darker. When I came in they were directly in front of me each with one elbow on the bar and looking at each other. Behind them the rows of bottles on shelves in front of a mirrored wall. I was wearing my seventies dress and Ellie's cowboy boots.

'Here she is,' said Sergei.

Jean-Marie straightened himself off the bar. He had enormous eyes and enormous lips. He planted a big kiss on both my cheeks. 'You are just how I hoped you would be.'

'No you are way too nice.'

'He is nice, he is so nice,' said Sergei.

We stood there all smiling.

'He thinks so much of you,' said Jean-Marie gazing at me from big eyes.

'Well and you. Your story is so romantic.'

'He is very romantic.' He looked at Sergei.

'He is amazing.' I looked at Sergei. I heard my voice come out low in a way that made me marvel. 'You are very lucky.'

'Stop it,' said Sergei. 'What would you like to drink?'

'Whisky straight up,' I said out of nowhere. It was an old man's drink but it was Greta Garbo's drink.

We sat in the back row against the wall. If I cocked my head back far enough I could see the light from the projector shooting out through a square hole just above our heads. It was full of moving dust motes. I imagined they were phantom images moving onto the screen and being replaced by new motes at quantum speed so we didn't realise they were different ones. It was funny how the moment the light left the square hole it formed a cone. Why didn't it come out the shape it was moulded into like extruded pastry? Or was it because the lens was round stupid? And if the lens were square? So why's the image on the wall rectangular? Then I looked at the screen and wondered where the old image went when the new one hit the screen a millisecond later. Then I looked at all the heads in front of me watching what was happening on the screen like it mattered incredibly. Then I looked at the back of the seat in front which was empty. When my eyes got used to the darkness at that level I let them glance below the seatbacks. I saw Sergei's knees and how they jutted out beyond mine and to the right of the knees I could make out that they were holding hands.

57

I pushed my suitcase into a corner of the hallway and went into the living room. I picked up the phone and dialled Dan.

'Hello?'

'It's me.'

I felt him readjust. 'Why are you calling?'

'I never thanked you for the roses.'

'That was months ago.'

'I know but it's not easy to call you.'

He didn't say anything.

'I've just been in Paris. Remember when we went?'

'Yeah.'

'Well so. How are you?'

'What I find strange, what I can't get my head around is that I'm not able to sleep with you any more and I'm sleeping with someone else and so are you.'

'I'm not sleeping with someone else.'

'Oh come on. I don't know why you bother to lie about it.'

'I still love you.' I hung up. I listened to the birds in the trees outside. The phone rang.

'Why did you say that?' he said.

'I don't know, I'm sorry. It was a wrong thing to say.'

'Well why say it then?'

'Because it's true.'

'So are you saying we should get back together?'

'No. I can't. I shouldn't have said it. I'm stupid and pathetic.'

'I could have told you that.'

'Sorry.'

'Do you know what? You are a total bitch. Fuck off and don't ring me again.'

He hung up. The birds gabbled outside. The same two or three notes over and over. I got up and went into the bathroom. I unrolled a length of toilet paper and blew my nose. The phone rang. I stood there staring in the mirror hearing the rings. I went back into the living room and snatched up the receiver.

'But what, you're allowed to ring me?'

I could hear him breathing at the other end.

'Dan? I'm sorry.'

'You are crying.'

'Who is this?'

There was no answer.

'Eric.'

'Yes.'

'I can't talk to you now.'

'Please.'

'Please just go away.'

'May I speak with you for a moment?'

'How did you get this number?'

'From your office. You have not worked there since a long time.'

'No.'

'Naomi.' My name.

'Eric I can't talk to you. I can't.'

'Please don't cry.'

I listened to the loud twittering of the birds in the trees. 'OK. Say what you have to say.'

Silence at the other end.

'How's your life?'

I thought I could hear his breathing.

'I'm asking because your letters worry me. You wrote that you'd dropped out of university. Left.'

His voice far away. 'Yes.'

'That upset me.'

Nothing at the other end.

'How do you survive Eric? What are you doing?'

'I write.'

'Do you have a girlfriend yet?'

He stuttered.

'Do you have a girlfriend?'

'No.'

'It's three years since I saw you. And you don't have a girlfriend. Are you listening?'

'Yes.'

'It makes me feel bad, do you understand? Remember what you wrote, how to live without love? On that piece of paper you left in my bedroom?'

A sound at the other end.

'Are you gay?'

'Excuse me?'

'Are you homosexual, you know, do you secretly like boys but haven't told your maman?'

'Naomi.'

I felt something tighten in my throat. 'Just answer!'

'No.'

'I bet you are. I bet you are and you're doing some weird subliminal shit on me. You need a therapist.'

'I don't want to lose pain. You are being banal.'

'Thanks. Have you ever had a girlfriend?'

Nothing.

'Answer.'

'Yes.'

'Did you write her poems?'

He hesitated. 'Yes.'

'Yes? Yes? Well that's easy then, go away and write them to her or someone else OK? You don't need me.'

Noises at the other end.

'Are you crying?'

I tried to control myself.

'Are you crying?'

'No.'

'Oh for God's sake.'

'I am burning.'

Honestly. Pathetic. 'Burning for what? You write poems to other girls. Why disturb me?'

'When I was sixteen. This is different. How can I tell you?'

'Eric I have to be cruel to be kind, you know this expression?'

'Yes. I understand this is what you are doing. You have a pure heart.'

'No. I am not the pure damsel of your dreams. You wouldn't like the way I live my life. I take drugs, I sleep with strangers.'

'It's not a question of that what you are doing. You cannot stop it.'

I hung up. I went into the bathroom. I blew my nose on a length of toilet paper. I stared into the toilet. I went back into the living room and lit a cigarette. Inside the flat it was almost dark. The birds were still at it in the trees. I smoked. I looked down at the patch of grass. Only a couple of weeks ago I'd gone onto it. You had to go round to the main road and cross the low wall to get onto the grass, you couldn't get there direct from the flats. I stood under the tree closest to the flats so as to be less visible from the road. The light under it was green-tinted. It had been raining that morning. I pressed the trunk and put my nose against it to smell it. Sour and slightly sad. I went up on tiptoe and broke off a bunch of leaves. They were surprisingly hard to break off, swishing about and the half-soft stem connecting them to the branch refusing to snap. The phone was ringing. They had dropped grime and small yellow curls on me and when I finally tore them off sticky white stuff oozed onto my hand from the snapped end. I looked at the phone. I couldn't believe how simple they were more like plans for a leaf than leaves.

'Yes hello.'

'It's me.'

'Hi Eric.'

'You are wearing a black on top, a leotard, and a skirt of white lace. The sun make the shadow of the lace to dance on your leg. I stare for maybe three minutes and it's true not only me but it's Georges who is looking at you also.'

'Georges?'

'The other one on reception. He turn to me and he say something I cannot repeat to you.'

'No go on.'

'It's too banal.'

'No tell me.'

'Then we hear your taxi stop on the street and Georges and me we make the same move to go out from the desk. There is a fight you don't see and I run pass you. But I go too fast and I run straight against the taxi. The driver put his head out of the window and say that if I want to end this life it is preferable to use a car that is moving.'

I laughed. I heard him laugh at the other end.

'I open the door of the taxi and you come and you stand in front of me. You look in my eyes and at that moment you say something I never forget.'

'Yes?'

'Thank you.'

I was about to laugh again but I didn't.

'It was three years on this day.'

I looked out at the tower block. The stairwell lights were on all the way to the top in a thin stack. Twenty floors forty lights. No, two weren't working. Quite a few lights on in the flats as well. People having their dinner on their knees in front of the telly. People having showers. Old people who lived alone. People putting their kids to bed. People not sure what to do.

'Eric, I don't understand why you are doing this. Sometimes I feel irritated by it. Sometimes I feel sad. Sometimes I think you have written the most beautiful things I've ever read.' I waited. 'I always think you have courage. Please listen carefully. It must stop now.'

He didn't say anything.

'I can't let it be because of me that you are ruining your life. Poetry isn't life. It's like its opposite. Have you slept with anyone in the last three years?'

He didn't say anything.

'Just tell me the truth.'

'No.'

I tried to console myself. 'Well you know I'm not sure that's good for you. Because for what exactly?'

He didn't speak.

'Eric?'

'Because it is a lie. How to treat someone like that?'

'Look I want you to be free of this. Me too. Stop writing the poems, at least the ones that need me.'

'They all need you.'

'But now things have to change.' I could tell he was in a state. 'Look Eric, I don't want you to stop writing poems. It's incredible what you've done. It's like a feat. Do you know that word?'

He didn't speak.

'But the price is too high. I've made up my mind. I won't receive any more.'

I heard him crying. 'By poetry I come near you.'

I made my voice harder. 'No. It's an illusion.'

Faint crying sounds.

'Eric?' I strained my ears. 'Eric?'

Nothing at the other end.

'Look. You can send me one more poem and I will receive it.'

'How?'

'What do you mean how?'

'Will you receive it into your heart?'

'Yes into my heart. But only if you promise to send no more and not to ring here again.'

'You don't know how much you are alone.'

'What?'

'You hurt yourself. You are not free.'

'That isn't true. I'm going.'

'No!'

'I'm sorry. I don't love you. I don't want this.' I had to raise my voice over the strange sound he was making. 'We will never be together, ever. I'm going for ever now.'

He was wailing. I hung up.

Tears began to roll down my face. I got up and went into the kitchen. I put the kettle on. The phone started ringing. I looked out of the narrow window into the well. It was completely dark in there. Ring. Ring. I got out one of the special thin cups and saucers. Ring. I opened the canister with the teabags. Ring. I opened the cutlery drawer and chose a spoon. Ring. Some of them were really tragic spoons ring that could break your heart. Free with petrol spoons ring. Pressed from some lo-grade metal. Ring. I looked for the really ring ring lovely spoons that looked as if they belonged to someone's grandma ring mine or Ellie's I couldn't remember. Ring.

I marched into the living room and grabbed the receiver. At the other end I heard the lightest movement that could have been him trying not to cry. I waited. It continued. I screamed into the mouthpiece and slammed the receiver down. I marched into the kitchen. I reached the countertop. It started to ring again. The kettle clicked to off. Ring. I poured the water into the cup with the teabag. Ring. Ring. Tears rolled down my face. I turned round and went back into the living room.

'Leave me alone.'

'Nay–'

'Fuck off!'

I threw the phone across the room. I grabbed the sides of my face and screamed something at the phone on the floor. I ran across and kicked the phone. It made small ringing sounds. The jack came out of the wall. I turned to the table and I saw the computer keyboard sitting there. I grabbed it and pulled it out of its socket in the display monitor and threw it. It smashed on the wall above the bar fire and fell on the floor.

58

7-Eleven came in. I was bundled up in a corner of the sofa holding a bottle of wine by the neck. Telly.

'Awright?' Taking in the bottle. He went and got himself a beer from the fridge. He threw himself down beside me. I moved slightly away.

It was a programme about wild horses somewhere like Hungary, somewhere I hadn't realised there were wild horses. They did things like rear up and fight on rocky outcrops. You saw them tossing their heads and galloping about under thunderstorms. It was like there were live wires whipping around inside them and touching off against each other. A young stallion raided an old stallion's brood of mares. He cut one out of the herd baring his crude square teeth and giving high-pitched screams, jostling and nipping her away until that was it, she was split off from her family and away with him on some bare mountainside.

'Anything else on?'

'I'm watching this. It's good.'

We watched the telly.

'You OK?'

'Yup.' I stared at the screen.

'Where's Ellie?'

'PR dinner. Some perfume shit.'

He got out some spliff started rolling. 'Something happen when you was over there?'

'No. Nothing. Watch the telly.'

He finished his beer. 'How's the wine?'

'Want some?'

'Don't mind if I do.'

'Get a glass then.'

He went to the kitchen came back with two glasses. Later we drank the other bottle in the fridge. We smoked a couple of spliffs. He made me laugh telling me stories about things at the Light Rums while I was away.

'So then Joanne right? She gets up on the table and she kicks the glasses off of it right? One after the other. Smash. Smash. Smash. Smash. She's getting to the last couple of glasses and he's saying do that one more time if you're bad, just do that one more time lady. Just one more time if you're bad. And she lifts up one of her feet right with these five inch heels, she'

I came to with a jerk like when you come awake and think you're falling. I realised that sometime during his telling this story or maybe the last story he must have started stroking my thigh. Because there it was his hand, big and unexpectedly light. I shook my head as if I was paying attention to the story. I pulled myself together inside. If I said anything now he would be hurt. He would tell me he was just relaxing, I was such a madam. When he had gone to such lengths to make me feel better, sensing I was low, making me laugh, making me drinks, offering to go and get a Chinese takeaway even, but I didn't want one. He was being kind and now because he was having a nice time and he was a bit stoned he was stroking my thigh, maybe he hadn't even noticed that he was doing it himself, maybe he was being matey. I decided to act a bit drunker and mored stoned than I was as though I hadn't noticed. Then in a minute when he'd finished this Joanne story, he was just a minute away from finishing this Joanne story, I could get up as if naturally and go and run a bath, lock the door. Until she came back. Just less than a minute from now.

'Think he done right?' he said.

I opened my mouth to reply. I saw his head coming at me in a blur, his eyes bloodshot and out of focus, his nostrils from this angle huge. I could see his teeth as they bore down on me and then his mouth was on mine. Half a second later his tongue bitter with weed and wine burst into me. I choked. I felt his body across me.

I thought, if you think about it, this is a pretty strange way to show that you are physically attracted to another person. What would they make of it in Papua, New Guinea? In Papua, New Guinea they would never put their tongue into another person's mouth. Over there they insert, they use, their fingers instead. But only the fingers of the right hand. The fingers of the left hand they use to wipe their arses. So if someone in Papua, New Guinea wants to really insult you he doesn't have to start shouting and swearing he just jabs in the direction of your lips with the fingers of his left hand. You go ape. It's war. The tongue. That goes into the armpit where it wiggles about licking off any human juices that the Papua, New Guineans love as much as a just-made cup of coffee. The light which had been blocked by 7-Eleven's head returned red through my closed eyelids. His weight slid half-off. I tensed against the sofa then I felt his teeth on my top, his nose pushing the fabric up. I felt his lips settle round a nipple.

59

About a third of the tables were occupied. I saw Sylvie by the back wall with her head leaning against chipped tiles across which galloping horses were painted. She was wearing a satin dress in a colour somewhere between peach and aubergine. When she saw me she stood up and I saw the dress was closed down the front by nothing more than a couple of carefully-placed kilt pins.

Almost the first thing she said was, 'You know Sergei and me are not talking?'

I said he had told me. Her face was strong, I decided, but in the close light of the candle there were shadows under her eyes and wrinkles at the sides. You should stop wearing kohl, I thought, at your age.

'Please tell me.'

'He seems to think you've let him down somehow. Sorry Sylvie. He sounded like he would get over it.'

'Get over it!' She poured me a glass of wine. I suddenly remembered the black ribbon round her thigh. All this time and I'd never found out what it was about. I started to ask but she leaned forward over the table talking quickly. How he'd come to her months ago desperate about the show. Brigitte was a nightmare, she was paranoid. One minute she wanted one thing, the next minute she wanted the opposite. It was his big break, he had never got his degree, he'd left college to go and work with Sylvie – she raised an eyebrow – he could handle the clothes, there he felt confident, but what about the mise-en-scène for the show? Would Sylvie help him? The waitress came for our order. Sylvie said I should try the rabbit in chocolate sauce.

'I was happy, Noy-me. I said of course. I have an idea inspired by a little art show I saw in New York. They project shadows of creatures on a white window, lighted from inside. You walk on the street and look at the window and you can see these small, but small, microscopic animals, moving like crazy. Only now they look as big as your head. Invisible things become visible as shadows. So I say I want to do it but with butterflies. The other one is better of course, but butterflies will work better for the Binet show. Sergei loved it.'

I let my eyes creep above her head. There were dark stains embedded between the tiles, on the grouting.

'We work on it. We have the idea of butterflies coming from the floor in clouds of colour. I research everything, you know, where to get the butterflies, which ones are good, which ones will still be alive at the time of the show. Some they must have a prolongation of their time in the chrysalide so they don't die before. I discover how, everything.'

Someone brought two plates to the table covered in a thick black stew. Bittersweet steam came off the plates.

'But then, before I meet with Brigitte, he come to me and he say she don't want to work with someone else. So he is sorry. I can't do it.'

I put a forkful of stew in my mouth. I tried to figure out if I could taste chocolate.

'I have spend weeks working only on this. So I ask Sergei, are you going to use my idea? Because if you are going to use it, you must pay me for that, you must make credit to me for that. So he go away and he come back and he say there is no money because Brigitte refuse to pay. She told him she never confirm that he can work with me.'

'For God's sake.'

'He said he don't know what idea they will use for the show. There is nothing more he can do.'

I scanned the grouting between the tiles. I could taste cinnamon, chilli, meat, maybe cream. 'But this doesn't sound like Sergei.'

'He told you about this?'

'No he didn't.'

'Is he using the butterflies?'

'Sylvie I can't, you know, I'm not supposed to talk about it to anyone. It's a job.'

Her eye looked ancient.

'Don't Sylvie.'

'So, he is using it.'

'Well. In a way.'

'I will speak to him.' She cut a piece of meat and pushed it to the side of her plate.

'If you talk to him he'll know I've told you.'

'No, I won't talk to him. My lawyer will make contact.'

I put my knife and fork down. 'He'll fire me, he'll have to. And he'll never speak to me again.'

'How can I permit he treats me like this? If I do something, it's wrong. If I don't do something, it's wrong. Why let him walk on me?'

'I wish I'd never got into this.'

'Me too.'

She rested her head against the galloping horses.

'Let me talk to him first,' I said.

60

Bright sun beaming off hi-gloss walls: snazzy studio Binet. Patches of black wavering on them: boys reflected. Surreal series of frozen hairdos: the boys. Kawaii miaowing: the sound system. Underfed over-long girls: the models. They stood around the big central melamine table waiting for their cue. One was wearing a string of paper butterflies round her neck. One had a couple of chicken-feather butterflies on her socks. Two held plastic butterflies by the legs between their teeth. One had a veil over her head with chicken-feather butterflies underneath. A couple had stiff wires going up from their wrists above head height with plastic globes on the end full of plastic butterflies.

Dieter gave the cue. The girls lined up tottering from side to side. One by one they launched into walking the length of the studio. Some stumbled. Some bumped into various boys. One hit the far end wall with her face but then it was so white and shiny maybe she was blinded.

'Why can't they just walk man?' Jude whispered to me.

I hunched my shoulders. Maybe they are stupefied with boredom. Maybe they are embarrassed to be so beyond beautiful that if they mated with normal men you'd get the human equivalent of mules. Maybe it's the shoes.

'Naomi. What works and what doesn't. The raz-cou?' Brigitte chopped the flat of her hand through the air. 'Cut it. The lips? Too goth.'

'But the Aztec goddess,' said Jude.

'What's razcoo?' I whispered to her.

'The net? It could work. The wire going up. Why the balls? The butterflies should be on invisible threads flying from the girls' fingers.'

'Much better,' said Sergei.

I swallowed. 'I know but I can't do that.'

'Naomi it's not difficult. You attach thread.'

A cute Japanese voice said Moto moto! Miaow miaow! Miaow miaow!

'It's not that. I'm questioning the whole idea of using butterflies.'

The boys all subtly turned their heads so they could see Brigitte and me in one look. The girls continued to lurch up and down staring at the end walls.

'What's wrong with butterflies?' said Dieter.

'Their wings will break. Their legs will break. They'll be crushed under people's feet. It will be a massacre.'

'A massacre of insects,' said Brigitte.

Moto moto! Miaow Miaow!

'Like flies or mosquitoes. Or cockroaches,' said a voice.

'Have you ever sprayed flies in your kitchen?'

'What if you had lice? Would you keep them?'

Some people laughed.

'You are Buddhist?' said the boy with the pinched-in nostrils.

'No I'm not Buddhist.'

'Do you eat meat?'

Miaow miaow!

'There's fur in the show.'

'Yes but I didn't kill it!' My voice going up.

Brigitte walked up to the nearest model and ripped the net off the girl's head. It caught in her hair. The girl half-ran after the net being pulled away in Brigitte's hand.

'Putain de merde!' She threw the net back in the girl's face and walked out of the room.

Moto moto moto!

'Naomi do you know about the silk?' The nostrils boy, Paul. He pulled his chair up to me. 'You know they boil the baby butterflies who are alive inside the cocoon.'

'I didn't know.' Upset that I didn't know about silk. Do I care about grubs inside balls of silk? Were they unconscious? Or were they like in a vegetable state, aware but unable to communicate? Did that matter because they were grubs anyway? But they were also butterflies? But pre-butterflies are not butterflies? Does that make them equivalent to embryos and silk-making like a mass abortion? A mass abortion of insects.

Sergei sat down next to me. 'Naomi it's not like they are puppies. I know they are beautiful.'

'I'm sorry. I can't. I can't do it.'

'Naomi.' He held my hand. I noticed I was shivering. 'They don't live very long anyway. They hatch from the chrysalis, they breed and after days they die. Some don't even have mouths because they don't live long enough to need food.'

'Great, anorexics,' said Dieter in the background.

'Well all the more reason why they need every hour they've got.'

'She's right. This is sick,' said Jude. She leaned into me from the other side and whispered, 'They eat fuckin horses what do you expect?'

'It was your idea to use living accessories,' said Sergei.

'I didn't think. It's because I didn't have time to think.' He stroked my hand. 'So I suppose I should leave now?'

He shook his head. 'Jude, you will be in charge of the welfare of the insects. I want you to work with the butterfly handlers to find a sanctuary for them to go to afterwards and also, to draw up a code of conduct for how we treat them while they are here.'

'No problem.'

'I can't do the thread thing.'

'We don't do the thread thing. We'll talk to the people who work with butterflies and we'll draw up a code.'

'Brigitte.'

'I'll talk to Brigitte. Is it OK Naomi?'

He was still stroking my hand.

'Yes it's OK. I'm sorry.'

Later I made myself go up to his desk. His head was bent over some drawings. His hand holding a pencil. Quick or you won't.

'I saw Sylvie last night.'

He was marking up the drawing with questions each identified by a letter inside a circle. A B C. 'How was she?'

'The truth is she was very upset. She said.' I looked round to make sure no one was in earshot, 'That basically you asked her to work on the art direction and she came up with the idea of butterfl'

'Lets go and have a coffee.'

He didn't look at me as we walked down the stairs and along the street. He walked along with his hands in his pockets. We turned the corner and went into the Moroccan café. I squeezed in to the same table as before. Sergei sat down opposite me.

'What did Sylvie say?'

I told him.

'You believe that?'

'How could I not believe it? It's Sylvie.'

'It's not exactly the truth. We had the idea together. We worked completely together every step of the way so that it would be hard to remember exactly which part of which idea came from who.'

'But the original idea she got from an art show in New York. That was her idea.'

'Yes she suggested to use something like those microscopic creatures. Anyone could have said that just in passing.'

'Yes but you hired her to come up with an idea and she did. She worked on it for weeks.'

'She started to do it, then it developed after she left. It didn't take weeks.'

'You should credit her for the work she's done.'

'What are you saying? There should be a name credit on the invitation and in every interview about the art direction?'

'Kind of.'

'In a fantasy world yes, but this doesn't happen in reality. It's my fault I know. I have to make it up to Sylvie another way but she won't talk to me.'

'She's really hurt.'

'I want to credit her but Brigitte won't have it. She calls her that crazy old woman.'

'She's a monster.'

'I know. What can I do?'

I tried to think of something more. 'You should make it clear anyway, if anyone interviews you or anything.'

'You don't make this stuff public. I will give her money but that's private between Sylvie and me. It's just a job. Sylvie gets carried away.'

I cast around for something. 'In a way you have to get carried away. It's that kind of job.'

'Did she tell you she doesn't work for Vogue any more?'

'I didn't ask.'

'You know I love Sylvie, I owe her everything. But I have to face reality.' I wanted to touch his face just for a second. 'I have a job to do, you too.'

61

I got a taxi from Waterloo straight to the Light Rums and saw Mo drying glasses behind the bar and Ellie already on one of the sofas at the back. I went up to the bar and ordered a rum toddy.

'Summer cold?' said Mo.

'Psychic ills.'

'Just the job.'

'Ellie?'

'She has her drink. You go over, I'll bring it.'

I pulled my wheelie-bag up to the sofa and gave Ellie a hug.

'How was it?'

'That woman. And then the animal rescue bit.'

'You told them?'

'Welll kind of. How's it been here?'

'Drama. Big row with Seven. We'll talk about it.'

I examined her face.

'And Eric, big dramas with Eric.'

'You spoke to Eric?'

'I spoke to Eric like hourly. But I've sorted Eric. It's all going to be OK from now on.'

Mo came up and crouched by the coffee table. He lifted the toddy off his tray. 'Here you go my lovely.'

'Are you OK?' I said to her. She looked pale, that was what I noticed. She had dark circles under her eyes. But then I thought, maybe she always has dark circles under her eyes and I only notice now because I've been away.

'I'm in a bit of a state. I got pills.'

'How do you mean?'

'From the doctor. I've been given anti-depressants.'

'Since when?'

'I've just started taking them.'

'But since when have you been depressed? I mean more than usual?'

She laughed.

'Ell.' I put my arm round her. 'What's up?'

'So Eric. Aren't you interested?'

'Yes but I'm thrown by you being depressed.'

'I'm more fragile than depressed.'

'It's not just the comedowns?'

'I don't think so unless they start to spread over the whole week after a while. The doc said I just needed some coping mechanisms until I could sort it out. So Eric.'

'Yes. What happened?'

'The night you went back to Paris he rang again. I know you said just to yell and hang up but I thought no I'll be reasonable. He said was I Ellie? and I said yes and that you weren't there.'

'But how did he know your name?'

'When he'd rung the magazine they'd told him that he should talk to me, you were staying with me. I suppose once he had my name he must have rung Directory Enquiries.'

'You didn't say I was in Paris?'

'No I said you were staying over at your boyfriend, Bison's – you see I stuck close to truths – and why was he stalking you like this?'

'That's a bit strong.'

'What do you think the police would make of this?'

'Officer officer a boy keeps writing me poems.'

'No but if he keeps calling all the time it could be harrassment. He asked all about you. I told him he was abusing your niceness. He said something about he didn't want to hurt you in any way. Then he had the cheek to ask if I would send him a photo of you. I said he had to stop sending you stuff. Then he got angry and said I didn't understand anything about love, about art, or about you either and that this was the most important thing in life. More important than life. So I said if you ring this number again I'll change it. I hung up and the next day he rang again saying he wanted to apologize and I told him to sod off with his saddo single male behaviour and I said you would never speak to him again. Then he just kept ringing hysterical saying he knew you were there and he had to speak to you. I had to pull the phone out of the socket. Then I did it, I got the number changed.'

'God Ellie what a nightmare.'

'It's fine. Just boring.'

'I'll pay for it of course.'

'No we'll share it.'

'No it's my deal. I'm really sorry.'

'It had to be done. I explained to him, by the way, that I was the one who had been bringing the poems from the office. And I said I was leaving my job so the poems wouldn't get to you any more. And by the way, I am. I'm going to resign.'

'What are you going to do?'

'Don't know yet, but I've got my letter written and everything. No more stupid beauty. I'm breaking out. Anyway then he said he'd send the poems to the flat. I said not to bother trying to find out because they never gave out that kind of information at work.'

'But the phone book.'

'Well I doubt he'll have one in Paris. But anyway, I've gone ex-directory. Quite a hassle for that boy.'

'Oh God Ell I'm really sorry about this.' I put my hands over my face. I saw him. The white face, tears, the glasses. I took the hands away.

'You know I'm moving out when this Binet job's done.'

'No I don't want you to go. I want that bastard to go.'

'Seven?'

'Yeah. He's not been faithful.'

She put her glass on the table and looked into my face. I closed my eyes. Behind the lids I remembered how I let him kiss me, how he'd started licking my nipple and I just sat there for a minute stunned and then I said stop that and tried to push him off and he pulled my pants aside and started licking between my legs. I got a leg free and shoved my foot against his shoulder and he fell back. I stood up. I said that was enough what did he think he was doing? I didn't want to do this, I was Ellie's friend, it had to stop. He propped himself on an elbow, his mouth looking as though he'd been drunk applying lip gloss and said oh that's right, yeah, you chose your moment girl, leading me on, letting me pleasure you and then like the fucking selfish cunt you are bringing out the line about me and my friend yeah well fuck that. And he grabbed me and easily pulled me down on the floor. I thrashed inside his grip. I couldn't believe how strong he was. Then I bit him as hard as I could on the shoulder and he clocked me and slipped on top of me like a big seal and jammed it inside me. It shut me up the way it felt like something cold and hard being shot into organs not designed for the purpose, the liver or kidneys.

I thought this is not happening, looking up at the ceiling, seeing him moving across in between seeing the ceiling. I thought maybe I should scream but my throat was dry. I could only get croaks out. At the same time an exhausted voice inside me said don't make a scene now when it's too late like you're stupid. Why didn't you push him off right away? That was a stupid tactic. Though don't think you pleasured me, you didn't pleasure me you bastard, you took me away from my programme about Hungarian horses which I was enjoying, pretending you wanted to be my friend and make me feel better when I was low but all the time thinking about doing me. Oh who gives a fuck.

Afterwards he went into the bathroom and ran a bath. He shut the door and put the radio on. I doubled up on the floor with saliva dribbling out of my mouth. I thought nothing like in semi-hibernation. Then I thought I can't stay here till she comes in from her PR dinner, what am I going to say? Watching him going up to her calling her babes.

Suddenly I got scared he would come out so I forced myself to get to my feet. I was exhausted but I grabbed my coat and ran out. There were a few coins in my coat pocket, enough to get the Tube. I had nowhere to go except to Bison's, so I went up there on the last Tube that went that far north. My legs felt weak as they carried me up the path to Bison's door. I could see light on in the window round the edges of the old blankets he used as curtains. I pressed the buzzer and he came to the door and saw me. He opened the metal grille outside the door and let me in and then got back into bed. There were orange-smeared cartons piled beside it, sweet and sour pork, shredded beef in black bean sauce, prawn crackers, and one of rice with some sauce on it. You just missed it he said, want me to call them get some more? I said it's OK I just want to go to sleep. His chest showed above the white sheet like a formation breaking through from the bedrock beneath the house. I got on top of the cover and put my head on it. His chest was so big I got a crick in my neck from having to bend it up like that. I glanced at the telly in the corner. A film. He touched my hair which was a rare thing for him to do. You don't look yourself girl he said, I'll clean all this shit away and make you a cup of tea. You OK? No I said I feel weird. What happened he said? I said nothing I just feel weird. He went into the kitchen and I sat up on the edge of the bed to take off my clothes. When I was bending over to undo my laces I caught sight of something just under the bed. I heard him coming back with the tea and I kicked it further under.

I opened my eyes. She was still giving me the funny look. Staring into my eyes as if she was looking under stones and in corners, her eyes not just looking straight but going from one eye to the other and back again like with a tiny torch, shining it into the shadows under the eyelashes and between the spirals of muscle in the iris, watching for something, a contraction, a dilation, a certain kind of blink. I closed my eyes again and as I did it I felt my eyebrows drawing together to show concern.

'No,' I said as if refusing to believe she could be made to undergo Seven's unfaithfulness, slipping away from The Light Rums behind my eyelids and seeing how later when Bison was asleep I got up. I got dressed as quietly as I could and then I reached under the bed for the thing and put it into my coat pocket. I tiptoed out into the hall and unlocked the front door and the grille. I wasn't able to lock the grille again behind me which I knew would make him mad when he woke up. It was only when I was almost out of the estate that I realised I'd forgotten to check his pockets for money. I didn't have enough on me for a night bus so I started walking down to central London. God I thought why this now as well? But then I spoke to myself firmly telling myself to shut up. People used to walk miles to their work every morning in your grandfather's day. Your grandfather walked three miles to work and three back and never thought anything of it.

I walked on. The streets up there were completely deserted. I didn't know exactly where I was since all I knew about the area was how to get from the station to Bison's flat. After a while I saw a big sign saying Central London which was just what I wanted so I followed it but it was too main a road so I plunged off into the quieter side streets where I was alone between the bushy suburban gardens which was a bit spooky but then I was away from cars which meant I couldn't be stuffed into one or even just watched. I didn't want to be watched. I walked down in the general direction. A man came out of a house ahead of me and got into a car. I kept on walking towards where the car was. He must have been doing something in the car because the lights didn't go on in it the whole time I was walking towards it. I knew the best thing was to keep walking without slowing the pace or showing any weakness. Head high. He was probably sitting there recovering from a row with his girlfriend. I walked by without looking into the car. A few seconds later the engine revved and the lights went on and he pulled out and drove away up the street.

I turned off into a smaller street with brick walls at chest height and small trees and bushes leaning over them. Semis still. A sign that I was still quite far out. A cat scurrying under a car. The road was tree-lined which made it very dark. I went down and along it and then crossed it to get to the other side of a street it made a T-junction with. As I crossed I saw someone was walking behind me at a fair distance and wearing trainers which was why I hadn't heard him. I just walked on in the general direction. I moved gradually towards more main roads and then I reached a main road and there were a couple of cars moving along it. I crossed it and continued in the direction I thought was London. I walked for what seemed like miles and met no one except a woman walking up the street towards me her high heels ringing on the metalled road like a leper ringing his little bell. Cars passed smoothly up and down at quite regular intervals.

Then I heard myself laugh way out on the outside. I stopped under a streetlight and took the flimsy scrap out of my pocket. I didn't need to verify it of course but I did it anyway, stretching it out along the palm of one hand, see-through pink with the squeakiness of the things themselves when engorged. I threw it into the next bin I saw not wanting to sadden the few scraggy bushes and green spaces of London by throwing it over the railings of the park I was passing. I was so desperate to wash my hands then that I risked going into the park to look for some water, a pond or maybe a drinking-fountain. Once I was in there away from the streetlights and people I felt different. The quiet was different. I knew it wasn't safe in the park but I also knew that nothing else could happen to me not now. I took off my shoes and socks and left them there and walked on the grass. It was cold and as soft as hair. Under it the earth was firm but clammy and not how I expected earth to feel. My feet clumped to the earth. My toes tried to suck it up into the spaces between them. It was darker in here and the wind moving through the trees plunged bodies of shadow towards me.

Then I felt exhilarated. I started laughing. I headed for the open grassy space with isolated groups of bushes dotted in it. The park was sloped and I could see the orange lights of London though not yet the middle of London stretched down in front. Orange clouds passed against the almost black sky. I ran and skipped on the grass. I felt stones maybe cutting the soles of my feet I didn't care. There was the rank smell of foxes around the shrubs, a wild smell you never expected to come across in London. I thought how I wanted the foxes to take over London. Everyone dead of the plague and the foxes slinking in and out of windows and doors barking and screaming. There was a bank with some sort of plant growing all over it and streaming in the wind. I went down on my belly and crawled right into the deeps of the plants and lay there with my cheek on the ground and my arms spread out on it. I opened up my coat so my body could get closer to the ground. The green leaves and stalks thrashed and waved around and I kept my cheek right against the ground and watched the patches of sky appear and disappear above the plants.

*

I opened my eyes. 'What gives you that idea?' I said.

I felt it coming as she started to talk and the moment it seemed plausible I looked away and right over my shoulder where I'd hung my jacket over the back of the sofa. I said mm hmm and knelt up on the sofa so I could reach down between the back of it and the wall, into my jacket pockets.

She was saying: 'I can't put my finger on it but he's been funny. He's down in clubs everyone knows him, lots of girls like him, he's generous and he's up for it, and he could have anyone he wants like that.'

She snapped her fingers. I was still fumbling in the pocket. What is good I was thinking is that if you put your head upside down like this it goes red anyway so when you turn back it will seem normal.

'What are you doing?'

'Nothing. Sorry. Just remembered I've got to ring someone and their number is on a piece of paper.'

I came up and sat back down beside her. I found I was able to look her in the eye. 'Sorry. Would it upset you if it was true?'

'Of course it would. Would you be upset if it was Bison?'

'Well it's funny you say that because I haven't told you this yet but I'll never bother with Bison again.'

'How come?'

'When I got back from Paris that last time I found a condom under his bed.'

'Why was that strange?'

'He never wears one with me.'

She looked hurt.

'Don't, just listen. So later I rang him and told him I'd found it and dyou know what he said? He mouthed off for a bit and then he said he'd lent the flat to his mother for a couple of days and she must have had one of her fancy men there, the old slag.'

Her face was blank. Then we both burst out laughing. Tears came into her eyes. 'His mum!'

I could hardly breathe. 'Blamed it on his old mum.'

62

He got up and put the telly off. He was muttering something to himself. I lay facing the wall. I heard him go into the bathroom, pee a couple of litres of piss. Into the bedroom. I heard the bedroom door click. I waited for his presence to leave the room completely. You had to be patient.

I got up and went over to the window. From up here you could see how the trees were moving at the speed of trees out of the shade made by the building. They grew up but also to some extent away from me. Sitting here in the fourth-floor window, how did I look to the trees? If trees had eyes I mean. Maybe every leaf was a simple eye, part of a huge compound eye like a butterfly's eye. They kept offering themselves to everything. Each tree holding thousands of eyes out in the sun and the rain. Then their eyes dried up and fell off like they were doing now. They went blind. Come spring they'd see everything with new eyes. I put my head on the glass. Cold. The wind got up and the trees made that sound they only made in autumn like they were covered with tinsel. Trees loved the wind most of all, maybe because it was unpredictable. The wind came and dandled the trees a bit. Whooshed through the branches touched all the secret parts of the tree every cold little joint of leaf and twig every underside of hidden leaves every crack in the bark. It went away. Then it came back rushing down the hill and tore a branch off. It slunk away. It roared back and lifted the whole treehead and pushed it so hard it almost hit the ground. The tree swang back. The wind slammed it down again. It screamed round the tree kicking its head in. In the morning little rags of wind moaning through the tree saying they were sorry.

Sometimes I would look at the moon if she was around maybe even in classic pose with clouds racing across her. Funny, Gothy, whooo. I'd listen out for cars. The building pressure as one approached from further up the hill or from down on the flat. The sound expanding as it passed under the window then dropping quickly to a purr. I'd examine the tops of the trees and look under the trees at their shadows. I'd check the tower block to see who was awake. Nineteenth floor. Maybe they always left a light on to keep the bogeyman out. Sometimes Eric came into my head. I'd wonder what he was doing. If he'd got over it yet. Gone back to study. Got a job. Fallen in love. I wondered if he was writing her poetry. Sometimes scenarios would come into my head. In one, it was Eric and me in another century. We lived on opposite sides of Paris. I went about veiled since the death of my young husband. Once a year I walked unveiled in the Bois de Boulogne with my dog. I would be feeling a bit queasy. In the woods Eric would be waiting for me watching from behind a tree. I never looked at him. He never married. In another scenario I went immediately to Paris. He came forward at the Gare du Nord with his white face and the dark frames of his glasses. We embraced and I realised that Doughgirl was right, I had just been scared of living love at this level. We went to live in a room under the eaves. He wrote at a little desk in front of our small fire. We couldn't afford much coal. Rain leaked into the attic and we put out a few pots and pans to catch it. I sat in an armchair wrapped in an old fur coat and stared at the flames and listened to the plinking of the raindrops and his pen scratching across the onionskin paper. He would come over, kneel at my feet and take my hands which he would turn over and kiss. Time passed very slowly and at the same time years went by and we hadn't noticed. After ages I'd realise I couldn't stay there under the eaves like that so I'd get a job at the Moulin Rouge as a high-kicker. I'd care for the orphelins of Nôtre-Dame by feeding them Mother Courage soups and teaching them Welsh border ballads. I'd post his poems to all the journals and cut the rejection letters into strips for toilet paper. I'd break into the lecture hall of the Ecole Normale Supérieure and push the prof off the lectern, then mount it and shout poetry before they carted me away foaming and epileptic, attempting to bite off their ears. The students would riot. We'd storm the barricades of jargon and Eric would be the poet of the hour and I'd be either a) tragically killed by a stray paving stone/enormous chunk of jargon or b) institutionalised.

63

You'd go up to a bolt of white satin and patches of it would blink and blunder off. You'd scan a chair before you sat on it and if you leaned your hand on the wall and felt your finger sinking into something squishy, you'd jump back, looking at the smear to check it was dead. Well-meaning giantesses tried to catch them in their hands, clapping them to death. Jude gave them butterfly nets and they galumphed through the studio smacking the nets on people's heads. The butterflies veered away from them in wave formation. As we worked into the night they roosted in the armholes of jackets, on coffee cups, in ponytails. In a storeroom at the back a hatchery had been set up with rows of chrysalises hanging off twigs. Beauties were reborn every morning.

The handler taught Jude and me how to catch and manipulate them. It was hard to attach them to objects. When we tried to wrap them in coils of fine wire they jack-knifed and cut themselves in slices. Sometimes we'd secure one to a hairband or eye-patch safely only to come back and find it had panicked and ripped its body to bits. Eventually we found two good ways. We wrapped the smaller ones in silk thread avoiding their wings and as many as possible of their legs. With the bigger ones the best method was plastic cable ties, the kind that ratchet to a close. If you got the cable tie to just the right tightness the butterfly was secure in a plastic corset. If you got it too tight they haemorrhaged.

The show took place at a warehouse on the outskirts of the city. Ours was the last show of the night. We ran late. Jude and me threw handfuls of butterflies under the veils of the braver girls just before they went on. We attached thirty Crimson-Speckled Moths to a sticky coating over one girl's bare breasts. When she came running backstage she was trying to flick itchy moths off her breasts with both hands. They had to be cut off with scissors leaving their legs behind. There was a standing ovation when hundreds of butterflies came out of the trapdoors. The moment the audience started to leave a group of us moved in to catch as many as we could with nets, brooms and the long cardboard containers they were transported in.

By the time we got backstage again most of the models had already left. Dressers and assistants rustled around bagging up the clothes and shifting the rails out the back doors to the vans. Journalists drank champagne out of paper cups while they waited to interview Brigitte. Some of them were poking about on the long make-up tables. The tables were littered with cotton pads, drink cans, hair grips and what for a weird second I thought were bright panting mouths attached to socks, eye-patches, rings, hairslides.

'I love it, I love it.' An American journalist. She carried the season's bag and a reporter notebook. 'Whose idea was the butterflies? It was awesome.'

'Brigitte's,' I said.

I picked a veil off a trestle table. It was full of legs and wings. I took the containers of rescued butterflies over to where they would be collected in the morning. I went back to the trestle tables. Jude was there, already snipping butterflies free. Someone brought us paper cups with champagne: Jean-Marie. He hugged me and left with Sergei. The journalists left. Brigitte left. Paul left saying he would come back later to help us. Then it was just Jude and me and someone wiping slowly at the floor with a squeezy mop and a bucket of dirty water. Then he left and it was just Jude and me.

'We're not going to make it to the aftershow party,' she said.

'No. I don't mind though, do you?'

'No.' She switched off the big overhead lights leaving just the bulbs round the make-up mirrors on. 'That's better.'

'I'm dying though,' I said.

'Me too. When did we last get any sleep?'

'I don't know. Night before last?'

Jude sat on a trestle table, I pulled up a chair. We got into a rhythm. The only sound was the scissors snipping and the almost-inaudible scuffling of the butterflies among the things on the table. I scouted around and found half a bottle of champagne behind a binbag. We drank it. We snipped.

'It was beautiful though,' said Jude.

'Yeah it was. It was really beautiful.'

We snipped.

'Fuck it's freezing. There's no heating in here,' said Jude.

'I know it's amazing how much everyone's body warmth heats up a room.'

We put on our coats. We wrapped spare binbags round our legs and our torsos.

'Paul left us a little wrap,' said Jude.

'Cool.'

She chopped it out. We got chatty.

Jude was a Buddhist. She had a thing for Paul. She was doing a year's work experience living in Paris. She loved it. Her dream was to go to Japan either to be a Buddhist nun or to work with Yohji. 'Or both,' she said, her binbag trousers crackling as she reached for a butterfly. 'Can you imagine being a Buddhist nun *and* getting to work with Yohji?'

'You'd have everything.'

'The Zen. The purity. The mastery. The folding. The cut. It's beyond.'

'Beyond.' I scanned the table. 'Time to start on the ones in the cable ties,' I said.

'It's gonna be a lot harder.'

'I know.'

'OK, I'll hold one in place, you cut off the tie. Better use this.' She handed me a scalpel. She picked up a butterfly with black-veined silver wings and steadied it in place in front of me.

'How do you know Sergei?' she asked.

'We worked together three years ago. I came here with a magazine to do a couple of shoots with Ryan. Steady.'

I sawed at the plastic tie careful not to cut into Jude's fingers on either side. 'You know Ryan, don't you?'

'Of course yeah. Oh Jesus.'

'No.' Green blood oozed onto the trestle table. 'Did I cut you?'

'No. Oh God it's in pain.' The butterfly arched its body. 'You'd better put it out of its misery.'

'Why me?'

'I'm a Buddhist.'

'I can't.'

'You have to.' She looked around. She handed me a huge gold can of Elnett hairspray. 'Use this.'

I took the can. I looked at the butterfly. 'I can't.'

It was moving its wings fast. They did that to get air in to their bodies. Panting.

'Do it.'

Inside I said, I'm sorry. I brought the can down with all my strength. There was thud mixed with the less defined sound of the butterfly's body mashing. I twisted the can from side to side to make sure. I lifted it and looked. Jude's hand flicked in and swept most of the body off the table. She reached for another butterfly, put it in place. 'Go on,' she said.

I leaned close to the butterfly. Its antennae almost brushed my face. It was trying to smell me. 'Yeah so, Sergei was assisting. Do you know a stylist? She was an editor at French Vogue till recently, Sylvie Hilbert?' I put the tip of the scalpel under the top of the plastic tie and applied pressure upwards.

'Sylvie Hilbert. She's amazing. She always works with him right?'

'Right.' I had cut halfway through. 'Hold it tight.'

I applied a last bit of pressure on the plastic. The bottom of the tie was yanked up underneath the abdomen. The abdomen snapped in two.

'Aw for fuck!' said Jude.

The two halves of the body jerked. I exhaled loudly. 'This is making me feel sick.'

'Don't think.'

I picked up the gold can of Elnett. I'm sorry. I slammed it down. I squished from side to side. I flicked the body off the table with the edge of the can.

'And Sergei was assisting her.'

Jude put another butterfly in front of me.

'I mean he was young then. A bit shy, very sensitive.' I made tiny passes at the plastic tie with the scalpel. 'But obviously very talented. And look at him now. But you know something?'

The scalpel slipped. I stopped. It was OK. I went on. 'I shouldn't say this you know.'

'What?'

'No I shouldn't. I shouldn't it's not fair but I'

'About them?'

'Yeah you promise not to say to a soul? It's that bitch Brigitte who's the problem.'

'Shit.'

'Not again.' I picked up the can. I smashed it down. She put another butterfly in place.

'Go on.'

'Well you know the idea for the show was Sylvie's? The whole thing with the lightbox, the whole butterfly thing, the trapdoors, everything. Sergei asked Sylvie to come up with something and then when she'd spent weeks working on it, Brigitte said.'

'Uh.'

'I can't do this any more.'

She passed me the can. I smashed it down. A crescent of gold-laced emerald wing sheered off like with a cookie cutter.

'One more.'

'OK. So Brigitte said she didn't want anyone working on it except Sergei, and Sylvie was told to fuck off basically, no pay, no credit.'

'That woman's a total bitch.'

'Total. And you know Sylvie   hold on   I had dinner with Sylvie and she asked me were the   were they using the butterflies and I told her. Fuck.'

I handed Jude the scalpel. I picked up the can of Elnett. The butterfly was already dead. I put the can down again. 'And every time the phone rang in the studio.'

I grabbed a butterfly. I placed it in front of Jude. 'You try.'

She doubled over the butterfly with the scalpel.

'Every time the phone rang I thought it would be Sylvie's lawyer saying she was going to sue. Because Sylvie was furious about the whole. Careful.'

'S'OK. No wonder. I mean wouldn't you have been furious?'

'Yes. But Sergei gave a kind of a different story. Shit.'

'Aw.' She wiped the hand holding the scalpel over her forehead. I smashed the can down. I swept the butterfly off the table.

'Sergei said they'd thought of everything together. Him and Sylvie. It wasn't really her idea. And in the end I didn't know what to think.'

Her tongue was sticking slightly out of her mouth. She made tiny rapid cuts. 'Come on baby.'

'And I think Sergei sort of hates me now. Because I told him about my conversation with Sylvie and I said he should do something about it.'

'I don't think he hates you.'

I drew breath. 'No it's OK. It's still moving. No but it's changed between us.'

'But it's not your fault. They have history. You know that.'

'Careful. Yeah she started him on his career.'

She had disembowelled it. Tiny organs. Perfect. I picked up the Elnett. I slammed it down. I put another butterfly in its place.

'Yeah but should she have slept with him? I mean he's like twenty years younger than her.'

I picked up the can. I held it against my chest. 'What?'

'Hold the butterfly.' Her tongue stuck slightly out of her mouth.

'What did you say?'

'You didn't know they were lovers?'

'He's gay.'

'Now yes. Tsk. Don't move.' She tried to hold the tip of the scalpel horizontal so as not to cut the body.

'But not back then. They say he was a virgin when she found him.'

'You say that.'

The blade slipped and sank into its back.

'You say that' I picked up the can. I banged it down. I put another butterfly in front of her 'as if she found him on the streets or something.'

'All I'm saying *is* if you do something like that' – her face was inches from the butterfly – 'you've crossed a line.'

It turned its face. It looked at her.

'Where did you hear that anyway?'

'Boys in the studio.' It had huge eyes. It was taking her in.

'Fashion gossip. You know what they're like.'

'Yeah.'

'I don't believe it.'

'Uh.'

'Oh no.'

She'd beheaded it. She sat back. I did the can just in case. I said goodbye to it. I put another one in its place.

'Take your time.'

'OK! OK come on girl.' Her tongue came out. Blue wings. Like a scrap of the Madonna's veil.

'You know people gossip that she sleeps with Ryan, now it's Sergei. It makes me sick.'

'I know. I don't want to badmouth your friend. Please. Please don't.'

'Sorry.' I held firm. 'I promise you it wasn't like that. You've no idea what it was like that trip I made to Paris.' It was bleeding from its wound. 'And she's happily married.'

I picked up the can. Blue wings fluttered one last time for ever. I hesitated watching the wings move. A mistake. I swallowed. Smash.

'Oh well. That's when people get really bitchy.'

I wiped the hair off my face. 'We haven't saved a single one of these.' I looked along the joined-together trestle tables.

We stopped. I lit a cigarette. Sylvie and Sergei and me making the garden. Her husband coming out of a river. Sergei looking at me. Me looking away. The oily yellow light in the studio. The thick smell of the flowers.

'Lets leave them like this,' she said. 'Lets just cut short any of the longer cable ties and leave them. That way at least they can crawl.'

We cut off the long ends of the ties leaving the butterflies wearing plastic corsets and put them in the cardboard containers. We stacked them with the other containers near the door. A make-up artist came in. It was six in the morning and the next show in the space was at nine. Soon the girls would start coming. The make-up artist started to bin the rubbish on the table and lay out her kit. We called a cab and picked up the three containers of Holly Blues and the four of ghost-like arctorius luctiferas. The sanctuary had said they wouldn't take these more common European ones. We got into the cab with the containers in two Carrefour plastic bags. It was warm and stuffy in the cab. I kept blacking out briefly. As we reached central Paris the dark was beginning to drain away, so slowly you couldn't observe the change but it was changing.

'Do you think he's in love with Jean-Marie?' said Jude.

'I suppose so, but I can't believe it somehow.'

'Why not?'

'I don't know. I just don't believe it. So maybe he still loves Sylvie. God I'm such an idiot.' I started to laugh.

We told the taxi driver to stop in the square in front of Nôtre Dame. It was deserted. The cathedral stood out slightly rosy against the dark grey sky and small high, lit-up clouds. As we stood looking at it the streetlamps went out. We walked up to the front of cathedral and squatted down.

'Do you think we'll be forgiven?' said Jude.

'I don't know. It doesn't say anything about butterflies does it?'

'I don't think so.'

'Ready?'

'OK. One. Two. Three.'

We opened the containers and shook them. Butterflies lurched out. A few of the Holly Blues set off like drunks with wings. The rest fell to the ground and started crawling. We went and got a coffee and a croissant and then Jude went to get the Metro back to her apartment in Porte de la Villette and I walked across the bridge to my hotel on the Left Bank.

64

On the bridge I stopped and looked down at the water. Maybe this was the same bridge where Eric had stood on the outside and thought about throwing himself off and I'd dragged him back, the me that he kept around. The women taking into their mouths roses of the pentecost of the tundra. The surface of the water was slicked over and reflecting the sky. The word dawn. It must be down there in the land of the dead with rose soul and star. It had carried a lot through centuries and it was all used up now. A shit word. But the thing itself, the real thing, it still worked if you could get the word and all the other words that went with it out of your mind. I still liked it that it was dawn without the word and that I was standing in it in Paris. I looked down at the big volume of water and metaphors slicked over on the surface and reflecting the grey and white of the sky. The way the river got caught on the buttresses of the bridge and rode up in a collar of water against them. It was at those points that you drowned. Someone had told me that once. Stay away from the buttresses in the river. If you stayed away from the buttresses that stood out against the flow then you could flow right down and out into the river mouth and out into the sea. Flowing down the river at dawn. But without the word dawn. I lit a second cigarette off the end of the first one. Trickling sounds in your ear instead of words, your hair swirling out in the current and your dress ballooning out, your body held and passed along. Your eyes seeing the sky passing and sensing the changing things on the banks as you were carried down. Weed, twigs, dead rats, plastic bags, swirling in the folds of your dress and your hair and then floating away. The current changing, the feel of the tide sucking you further out, seagulls, the docks, the big ships at anchor in the bay stinking of sewage and tar, you glide past the steep steel hulls, far out past the foghorns and all the way out. I took a last couple of drags and flicked the rest of the cigarette off into the air and watched it drop and the light phut out as it hit the water. In a second the small white shape was carried under the bridge and disappeared. But the fresh lovely river wasn't fresh for me. Eric had got here first and tagged the whole thing with poetry. I could never have it undone again. The smooth humps of water bulged where they were pummelled by eddies. It was turbulent underneath you could tell. The whole riverbed lined with decaying poems. Words coming loose and flowing into the current. I wished he'd left it alone.

65

God save me.

I can't. I'm fucked man. I'm really fucked.

This'll sort you out ladies.

No.

Naaaah nah nah nahnahnah*nah* nahnahnah*nah*. Nana Nah.

Yar lightweights.

Women innit. 7-Eleven laughed.

You having a laugh? she again.

He laughed again. He had such a deep laugh.

One of their faces came right in front of mine. For a minute something weird. Like a curtain pulled back on weird panic and sadness. Then smoky hazy. Laughing at the face of him. Goo-oof! Big round eyes and proper little boy skin white with rosy cheeks. Hair sticking up little boy hair. Rah hair.

He turned to 7-Eleven. Goof smile. She's up for it. Aren't you babes?

Aunt you. No. More painfully aaaawww. Slight dentist thing. Like when he's hit a nerve drilling and you go aw aw with your mouth open wide trying to tell him that hurts.

Don't babes it that's Bison's, said Seven.

I nudged 7-Eleven shurrup.

Not seeing him any more.

Heard mine coming out fast shrill.

Good pills. I to Ellie.

Good good goody good good, she said.

Safe, said Seven.

She snugged into my side more. Hooooooome.

You sleecefully peeping?

She smugsnuggled into the side of me. Happy. Safe. 7-Eleven always *smells* so nice.

What's your aftershave 7-Up?

He sucked teeth: Feary-moans.

Uh I said biting a finger all scaredy.

Hoooooooome, into my armpit.

But not before, said the other one. Not as goofy as his mate. He looked from somewhere else maybe India but same accent. Bollywood Brideshead. The Eliot-through-a-megaphone scene done as a big dance number. Busty wet saris rolling their eyes and shaking chicken dopey-ass-ah in front of dreaming spires. Do I *derrre* to eat a peach? Oh oh! Roll the eyes. Urr to wuk upun thut beach? Roll roll. Thut big old peachy-bie! Thut jubbly beach!

But not buffaw.

He was quite handsome.

Not before what? Ellie.

But it was how he was dressed. That fucked him.

Let me style you. Heard self say.

Come on we've gort tuh pahtay, he went on. We've gort tuh like.

He reached for the pipe from 7-Eleven.

What, said Ellie, is that all just a plastic Evian bottle?

7-Eleven coughed out smoke. It smelt high-pitched poison. Shit, I said, that's killy. Respect.

He pounded his chest with his fist. Between chesty coughs: Save designer one Christmas.

The Bollywood one's a smug piss face holding in smoke. He fanned hand in front of his face holding. Belched it out.

Sheeeeeesh.

Kebab, I said. I looked round. Didn't mean. Just goes with Sheesh.

Put lips on the straw, 7-Eleven laughing at me. I go for it.

EEEEEEEEEEEEEEEE!

Comes right back up spring-loaded and behind it bumping it pushing it and lashing it with its ten kryptonite tails as it streaks past the crack screaming in a shatterglass soprano.

I lay back and felt it run me.

How you doin babe? To my girl.

Aow.

Yeah.

Love you though.

Not the drugs talking?

Nut.

We lay back. I took in the ceiling. It was all speakers. Closed my eyes and opened them again. For true.

What happens if you turn it up, I said.

Blurwahuhwindah.

Sorry?

Blur art uh windeow.

Go on then.

Time passed.

Fucking turn the dial up, yelled Ellie.

She angry. I got angry.

G'on mate. It's 7-Eleven, he still here.

I saw a goof rise up in his unbaggy jeans and move towards a console.

Speech bubble escape my lips. Let me style you!

Kiss you, said the one next to me. He fumbled over me.

I said, yuch, and, 7-Eleven! His arm came down and batted away the feeble goof body.

Time passed.

Seven?

Yeah?

I love you.

Time passed. He laughed from his boots.

A beat. Then my head getting crammed up with

FEEL IT IN ME

like when your head gets crammed up with snot in a cold.

Bouff bouff bouff bouff *I wanna feel the music* I wanna feel **bouff bouff bouff** *wanna feel the music.* Ah feel it in meeeeeeeeee. Goof dancing by the console table. Arms hanging out to dry.

Time passed back once again back once again back once again. Uh u-uh. Breathe. Uh u-uh. Fall. Uh u-uh.

Uh u-huh. Uh u-huh. Uh u-uh. Goof dancing by the console table.

Reload.

Reload.

When I say come you come to me
when I say go you go away
I am your obsession no rules involved

A feeling of crystal beauty passing through me in pins and industrial diamonds. A feeling of extra strength wellness. Hurts Aaaaa in a good way. I fell back on plumpy cushions. Soared up in shape of a soundeee eeeeeeeeeeeeeeeeeeeeeeeeeeeeeeeeeeeeeeeeeeeeeeeeeeeeeeeeeeee

Stayed up there bobbing. 7-Eleven going on and on and on. I couldn't really hear it for feel it in meeeeeeeee! His voice like a big bassoon going bwoom bow woom bowoom wah wuh woom and Know uh un sayin?

The goofs leaning right over him concerned, sicky coloured.

Know uh un sayin?

Same thing hepind to me mate. I mean you kneeuw what I'm sing?

Yeah, said 7-Eleven. Like cunt.

Like tay tilly cunt.

Like tay tilly cünt, said the other goof. Which I liked.

Time passed. Pipe passed.

Hey Ellie you still there? to my girl and

Her voice came out the pillows.

You lickle freebie, she said, fly away fly away home.

She butted head into my ribcage. No no. From home. Fly away from home.

Flying aways home, I said.

Someone switched the music up. Parts of the ceiling started pursing their lips in and out other parts zzzed. I watched a glass someone had left on a white perspex cube that was lit from inside so it went from violet to blue then fairy glade green. The glass shimmied to the edge of the cube and havered for a really fascinating bit of time. It fell.

Deownt!

One goof launching at another goof's back. They fell wrestling on the floor in shambly goof moves.

7-Eleven loped to the console and flicked the switch. Ceiling froze. He flicked CDs. He shoved one in. Chilly café.

Eh Christian got another rock bro? he said.

I did cynical brays of laughter. I did it as a gift, a treat of carefully controlled sensurround. As if he didn't have more rock in stock. He kept them in his gnarlies. Christian and him fumbling setting it all up.

Pipe passed.

Crystals of extra strength beauty needled my guts and suddenly.

I sat up. A feeling of extra strength wellness.

The goofs laughed together like a small flock of wineglasses.

Dyou have any water? I said sensibly.

The Bollygoof smiled wetly and left.

Are you thirsty? I'm really thirsty, I said.

Yeah really thirsty. She sighed. What was I trying to say was that what I know in my heart is.

We both turned to look at the half-open living room door. Horror flick sound from the hallway. Not body, too clinky clunky. A large automatic weapon bumping across stone-flagged floor. A thumpy chest full of bank notes.

Clunk. Krrrrrrrhhhhh. Clunk.

Where are we? I said. Tried to realise. Taxi. Snapshot to the band's party. What band? Some band that knew Doughgirl. Snapshot to Doughdough and me dancing discopelvic in front of DJ booth. Snapshot to me and Doughgirl doing tequila. Snapshot to another 1-2-3 E! Snapshot to nothing.

Bollywood boy entered dragging a bottle. Putting his back into it heave-hoing. 7-Eleven grinning. Bottle comes up to Bollyboy's groin.

Bolly innit? 7-Eleven makes that noise with his fingers. I practised when I was waiting for coffee to boil but I couldn't. Sad sad. For me the finger thing was like the splits or cartwheels too late for ever now.

Where is this? I said.

Alice in Wonderland's bottle of champagne, said Ellie.

Paleface goof zumpfed in front of me. Oh Duyus saatch a she-ef. He closed his eyes. Opened. Thank *Gored.* Closed.

Duyus and 7-Eleven and Ellie crouching over Alice's bottle. Bottle yanked tipping on its round edge near-plunges. Fuck! Fuck!

Deownt!

Eek eek eek: Ellie. I felt the same.

Come on, said Christian unzumpfing, lets get some glauhsez. He hauled me to his feet and out into hallway. Air fresh out here. I realised how much more together I was than I had thought.

Hey I said, you're Christian right?

Yuh. Yuht.

You're sweet as.

I said it because. I don't know.

I just need to know. Where did we meet you?

He was holding my hand. He had damp hand of someone who has been out for hours. He laced finger in between finger. I let my mind wander.

You deownt mumba? He looked me in a joke way.

Just tell me.

You mean you deownt remumba the ahs and ahs I just couldn't shake you orf me. It was embursing.

I looked down at the stone flags of the floor. Blank. Blank. I looked back at what was his name? Where was Ellie? Footsteps echoing. Us. I looked up. The stair. We're on it. It goes up like inside a shell.

Wow I said. Looked up. This place is shunusual.

He made a sudden move to the left still holding my hand very tight-laced.

Would you like the grand toah?

Giving me the Regency buck eye. Ooh yes kind master. A lock of his hair, because boys like that have locks of hair fell over his forehead which was clammy. In a good way.

We climbed the big insideshell stair together hand in hand in Aliceland.

I heard myself sing to the music coming out from the ceiling downstairs *like a feather in beautiful world.*

Shall we start utter turp and wuk darn?

OK but should we get some champagne?

Well snot as if they can drink all that beef awe we get back darn.

I put my back to the banisters. I'm really really thirsty.

Flopsy mopsy locksy. Sweet eye rolling as. I watched him lollop down in giant bunny strides. I turned and ran up the rest of the steps two at a time to the top *run run run run ruuuuuuuhun.* Up and up at the top I stopped and there was a glass dome above my head. The light off up here. Rainwater running down outside of the dome. There was the moon. I looked down over the banister. Stone slabs of the hallway were at the bottom and at each corner of each slab a little black diamond-shaped stone like a speck of dirt. Lovely little specks pushed open the door in front of me. I felt the inside wall for the light. You didn't flick you turned a knob and light went up and down like a volume. There was another knob underneath. I turned it and music went wwwwwwaaaaaawwaaaaaaaaaaaaaaa and I laughed to see such fun. Bedroom right out of the interiors section of a mag. Ticking glossboxes.

Vast, above all, high bed ✓
Coronet on wall above bed with hand-printed fabric cascading down ✓
Matching floor-length curtains at windows ✓
Metal expensive old things to tuck curtains behind ✓
Bold wall colours (never 'with a hint of') ✓
Carpet texture of chinchilla fur ✓
Carpet colour of chinchilla fur ✓
Bed throw of chinchilla fur ✓
Tray nearside bed with antique flask half-full of water ✓
Drinking-glass doubles as stopper for flask ✓
Ditto far side ✓
Enormous chest of drawers with cornucopias, putti ✓

Plexiglass ultra-mod shelving ✓
Enormous telly facing bed 'on' ✓
Images from telly reflect on window glass ✓
Rain on window glass ✓

Cross the room and through an inner door and it's a bathroom. Ticking hitting me like automatic weapon fire. Ten-speed shower Boomf! Big shallow sink Boomf! Heated towel rail Boomf! Waffle towels Boomf! Boomf! Penhaligon bath oils Boomf! Diptyque scented candle Boomf! Flavour 'bois ciré' Boomf! Boomf! Boomf! Sunken bath Boomf! Under floor heating Boomf! Travertine floor Boomf! Piped music Boomf! Fold-up blinds in same chinoiserie hand-printed fabric as bed Boomf! Other boomfs!

I went out into the bedroom. Images from the TV ghosting black wet glass. *And some are lost in darkness* Out onto the landing. Looked down. Voices music tiny specks of dirt. I opened another door. Turned the knobs *keep my eyes.* Same. Big vast bed tick this time a mod four poster tick hung in black swags tick matching curtains tick big telly 'on' tick reflected in window glass tick chinchilla throw chinchilla-feel rug plexiglass shelves tick tick tick tick and the bathroom door. I go through. Tick. Tick. Waffle heated scented sunken 'bois ciré' rain on fold-up Penhaligon ten-speed heating. I dialled the music to full *Youth* then sunk it back to whine.

I open the two other doors on this floor. Same. I go down a floor. Same. It's like in a hotel. In every room tellies are 'on' with the sound turned down. Some have mod beds some have old *and some are lost in darkness.* In between I look over the banisters. Voicesmusic getting louder and louder. Specks of dirt getting bigger. No sign. I go down a floor. Vast grandee bed hung in crimson dyspeptic mothrag dusts of ancient costive costliness. Silver-framed photos of Jollymums and Bollydads. I look at the bed. It actually has a little set of steps for getting high enough up to launch yourself onto the top wearing a nightie and a Wee Willie Winkie hat. Wee Willie poor Wee Willie. Fly away fly away fly aways home. I could launch. I could lie there in crimson dark splendour and moan the words to old Smiths songs. But they might forget they've left me somewhere up here and go and not be able to remember where they had been in morning. I never escape. A wheedling Filipina will bring in trayfoods calling *Rune sorebees!* I become the sex prisoner of gosh mummygoofs whose skin eventually takes on a tint of sparkling rosé and whose paps became chateauneuf.

Down a floor. There's a set of old hickory-smoked double doors that I fling open with a ta-da higher than the human hear. Now I realise. Now I know. What they're hanging around in downstairs is more of an antechamber. Almost a cloakroom. This is the biz. The McCoy. A drawing room maybe called that because once upon a time it only seemed to exist in drawings and now still on paper in shiny shiny synthetic-smelling pages of places that you can never never go. Places you have to fall down into through a womb. You can't get there by setting out. Unless you strike lady luck and fall backwards right on time. Yikes! You either break an ankle and stumble onwards Ms Gritty-Realism or you're that lucky lady whooshing down wormwise into the netherworld of the Drawing Room the parallel universe where they go aow aow!

No knobs I had to switch on lamps one by one for real. Tiny pools of light like puddles in the taiga. Dark wood panelling. Maybe they ripped it out of old Scottish castle. Bollyfolly behaviour. Sofas made out of kindly old moleys with impeccable silver spoon manners and pince-nez specks and claw feet. A sort of alcove off. A set-in nook double of Ellie's living room walled with vasty bookshelves groaning with leatherish books. In front parchment maps in piles like where be dragons on a renaissance coffee table. Not exactly a bed but a kind of vasty deep maybe it's called a daybed, maybe it's more of a liferaft set into an alcove within the alcove chokka with plumpy cushions. Shallow pointy shaped alcoves within the alcove within the alcove holding dimmering brass vasepipes for smoking rare orientoxic narcotics. Laugh druggishly and climb aboard.

Just pee ogs. Some pee ogs they dogs
the and smelliness dogs they don't it they love it
wet dogs dog hairs on the sofa licky dogs ju after they

have vry last flake of gy arseholes up and slobber basting flew half half fied dog shite.

I saw squidge shapes I put my hand on one my hand on another fleshsquidge felt Elliearse lovely Elliearse in front me like a portcullis a portcul.

Ellie?

Hello darling you back?

Where've I been?

Up here you silly bill. We couldn't find you for ages.

I love dogs I said but do you have to?

She hugged. Get her a glass of that will you?

I sat up. They were all there with me in the alcove on the Arabian Nightsraft except there was the goofarajah lying across the Jacobean coffee table with parchment maps jumbled on it with the straw coming out of the side of the Evian bottle at his lips.

I held out my hand for the Evian thing. I must wake up, I said, or I'll die.

Zompfed picking at something on the itchy carpetlike cover of the Arabian Nightsday.

Christian, I said. *I jus wanna be*

He turned his eyes up on me. Side of his head parallels bedtop.

A woo oo man

What happened?

Nothing dulling you nodded orf.

I took the pipe. Mouthparts on mouthparts off. Oh crystal clarity of swans! Oh ringing tones of edgéd lungs! Oh bright oh frosty morning!

Is he your boyfriend? I said to Christian.

Those people accept dogs just as they are they don't want to change dogs the way they piss up the sides of things like cars like bins like you know things you don't want them to piss up or wank on sorry but people's dogs do do it you are there with your legs crossed having a cup of tea with your friend at her mum's house and a mangy old Lab comes out of its basket and grasps that's the only word for it

Ellie.

Your leg and goes at your tights with its willy the way

Stop it!

They have willies that look sore and shiny that they just pop out from what you thought was their

Sh'up.

Willy shiny and sore like little livers that they just slither out of a witherlily

What?

Wither what you thought was their willy but is actually a willy-casing round the liverwilly all red and sh

Shu'rup!

Iny like in the alien when it pops like an extra head a raw head all red and shiny from a plain looking bit of body where you weren't expecting a raw

Give it a break girl. 7-Eleven.

Head to break out. She leaned forward at Christian. You never seen that?

I'm a cat parson.

He scratched at the itchy cover maybe pretending to be a cat.

Yes you are a cat person and other people are dog persons and that's right coz what I'm getting at is just like there are cat and dog persons there are man persons and I am a man person. Always have been can't help it. I like being around them I like the sound of them the smell I mean it. I love mansmell. You listening?

Yeah babes, said Seven.

I know this sucks from a feminist perspective but I like the way they are big and strong and I like beer bellies. I find that something I want around me in a man because it's about volume density big gestures and not saying much and what they are saying I could chew over like bits of jerky for the rest of my days.

Fufucksick shut her arp someone, said Duyus.

Watchya mout.

Bollygoof slumped back onto parchment.

G'on babes.

It's been that way ever since I was a little girl you know when all the other little girls wanted to be in the kitchen with the mummies piping pink icing onto itty bitty cakes and hundreds and thousands.

I love hundreds and thousands, I pipetted.

Me too, said Ellie.

But only the silver ones not the multi-coloureds.

That's coz you're a stylist babe.

I'm a cat parson, said Christian.

I looked up at him from where I'd sunk to contemplation behind Elliearse. That bastion. That staunchfleshion.

He sagscratched at the itchy coverlet.

I said watch ya mout, said 7-Eleven.

He didn't say anything, I said.

E's being funny.

Durys my evuh fanny?

Neow.

Dhurrie Us? I said.

Dah. Ius.

Is that Darius like an ancient Roman?

Niaow.

I shot up. I jumped up and down on the thousand and one beds. I've got it I've got it. They're cat people! That's why they talk like that. Cat people!

I would be in the sitting room with my Dad and his pals while my sister and her little friends were making fairy cakes and I'd have to sneak in because they didn't want frillies coming in and stopping them doing man stuff stopping them being free to do and say the secret stuff men do and say when you're not around and there they'd be watching the racing on a Saturday afternoon and you wouldn't believe how much smoke was in the air like zombie candy floss and their voices would come out in blurts saying things like G'on my son   Silly old moo   I wus robbed   He's a bit light on his feet when it was a jockey they didn't like. Just the sound of their voices the rhythm of how they raised the beer bottles to their lips the rolling tobacco g'on my son the gruffalo sounds and the smell of tobacco and Wright's coal tar soap from Mr Gibbons all the Gibbons family used it I used to play with one of the boys and I tried to get Mum to buy that yellow mansoap so I could rub their secret power on me in the bath newspapers everywhere getting the arms of the couches grubby and the way they sat forward with their legs apart and their fists up at jaw level rocking like jockeys and making ooh ooh ooh ooh monkey mad sou

She stoppeth one of three or something? said Darius.

Who's got the pipe, I said, the pipe.

Chris? Got another rock mate?

I'll hef to make a caul. Bagah. You got nothing orn you?

Nah mate never carry it.

Don't think I don't know what you're on about, said Ellie. And no you can't have another rock we're going home actually and I haven't even told you yet what I was going to say.

Yeah, I chip in, you can stoppeth that stoppeth shit right now.

She knows all about poetry. She loves poetry. She *is* poetry. Spake Ellie. Can I have a glass of champagne? Please!

We need powershit, said Darius, if you're cauling.

7-Eleven, I said, you've got

Shurrup girl.

No but fess up y

Shurrup. Mind your own.

Who thicks men's blard with curled, said Christian. Lying back on red and gold velvet cushions with his head dropped back. His skin a bit damp from the effort his body was having to make with coping with everything he was throwing at it. His T-shirt half up and I could see his belly which came up just a little bit in a mound from where it scooped down by the hips and was covered in blonde hairs that stood out with tiny shadows on one side. I bet he had a blonde. I'd never seen one. I poked him with a toe. Didn't like the idea of it all blonde. Blond I mean. Blond. Or was he blonde?

Champagne. She needs champagne. Big toe rousing the dear dolly goof. Mrs Wolly Toddle's Leather Widdle Paddle.

Kont.

You can.

Kont.

Christian slid down the cushions still with his eyes closed and his feet touched the floor. His legs buckled. He opened his eyes and sat up.

Heuld uh glars.

I grabbed Ellie's and got down off the hundreds and thousands and ones. I squatted on the floor holding the glars with both hands. I looked up. Christian grappling the neck of the bottle so it tilted down. It was still far above the glars. I lifted the glars further up. A jet of foam shot out and pissed on my foot.

Fark!

7-Eleven grabbed the glars with one hand the bottle with the other and poured the champagne in. I passed it to Ellie and handed him another glars and another one.

I kneeswalked across to the oaken coffee table where Dawius was laying propping his forehead on an upturned palm. Dozing? Despairing?

Who ish sheesh boish? Over shoulder to Ellie.

I gave him a glars. He said ta very much. I put my back to one of the legs of his table and stretched out me old pins.

It's just a dream, she said, they're succubuses.

The nightmuh life in death is she, saith Christian.

Suck ya pussies? When 7-Eleven laughed it was like someone idling a sports vehicle.

Quotus quotus stoppeth stoppeth. She shaked her head all dimplyash. You think I'm just clubtrash cute as a button don't you?

Eow shorely nort.

Spend my whole life dreaming. Aaaah.

Water water all around? I held up a bottle of Volvic spotted under the Jacobean oaken coffee table. no one laughed. Oh well. Gave self small gold star.

More like suckers innit, said 7-Eleven. Gave it a bit more throttle.

Hwart's your point here Nellie? It's not a farking romentic simpaysium. Dayus.

Ellie reached a hand out for the water.

E bothering you? 7-Eleven.

She teethsucked.

I thought you liked men, I said a bit more loudly, their smell their rhythm their liverwallies.

Men yes. I like their rhythm. Do you like my rhythm?

Oh epsilootlay, said Darius.

Do you like my rhyme? she said.

Rhyme me a rhyme lady mine.

She stretched across the day for night bed her feet up on Christian's. She swivelled her head and stared up at the ceiling she said

The trees are in their autumn beauty
The woodland paths are dry
Under an October twilight the water
Mirrors a still sky.

She swivelled the head back down and around. Sucked pipe with smirk.

I see you're a lava of purtry.

We all are here, said she tween sucks. My massive anyway. Don't suppose the Eton Square poss-ay stretch to much more than a bit of old Sammy Skagman and other jabberwanky.

Bee wayah! Bee wayah! Cushions. Muffled.

Rhyme me a rhyme mystreow, Darius to 7-Eleven.

Lighter on lighter off lighter on lighter off. 7-Eleven held it in as long as possible and blew it out in rings. He closed eyes and savoured, said slow

Crazy like a fool. Daddy daddy cool.
Me: Daddy Daddy Cool.
Ellie and me: Daddy Daddy Cool.
Altogether now: Daddy Daddy Cool!
Daddy Daddy Cool!
Daddy Daddy Cool!
Daddy Daddy Cool!

Wavering from red and gold cushions:

Brown girl in the ring. Tra la-la la-la.
Brown girl in the ring. Tra la-la la-la-la lala.

It frittered away friggingly.

Stopped.

Pass the pipe, it said pipingly. Sound of someone sipping hot soup. Cough cough. So you were ship at the shrine of the meows?

Which one? said Ellie cool as.

Rato spose or is dear old Calliope more your thing?

Calliop *pee*? says I reeling.

Yarp. Muvvav orf Orpheus – Hot soup suck – End orf Hymen spose.

Goddess of Brides and Setting Up Home? Ellie gobbed finger.

I went rhn rhn rhn.

Upon the bwimming wartar among the sterns are nine and fifty swuns. Duyus clicked fingers at the cushions. Chrissie.

Whart?

Give it to pappy diddums.

I saw before um um I saw before no. Ellie smacked lips.

Hand emerged from sea of red and gold. Holding pipe up. I took it.

Scatter wheeling in great broken fuck.

Lighter on lighter off.

She rapped fist on forehead, lower teeth grabbed upper lip.

EEEEEEEEEEEEEEEEEEEEEEEEEEEE! A snowburst of extra fine needles. A shower of sharpdropping diamonds. I passed pipe to Darys.

She got to her feet.

Brimming water among the stones.

On the reds and golds Ellie ascendant.

Brimming water among the yes are nine and fifty swans. Yes. The nineteenth autumn had come upon me when I first made my count. Yes Yes.

She wobbled on the bed of Araby.

Saw before I had well finished all suddenly mount and scatter wheeeeeeeling in great broken rings.

Pawing air. Heaving arms round. It's broken rings. No. Flapping. Doing wings. She's doing wings.

Upon their clamorous.

Their stammerous (from red and gold deeps) their truly stripey pyjamerous.

Wings. She teethsucked. Clamorous *wings.*

Mental, said 7-Eleven.

Darius take it away my man, she said.

Darius bent forward to light a cigarette almost in my hair. Smell of Happy Ever Aftershave. Maybe I'm a man person?

Is that Pour un Homme? I said.

Gentleman. Jivanshee. His lids fluttering over turned-up balls in stutterous wings of mothly mutterings and papery hymens of pastry cupperings.

What's hair look like inflammabus? I asked.

His head falls back to rest on palm. Other hand sails through air in perfect parabola to pluck sucked fag from fleshly lips and bear it slowly away in perfect reverse.

Yeats sayo baw ring. Con't we do something a little maw neonced? He opined.

It is neonced says she. Its full of them.

Reuwsy crosses and suchy like? Mused Chrisions.

Well first off obviously its about how swans pair for life. They're married. Ellie.

That's not a neonce.

I think they're just living together, said Chrisions from cushions.

The blackness of darkness forever

And he is wandering about in the autumn woods and he sees them unwearied still lover by lover. Uh lover by lover. By lover. Darry?

They peddle in the curled compenionable streams or claim theuh, their hurts have not greeurn eold, peshun or kon kwist wander whirr they will, attend upon them still.

Big swanny soar streaming white smoke.

Ooh can I have one, I said.

Whereas for him, says she, all's *changed* since I hearing at twilight the first time on this shore the the clamorous

Duwius: Herring at twilight the fast time on this shaw, the bellbeat of their wings above my head, trod with a lighter tread.

Cushions: Sod what the blighter said.

See? See what a fucking arsehole Yeats is? She legs apart swaying on the bed of night.

Yah just look at the fay toes, said Cushyuns.

Arse. Like he has the swans not growing old. Whereas in actual fact right. In actual fact.

She made scrabbly motions to call pipe of peace to her.

After nineteen fucking autumns most swans are dead. He's the lucky one not the swans. Lips on. Hot sucky soup sound. Lips off lips on. Suckier soupier.

Me: Yeah but his point is that his love is gone but they don't get sick of each other.

She propels polluted air through funnelled lips. Looks round bulgy-eyed barrel-chested. Hand over mouth. Chipmunk-cheeked. Taps foot on Christian. Hold hold. EEEEEEEEEEEEEEEEEEEEEEEEEE. Out.

That's the arrogance of man innit?

I thought you were a man person, saith I.

She passed pipe down to cushion hands.

They auh eehmohtul. Neow wurnus uv death hence eehmohtul. Chrision his cusions. In manuv speaking.

Yes I am *a* man person but I'm not *Man* person. *Man.* Different. Swan is kind of Man for him. Swan is swan never this swan that swan. One dies it's replaced by swan, it's so third man!

Ee myrtle!

Hey Chris? Got any skag snuck away ere mate? Said Seven.

Nine and fifty sucks as well, I said.

Chris mate.

Why not fifty-nine? That's where poetry annoys people.

Oi wakey wakey.

Coming from you Callio pee? she said. I thought you liked it poncey.

Chris mate.

But you're on to it. You're on to it girl. She pointed at me because I was a girl and I was on to it. Unwearied still, lover by lover right? They paddle in the cold companionable streams and climb the air. Love that. Two most beautiful lines in the English language and they've got paddle in them.

Christian. Mate. Said Seven.

And compaddleable. But wait a minute. How can they go lover by lover all fully of the swanny joys? There are not fifty-eight swans. There are not sixty swans, says she.

Theuh nort sixty-two swuns. Theuh nort foughty-fough, continued Bollydar.

Exactly. He has forgotten that there is one sad lickle swan all on his tod.

It hit me. Oh no the fifty ninth swan!

Or has he? Either Yeats is so fucking arrogant he doesn't even notice he's fucked swans again.

Chris sat half up. I'm a ket purrson.

Oi Chris mate got any downers?

As long as he's got that thing going with nine and fifty and nineteenth. See they're not bothered about sense are they? They don't give a fuck about that. So people think they are deep! But they're just not bothered. It leaves loads of elbow room for others to shove in and dig out the deeps. I mean did they point that out at school? The little autistic swan all on his own? What happens to him when the others set off to climb the cold companionways eh?

She staggering on the reds and golds in my 20-hole Doc Martens and spangled loincloth cumskirt. She steadied on the books.

It's prubbly Yeats, said cushchris.

We all know its fuckin Yeats, she rrred a furstated face down at him where we couldn't see him him having backed away down. You're out of your box mate.

Wicked, said Seven.

Chrisions: That fifty-ninth swun it's him.

She steadied on the books there facing Darius and me.

Does he just stay behind when they all suddenly mount and stretch out his neck on the brimming water and as the October twilight turns to night does he just die there all alone?

She fell on her knees on the bed and put her face in reds and golds in cushions.

Time passed.

I looked away and saw a strip of light between drawn curtains at the other end.

She came up out of cushions livid.

How could he get the Nobel fucking prize!

All utists uv turble egos, said Darius.

Pipe passed. She swung dark blonde to sup pure poison.

Mentalist, said Seven. He scratched neck under back of her hair.

Darius sighed. What's sweet he said, what's chumming is that the hwild swuns are at cool with an e.

7-Eleven did the one-hand clapping thing.

I'm cool with an E man.

You see? 7-Eleven cuts to the chase as you zhewel. In the Baudelaire by the way. Seven? Utterficial purrdises somewhah in the middle.

Darius waved his hand at the chokka block books behind 7-Eleven's head.

Say again man.

Do you think it's wilde swans? I said. With an e?

Laughly. Paps that would explain the extra sworn.

Everything's good with an E, said Ellie. Pop with an e is pope. Star with an e is stare. Dog with an e is doge.

Neow, from cushions, dog popstar!

You saying you stash is back ere? 7-Eleven waved a large hand behind him.

Dog backwards is God, I said.

Love, said Ellie.

Orlready has a knee.

Yeah well that's why.

Duyius closed his eyes as in pain.

What book? Tell me the book sweetboy, said Seven.

He prodded a cushion. Chris! Hey Chris mate got a rock?

Or that extra swurn, said Chrisions, could be Mored Garn.

I foregathered. Maud Gonne! His muse. We love her don't we Ellie?

Love her.

Ellie picking and picking at itchy coverlet. Staring at itchy coverlet with itchy eyeballs.

This picture she's got like two pigeons colliding on her head. Crashing pigeons. Why isn't there a band called that? said Ell.

Darboy? Da book, said Seven.

Or Mored Gonne? Said Chrisions.

Bode lair. Another lust of the romantics. You neow 7-Eleven, smirked Darh.

Amazing woman, I held forth, great beauty, major political activist, crazy hats, something to do with the post office, rejected Yeats but he kept on writing poems to her all his life, she was the lifeblood, the soul.

What shelf mate? Just point.

All that time holding a candle and we don't even know if he had sex.

Book boings Chrision's hip. Seven lobs another.

Lower darn lucky Seven. Next ta the Jerries, says Rosychris.

Fuck the Jummuns he's nohwané ah the Jummuns.

I put him thuh.

Mummy moved him.

What not big mummy? Check the pichuhs, he added, didn't look like he was getting his end away.

Maagic without love

But in those days they never did, I went on. They looked as though they didn't have ends just inflatable liferafts under their seats that they tied in a double bow at the side.

Mud Gun wasn't Ourish, said Chrissie O'Cushy.

I hated him sweating sarkily in those cushions.

Get up, I said, stop being so feeble. Get up and get us a rock.

Bawn in Guildford. Think her Dar was échillé Scotch to boot. Anyway, nowt bog.

Ellie swimming up sublunar: She was. She was. So.

Sshwayed. Scrabbled fluff. Said it. *Wilde.*

Roun bout ere? Seven stands six foot five on the nomadic nightbed pulling book after book off a shelf and letting them thud on said bed.

Well read the spine dulling. Baudelaire. *Charles* Baudelaire not thuther one.

He was the lorst romantic, muffled Chrisions.

Books boffed him.

Aow aow.

Eaton square pussé.

Ellie scrabble. Scrabble. Hey. Here's a bit.

She held something up to Seven. He peered. Picked it off her palm. Turned it over. Sat back down again dangling. Prowled over his hand. Got the plastic water bottle off Christian's bare belly. Prowled. I felt my whole mouth fitting over Christian's belly and sucking on its slightly fatty douxness. Days of tongue licking out a walnut whip those days of infant yore.

Elllie went   cluck cluck   cluck cluck. Being a hen.

Surprisingly I jumped up. Jumped on the bed of wibbly wobbly wonders. Not to Chrisions where he lay. To the labiarinth and that text which is not one. Ran fingers along spinestrings. Plink plink plonk plonk plink plink plonk.

Oh you've got Rimbaud.

Flicking page page page.

Page page page. Quoi? – L'Eternité oisive jeunesse l'âme pourrie et l'âme désolé Quel rêve, ô pauvre Folle! avait un large trou un Génie inconnu SOLDE à la cime argentée je reconnus la déesse Douceurs! Feux pluie diamants jetées par le cœur

I love that boy Rimbaud, said Ellie.

G *(gén pl) (-sucrerie)* sweet; *(= flatterie)* sweet talk *(NonC)*

Give us the one about the arse, said Chris.

Your ass is mine, said 7-Eleven. His hand going under Elliearse. Throttle revving.

The goofs guffcawing and clawing the air in feeblie motions.

I looked back at the book. Délires II.

What's it called again?

God didn't make Rimbaud, I made him.

Guffcaw guffcaw. Beef awe.

I dropped Rimbaud on doux Chrision. He gunked. Grabbed.

You find it. Or do you know the arse one by heart?

Plink plink plonk plonk plink plink plonk.

Is there any logic to this bookcase? I asked sensibly.

Farknose.

And then right before my eyes. The abode. The lair. I deshelved it.

What upsets me, I said, what worries me is poetry.

She's a worrier, said Ellie, and it gets to her. Poetry and the rainforest. She can't sleep.

I went page page page. Page page page. Viens-tu du ciel profonde ou sortes-tu de l'abîme, O Beauté? Tucked into the gutter and drooping like a paraglider over caressant son tombeau a neatly-folded oblong of tinfoil. I flicked it across mon unique reine to the edge.

Do we rate it because of old bye bye nostalgia? Said the one cold eye.

Held slim silver in my tips and slid it behind the black leather wristband decorated with the designer's teethmarks (each band unique) on the wrist of the arm holding the book.

I turned. Trod with a lighter tread. Leant against the bookshelves.

Right I said. Ell? Open this any page read a verse.

She swapped pipe for it. Peers. Flicks.

Lighter on. Lips on.

Inflate gonfle hold kont *can* holding holding
Vigour of venomous pins and arrows
Hurtling my blood with heady
Whwhwhwhwhwhwhwh I said any page, I said.

She obliged.

Je t'adore à l'égal de la voûte nocturne,
Ô vase de tristesse, ô grande taciturne,

She looked up.

Right. Can you translate that in any way? I said.

It's got it here at the bottom. I adore you no less than the vault of Night, capital N, itself, O urn of sadness, O monument of silence; and I love you the more, my beauty, the more you elude me, and the more. Stop that! The more, O grace of my nights, you seem ironically to multiply the leagues that deny my arms the blue immensities of heaven. Hey!

She rounded on 7-Eleven. He fell back on reds and golds all goggly.

What utta rubbish, from cushions.

I can see right up your skirt girlie Seven to me.

Right, says I, I adore you no less than the vault of Night itself O urn of sadness. I mean can you imagine anyone getting away with that now?

A creepy-crawly on my leg.

I looked down.

Wooooo. Heh heh, said Seven.

I pushed the hand off.

Heh heh.

Give me that bit in French again Ell.

Je t'adore à l'égal de la voûte nocturne ô vase de tristesse, ô grande taciturne.

I udaw you as much as the noctahnal vault, said Darius, Night's not pissonafide. O vars of sadness. Vars! Ahns aunt in it. They always have to piss about with a tronslation. Such a baw.

Same with my beauty copy, said Ell.

So Dar if I had just written that poem just now you wouldn't think oh my God, the great fucking Baudelaire de nos jours would you? I queried.

Eh? said Seven.

A genius has been born? I go on. No. You'd think pretentious. Exactly how they tell us not to write. Lofty. Big up.

Wuds wuds wuds.

Is that It?

Get off me, Ellie slapping.

Give it ere.

Get off Seven. Just a minute. So are you saying Baudelaire was shite? She to me.

OK sex me then, said Seven.

Shurrup.

If you're going to damn him, awnment de may nwee, damn him on his laurels. Throat here Elsie, spake Darius.

Oi!

She flunge the booke uppe and forwarde but Seven's bigge arme was alreade there hanging overe it. The hand closed shut like the crab on the end of a crane and brought the book round to him. He moved it about between all ten fingers.

Bow. De. Liar. Zis it?

He shook it suspiciously then started turning the pages with a long fingle.

Are you listening anyone? (i)

Cat paw sin, said Cushions.

Cos I just wanna know the truth. Was the nineteenth century just a more poetical age?

Poetiquettical, murmuttered Chrisions.

Get up, I said, and get us another fucking rock.

A mountain in Mexico, said Darius.

Christian reared with peaky hair burped and subsided.

You know, I go on, we look back and we think oh it was OK to write like that *then* they wrote differently *then* poetry was 'poetry' then. Or what I'm wondering is. Was stuff like that always embarrassing at the time? So most people thought this is not of our world. Only after time passes we imagine a lost time when somehow it fitted. We allow it we revel in it so long as it comes from *then*. Or it's like there over there. You know when you're on holiday and you hear voices and you don't know what they're saying but you feel they are talking about different things than you do at home and in like prelapsarian language?

Chrision from his cushions: Uh-uh. Canter knees. Cats having sex. Suits me.

Everything you've picked is nineteenth century, said Ell.

Other centuries then. Tenth eleventh seventeenth. Hit me.

Duyius sagged half-off coffee table lighting a fag. Said.

Off with those shooes and then safely tread

In this loves hallow'd temple, this soft bed.

Oh sweet, said Ell, sweet.

License my roving hands, and let them gaow,

Beefawe, behind, between, above, belaow.

Pipe Seven, piped Christian.

But now it's got to be they fucked you up your mum and dad, I raved.

Brute brute heart of a brute like you, Ell added.

I puffeur un cœur tendre qui haït le néant vaste et nwah.

Slap me on the patio, said Chrisions.

Oh var good sgot the same sawlt 'n' vinegar flayvuh as those bittuh little French poe zeurhz.

I'm not saying they're not good today especially Sylvia we love Sylvia, said I.

No we don't, said Ellie.

They're all gawn, said Darius. You haven't got a today one cept mistuh misrable gnarl.

Ell you got a today one? I ask.

Um.

I looked away and saw the bleeding between two sides of black at the end.

No.

Darius?

He drooped on parchments. O du verlorener Gott! Du unendliche Schpoor! He pulled a parchment from under his neck and laid it on top of his face.

Added: Saul pop gnarl.

It's not in ere mate. Dar. Said Seven.

I trod on Seven's arm and fell to my knees on love's hallowed temple. Slap you on the patio is that better than the nocturnal vault? I said.

Chorus: yes.

I strenously in damp paste of Christian casing. Remember a lot of poets were laughed at or ignored when they were alive. I mean was it ever a cool thing poetry? Much?

Dontay loved spected in his day.

Bed boings up pushing me into Chrisions. He pastes. 7-Eleven loped to Darius.

Really? Going on about this housewife Beatrice as the queen of heaven? Can't you just see everyone going who does he think she is? Behind his back all liaisons dangereuses?

Seven dropped the flowers of evil on Darius.

Look I've read the whole book mate and it's clean.

I wrestled with Christian meekly. Saying.

Maybe whether poets are of their time says more about the time than poetry.

Our time is art of joint said Darius from neath parchment.

Innit?

Whethuh in crystal rocks ye reove beneath the bosom of the sea wand'ring in many a coral greove fair Nine fuhsaking Purtry!

Say gain? Seven swiped parchment off his face. Darius flinched but only very slightly. Kept eyes shut declaimed.

How hev you left the ancient love that bahds of eould enjoy'd in you! The lenguid strings do scowrcely move! The sound is fawsd, the notes are

Seven shoved him. Dawius' eyeholes oped. Yar you're right I got the book wrong.

7-Eleven's hand jerks to booky nook behind.

You mean it could any one a these?

Try Uving Waughsh, said Dawius.

Licking my neck in little cat licks. Crisions is cat person warm and sticky.

Blood clart!

I press on: A poet might be ahead of his time but what if he's behind it. Why's that more wrong? Is fashion to blame?

I unstuck with suction sounds and made my way on my knees to the bedsedge.

I stood on the bedsedge. Wibbling wobbling but up.

Eurgh lift em back in with warm spoons, he groans clutching a pair of plumpy cushions.

Rubbish blehhing on the street, said Darius, fark awrf awl uv you. Where I come from purtry is for talking to Gored.

Signals to ighter space, opined Chrisions, mayswell flush yours away with thuther shite.

Yeah, said 7-Eleven facing me now. Yeah I see you lady mine.

But then I think no, I said, because if fashion actual fashion felt it had to change at that level it would be constantly reinventing the very forms of fashion. The pant.

You are one b   itch. The way Seven said bitch like he put a finger in his cheek and popped it.

I go on: Instead of accepting that the pant is perfect and just proposing various takes on pants but still pants.

With a twist, said Ellie stirring blonde strands.

Popitch, said Seven.

Well yes with a twist yes but not like adding an extra leg to make it new.

Why not? Spake Chrisions from deep in cushions. A dozen legs. Run them up on the machine!

7-Eleven very near very tall. I wobble on the bedsedge.

Came in right next to me startled me so near.

Worked slugs round my earhole.

Sent a hot breath eddying inwards blades of a fan.

Sex me popitch.

Lurch back. Wipe ear. Finger in to itch it out.

He put his arms round my thighs and I was aloft. I liked it.

Accept, I said to the gathered below, that the pant matches man.

Oh ferk uf, said Darius putting parchment veil on again, there's noah for your cock to gayoh.

Merely matches.

He's right that thing of left or right dresser sir shows how crap trousers are for men, she said.

I put my hands up in the air taller. I spit on pants I shred pants. I am for poetry and the gabbeldy-gab of poetry!

Different fur guls, said Daryus.

Seven shifted so I hinged. My top half falling headfirst. Banged his back.

Firebomb fucking fashion! Half-smothered in Seven's sweatshirt.

Clearly you've never had your beaver split by a gusset. Ellie.

Stop you're giving me a haar dawn.

The fifty-ninth swan flies free!

Men.

I saw her moving away golden haired in the golden pool and the red and gold of Chrisions's tousled limbs and Darius laid out before them the shadow of his skull through parchment.

I thought you were a man person, I shouted.

Like riding a camel like what they say that's like but upside down.

Let me down, I said.

Popitch.
Lets face it the pant needs a major rethink.
Her voice going further away.
I felt cold go up my legs and touch my crotch.
I saw the edge of the door go by me.
No! Across the dark taiga. Scared suddenly.
Christian!

Colder darker. Going up and up the sound of needles furring plastic.
Going up and up cold marble.
Look stop this.
I buck and flutter to free legs.
I beat his back pom pom pom.
Still or you fucking pay. 7-Eleven.
Swooshing sickening
a new atmosphere low light realisation
of rain arcing up through colours rushing
whoosh and thump. Bed. Hurts
sfingers tightening on wrists
Where is it popitch?
Flip and flap buck and curl
Butterfly stroke in combo with chaos
Let me go! Try to bite it.
Hurts hurts. He not even trying
Yet. His strength. Slap.
Let me go, I'll show you. Half sob.
Release not immediately realised
Then exultation of untouchedness.
I squirm it out from covert
Black bitten leather wristband
It falls on chinchilla tick bedspread a silver
Promise of magnificent slow rivers of mind
Or so I'm told. He laughs low
As expected. His great side of beef
Pushes me over and pulls down my knickers

Cold punch to the heart I scream
He slaps buttocks that wubble and flotter
Resounding flat echoes of atonal melancholy
Gets up leaves.
Time passed.
Lay sickish on the bed heart racing
Humming pop nonsense telling self s'OK sOK
Then
Chrisions pale gold and pale
You OK?
Yeah.
You called.
Did I?
Come here.
He wraps me in his arms and I
Present my breast toast to paté
Spreads his warm meat upon my chest
Alive and full of other organs
We kinetikiss
Sdrugs in spocket
Laugh. Oh God I say never leave me
You in your small corner
And I in mine.

Then a flare round bent heads
We dribble dark brown tars
Smoking down sheets of silver
The air fills with cut flesh finer
Fuller than spirit
I hover on sustained note
Before behind above below
Pure and impasto with Chrisions
His ions glow in beef ore
Fuse and spill

66

January was even colder than December. I'd lie for a bit feeling wide awake but different because of having been asleep. I looked at the ceiling. The sounds were cars mostly, coming down the hill also going up the hill and some of them stopping at the lights a bit down the hill from the window. Some turned into the road that went away past the tower block. The sound the cars made coming down the hill. I tried to locate the beginning of the noise but I was never able to pinpoint it. The way it grew. The shape of the sound had a tail to it like a comet. As the car got nearer the sound got rounder. Then the increase in pressure and the way it burst just under window and dropped quickly on a line of sound. The more sustained low soundshape of the cars going along the side road by the tower block. The window sash shadow on the ceiling. Slightly waving as if it were made of water. The orange light from the streetlamps on the ceiling and top bit of the wall rippling and twisted in plaits of pale light-filled shadows revealing flaws in the window glass you couldn't see any other way.

I sat up. I wrapped the blankets round me and got the cigarettes and the lighter. I went over to the window. I crouched on the dining-room chair. Sometimes I got into a position where I turned the chair round and I half-sat on the windowsill and half on the seat of the chair. This way I could press half of my body and my face right against the glass and feel outside through it. Sometimes I let the blankets drop on that side. If it was warmer I would take off the oversize T-shirt and press my skin against the glass. It was burning cold. I'd shiver and my teeth would start to chatter and I'd let them. I'd really let the teeth go while I scanned the patch of municipal grass and the trees. After a while sometimes after ages the teeth would stop and the cold would run through me unopposed. Then I'd become the bit between in here and out there.

Everyone loves snow and frost but I only saw it once. That was a freezing night. The snow trying to find places to land on the bare branches, light snow building ridges very very delicately. First the air was full of blots flying at an angle because of a wind, but you couldn't hear the wind something about the snow veiling things audibly as well visibly. I stared out and saw the blurry balls of orange light from the streetlamps dimmer and fuzzier in the snow, almost disappearing looking like they could be at the north pole. An amazing amount of time passed without me noticing in the normal way. The wind died a bit and I watched the snow fall at less of an angle. I saw it build up in the grass, above the grass. I watched it shape to the trees down a bit of one side like shading, set like that because of the wind. How it lay along branches twigs. Later how it hardened like in an oven of cold, cooked-hard snow and the harder it got the more it glittered. Then it was just there on the grass the trees the top of the lamp-posts which looked coldest, snow and metal and the bleakness of orange light. Maybe they made streetlights orange because orange is the colour of the hearth and they wanted to make the city cosier from a psychological point of view. But the orange of streetlights is cold. The snow landed on some of the windowsills of the tower blocks I thought I could see if I stared hard. I could see it on the windowsill outside just inches below me. The glass was burnt into my cheek and the side of my body. I smoked a cigarette. Another cigarette. The trees withdrew inside the trees to endure the snow.

The moon amazed me. I'd never spent much time looking at it. It was wild, possibly hostile, though also just a lump of rock an asteroid or something stuck in our force field. It was a shock how out of place it was lit up way up in the dark. It was changeable. Small hard, big yellowy, sometimes it was seamed with red. Changing even in the course of the night. I like the way they used to call it a she. She was, big and full, yellow and the word they always use for the moon, serene and no doubt reflected in all kinds of lakes all over China and in Siberia where I'd read there were 27,000 rivers and bodies of water. Then I'd look at the trees for a while and the tower block and other things and when I really looked back properly she'd shrunk down to a mean white thing going up much more remote into space. As well, she was never the same shape in the sky from one night to the next in the month. Still when I got up and went to the window and was able to see a section of a circle drawn with scarce light in the dark I knew life was worth precisely that.

I smoked quite a lot at night and there were never better smokes. Even those smokes on a pill, even those ambrosial smokes were surpassed by the night smokes though I never analysed in what precise way. I watched the smoke turned by the cold glass and curling back into the atmosphere of the room. Some nights I was in a mood where I would hum things under my breath, pop songs, old Welsh songs, and sometimes a whole series of nursery rhymes. Old Macdonald Had a Farm, Hushabye Hushabye, Nick Nack Paddywhack Give the Dog a Bone.

67

I tore open the metal-backed pockets and dropped the big Solpadeine discs into the water. They hit the bottom and began to boil. I recognised the kind of hangover that gets worse in the afternoon. I poured a second glass of water with less water. I opened the drug drawer and got out the soluble C. Plop into the second glass. Thick streams of tangerine bubbles. I looked at the Solpadeine. Painkiller vapour torquing above the glass carrying in it some larger more visible particles that seemed to itch in the air. Inside the glass the pills spun and started to come up slowly through the cloudy water. I closed my eyes. The coffee started to make the noise in the pot. I drank the Solpadeine. Felt sick. Suppressed it. I put one glass down and picked up the other. The doorbell rang. The kidney-shaped bag of the season in red. The Must Have. I glugged the vitamin C. I'd have to face it.

'Just a minute.'

I went into the bathroom. A sight. The hair crushed flat to the side of the head. Snarled and fluffed on the other side. Blotchy cheeks. Blue indents under the eyes. Mascara smudged everywhere. I wetted a finger under the tap and rubbed it in the cake of soap on the sink. I dragged the finger under each eye and wiped it on the dressing-gown. The bell again. I stuck head into hall.

'Just coming.'

Back in. I saw Ellie's brush made out of nails. I dragged it through the hair on my way to the door. I pulled back the latch but she'd done the other lock on her way out. Sifting through piles of junk mail with one of the Daffy Ducks.

'Just a mo. The key.'

Into the living room. Jacket on the back of the chair. The pocket. Got it. Back to the door. Wave of nausea. Suppressed it. I stuck the key in the lock and turned it. I looked through the peephole. A white face distorted by the lens so the nose looked bigger and squashier than it was. Something on the margin. A boring thing like brushing your teeth. Exhausted, I leaned my head against the door.

'Who is it?'

There was no answer.

I put my eye back on the peephole. He was looking down.

'Who's there?'

'Someone.'

'What?'

'Someone.'

The boring thing hovering on the margin. No motorcycle helmet. No big puffy jacket or leathers. Maybe he wasn't a motorcycle courier. Maybe one of the Irish boys wanting something, milk. Someone. They were in a band. Being cool. A thought articulated itself with difficulty into a word, amassing a letter from over here, another from there.

'Eric?'

The voice behind the door. 'Yes.'

Yes. He said yes. He is here. He is standing outside my front door. Someone is Eric. I backed away from the door till I felt the boiler cupboard at my back.

'Naomi.' A name spoken on a different plane. Nausea.

I looked around the hallway. I spoke to the door.

'What are you doing here?'

'I must see you.'

'You can't.'

'Naomi.'

The way he said that word. He's breaking down. He's wrought up. He's come over. He's actually come over. Look at the state of me.

'Eric please go away. I'm not letting you in.'

'Please.'

'Not now. Come back later.'

'I will wait.'

'Wait somewhere else. Please.'

There was no sound from the other side of the door.

'OK? Come back this evening. Come back in three hours. Please.'

He didn't say anything.

I walked round the bend into the short bit of the hallway off which the kitchen, bathroom and living room opened. Nausea. Suppressed it. I went into the kitchen and poured coffee into the cup, stirred it. I took it into the living room. Grey day. Light drizzle. The buds on the trees swollen but still like scabs. That phase could go on longer than you'd think. I switched on the computer. A slot appeared slowly filling up with grey. I drank the coffee. I opened a blank document. I looked out of the window. Thick white cloud. I looked at the cursor blinking on the screen. Imagine if I'd opened the door. Imagine if I hadn't for some reason asked who. I had to get going. I went to the magazine rack down the side of the sofa. I had the press release at least. I got the big hardback A4 envelope and slid out the release. Shiny. Luxe. Anti-depressant colour. Grey days, red bag. I took the press release over to the computer. Red Leather Days Anti-SAD Bag Small Bag, Big Colour Small, Chic and Red All Over Red Bag of Courage. The women taking into their mouths]roses of the pentecost of the tundra[

I got out from behind the table and took off the Daffies. I crossed the room and out into the hallway. At the bend I listened. It was about twelve feet from the bend to the front door. I went slowly placing my feet carefully. I breathed through my open mouth so it was inaudible. I reached the door. My eye settled on the peephole. Nothing. Black blurred smeared. Black pulsing. Pulsing hole. Black pulsing hole. It collapsed vanished. Spasm of polyps. Then just black hole. I jumped back choking.

His eye.

I ran into the living room and stood gagging on my hand. Suppressed it. I picked up the cup and bustled out noisily into the kitchen and poured another cup of coffee. I hummed as I took it into the living room. I pushed the living room door as shut as it would go. It would never quite shut, the wood was swollen. I sat down. I looked at the screen. His eye on the peephole. I opened the press release. I underlined several key points on the release. I looked back at the cursor beating on the screen. I wrote. Wear Your Kidney on Your Sleeve. I read the press release again. I looked at the words I had written. I held my middle finger down on the back button and deleted the line.

Red
Kidney
Detox
Shock
Drainage
Organ
Heart
Bag
Open

I put my finger on the back button and held it down until they had all gone. The cursor beat on the screen. I listened. Nothing. I went over to the sofabed not yet made back up into a sofa. I lay on it with my head on two cushions. Some mute emanation seeping into the room, pressing on the walls and on the sofa. Him. I sat up. I went out into the hallway and stood a couple of feet from the door.

'Eric.'

I glanced at the letterbox. Him opening it. His eyes moving in the slot. Seeing me. No. I tried to stand a bit to the side, in case.

'Eric are you there?'

I sensed him fondling my voice pulling it in.

'I need to see you.' The broken bits of his voice.

'You can't just turn up like this.'

I moved back towards the boiler cupboard.

'Is everything all right?'

Nothing. Then, 'No.'

'What's the matter?'

'I suffer.'

A wave of repulsion. 'Go away. Go away now or I will call the police.'

'I don't want to hurt you.'

I made my voice harsh. 'You are making me a prisoner in my own home. Fuck off!'

I marched into the living room. I picked up the phone and rang the PR agency where Ellie worked now.

'Hello, Care Communications.'

'It's me.'

'Why are you whispering?'

'Eric is outside the door.'

'Who's Eric?'

'The poet.'

'Fuck. What's he doing here?'

'I don't know. He's turned up.'

'Did he say what he wants?'

'No. I nearly opened the door I thought it was a courier.'

I felt the edge in my voice.

'Calm down.'

'He sounds like he's having a breakdown.'

I put my hand half over the receiver.

'Did you hear that?'

'No.'

'I'm frightened Ellie.'

'Wait.'

'Did you hear that?'

'Christ.'

'Oh God.'

'Sit tight I'll get 7-Eleven.'

'Where is he?'

'Probably at the garage.'

'Can you get him to hurry?'

'Calm down. Whatever you do don't open the door, OK?'

'OK. Hurry.'

I looked out of the window. The three trees bare, budding. Almost budding. When you pulled out the latch but the door didn't open because the other lock was locked then the door stayed out of alignment with the door frame. The trees stuck in the ground the same old ground. The wood dried-looking and scabby. The latch-bolt couldn't click back into its hole in the door frame. It rested on the edge instead. White glare sky. Sometimes if you pushed the door snug against the frame again the bolt clicked into its hole. The buds scaly, the wood the colour of dirt. Sometimes it didn't. The latch was old, it got stuck. Sometimes you had to bang the door against the door frame a couple of times to get the bolt to spring out. When I'd gone to the door the second time and unlocked the other lock with the key had the latch-bolt clicked into its hole? Was it on the edge, ready to click into the hole if I pushed the door? Or was it stuck, jammed back? What if he knocked hard on the door? What if he leant on it?

I walked lightly across the room and took the living room door by the handle. I pressed down with my bare foot on the carpet in front of the door's trajectory and pulled the door in and as up as I could at the same time. It made the swishing noise on the carpet. I stood still. The slight squeak as the front door swings in. His breathing. I strained my ears. He must be in. He can't see me round the bend of the hallway but he's in. I stepped very carefully onto the carpet past the living room door. I was outside the living room. There were creaky bits out here I had to avoid. I hear him clear his throat. He says my name. Naomi are you there? I say yes please don't frighten me. He says I would never never frighten you, my heart. May I just come round this corner and set my eyes on you? Don't, I say. I stepped slowly deliberately towards the bend in the hallway. You don't know how it's been for me, he says, I suffer. I reached the bend. I saw the curve of the bolt resting on the edge of its hole in the door frame. He comes round the bend. He sets his eyes on me. I stared at the poised bolt. If he just leaned on the door it would swing open like magic. He is pale, tall. The way he presses his lips so his chin comes up holding in emotion. I concentrated on the back of the door. If he so much as rested against the other side it would open and he'd see me standing here. Do you want a cup of tea? I say. Trying to keep things normal. I make tea, talking all the time. We take the tea into the living room. He gives me a poem. He says this is the last poem as you requested. I take it. I placed the ball of my right foot on the hall carpet. I look down and pretend to read the poem. I pressed down with the foot. Underneath the carpet a floorboard gave a sharp crack. He takes out a flick-knife. Flicks. I cry out. I froze with the heel still up. I think, my young life! He's going to take it. I took another step. No sound, nothing. I lifted the back foot off the creaking floorboard. Eric please God don't hurt me I have never done you any harm. Eric I read every poem. I couldn't take my eyes off the back of the door. All I had to do was reach it before he knocked and felt it give. Eric listen to me, I say, not believing it's happening, thinking, Why didn't I listen to the inner voice? His eyes show the whites all round. A sound. He was sighing on the other side. He holds the knife with his elbow bent, the tip pointing at the ceiling. It was so quiet I could hear the movement of air in and out of his body. I reached the door. I had one chance at this. The whites showing all round his eyes behind the glasses. Our love can never exist in this world he says. If I could push the door quick the bolt would click into the hole before he noticed. He lunges with the knife. I breathed through my open mouth. Someone is lunging at me with a knife this is not a dream this is not a film this is not. Although it might stay stuck. Quickly quickly. My arms are out pushing him off. I am up off the sofa. I get behind a chair, lift the chair. I need to think quickly, you can lose your life through being careful. One chance, it had to make the clicking sound or I was done for. Through the bars of the chairback he stabs me. I breathed through my open mouth. I feel something moving through a place where I've never felt anything before. My young life! It was so quiet he might hear my heart. He was an uncanny boy. I hold onto the bit of the blade that sticks out from my chest and try to push the knife out. I was only going to have one chance. Blood springs out along the crease of my palm where it holds the blade. He thrusts. It was almost in the hole. If I pushed a few millimetres it would slide over the lip of the hole and in. The knife moves backwards inside me with a strange sensation. I placed the side of my body against the door. The knife tugs on a membrane lining my insides. He jerks it out. He holds it up at shoulder level. I looked at my arm in the pink dressing-gown fabric with the fuzzballs. My hands on the wound cup blood sliding over the lip of the cut. I put my hand flat on the latch. Now. He stares at me. He slashes his throat and falls forward with blood spritzing from his neck. I pushed against the door with the side of my body. It splatters my face and my arms. I looked at the latch. I'm bleeding badly but I could live. My mouth stretched wide. The bolt was still stuck back. I go round him on my knees. I threw my body at the door, feeling it thud back against me. I could live. I heard myself shout, feeling his body against mine through the door. Click. I could live! I jumped back. It was in, the bolt was in its hole. I reach the phone, dial 999 with wet red fingers. I reached up and rammed home the old-fashioned bolt at the top of the door as well. Help me, I'm dying! A howl through the wood. I ran into the living room. I snatched up the phone.

'Ellie!'

She started to cry at the sound of my voice.

'What is it?'

Couldn't get it out. Gasping.

'He tried. To push the door in.'

'My God! Is he in the house?'

'No.' Sobbing.

'Is the door locked?'

'Yes. Yes I think so.'

'Calm down. It's OK.'

'Where's Seven? Where is he?'

'It's OK. He's on his way.'

'For God's sake. I think he's going to kill me.'

'It's OK. He can't get in. He said he'd be half an hour.'

'Please tell him to hurry.'

'He'll be there any minute. Calm down. It's OK.'

'No.'

'Go and make yourself a cup of tea. He can't get in.'

'Maybe he can.'

'How?'

'I don't know.'

'It's OK. Just wait.'

I went into the hallway. I went up to the door, flinching, and put my eye against the peephole. The corridor stretched away mushroom-coloured to where it bent gradually round to the left and the shadows of the lift area spilled out into it from the right. It was empty. A movement caught my eye. I stood on tiptoe and looked down. He was slumped on the floor with his back to one wall and his feet against the opposite wall. The top of his head medium brown. Black-rimmed glasses on a white face. He was looking at the wall. He had a bag with him, a kind of rucksack. I moved back. A faint ping. Squeaking sounds on the linoleum. I went up again and looked through the peephole. 7-Eleven was shambling along the corridor bleared by the lens. He stopped and I saw him looking down.

'Lo mate.'

'Hello.'

'What you doing down there?'

'I am a friend of Naomi.' The quavery voice.

'She don't want nothing to do with you mate. Gotta give it up.'

'I have to see her.'

'She don't want to see you mate. You can't sit here.'

'I must see her.'

'Can't have it mate.' 7-Eleven reached forward and his body obscured the lens.

'No.'

They reappeared. He had an arm under Eric's arm hoisting him. Eric resisting, his legs going. They started to scuffle. I put my back to the door. Eric going no no and the sounds of their bodies scuffling. A kick on the door. It went quiet. I heard 7-Eleven talking and Eric crying. A knock at the door.

'Naomi you there?'

'Yes.'

'Open the door will you.'

'I can't.'

'Don't be like that he says just come out and let him see you and he won't bother you no more.'

'I can't.'

There was a noise in the lock but the top bolt was still drawn across the door.

'For fuck's sake girl. He won't do you nothing. He's all right. In't you Eric?'

I made my voice hard.

'It will make him worse. He's sick in the head.'

'Just let him see you what's the harm?'

'I told you I can't. Take him away.'

There was no answer. I looked through the peephole. 7-Eleven was crouched down beside Eric talking to him. He stood up.

'Don't be hard-hearted girl. He's come all the way.'

'I don't want to.' My voice rising.

'Bloke'll do what I say. Won't you mate?'

'Yes.'

'Please Seven, I don't want to.'

'Come on. It ain't that hard. I'm here.'

I put my head against the door. 'Will he go away?'

'Yeah.'

'No but if I come out does he promise to leave and leave London as well and leave me alone for ever?'

I heard 7-Eleven mumbling to Eric. 'Yeah he says yeah.'

'I need to think about it.'

68

All I had to do was come out from behind the door and let him set eyes on me. I felt every nodule in my gut contract. That was all I had to do. It would take five minutes. Go out. Let him look at me. Let him say what he had to say. Nod, humour him. 7-Eleven would be there. Go back inside. He would go away for ever. Life is like this. Always making yourself do something you don't want to do, swallowing it down, so you can get to the thing you do want. That's how it works. I went up to the door.

'OK. Give me five minutes.'

I went into the bathroom and put the shower hose over the bath taps. I threw the dressing gown and the outsize T-shirt off and squatted in the bath. I soaped under my arms, between my legs, my feet, scoured the rest quickly with the weak streams of water. I dried myself with the nearest towel. I went into the bedroom. I remembered the white rubberised lace skirt he first saw me in, the skirt like a little hanky. I still had it somewhere. Stupid. Mad as he is. I opened the wardrobe. The thing is to be neutral. Jeans and a top. And a jumper. He hasn't seen me for almost three and a half years. I went back into the bathroom and squeezed toothpaste on the end of the brush and stuck it into my mouth. Back into the bedroom. I ran the other hand through the rack while I brushed. The Dolce dress from a journo sample sale. Nun-coloured. Body-fitting to the hips then flaring like something from an Italian film. Just below the knee, long sleeves, high neck. I went into the bathroom, rinsed the mouth. Soap water. Eye make-up remover lots of it. Moisturiser. Back into the bedroom. I slipped my arms through the dress. I found hold-ups in a drawer.

Ellie's best day shoes were under the bed. I pushed my feet in. Back into the bathroom. I ran a finger along the perfumes. Angelique Encens. One Ellie had brought back before she left the mag. So precious it came wrapped in white leather. I leaned my head down and brushed the hair hard from underneath. I tossed my head back and the hair flowed in waves.

'Naomi?'

'I'm just coming.'

Eyedrops for the reds. She had the best ones, the ones that ran down your cheeks milky blue and stung. I dropped them in. Blinked hard. Milky blue ran. Red evaporated like magic. The make-up artist foundation, the one that looked like you were wearing nothing. I patted it on with tiny movements smearing at the edges to blend it in. I applied another, thicker layer on the blue hollows under the eyes. They disappeared. Younger. A faint colourwash over the eyelids. Chestnut. Dark grey eyeliner just very subtle to ring the eyes to blend into the lashes at the root and make them look deeper and more mysterious so when I turned up the eyes he would look into them and see. He would look into them and see. I looked in the mirror. My eyes coming forward to meet their glory. My little mysterious smile.

I closed my eyes. Opened them. I picked up the soap and ran water over my hands and lathered the soap up. I looked back in the mirror. I put my soapy hands on my face and rubbed hard. Scrubbed at my face. I bent. Splashed. Looked in the mirror. You. The veiny blue pits under your eyes. The bulb of your irregular-shaped nose. The red vein that runs up one nostril. The fleshy sides of the nose prickled with blackheads. I leaned closer to the mirror to get a good look. Your skin grey-white and blotchy red. The almost-white fur that covers the sides of your face on the jawline. The crease beginning to show between the eyebrows. Blown pores. Above the corners of the lips, shadow-hairs. On the sides of the cheek and there on the sides of the forehead dried-in bits of dead skin clinging in patches to the rawer skin underneath. I turned the face from side to side. I started to laugh. Mascara! I pulled out the wand and worked it crudely back and forward under my eyes. I threw it in the bath. Rubbed the mascara into the skin with a finger.

The brush of nails. Snatched it. Sawed it through the hair. Rubbed it round the top of the head in circles banging the scalp. I grabbed bits of hair and backcombed them randomly into rearing tufts all over the top and sticking out at the sides. I laughed. More. I picked up a comb. Snarled it in and backcombed harder. I threw it in the bath. More. I grabbed at the hair and tugged and slapped it about on the head till it stood up in twists and spouts. Laughed. I looked around, opened the bathroom cabinet. Chanel. I turned the base and it came up bright red. I looked in the mirror. I yanked it across the lips. I laughed. I worked it back and forth rough on the lips. I saw my teeth. I worked it red across the front teeth. Once. Twice. Big slashes. It tasted thick, waxy. I laughed. I pulled the dress off over my head and threw it on the floor. I got back into the Number 47 T-shirt and the pink fuzzballed dressing-gown. I left the bathroom tying the dressing-gown cord. Oh wait. Fragrance. I went into the kitchen and opened the fridge. Milk, wine, mayo, salad bag, yoghurts, tub of potato salad, jar of pickled herring. I opened the jar and scooped out some herring. They squidged between my fingers. I rubbed them over my chest and neck. I lifted the T-shirt and mashed them on my belly and between my legs. I threw the remainder in the sink. I strode out of the kitchen and up to the front door wiping my hands on the dressing-gown.

'Here I am!'

I threw back the bolt and stepped outside laughing.

He was still sitting on the floor with his back to one wall and his knees up, his trainers propped against the opposite wall. I straddled his calves leaning back on the wall. I forced myself to look down into his face.

'Look Eric. This is me.'

He wasn't looking. I stuck my head out and forward. I moved it about to try and catch his eyes.

'Satisfied?'

He lifted his head. My eyes gripped his.

'Is this what you want? Is it?' Strength pounded in me.

His eyes moving closer and closer like they were swimming up through water.

'Well. Say something.'

His whole face moving up and towards me, his eyes getting wider and wider like mouths.

'Come on. Out with it!'

I forced my eyes to narrow hisses.

'Say something!'

I grabbed handfuls of my hair and pulled it, screaming in someone's else's voice, 'Is this what you want? Is this it?'

I felt something pull me and pin me to the wall.

'Ease off. Look at the state of him.'

'What about the state of me!'

Jabbing at my own chest. My voice tearing. I forced myself to look back at Eric. My eyes struck into his.

'You need a doctor. Sick! Sick!"

I jabbed at the side of my head with a finger. He slid across the linoleum on the seat of his jeans keeping his eyes wide open all the time. His hands reached my dressing-gown and worked their way up the front while he stared up into my face. I screamed. I beat his body with my hands and my knees. 7-Eleven pushed me back against the wall with his body and prised Eric's fingers off my dressing-gown.

'You are one evil bitch,' he said.

He let me go. I stepped over Eric's body and into the flat. I shut the door and pulled the bolt. Noise from the other side. I looked through the peephole. They were at the lift area. Eric was using his whole weight to try and sit on the floor, his feet using the corner of the lift area as leverage. I saw 7-Eleven pick him up by the underarms and drag him and they disappeared.

69

I stopped as we were coming down the stairs. A man with a droopy moustache stood behind the bar below us polishing a glass with a tea towel. Against the opposite wall high-backed booths with burgundy velvet banquettes. Gypsy paraphernelia was tacked to the walls above the booths: painted plates, bits of horse tackle and brown-flecked photos of an old-fashioned city. Three steps at the far end led up to an area of candlelit tables that disappeared round a corner. It wasn't very busy.

'Why here?' I said.

'You said somewhere we'd never come back to.'

I followed her to a booth and slid onto the banquette opposite her. The barman came over. I ordered a glass of wine. She asked for a vodka and tonic. Someone started singing in a throbbing voice. I craned my neck out of the booth. Two men and a woman were standing round one of the candlelit tables up the three steps. The men were playing a fiddle and an accordion and the woman, in a floor-length flowery skirt, was singing. In between phrases of the song she smiled but with her eyebrows drawn to show pain. She beat time on her thigh with a tambourine.

'This is a bad idea,' I said.

Ellie swayed to the music. I picked up a menu to pass some time. I put it down.

'I think we should go.'

'Relax.'

She started snapping her fingers and humming, eyes shut. I picked up the menu again. It was the kind where every page is protected in thick plastic. The word meatballs repeated a lot and cabbage. Above the edge of the frayed plastic cover I saw the V of flesh in her body-fitting sweater moving to the left, to the right, to the left. Romani Khoniji. Gibanica Cesnica. Stuffed Cabbage Rolls. Between her breasts a zircon vibrated on a piece of invisible fishing-line. Charbart Pasulj. Meatballs with Pickled Cabbage. A feeling crept up the back of my neck. There was an oval woodcut at the top of the menu of a gypsy woman with downcast eyes and arms covered in gold bells. I examined the woodcut. I saw Ellie's out-of-focus breasts move in two or three swings further across to the right. I examined the gypsy woodcut more closely. Someone was coming into Ellie's banquette from the left. I counted the ripples in her gypsy hair and the spikes of woodcut light outlining her body. Some kind of nondescript jacket and under it a faded dark blue shirt. It was getting to the end of the period when I could feasibly keep looking at the menu but I couldn't pluck my eyes away. She was my dream gypsy woman like the woman on the packet of cigarettes. I focused more on the shirt. I saw a little burn hole on the pocket. I met his eyes.

'Hello Naomi.'

Dark blue. He smiled.

We got him a drink. Ellie immediately started chatting away to him. I looked up the length of the room. The trio were standing by another table. I wondered if she were singing in Romany, if that's what that was. Was Romany the national language of Roumania? I heard Ellie asking him what he had been doing since he got here. He said that he had been to the National Gallery that morning.

'Good for you,' said Ellie, 'not just pining away then.'

He was looking at me.

'What did you like best?' I said.

'I really like the Madonna with the Bambino by Bellini. It is the one where she is sitting and he is lying on her stomach.'

'And he's sleeping. Yes it's. I know the one.'

'Hey garçon!' She clicked her fingers in the air. The barman kept polishing the glass with the tea towel. 'Garçon. Hey!'

The barman came out from behind the bar and over to our table. He stood looking above our heads at the photos on the wall. He had his hands crossed under his apron.

'Hi. Have you got any cigars?'

He said what he had.

'Cool. I'll have a Romeo y Guilietta. Eric?'

He shook his head. She nudged him with her elbow.

'Go on. We've got to celebrate. This doesn't happen every day.'

I looked at her but she didn't meet my eyes.

'She's very nice your friend.'

'Yes. I wouldn't have come if it hadn't been for her.'

'I didn't want to cause you pain.'

'I know. That's what I wanted to say. I'm sorry I got so upset.'

'It's my fault.'

'Why did you come?'

'Ah!' said Ellie.

The barman held out a box and she reached across Eric and took one. She held it under her nose and ran it back and forth through the air with an expression of satisfaction.

'Eric what do you do these days?' she said.

'I write poems.'

'No job?'

'No.'

She leaned under the table and hoicked her skirt up. She began rolling the cigar up and down her thigh. 'Ah, you're wondering what I'm doing.' She smiled. 'It softens the fibres of the tobacco leaf. It gives a moister smoke. Go on, get one. I'll soften it up for you.'

He laughed and I laughed as well. She winked at me across the table.

'So how do you survive Eric my love?'

She popped the cigar between her lips and held up her face. The barman leaned across and struck a match under the cigar.

'I go back to live with my parents. Sometimes I take a job at the factory.'

Ellie moved her chin so as to be sure the flame didn't touch the end of the cigar. She sucked hard a few times and the end of the cigar began to smoulder.

'Thanks mon brave. Really? You gave up your studies and you moved back in with your mum. All for love of our darling Naomi?'

He looked at me. I could tell he was enjoying her.

'Yes.'

'Aw ain't love sweet. Here have a puff.'

She inserted it gently between his lips. He took a couple of draws and held it out in his hand to look at it.

'It's good. But I like to see you do it.'

He passed it back.

'But Eric. That must be hard at your age,' I said.

'It's not so perfect. I go out or I spend a lot of time in my room.'

'Do you have a girlfriend?' she said.

I caught his eye and looked away.

'I think I cannot answer.'

'That means you do. Come on, tell us a little bit about her.'

I stared at her but she didn't see.

'You know my situation.' He was still looking at me.

'But that's got to change. Your parents must be worried,' I said.

'I explain my heart belong to someone.'

'I give it back.'

His drink arrived. We said cheers. She took the cigar out of her mouth and picked little shreds of tobacco off her lips.

'One end is always a bit narrower and that's the end you put in your mouth,' she said.

'What does your mother say?'

'She know from the first day she see me that summer something has change.'

'She found the poems?'

'Only you see the poems.'

He was bathing me in his eyes.

'Eric that's insane. They're so beautiful. They stun me!'

She put her hand on his forearm.

'You must publish those poems. He must get them published mustn't he Nay?'

'Maybe it's irrelevant,' I said.

'What will you do now Eric? Will you keep writing?'

His face changed.

'No.'

The gypsy ensemble were standing at our table. They bowed and hoisted their instruments. Then, nodding to each other with sparrow eyes, they began to play. The woman's voice undulated over us. Ellie whooped. She said a word that could have been polka! it was hard to hear above the music. The pills again, I thought, they've still not got the dose right. She started clapping along.

Eric rummaged down the side of the banquette. He sat up and put a black binder on the table and pushed it across to me. It was the kind of binder with clear plastic presentation sleeves open at the top so you can slide a sheet or two of A4 into each one. I opened it. The first page was one of his poems on the familiar thin paper. I turned over. On the left hand page was a photocopy from an English language newspaper reduced to A4. On the page opposite was a small part of the same page blown-up big. This Week's Must Have. It was the one where the Must Have was a chunky identity bracelet with DIOR picked out in diamente. Just under the title was a small byline picture. The picture was blurry from being blown up and copied. It was hard to tell it was me.

'Ellie?'

Her head with the cigar clamped between her teeth tossed from side to side in time to the music. I turned the page. It was the masthead from the magazine I'd been working at when I first met him. My name halfway down. On the facing page he'd enlarged the bit where my name was. I turned the page and it was the contributors' page from a magazine I'd done a shoot for just after I'd left my job. It had been a swimwear shoot. The picture of me was a terrible snapshot. Dan had thought it would be a good joke. I was wearing a bikini and holding up a six-inch fish I'd caught. Making a stupid face. My knees knocking together. On the facing page he'd blown up just the bit showing my upper half with the fish. The image breaking up in a glut of blots. I turned the pages. More Must Haves. My name credited on a couple of shoots and ringed in red crayon. A page from the shoot Sylvie and Ryan had done in London. It was a black and white of an old East End pub with the bar running across the shot, gilt mirrors tilting in. Two ash-blonde girls leaned on the bar in fantasy get-up with pints of

Guinness. Krysta and Boukje. In the darkish picture they shone. I was standing in the shadows to one side talking to an old character wearing a flat cap. I'd been drafted in as a 'real person'.

'Ellie.'

'Bravo! Bravo!'

'Ellie. Please.'

She held her hands high in the air and clapped them loudly. She nudged Eric and dipped her chin to show him he should clap. He laughed good-naturedly and started clapping.

'Ellie.'

The gypsies looked at each other. One of the men held his accordion grinning open, the other rested his bow on a string. They bent their knees and nodded to each other at the same time. The woman threw back her head and throbbed her throat at the ceiling.

On the next spread he'd blown up my head. It was hard to recognise it was a face it was so blown up. I turned the page and he'd zoomed in closer on the photocopy. A meshy black and white diamond took up most of the page. It took a few seconds for it to resolve into a cypher of my eye. I turned the page. A field of black squiggles and dots disseminating and eroding. I turned the page. A crabbed ancient script written in frantic panic thousands of years ago. It was vibrating like some kind of optical illusion. I turned the page. A labyrinth with no centre bleeding off the sides. Swarms of walls, angles and dead ends disintegrating into formless extensions of black. I looked for something to focus on. Blanks in a black disorder. Maybe a grossly enlarged reflection from my eye. I turned the page. Clusters and dispersions. I turned the page. Steady white rain, beginning to merge bottom left. I turned the page. He'd zoomed in on a few of the white blobs. Dits specked their whiteness. I turned. White holes emerging from black holes floating in white holes. I closed my eyes to make it stop. I felt sickish even though I knew that if you keep magnifying an image as you photocopy there comes a point where all you are recording is the pattern of dust on the photocopier that day. Somewhere, way back, I'd disappeared.

I felt a hand land on the open binder. 'Aren't they brilliant?'

She lifted her hand and the last few pages turned by themselves, drawn by the weight of the others so that the binder lay open on the last page. It was a sized-up photograph. A single bed in a corner of a room. A bedside table with a lamp on it and piles of books on the table and on the floor. Eric was sitting in the middle of the bed with his back to the wall and his legs dangling off the bed. Behind him the wall was covered with pictures. The quality of the image wasn't good and it took me a while to realise that they were his originals of the pictures that he had stuck in the binder.

The gypsies stopped. Eric and Ellie clapped. I pushed the binder at her. 'Look at this.'

She held up a finger then struck a match, making sure the match flame didn't touch the tobacco leaf. She puffed away and started flipping through the binder. The ensemble started up a few tables away. Eric said something. I watched her for a sign.

'Sorry Eric?'

'God how could you let them use that?' She pointed to the one of me with the models. 'You look terrible.'

'Look at the last page.'

'Hello darlin.'

He squeezed in beside me wearing a baseball cap and smelling of aftershave. He glanced at Ellie then gave me a smacking kiss on the lips.

'Eric this is 7-Eleven, Naomi's boyfriend. You met the other day right?'

Eric reached across and shook Seven's hand. 7-Eleven put his arm round me and pulled my head into his shoulder.

'Take it from me sta she's not worth it.' The lazy laugh.

I signalled to Ellie flicking my eyes down at the binder and up to her eyes. She looked at me, then sideways at Eric, putting her lower lip out and drawing her eyebrows together to say 'poor baby'. I looked at my watch.

'Well. I'm glad we did this but we have to go, 7-Eleven and me. We're going to a gig at Earl's Court.'

'Eh, I've not even had a drink yet.'

'We'll get one there babe.'

'Yeah you'll get one there. So I guess you and Eric better say your goodbyes,' she said to me.

'Can't you stay a little longer?'

'Just a couple of minutes. I'm sorry.'

He stood up to let Ellie out from the booth. She wiggled along it, the zircon bouncing and flashing between her breasts, then stood beside the table smoothing her skirt. He sat down again.

'Unless you want to hang out with me and have another drink when they've gone?'

'Another day I love to have a drink with you.'

She skipped over to the bar motioning to 7-Eleven to follow her.

We sat facing each other. His hand was resting on the table so that his middle finger was almost touching my index finger.

'You will leave me alone now?'

'Yes.'

I looked down at the table, at his hand.

'Why me?'

'Sometimes you are lost. Then you meet someone's eyes and it is like the sacrament.'

I concentrated on the space between our fingers. I will have you full on the end of my fingers what a dream.

'I know that you understand but that you are afraid.'

'Yes I understand.'

He passed an envelope across the table.

'What's this?'

'The last poem.'

'No. I can't.'

'I ask you please. It's important.'

I picked up the envelope and looked at my name written on it in his small, incised handwriting. I put it in my pocket.

We went up to Ellie and 7-Eleven at the bar. The way he leaned forward to Ellie who was offering him her glass to taste out of. The way he laughed at something 7-Eleven was saying. I started to climb the stairs. Behind me Ellie linked her arm with Eric's. I reached the street and saw 7-Eleven's car pulled up on a double yellow.

'Can we drop you?' I heard her say.

'No we've got to run. We can't drop him.' I walked over and stood by the passenger door waiting.

'Sorry mate. Give us a shout if you come back right? I'll keep her warm.' 7-Eleven came up and reached his arm round my shoulder and out of sight of Ellie and Eric slid it down my back and put his hand under the waistband of my jeans and under the elastic of my panties. Eric had stopped further back on the pavement, his hair lit up from behind by the light coming out of a mini-market.

'Goodbye Eric,' I said. I looked at his face without focusing. I felt 7-Eleven move a finger up and down between my buttocks. I clenched them as tight as I could but his finger was stronger.

'I have a request.'

He opened the plastic bag and got out a camera.

'I like very much to have a photo.'

'No.'

'Aw come on, let him have just the one,' said Ellie.

'No!'

'You're so hard-hearted.'

'Yeah go on girl. Let him have a picture.'

'I can't.'

'Come on it's nothing. Come on.' She grabbed my arm and pulled me towards him. She arranged me next to him then took the camera off him and backed away to lean against the car.

'This button? The one on the top? Is the flash on? OK.'

I felt Eric's arm on my shoulder.

'Cheeeese!'

I lunged forward as the flash went off and pulled open the front passenger seat. 7-Eleven got in the other side and put the key in the ignition. Ellie was standing beside the car, waving at Eric.

'Bon voyage Eric. Bon voyage!' She ran forward and gave him a hug and came back and stood by the car. 'Bye! Bon voyage.'

I banged on the side window. She got in the back talking. 'I can't bear it. He's no money. You know he walked to Calais? Yeah he walked to the ferry. What is that? Two hundred miles? Think of him now going to some room alone in a youth hostel.'

'I don't want to hear it.'

'And he's so sweet. God, he's so sweet. You're such a drama queen, know that?'

He was standing by a streetlight with the plastic bag leaning against his leg. People strolled in front of him and behind him, and further back behind him there was a rack of London postcards outside a newsagent and the steep banks of fruit and vegetables outside the mini-market. To his right the door led down to the gypsy place. There was a neon sign of a gypsy's head above it, her left eye blinking on and off. I turned to face the windscreen. Out of the corner of my eye I saw 7-Eleven look over his shoulder to see if it was safe to drive out into the traffic. I knew he wanted me to look back and meet his eyes one last time. I kept my eyes to the front. I wanted to hold on but I couldn't. I started to cry. We coasted out from the kerb and I saw 7-eleven stick his finger in his mouth.

'Ah juice juice,' he said.

I turned round suddenly but he was obscured by a parked van and then I caught a glimpse of his legs with the plastic bag leaning against them through a parked car's window and then we accelerated up the road and I rolled down the window an inch or two and threw the poem into the stream of traffic.